The Gramophone and the Voice

The Gramophone and the Voice

by John Steane

To colleagues and staff at ***Gramophone***
present and past

Copyright

First published in Great Britain in 1999 by
Gramophone Publications Limited

Production

Editor	Mark Walker
Designer	Birge Frommann
Art Editor	Mark Jubber

Gramophone Publications Limited
135 Greenford Road,
Sudbury Hill,
Harrow,
Middlesex HA1 3YD,
Great Britain

Printed in England by William Clowes Limited,
Beccles, Suffolk NR34 9QE

First edition

British Library Cataloguing in Publication Data.
A catalogue record for this book is available from The British Library.

ISBN 1 902274 07 5

Contents

Bold type indicates a complete Quarterly Retrospect. These are laid out in two columns throughout the book.

contents

Foreword

by Graham Johnson

Great songs and operas will surely outlast their singers. Few now remember the names of the vocal celebrities courted by Franz Schubert as he tried to interest them in his compositions, often without success. But such is the power and immediacy of the human voice that those singers, for a short while at least, have seemed the real stars. Only too soon, these will be replaced by the new, but not necessarily better, sensations. The music, printed in leather-bound volumes, remains a constant; but this holy writ, like any other, needs interpretation; and the list of singers able to offer musical revelation to the listener is always changing. (How often? 'About every three months' readers of the 'Quarterly Retrospect' will reply.) In the middle of confusion, pretension, spin and hype, someone has to keep his head, defending the old (when worthy of it) and greeting the new in the context of the achievements of the past. Enter John Steane. For 25 years, in the pages of ***Gramophone***, the author of this book has been on hand to salute the lark ascending and to draw our attention to its youthful song. But he is too much of a wise old bird to forget the vocal glories of past summers.

'Remember me!' says the great Carthaginian soprano Dido, but that is easier sung than done. The ever-changing history of singing is written on air, rather than water. In most cases it floats into one ear, and out the other; occasionally it curls around the ear-drum and insinuates itself on the heart. Even if captured on a disc, that sound can remain trapped on a shelf, silenced until our technology needles it into life. And yet, somehow or other – and this is his unique achievement – Steane has found the means of recording, in words, the recording of voices. His writing, like the palimpsest of the Anglo-Saxon chronicler, takes account of new events in the context of the old: parchment in praise of shellac is embellished, after much deliberation, with accounts of more recent famous victories on vinyl and plastic.

And Steane writes like an angel – a recording angel, naturally! He writes on singers in a way that the rest of us dream about writing anything: with knowledge and understanding (these two are by no means synonymous), wry humour, compassion – and with just a hint of that apologetic diffidence that marks out a gentleman of the old school. English language is his professional skill, music his private passion but, in the manner of that dying breed, the British amateur who outclasses the academic authorities, he has combined them in a hobby which has brought him world-wide fame.

I have been a fan of his ears, and of his prose, since the publication of *The Grand Tradition* in 1974. The quarterly articles considerately provided by ***Gramophone***, a selection of which are printed here, were welcome updates and amplifications of that classic work. After some years, when these Quarterly Retrospectives began to contain occasional evaluations of my own playing (he kindly includes singers' pianists in his interests) one could always tell that he had listened carefully. He was (and is) fair, which is not the same as impartial. One of my favourite singers has remained, to my regret, a no-go area as far as he is concerned. He has remained silent on artists who seem, to me, indispensable. On the other hand, a number of singers whom he adores mean little to me. *Tant pis.* We have had our differences, and this is the inevitable divergence of opinion of two musicians with varying tastes. But it is impossible to bear a grudge against someone who loves music so much, and who writes so well (George Bernard Shaw's victims must have felt the same) and there has also been gratitude for words of support, A favourable mention in 'Quarterly Retrospect', after a damning initial verdict, was like winning the day in the Court of Appeals.

'Retrospect' is a noun well suited to his occasional writings, because retrospection is Steane's great *forte*. The word implies a patrician sense of perspective, with time taken to evaluate the recordings with the necessary *gravitas*. Phrases like 'summing-up', and 'directions to the jury', come to mind, and in giving him the last word, ***Gramophone*** signified its confidence in his judgement. It was confidence well placed. Once you have read the pieces reprinted here, I urge you to try *Singers of the Century* and the fascinating *Voices: Singers and Critics* (Duckworth). Steane has assembled a famous library of recordings and, with it, a cunningly varied array of literary means to describe and differentiate something as elusive as a pair of rival voices, whether contemporary or of the past. In his word-portraits of famous singers, he manages, in a few admirably concise pages, to sum up the essence not only of a disembodied voice on record, but the human being behind the vocal chords. His chapter on Peter Pears (*Singers of the Century*, Volume 2) brought that great artist, and friend, back to life for me more vividly than anything else I have read. I did not agree with every single one of his evaluations, but that did not seem to matter – it was the broader sweep of Steane's perceptions which carried weight. He had listened to the voice intently of course; but he had then stepped back to assess the broader resonances which differentiate a fine singer from a great one, a first-class vocalist from a key artist of the century.

There have been other urbane writers on vocal matters – I think of names as far back as Reynaldo Hahn, the American *aficionado* W. J. Henderson and, more recently, the authoritative Henry Pleasants. But Steane is somehow more hospitable than these, and many others – he enjoys singing too much to play the role of outraged guardian of so-called legendary values. He lives in the real world and is aware that singers, like all of us, change and develop, and that vocal chords are not black and white. He is aware that the conditions of modern life and music-making pose considerable threats to the standards of singing, but he is too much of an optimist to retire into his library of 78s, muttering darkly about the incompetent young. Despite the Jeremiads of the 'golden age' brigade, there are modern-day miracles, as the pages of this book testify. He is irremediably in love with records, but he also attends concerts assiduously, relishes live performances, and balances his judgements between the two different worlds of achievement. Steane gives every school of classical singing its due – he seems equally at home with the Italians and the Russians, the French and the Germans. The Scandinavians and more recently, the Americans receive their proper attention and consideration. Not bad for an Anglo-Saxon chronicler, I say. It seems to me that this voracious catholicity of taste stems from his sheer determination to understand and assimilate everything within his chosen field of interest – to impose order on chaos, and to end up with a coherent world-view. If there could be such a thing as a dictionary of vocal timbres, here would be the man to write it.

It happens that John Steane's own listening career has coincided with much of the history of the gramophone (as well as ***Gramophone***), and it is this span of experience which gives him his authority and his perspective. The field has now become so large, and so diffuse, that it is impossible to become a renaissance man, even in a field as specialized as classical singing. You have to be one already, like Steane, who, against the odds, has managed it, and continues to keep tabs on developments. But I doubt that we shall see his like again. Read him while you can.

Introduction

John Steane

One hundred articles, 25 years: the numbers seemed to be saying something. I searched long and hard for the message and at last (as indeed at first) construed in it the magic word 'retirement'. 'Nobody would *want* you to go,' said Chris Pollard, which I thought was encouraging and which took me back a quarter of a century to his father's equally encouraging words: 'Try your hand at it.'

This was early in 1974, when I had not been long on ***Gramophone***'s then much smaller panel of reviewers. My hand, it must be said, raised no objections; doubtless it appreciated the opportunities of what my old friend Captain Grimes (E. Waugh, *Decline and Fall*, Ch. 13) would have described as 'God's own job.' What it involved was, in the first place, a lot of listening. The vocal records of three months were to be heard and appraised. They were to be sifted and placed in a larger context, and the original review itself was also to be under scrutiny, because if injustice had been done here was the chance to put it right.

This was the purpose of our founder, Compton Mackenzie, who made a special point of it in his Editorial in the first number of ***The Gramophone*** in April 1923: 'The critical policy of ***The Gramophone***,' he wrote, 'will be largely personal, and as such it will be honest but not infallible, while the errors will be mostly on the side of kindness ... every three months we shall deal very critically with the output of the previous quarter.'

So that was the Quarterly Retrospect's origin and rationale. When I took it on I don't believe that it was ever suggested to me that part of my purpose should be to 'deal very critically', any more than when starting as a reviewer I was instructed to err, if at all, 'on the side of kindness'. In both instances I assumed (and I'm sure rightly) that what was wanted was an honest opinion arrived at after conscientious and sensitive listening. The 'Quarterly' did, however, involve an additional operation, for it was to provide a second opinion, obliquely or overtly (therefore) judging the judgement of colleagues.

Whether owing to my tact or to their tolerance or indifference I do not know, but in all those 25 years I received only one complaint.

My predecessor, with a brief gap in between, was Desmond Shawe-Taylor, for many years the greatly respected music critic of *The Sunday Times*. He himself had experienced difficulties of this kind, and his friend and colleague Philip Hope-Wallace had once written about how he and his fellow reviewers had to watch their step or they would have Mr Shawe-Taylor coming down on them like a Headmaster out of his study. What that really meant was that the writer of the Retrospect had to be on his guard to avoid any such charge, however humorously made. DS-T also warned me that the title 'Quarterly Retrospect' could be misleading: it was, in fact, a job for all the year round.

He had devoted himself to it from 1951 to 1973. That was the period which I dare say some older readers will regard as ***Gramophone***'s golden age, when the non-vocal retrospect was contributed by Edward Sackville-West, co-author of *The Record Guide*. His successor was Robert Layton, who like myself had the whole field for survey. It was not until the 1980s that parts of the territory were dealt with in separate quarterlies by experts in areas such as early music and baroque. I quite saw the point of this, and was in some ways relieved because by then the sheer output of recordings was becoming unmanageable; all the same, it seemed to me that these parts of the repertoire should not become too rarefied, and so if notes and queries arose out of my listening I would still from time to time venture an observation. I mention this now because readers of the selection in this present volume may wonder what has happened to the middle ages or (for instance) to Handel's operas.

The selections have been made mostly as a matter of personal choice – they are, on the whole, bits I liked or thought had some interest beyond the immediate one of the records under discussion. Some of the articles are reproduced whole, so as to give samples of the coverage; many are extracts, and these have been chosen also with an eye to the variety of their subject-matter. Possibly this will be deemed too wide for credibility: there exists, I fear, a ready suspicion that if you profess to know something about areas outside your immediate expertise then you can't really be very expert in that either. Robert Louis Stevenson has a good sentence on this in his *An Apology for Idlers*: 'That a man has written a book of travels in Montenegro, is no reason why he should never have been to Richmond.'

It has all been (as Lady Mary Wortley Montagu said on her deathbed) most interesting. I always felt it a great honour to be entrusted with the task, especially as I saw it in line not only with my illustrious predecessor but also with the legendary Herman Klein and Compton Mackenzie himself. Klein, who was the doyen of so-called connoisseurs in his time, did not actually write a vocal 'Quarterly', but his monthly articles, from 1924 to his death in 1934, were headed 'The Gramophone and the Singer', which Desmond Shawe-Taylor adapted as 'The Gramophone and the Voice'. Liking such links and traditions, I took that over in turn and when, one month early on, it disappeared, I for once (rare occurrence) insisted. It now becomes the title of this book, and the line passes to my distinguished successor Patrick O'Connor: I hope he finds it all as interesting and enjoyable as I have done.

JBS, May 1999

The Gramophone and the Voice

Quarterly Retrospects **1974-99**

1974

Pfitzner's Palestrina

There is joy in discovery, and deferment intensifies pleasure. Hard, then, to exaggerate the delight of finding this *is* the masterpiece that Bruno Walter, Thomas Mann and so many other good judges always said it is. Appropriately and creditably, the first commercial recording comes from DG; outside Germany and Austria all sorts of silly reasons have been found for ignoring the work (Ewen's *Encyclopaedia of Opera* lists 'lack of love interest … archaic flavour and long stretches of dullness'). More considerate objections centre on the Second Act, the meeting of the Council of Trent; yet it brims with musical invention, richness of theme and orchestration, as well as interesting, well-rounded characters and an inexhaustible interplay of light and shade. It could be scrappy, with second-rate voices in the smaller parts or lack of cohesion in the playing; but, led by Karl Ridderbusch and Bernd Weikl, all these roles are finely sung in the present recording, and Rafael Kubelík's direction is masterly in its feeling for changing mood and colour. Musically, the Second Act provides just what is needed: a vigorous, abrasive, extrovert contrast to the reflective 'inner' music of the First and the Third Acts. Dramatically, it contrasts the public world with the private: amongst these bustling, fretting vanities, personal, national and religious, Palestrina's timeless Mass is 'that little work' of an artist whose name the great churchmen hardly know. He himself is absent from the stage, but the news of his imprisonment shocks brutally, while attention is focused on the opera's other main character, Cardinal Borromeo. Fischer-Dieskau presents this many-sided man with authority, zeal and tenderness; he catches the sense of historical vision, the growing exaltation of his exposition, the imminent horror of art's annihilation. As against this dynamic force, Palestrina appears for so long to be static; kindly, but grey and withdrawn. This too presents challenges to the interpreter. Gedda, touching in his self-discipline, allows his tone to flower only when hope and inspiration are reborn. With a yearning, tender intensity, the voice is always convincingly that of the old master; one can inwardly hear his great predecessors, Erb and Patzak, in the role, and Gedda must surely stand with them, vivid, sensitive and deeply human. Pfitzner wrote beautifully for the voice, and his score brings out the best in a worthy company of singers. The whole performance glows; the recording is clear and warm. The gramophone has atoned handsomely for its half-century of neglect.

Monteverdi: Madrigals and Church Music

Amends to Monteverdi for centuries of neglect by the whole musical world are carried a stage further with the recording of Books 3 and 4 of his madrigals. Raymond Leppard, as in earlier records, directs an expert group of solo singers, giving, in this set, some of the madrigals to a chorus. The solo voices are so very nearly ideal that it seems churlish to grumble, but I think I would prefer either a purer tone (further reducing vibrato) or a more full-blooded Italianate sound. Still, they are fresh-voiced, finely in tune and consistently intelligent; and what riches they put before us. Nothing here is routine. The rhythms may dance or languish, the harmonies may be joyful or tortuous, but all will be in response to the particular text. The fifth side is perhaps best for sampling (and here I really do have a grumble: why don't Philips label their box-sets sensibly, giving the figures 1 to 6 in the large type which they now reserve for the quite unnecessary 1 and 2?). Or one might sample the settings of Tasso in the earlier records, or *Rimanti in pace* (Side 3) with its explorations into darkness, or *Si ch'io vorrei morir* (Side 6) with its sexual thrust, or the last of all, *Piange e sospira*, with its rich harmonies and haunting ending. But each of these madrigals is a gem – the only danger is that, hearing so many, one only half-listens.

This is rather more likely when it comes to the 16 sides of religious music comprising a fine album issued on the Erato label by Michel Corboz's singers and instrumentalists of Lausanne which have earned double gratitude this quarter, for from them come also the 'little' Masses of J. S. Bach, full of glorious material. With Bach one always (nearly always) listens; with Monteverdi one sometimes, very pleasantly, nods off. There is that courtliness, devotion made easy by sumptuous harmonies, rich decoration, beautiful voices, and string accompaniments that suggest the palace and the villa rather than church. Yet the collection is inexhaustible. The meditative, languishing, feminine *Magnificat* (Side 4), or the very different, rhythmical, 'new-style' setting on Side 6; the religious madrigals with their wide expressive range; the charming *Confitebor* and its simple, scale-built Amens, sung with the clearest of voices by Wally Staempfli on Side 9; and on the same side a playful, almost childlike setting of the start of Psalm 126, later deepening, gaining in physical energy with the 'sagittae in manu potentis', syncopated in 'saecula saeculorum', profound in the 'Amen' … all receive careful, pleasing performances. All, moreover, leave one amazed at the fertility of invention, and at the centuries of neglect.

Nineteenth-Century Opera

Not so long ago, Berlioz was also found in the ranks of the great neglected; certainly where his operas were concerned. Now they are two-a-quarter. Here, for instance, is Nicolai Gedda recording his third *Damnation de Faust*, this time with Colin Davis. It must be said that he was in fresher voice in the earlier versions; and also (when one comes to compare) that the present Méphistophélès, Jules Bastin, does not match up to either Souzay or Bacquier as a singer (he characterizes well enough, but the tone is thin and unsteady). There is, however, the pleasure of hearing Josephine Veasey, whose Marguerite develops in vocal character from the first solo to the last: intense in the feverish 'Je suis à ma fenêtre' and most affecting in the repeated 'Il ne vient pas'. The whole work is finely conducted, played and recorded; and Gedda, Faust-like, seems to rediscover his own youth in the love music. About the *Roméo et Juliette* (not really an opera – and nor perhaps is the *Faust*, but a 'dramatic symphony') I am less happy. For myself (though not, I see, for John Warrack, reviewing it in the February issue), the great pleasure of this performance was in the singing of Nicolai Ghiaurov on the last side. His tone is magnificent and his legato quite exceptionally fine. Michel Sénéchal is characterful, but rather dry-toned and unsmiling in his Queen Mab solo; Christa Ludwig sings well. The chorus work has been much better done. The Vienna Philharmonic under Maazel catch the excitement, but not the warmth and nuance of the score.

A muted welcome, too, for the new *Simon Boccanegra*. Domingo seems to me to be head and shoulders above the rest of the cast. This is a rare voice, not only in quality but in kind, having a roundness and richness that seldom, as with him, go along with effective, free projection. His style is fine, both in declamation and in the lyrical passages, and he sings with sufficient intensity to make Gabriele Adorno the focus of the whole opera. Amelia, Katia Ricciarelli, also comes to life in a vivid and heartfelt portrayal. Much of her singing is good too: not in the opening aria, I think, which is lumpy and charmless, but in the duets (surely a greatness about her in the 'Orfanella il tetto umile' passage). In fact, the lovers come right to the centre in this performance, for the Boccanegra and Fiesco make little impression. Ruggero Raimondi, with one of the finest bass voices of the day, is ungainly and flatfooted in Fiesco's 'Il lacerato spirito', though much better in his duet with Adorno. Piero Cappuccilli as Boccanegra seems to me, I'm afraid, to be quite undistinguished; his voice is often unsteady and yet has no special character of its own to compensate, and the portrayal of (after all) one of the great acting roles is no doubt sincere but rarely imaginative. Perhaps we have been spoilt by knowing Gobbi and Christoff, who were at their very finest in these roles. There should always be a place for *Simon Boccanegra* in the record catalogues, but, at least until something better comes along, it is Gobbi's recording that should fill that place.

No problem about a place in the catalogues for the remaining opera; there'll always be a *Tosca*, so to speak. And this new one is an all-star performance, ably conducted by Zubin Mehta and sung by three of the best in the business, Leontyne Price, Domingo and Milnes. But there is a world of difference when you go back and compare the Karajan/Price recording of 1963. Take Tosca's arrival and first solo in the Love duet. The added chesty maturity of Price's voice in the new version creates an unendearing first impression, and one feels that what she sings is not addressed. In the earlier recording the voice is fresher and the impersonation has far more life. There is a smile and a seductiveness about it; the passage 'Dai boschi, dai rovete' swoons amorously, and one understands why Cavaradossi could not possibly refuse the invitation. But, of course, Karajan helps much more than Mehta with the persuasion. The orchestration of that passage is magic in his version, and the feeling for the climax has a fullness of emotion which in turn helps di Stefano to conjure up beauty and affection with his 'mia sirena'. This is love for the music; the other is high-class routine. Price is certainly more tender in the last Act, where Domingo sings beautifully and where there is some inspiration in the playing. But the greatest source of enjoyment and interest, I think, lies in the Scarpia of Sherrill Milnes. He is in excellent voice and gives a more vivid and convincing character-portrayal than I can recall on his earlier records. The whole set is splendid in recorded sound; but personally I would not dream of exchanging the Karajan for it or the first Callas-Gobbi recording or the second Tebaldi.

Recitals

Domingo and Milnes sing together on another record; they also conduct for each other. There being no world-shortage of competent conductors, their conducting does not matter. Their singing does, and Domingo sings poorly for the first time on records. Or rather, he sings insensitively. The stream of golden tone flows on, but the *Rigoletto* and *Traviata* arias in particular register as spirited but crude, thoughtless performances. Milnes contributes a good 'Nemico della patria', but neither singer, as conductor, brings out the best in the other. More interesting is another and very different recital record for tenor and baritone, a collection of Victorian drawing-room songs and duets called 'The Dicky Bird and the Owl'. André Previn appears as a stylish accompanist at the piano, and among the items I liked Robert Tear in *The Death of Nelson*, Benjamin Luxon (sounding unexpectedly like Noël Coward) in *Cigarette*, and both in *Excelsior*. But this is the sort of singing in which we collectors of old records have standards — and this is not the way Peter Dawson used to sing *The Siege of La Rochelle* or Heddle Nash *Two eyes of grey* (try 'Great British Singers' on Rubini, which includes both). It is a matter of voice-production, and it seriously limits my enjoyment of Robert Tear's solo record, which couples Britten's *Nocturne* and Mahler's *Lieder eines fahrenden Gesellen*. I can't really see the point of issuing another recording of the Britten unless it is by somebody whose way of singing is quite distinct from that of Peter Pears; Tear's vibrations, colouring, vowels and consonants, his use of the head voice, are all uncannily like Pears, whose record with the composer is still markedly preferable in matters of interpretation. In the Mahler there is certainly much to admire (including the playing, with a rare lightness and transparency, of the Academy of St Martin in the Fields under Marriner). But the texture of the voice leaves me yearning to hear again the evenness of old Heinrich Schlusnus in a recording he made just before his death when he was over 60. I play it, and have to affirm 'This is what I call singing.'

It is the kind of contrast that comes to mind also while listening to a recital by another veteran, Hans Hotter. There are some lovely and rarely-heard songs here (Schubert's *Alinde*, Wolf's *Schon strecht' ich aus Bett*, for instance) and Hotter sings with humanity and skill. But the voice is very, very unsteady. A great artist, whose art is best recalled, as Andrew Porter remarked, on other records. Fischer-Dieskau, however, is on top form on a record of little-known settings of poems by Goethe. I liked Zelter's settings rather more than JW, and Reichardt's a little less, though the last one, *Tiefer liegt die Nacht um mich her*, matches up to the great challenge of the poem. The Seckendorff and Beethoven songs come to life wonderfully, as indeed does everything that Fischer-Dieskau touches. And he, I fancy, has pointed the way to the kind of interpretation which Peter Schreier gives of Schumann's *Dichterliebe*, coupled with the *Liederkreis*, Op. 24. He emphasizes the neurotic, unstable character, sweet and sour side by side, with the apparently jolly songs, like 'Ein Jüngling liebt ein Mädchen' and 'Aus alten Märchen', overlaid with a bitterness that is almost fierce. Similar sharp contrasts paradoxically unify the *Liederkreis* too, and make it more convincingly a cycle than usual. Particularly fine is the Schumann song, *Der Nussbaum*, in Janet Baker's recital. A lovely record, this; whether in the bold, outward-going way with the German songs (no microphone-coddling here), or in the charm of the French (with a brilliantly resourceful arrangement by Bax of a traditional song), or in such open-natured and craftsmanlike English songs as Parry's *O mistress mine*, this is singing for joy. A word of appreciation also for one other piece of Englishry, Elgar's 'Music for the Theatre'. Cynthia Glover touches the soft high notes beautifully in *The Starlight Express*. One of the charms is pure nostalgia – the kind of music that has disappeared along with the theatre orchestra, matinée tea-cups and genteel copies of *Playgoer*. But there is plenty of heart and spirit in it too.

Choral

My own favourite among all single-record issues this quarter is a choral one, the performance of Stravinsky's Mass coupled with some Poulenc motets by the Choir of Christ Church Cathedral, Oxford. Entirely apt for the Stravinsky, perhaps less so for the Poulenc, the choir produces a tone as 'straight' and drained of vibrato as any I have heard. Balance, intonation, rhythmic sense, range of dynamics, all are superb. One wonders if they are capable of warmth: but yes, the start of 'O magnum misterium' with some perfectly poised treble singing, is quite lovely. Simon Preston is surely producing one of the best choirs in the country. Louis Halsey, too, has added another distinguished choral record to the catalogue: motets by Gabrieli, Monteverdi and Schütz, all done with fine precision and devotion. It's a little bit unsmiling: Schütz's *Lobe den Herren* and Monteverdi's *Cantate Domino*, for instance, have an almost fierce intensity which sorts oddly with such happiness in the music. Very fine, though, is the sense of personal urgency in the last, unaccompanied, Schütz motet, sensitive to the spontaneity and flexibility of the writing.

Reissues

The complete *Thaïs* brings a surprise or two. A pleasant one is that the little aria 'Qui te fait sévère' develops a chorus and starts to waltz away like Lehár. On the other hand, confirming one's worst suspicions is the discovery that the celebrated 'Méditation', usually heard as a violin solo among palms no further east than Eastbourne, owns a heavenly chorus. Renée Doria, rather shrill on high notes, sings with much of the glamour of voice and temperament that the part requires, Robert Massard is reliable as Athanaël, and the recording (from a Vega original of 1963) survives well. As does Toscanini's *La bohème*, taken from broadcasts in 1946 and reissued as number 13 of RCA's 'Toscanini Edition'. It is one of the happiest of the Toscanini operas; even so, one marvels that the soloists (especially Licia Albanese, at her very best here) can give such characterful performances under such stress. It's all terribly robust; there's no charm, fragility, repose. But electricity is almost a visible presence.

A 'queen of song' worthily celebrated this quarter is Adelina Patti. She was over 60 years of age, and so are her records. But they are all that is left of her, and are superbly reproduced in a limited edition which I learn from EMI is still obtainable. As well as singing some of her favourite songs and arias, the elderly lady also speaks a New Year's message to her husband. In deep, measured tones, she signs herself 'Your loving Adelina, otherwise Patti.'

The Knot Garden

In a season of plenty the greatest richness of yield comes from what is to me an unexpected source. I had seen *The Knot Garden* twice, listened twice to the records, and still thought of it as fulfilling only the arid promise of its title: a joyless, 'clever' opera by a composer I had loved (and lost in *King Priam*) about people I didn't care for. Its 'cleverness' seemed sometimes silly, sometimes embarrassing; more seriously, the progress of these seven characters towards grace, acceptance and fulfilment seemed illusory both in the mechanics of the fable and in actual (as opposed to theoretical) musical effect. But things grow in *The Knot Garden*, and once they start the growth-rate is alarming. There comes a point when, drawn back to the records by a half-memory or a critical comment (Andrew Porter's review in the April issue sent me back immediately), one returns to find that the mind has been responding, sifting and collating after all; suddenly the music catches at the heart. And by that time one is there in the maze with these unsatisfactory people, and the desert has rejoiced and blossomed as old Isaiah said it would.

Records are invaluable with this sort of work. In the accompanying booklet Tippett himself assesses the gains and losses of recording compared with experience in the theatre, but in this instance the advantages seem to me to be overwhelming. One has to take it slowly. Thea's music probably speaks first, homely, tender, comfortable as moss on a garden path, deepening with her solo in Act 3 ('I am no more afraid') where one recognizes the Tippett of Sosostris's music in *Midsummer Marriage*. Then Denise (and a superb performance by Josephine Barstow): the recoil from a sense of gratuitous shock once over, her aria is profound and vivid, a compassionate exercise by the composer of

A Child of Our Time, now so much more complete in his mastery of resources. The duet between Mel and Denise in Act 2 then takes its place at the emotional centre of the opera, with both the depth and exaltation that are Tippett's peculiar gift, made possible (one comes to realize) by all the chattering counterpoint, percussive instrumentation and jagged writing for the voice that had originally played their part in repelling enjoyment. Bit by bit, one assimilates Dov and Flora. Perhaps a time will come when I shall find something in Mangus and Faber.

As for the performance, recording exposes the rough voice-production of the baritones, but presents Robert Tear's Dov as a vivid, sensitive portrayal. The women are excellent: Jill Gomez, Josephine Barstow and Yvonne Minton all fully within their parts, with Barstow's account of the extremely difficult solo ranking with the finest operatic singing on record. Colin Davis and the Royal Opera Orchestra play the score with conviction, mastery and insight. A recording to earn ever-increasing gratitude.

English Siegfried

Much gratitude, too, for the eagerly awaited first instalment of Sadler's Wells's *Ring*, a joyfully triumphant *Siegfried.* The success of EMI in recording from live performances, the great distinction of Reginald Goodall's conducting, the generosity of Peter Moores's endowment, and the fine quality of the singing and playing, all have received general acclaim. The Brünnhilde of Rita Hunter also has emerged from the whole cycle as an achievement of international stature, her tone bright-edged as the sunlight to which she wakens, strong as the sword which has won its way to her. But my own joy in this performance of the opera, above any other I have known, lay in the singing of the protagonist. I used to hear Alberto Remedios a good deal, ten or 12 years ago, at Sadler's Wells in Islington; his voice as I remember it was at that time strong and penetrative but hard and shallow in tone. Now it has put on flesh and become a quite beautiful musical instrument, under fine control, entirely steady even in the loudest passages, and softened without breathiness or loss of definition. He gives the vowel-sound its full length (which Lauritz Melchior used sometimes not to do) and, helped by Goodall's slow tempos, he presents Siegfried's music with a lyrical breadth it has possibly never known before. The character also gains immeasurably: a simple, instinctive person still, tireless of energy (as of voice) but responsive and reflective ('But I am quite alone, have no brothers nor sisters', beautifully softened tone for this). The 'Forging Song' too, very deliberate in Goodall's reading, gains dignity, and there is real meaning in 'Nothung, sword of my need'. Remedios has given us one of the very few completely satisfying performances of a Wagnerian tenor role on records, and he has done it using the means I value most: a scrupulously unforced, even emission of tone, breadth of line, and care for the voice as a musical instrument.

Rita Hunter is a Brünnhilde to match up with this Siegfried, and it is good to hear how she can moderate the sword-blade brightness of her full voice. Norman Bailey's Wotan is intelligently conceived and presented with authority, but there is often a kind of fuzz over his none-too-steady voice. Dempsey's Mime is grindingly strong of voice and clear of diction; Hammond-Stroud's Alberich is more recognizably Mime's brother than usual, but lacks darkness and solidity. Anne Collins takes her high notes with style but has not quite the contralto's weight needed for much of Erda's music. The orchestral playing, for much of the time, is inspired; so is the audience.

Song Recitals

Two tenors have recently recorded *Die schöne Müllerin* and they make an interesting comparison. Ian and Jennifer Partridge delight the ear and feel the songs in detail as well as in their inter-relationship. But Peter Schreier and his pianist Walter Olbertz make us picture a particular young man and listen to what he is saying. As in his recent *Dichterliebe*, Schreier characterizes the 'I' of the song-cycle as deliberately as he would an operatic role, presenting here an energetic, ingenuous country lad, and he makes sure that nothing gets by as 'mere' melody or as a song that can be properly understood outside its context in the cycle. The drawback is that his singing is so often ungainly; the soft, intimate singing is sometimes breathy, sometimes pallid, the louder notes often have an odd kind of throatiness, and the rapid, emphatic enunciation of words (as in 'Der Jäger') brings an effect too like speech-song, or even patter-song, for my liking. Partridge never sacrifices the singing-tone; at a *forte* his voice has a good ringing edge to it and in soft passages a rare warmth and natural gentleness, but it is all one voice, a well-treated instrument. Certainly Schreier is better at making sure that in 'Eifersucht und Stolz' we see him satirizing the maiden craning her neck to catch sight of her fancy huntsman; yet comparisons of interpretation do not always work in his favour (the gaiety and rhythmic spring of the Partridges' 'Mein' is surely preferable). And comparisons that concern themselves with the singing voice as a musical instrument rather than as an alternative mode of speech will I believe consistently favour Partridge.

On rather similar grounds, when William Mann (May issue) compares Benjamin Luxon's voice with Hüsch and Janssen, I reach for my old Wolf Society albums. The *Mörike Lieder* afford only a few songs for direct comparison: 'An die Geliebte', for instance, and what a contrast! Compare the very first notes, or indeed any note: loud or soft, Janssen's voice and its production are one thing, Luxon's another. Luxon has much more in common with Fischer-Dieskau. Still, the album makes a handsome contribution to the repertoire, and Luxon's collaboration with his brilliant accompanist, David Willison, provides some exciting performances of dramatic, rarely-heard songs like 'Lied vom Winde', 'Der Feuerreiter' and 'Die Geister von Mummelsee'. Exciting is also a word for Marilyn Horne's account of Falla's *Seven Spanish Popular Songs*. And here I may risk incurring the wrath of collectors of 78rpm discs for I hear a richness in this voice comparable to Ponselle's; and after her Carmen, when the voice had lost some of its firmness, she seems to be quite back on form. It is a marvellous sound (lovely in Nin's carols and in Bizet's songs too); but somebody should have dissuaded her from that shriek at the end of 'Polo', and somebody should probably have tactfully persuaded both artists that Debussy's *Bilitis* songs would be best postponed. The singing is often fine though she will assuredly do better with them in years to come; but the pianist, Martin Katz, is quite unidiomatic (comparison with Moore or Cortot makes this clear).

1975

Verdi

Time selects, but it also levels; and I don't think it is on the side of the big tunes. Thus: it picks out Verdi and confirms him, but for a genius that is pervasive. It also weakens our inclination to whistle 'La donna è mobile' and the Anvil chorus, but strengthens our pleasure in the whole style or idiom of the composer's work. So the record companies can in the same few months give us *Un giorno di regno*, *I vespri siciliani* and *Otello*, and, instead of finding that the one undoubted masterpiece eclipses the two lesser operas, we are likely to be struck most forcibly by the evident genius at work in all three. The relative absence of 'big tunes' means less the further we get from the nineteenth century; and all the time Verdi himself becomes fresher, richer and more subtle.

Un giorno di regno, his second opera, written against a background of personal tragedy, and a failure at its first performance, is sheer joy. The great thing about it is that the sparkle is sustained: you begin by thinking of Rossini and Donizetti, and end by thinking of Mozart. It has that kind of thorough workmanship and a sort of musical stamina that already exceeds the other Italians. *Falstaff* becomes the logical (as well as the miraculous) end to the career which so early on could produce this *melodramma giocosa*. The performance under Gardelli sparkles too, with spry, stylish playing by the Royal Philharmonic Orchestra, excellent chorus work by the Ambrosian Singers, and warm, clear recording. Jessye Norman and Fiorenza Cossotto are finely contrasted, though matched in accomplishment, in the female leads. Cossotto's brilliantly projected, brighter, harder voice copes marvellously well with a tessitura that is high for it: she is perhaps most impressive in the cabaletta of her aria in Act 2. Norman is velvety, rich and gentle, lovely in her first solo where she holds long notes over the chorus in a passage which would be an irresistible extract played on a radio review. Ingvar Wixell sounds like a genuine Verdi baritone (rare these days): both he and the tenor, José Carreras, are particularly good in their cadenzas. And the *buffo* duets by Ganzarolli and Sardinero go with plenty of zest. From all points of view, the album is a delight.

Similarly, hearing the *Vespri siciliani* is an impressive experience that brings as a by-product the great questions 'Why so rarely performed (never seen, for instance, at Covent Garden)? Why so unpopular?' Perhaps it is because there are few 'big tunes' by nineteenth-century standards (plenty by ours). Perhaps it is the harshness of the subject-matter, the background of fierce struggle which is insistently real and does not lend itself to jolly soldiers' choruses. This hard, menacing, militaristic quality characterizes James Levine's reading of the score. He secures playing of the greatest brilliance and energy from the New Philharmonia, and indeed only with a virtuoso chorus to match (it is the John Alldis Choir on top form) could he have risked such speeds. But it is all a bit unyielding: a Toscanini-like drive that probably does much to bring out the peculiar flavour of this opera, but which I should hope would go to work very differently on *Traviata* or *Rigoletto*. The soloists respond well, with Domingo again outstanding, as he was in the recent *Simon Boccanegra* set: firm, beautiful tone and an inspired reading of a highly demanding role. Arroyo's upper middle register seems to be loosening and she is taxed by some of the florid passages; nevertheless much of her singing is very fine indeed. Raimondi makes a better Procida than he did Fiesco in the *Boccanegra*, the upper part of his voice excitingly ample, rising gloriously to the great phrase 'Ah! sia salvo il caro suol, poi lieto morirò'. Sherrill Milnes, on the other hand, produces curiously lacklustre tones; the characterization is well enough, but the vocal style is undistinguished and the voice sounds tired. Verdi himself never does.

Nor, in the new *Otello*, does Herbert von Karajan; on the contrary, his insight is constantly revealing fresh detail in the score which again reflects the inexhaustible vitality of the composer. What does not reflect it, to my mind, is the Otello of Jon Vickers. One must put this personally for, obviously, the performance has many admirers, including Andrew Porter (October issue) who wrote of its nobility, grandeur and intensity. To me, it is quite unsatisfying and particularly disappointing when I think of the great things that seemed to be promised by his earlier recording. It seemed then that stage-experience, working the role into the system, would transform a notable Otello into a great one, but such development as one can trace has taken a curious form – a vocal characterization of dreamlike quality (emphasized at Covent Garden by the continual slow stride across the stage), interrupted but not interpenetrated by passages of anger and grief. There is no space to argue this in the detail which is necessary to substantiate the point, but it could be done. Comparing the two performances, I find the later version rather more intense in the Act 3 duet with Desdemona ('di che sei casta' for example), and the more open vowel sounds allow a little more sense of exultation in 'Esultate'. But often there is a loss (compare, just as one example, the phrase 'se dopo l'ira immensa vien quest' immenso amor' in the two versions of the Love duet); and there is nothing to compensate for the deterioration of voice (compare the notes at the start of 'Niun mi tema' or the tearing sound on the top B of 'dispersi insieme'). Again, for Glossop's Iago, I'm afraid I could not find the admiration which AP felt (and I have greatly enjoyed his stage performances). 'Era la notte', for instance, seemed unsubtle, and I could not catch the bluff 'onesto Iago' in this recording either, though parts of it are vivid and much is well sung. Freni's Desdemona, however (again differing from AP), did give me a lot of pleasure, but for her habit of taking notes from below. Then, to complete the account of disagreements, my struggles with the metronome found Karajan's tempos, as

I'd suspected, very markedly at difference with the score. And his second cut – slicing into the middle of the great concerted passage in Act 3 to an extent which not even the old Metropolitan performances used to do – is surely unforgivable. Remarkable indeed that at the end of the whole performance one is still overwhelmed afresh by the masterpiece which the work itself is. I liked the story of Toscanini returning from the première to call his mother up out of bed with 'Get on your knees, mother, and say "Viva Verdi".' She duly did; and so should all of us.

A Great Choral Record

Turning from opera to other vocal music, one wonders afresh whether the particular excellence or contribution of our present age to singing lies in the work not of the soloists but of the choirs. Every month's records bring new beauties, and the general level of accomplishment is very high indeed. Yet even by these high standards, the Choir of Christ Church Cathedral, Oxford, under Simon Preston, is exceptional. A year ago there was the superb recording of Stravinsky's Mass coupled with motets by Poulenc (July, 1974). Now, and I do believe it is still finer, there is De Lassus's *Bell' Amfitrit' altera* Mass and his setting of the Seventh Psalm. The intensity of these performances, the control and responsiveness of the choristers, the sensitivity and vitality of interpretation, all are immensely impressive. The dance-movement of the 'Osanna' expresses joy with a sort of subdued excitement; the sinking down of 'similis descendentibus in lacuna', or the rebirth of 'et vitam venturi': there are so many special moments. And yet the overriding merit is that this is a total reading of the works, that most of the dynamics are in changes of nuance, and that there is no imposed interpretation. Choirs and their directors receive little public acclaim compared with orchestras and their conductors; but in an instance like this the creative achievement compares with the greatest.

Gurrelieder

The discovery of Schoenberg's *Gurrelieder* (how late in the day) satisfies a half-articulated, long-felt wish for the existence of a work which draws upon the nineteenth century, its warmth of melody and harmony, its richness of orchestration, its breadth and seriousness, and yet which will blow the fresh air of the new century through it, to produce love music whose spirit is chaste: that is, that it has not palpable erotic designs upon the listener, that it is not mawkish in its lingering or morbid in its chromaticism, and that it nevertheless expresses tenderness and passion with all the resources which European music had so wonderfully evolved for these purposes. And now here we are, quite suddenly with two recordings to choose from, and a third to be released this month. My own introduction came through the Danish performance under János Ferencsik. Just possibly, if it had been the other way round, then I might have been drawn to the recently reissued Kubelík version instead but repeated comparisons make me doubt it. The very first pages tell of the difference. With

Ferencsik there is a pastoral sweetness, something of a Ravel-like delicacy; Kubelík is firm, clear and businesslike, and his players are entirely efficient, but the mood is lost. The deeper sonorities of horns and trumpets on their arrival (bar 14) are not felt as a new, expectant ground-swell; the strings (bar 27) do not sigh. Then when the Waldemar starts to sing, he has no poetry whatsoever: this is Herbert Schachtschneider, whose tone and interpretation lack beauty and imagination. The Danish performance has Alexander Young, who is taxed by the part and whose voice has loosened somewhat since the days of *The Rake's Progress*, but who understands and feels the music and who has the lyrical style at command. In certain brilliant passages of the score (after Klaus Narr's solo, for instance) the Germans have the virtuosity and their recording has more of the needful clarity. There is also the insight and magnetism of Inge Borkh's Tove, where Martina Arroyo, though fresher-voiced and broader in phrasing, makes less impression – the part really wants a Lotte Lehmann. And perhaps both recordings will be superseded when Boulez's appears. But then will come the test, and I believe that there will remain something special about the Danish performance (perhaps only in Janet Baker's glorious Wood-dove, but I feel that it is more pervasive), and that, although we may not hear all the notes of this infinitely detailed score, we still capture the spirit, the poetry and the love of it in a way that may not prove so dispensable.

Gurrelieder

The April Quarterly calls for a postscript. The issue of the new recording of *Gurrelieder* under Boulez has meant comparing it with the two versions discussed last time; and it has also brought the opportunity of going back to the famous pre-war Stokowski as well as to the 1954 Leibowitz. Such listening becomes obsessive and when all is over, first love is still last love. Perhaps the fact is that when one comes to know and love a piece of music gradually over a period of years then it exists in the mind independent of any single performance, whereas a work that has hit hard and suddenly (as this did) remains inseparable from the artists through whom one first came to know it. Perhaps it is sheer obstinacy. I see that Jeremy Noble (April issue) stays faithful to his Kubelík, and I fancy that those who were brought up on the amazing Stokowski will be unlikely to forsake that. For myself, it is still Ferencsik.

Yet this summary is misleading in that it denotes the recordings by their conductors. These are the *songs* of Gurre, and they want singing. No pleasure, but none at all, lies for me in the singing of Jess Thomas, Herbert Schachtschneider and Paul Althouse who as Waldemar with (respectively) Boulez, Kubelík and Stokowski have half of the poems to their share. Thomas's notes bulge, lose their shape; and the emission of steady tone is not a prominent feature of Boulez's soprano Marita Napier either. The difference when Yvonne Minton begins to sing is clear; she is the Wood-dove in this new recording, a glorious performance, finely sung in the way that Janet Baker's is in the Ferencsik. And the Boulez version certainly has other strengths: there is the expressive Speaker of Gunter Reich, there is much insight and brilliance in the orchestral work, and the recording as such is a triumphant piece of engineering and production. But if you can't love the lovers of Gurre, the impulse of this impassioned score is much diminished. I go back to its affectionate reading by Ferencsik, and to the intelligence and lyricism of AlexanderYoung's Waldemar.

Celeste Butterfly

When we come to Italian opera there are two recordings that shake up the hierarchy a little. With the new *Aida*, it is a matter of individual performances, or parts of them; with Karajan's *Madama Butterfly* it is a total experience, vivid and special from beginning to end. *Aida* with Caballé, Cossotto, Domingo and Ghiaurov has something like the ideal modern cast. Much is magnificent. And yet I left the gramophone at half-time, after the Triumphal scene, without quite that elation that sends one off clattering down the stone steps at Covent Garden out for a drink in the interval singing away to oneself or to anyone else unfortunate enough to be within range. And at the end of the opera, despite the celestial voices singing their farewell to earth in G flat, there was never the least question of drying the furtive tear. The fault, I think, lies essentially with Riccardo Muti, the conductor, who hurries both the triumph and the tragedy. The Grand March loses its swagger and style, the dances are not allowed to breathe; and then, after the 'fatal pietra' has locked the lovers in, it is a case of 'si schiude il ciel' in shop-shutting four-four and no-nonsense. Still, this is not the whole story, and fortunately the conducting seems genuinely sympathetic in the Nile scene in which Caballé especially is so superb. Her voice in itself makes possible the most lovely 'O patria mia', but then there are also these long, long phrases which are now so marked a characteristic of her style, floating up into the air and straight through to the softest, moonlit top C. Nor does she lose focus in the louder, more dramatic passages, as Zinka Milanov (otherwise rather comparable in her recording) tends to. Domingo's golden tone and Cossotto's firm, unified and brightly projecting voice are great assets; and the recording is fine. But comparisons with Solti and Karajan show readily enough how much more imaginatively the score can be read.

The special qualities of an overall conception and a newly perceptive attention to detail do distinguish the Karajan *Butterfly*. One feels the play of tenderness and cruelty more acutely through this performance: the one in the delicacy, lilt and sweetness, the other in the sharp edge and thrust of the brass. Mirella Freni gives a lovely account of her role, surely her strongest on record. She is not one of those singers whose unmistakably personal tone gives that pleasant shiver of recognition when she first sings, and maybe hers is not one of those performances that become etched upon the music in one's memory. Yet at whatever point you test it, it affords something lovely and imaginatively apt. Pavarotti, on the other hand, is going to stay with me in Pinkerton's music. Many individual phrases become newly vivid. How (for instance) he takes up the challenge, in the Love duet, or Butterfly's prescient cry about what they do to butterflies in his country: 'Yes', he says, 'it's so that you won't fly away', and that amorous pinning-down is almost visible. His voice has all that ardour one has loved in the best Italian tenors of the century, and he sings with a style that only a few of them could command. Like the *Bohème*, Karajan's *Butterfly* should become a classic of the gramophone. Might we urge upon him and his team the desirability of a new *Trittico*?

Missa solemnis

Let not the sun go down upon thy disaffection with a masterpiece. I did; it was the *Missa solemnis* in Karl Böhm's new recording, and a curiously hollow experience it had proved. Occasionally in opera house and concert hall, art gallery and study, the malignant spirits of denial emerge from their shadows to observe that greatness is an illusion, or, worse, to boom as through the echoing cave 'Everything exists, nothing has value'. That evening the *Kyrie* whispered it and the *Gloria* shouted it, with Beethoven striving and straining, sending his sopranos higher and higher towards climax after clamouring climax, never really achieving the fulfilling power and release of melody until the final prayer of the whole work, the 'Dona nobis pacem'. Genius making superhuman gestures stresses its own mortality; the listener stays earthbound and wonders what is wrong. I went to bed profoundly bemiserated.

But this present quarter is the *season* of the *Missa solemnis*. After Böhm there were still two other new recordings to hear, and from a noted and reliable tipster had come the recommendation to try again the 1970 Jochum. And I must say that under Jochum the *Kyrie* next morning sounded very different: Böhm's slower tempo, underlining the 'solemnis', had dragged, and Jochum's Netherlands choir was a great deal better than Böhm's Viennese, with their scrawny, tremulous sopranos. So I unwrapped the RCA album with Masur and the Leipzig Gewandhaus Orchestra and HMV's Karajan and started afresh. During the course of that morning, the music more than regained all it had lost the previous night. And the agent, again and again, was Karajan. Take the 'Christe eleison', for example. Karajan shapes it; he gains buoyancy by giving the repeated rhythmic figure in the bass a degree more prominence and more sensitive regulation, and he moves towards the *fortissimo* climax (bars 22-3 of the 'Christe'), the modulation from D major to A minor, bringing up the brass in the bar marked for crescendo, having his soloists swell and mould their rising and falling lines, controlling the gradual *diminuendo* as the music lovingly plays itself out and comes to rest on the last chords, *ppp*. In their different ways, all of the other performances miss the special character of this section. Nor do they secure such beautiful and enlightened playing in the last pages of the movement. Much more than the others, Karajan has observed the insistency of the markings – *pp*, *sempre dim*, *più pp* – and so a wonderful hush lies over the passage, while the suspensions, so much of the essence of this music, are played with many-tinted changes of woodwind sound. It has a beauty that is quite special.

This is so throughout the work, with one strange exception – the start of the *Gloria* brings a hazy rush of noise, even a feeling of perfunctory direction. Elsewhere the recording very deliberately balances claims of orchestra, chorus and soloists, so that one hears them in genuine concert-hall perspective. The chorus sometimes goes behind a cloud, as at the start of the 'Et incarnatus'. Yet, typical of this recording, it is then followed by an illumination to which the others seem quite blind – that is, the *pastoral* sweetness of the quartet, with its flute brought into balance with the soloists. In Böhm you hardly notice the flute, yet it is the essence of this passage. Going back to Böhm, I found the one unfailing pleasure to be Margaret Price's singing of the soprano solos. Back to Masur, one can rely on a workmanlike, unostentatious performance, and enjoy a clear recording. Jochum I think is better than either of these, with Karl Ridderbusch outstanding among his soloists. But with Karajan there is the feeling, or, rather, the solid evidence, of quite special interpretative insight. It focuses not upon the superhuman gesture but upon the great beauties of composition, and it does so with the freshness that most justifies a new recording.

Venetian Splendours

The other record that gave me comparable pleasure this quarter – that is, the experience of a great work newly illuminated – was John Eliot Gardiner's presentation of Monteverdi's *Vespers*. Again there is the sense of a man with something special to say about the score. It is a passionate, urgent performance, with dancing rhythms and sumptuous colouring. And once again comparison serves only to confirm and clarify the excellence. Jürgen Jürgens has directed a scholarly recording with the Vienna Concentus Musicus, but it has only a fraction of the vitality of Gardiner's.

The difference in spirit is clear from the start. With Gardiner the tenor soloist (Robert Tear on top form) gives out the opening text with fine ringing command, the choir and trumpets have splendour, the ritornellos dance, and then there is a marvellous way of bringing out the character of the last Alleluias, soft and smooth with the new, unexpected richness of harmonies, then a great growth of sound leading to the close. Jürgens offers little of this, the tenor enunciating with a monkish tone and emasculated style, the choir giving no comparable sense of presence, and the Alleluias unresponsive. Or take the 'Laudate pueri'. Gardiner has the opening phrase sprung as a lively dance rhythm, where in Jürgens it is taken quite dully legato and consequently little contrast is possible with the suave, caressing passage that follows. Later, at the marvellous phrase 'ut collocet eum', Jürgens's performance is tender and meditative, but there is none of that sense of the mystery of God's ways which is present in Gardiner and in Monteverdi's exploring harmonies. Innumerable, in fact, are the wonders of work and performance. Gardiner has a fine way with everything I want to hear in Monteverdi; the essence of it, I think, is the way the strong dancing energy of one section can go side by side with the darkened harmonies and mystical, sinuous line of another, yet all be one – the energy, mystery, solemnity and splendour of God's works. So, whether it is the fervour of the 'Lauda Jerusalem', the mysticism of 'Duo Seraphim' or the blessed quiet simplicity of 'Ave maris stella', all is there in full existence, with every bar living to capacity.

The Missa *In illo tempore* was published in the same volume of 1610 as the *Vespers*, but the style is very different. So, I'm afraid, is the standard of performance by the Scottish Chamber Choir; at their best in the *Agnus*, they need to secure a better blend, particularly among the sopranos. Nor do the Tölz Boys sound really firm and secure in the high tessitura of Giovanni Gabrieli's *Quis est iste* with Bruno Turner's Pro Cantione Antiqua; a fine record nevertheless, with the more sombre polyphony of Lassus contrasting with the springing rhythms of Gabrieli.

But glorious and on no account to be missed is the Venetian Festival Music recorded under David Willcocks by King's, two other choirs and the Wilbraham Brass Soloists. Germans in Venice learnt to do as the Venetians, and there is Samuel Scheidt's triumphantly trumpet-laden *In dulci jubilo*, while Schütz springs all sorts of surprises, harmonic and rhythmic, in Psalm 150. But most of the music here is by Gabrieli, and again the richness of sound, devotion and ceremonial testifies eloquently to the quality of a civilization now lost.

Bach in Plenty

A whole civilization also lies within those weighty albums in which DG are issuing their Bach edition: 11 volumes in all, between seven and 11 records in each, some old, some new, all attractively priced and presented. In one of these are the Passions, in another the Masses and Motets, the latter being a reissue of the splendid recordings by the Regensburg Choir. In *Jesu meine Freude* I prefer them quite markedly to the performance in the Louis Halsey Singers' new album, expert and musical as these are. It is rather like the excellence of the Karajan and Gardiner performances discussed above: there is a special realization and energy. The phrasing, the shaping, the splendid affirmation of 'I am free' in the second chorale, or the swaying rhythm of number eight, the full-hearted climax of 'Jesus, tritt herein … mein Freudenmeister': the Regensburg performance is rapturous. The Halsey Singers don't mean as much in their singing; nor do they in *Komm, Jesu, komm* which the Regensburg Choir address as a real plea. They are a highly able group, the English singers: admirably clear, for instance, in the intricacies of *Lobet den Herrn*, and of rare accomplishment, having sopranos who can actually trill as one voice. But Regensburg has some of that quite special life we used to hear in the recordings of Bach by the Berlin Motet Choir. I think they are still finest of all in *Singet dem Herrn* and surely (despite some faults) are due for reissue.

The great Mass and the Passions in the Archiv albums are reissues of performances recorded several years ago under Karl Richter. The *St Matthew* survives least well; I thought the sound rather harsh and some solo work unacceptable. Much to enjoy nevertheless, and more in the *St John*, which dates from 1964. I found myself rather more engaged in the listening than I was by the new Decca recording under Münchinger, though that makes a stronger, more intense appeal at first. The great asset of Richter's company is, to my mind, his Evangelist, Ernst Haefliger, and I wish he could be prescribed study for tenors undertaking the part. He has depth, command, skill in narrative, all these things; but the great distinction is that he doesn't squeeze, wail or wobble, but produces his voice with care for its evenness and with a virile tone. Dieter Ellenbeck, with Münchinger, does the usual sort of thing (though very well). Münchinger's other tenor soloist, incidentally, is Werner Hollweg, who sings the arias finely, and without that feeling of constriction and hardness that spoilt some of his earlier records. Still, both recordings, Münchinger and Richter, leave one with the marvellous feeling of exhilaration that there is in the *St John Passion*; bracing and dramatic in a way distinct from that of the *St Matthew*, for all its greater weight of sorrowfulness and meditation.

Turning to the Masses, I must include a reminder of Johannes Somary's recording of the B minor, highly spoken of, though, regrettably, I have not managed to hear it. Richter's performance (1962) survives well (choir and orchestra both splendid in the *Gloria*). And the album also includes fine new recordings of the four Lutheran Masses under Martin Fläming, and 26 *Geistliche Lieder*, whose purity is unblemished in the singing of Elisabeth Speiser and Peter Schreier and the accompaniments of Hedwig Bilgram. And what a cultural history they also embody, with their straightforward faith and unadorned devotion.

English Church Music

Among the English composers represented this quarter the one nearest to Bach in spirit and perhaps in workmanship is none other than Sir John Stainer. Bernard Rose's choir at Magdalen does him proud, and at this date it is quite a treat to hear genuine old-fashioned lay-clerk beefiness among the basses of the choir. At his best in the contrapuntal *Gloria* of the *Magnificat* in B flat, Stainer is generally too untroubled, too drawn towards the thin piety of his treble solos, too content to proclaim *I saw the Lord* as though He were W. G. Grace bicycling down The High. Before and after Stainer, however, English church music has included much that the plain Anglicanism of the eighteenth and nineteenth centuries generally excluded. There is the high Cavalier style of John Blow, splendid in some occasional pieces like *I was glad* written for the opening of Wren's St Paul's in 1697, inspired and sometimes breathtaking in *Blessed is the Man*: attractive performances by the Choir of King's College Cambridge with the Academy of St Martin in the Fields. Earlier, back to the first of the great English composers, there is a collection of motets by Dunstable, with flowing, sinuous lines that nevertheless sound austere compared with the sweeter writing of Dufay on the other side of the record (Pro Cantione Antiqua on Archiv). Then later, in our century, a notable affinity with the modality of the middle ages is there in composers like Vaughan Williams and Herbert Howells, whose *Magnificat Collegium Regale* is a lovely and thrilling item in an outstanding record by the Choir of Chichester Cathedral, originally released in 1966. Mention of Chichester brings us further up to date with the Psalms written for them by Bernstein and coupled by King's Choir with Britten's *Rejoice in the Lamb*. With organ, harp and percussion, Bernstein's work sounds more attractive than in its original recording with full orchestra. The spices and dances of the east with a hint of westside jive, circulate in the choir stalls. Most unanglican: one wonders what Sir John Stainer would have made of it all.

Grandfather's Grand Opera

Any well brought-up late-Victorian would know perfectly well what to make of this quarter's operatic fare. Bellini's *I Puritani*, Rossini's *L'assedio di Corinto*, Massenet's *Thaïs* and *La Navarraise*, with revivals of *Luisa Miller*, *La forza del destino*, *Un ballo in maschera* and Bizet's *Les pêcheurs de perles*, it might well be a grand fortnight arranged by Augustus Harris or Maurice Grau. What about the singing, though? Mesdames Sutherland, Sills, Moffo, Popp, Price, Milanov, Micheau and Verrett; Messrs Pavarotti, Vanzo, Bergonzi, di Stefano, Gedda, Cappuccilli, Souzay, Merrill, Bacquier, MacNeil, Tozzi and Ghiaurov. Not such a bad line-up, one might think. It will not satisfy your real golden-ager, but then probably nothing ever will.

The *Puritani* is a fine, first-night gala performance, with Sutherland brilliantly and beautifully in the lead. Her duet with Ghiaurov in the second scene is a joy; and the baritone, Cappuccilli, if no Battistini, nevertheless negotiates his runs honestly and produces some well-nourished tone. Pavarotti combines a lyric tenor's ease in the tessitura with the ringing power of a spinto. Even so, there is more to the singing of Bellini than this, as is clear if one compares his performance of 'A te, o cara' with Bonci's and Lauri-Volpi's. It isn't technique but style; the play of light and shade, the little lingerings and *diminuendos.* Perhaps this is what grandfather would most miss if he compared these with the performances of his own day; singers could hold out a moment as lovely and precious in itself, and listeners could savour it.

With the rest of the new productions, however, grandfather might well consider cancelling his subscription. *L'assedio di Corinto* gives patchy pleasure as music and drama, but much depends on the prima donna, who is Beverly Sills; and, however accomplished the scales, staccatos and trills, one flinches as the now apparently shrill, shallow tone is made to sound notably more powerful than in the opera house. It is harder still to compliment the prima donna of *Thaïs*. Anna Moffo appears to have added to her vocal effects a sort of vibration normally cultivated by popular singers of another kind. Maybe it is an interpretative device intended to suggest the character's sensuality, in which case it should have been renounced after her conversion. Massenet's excursion into *verismo*, *La Navarraise*, is more enjoyable. I imagine that when grandfather saw Emma Calvé in the role he came away with more to remember. Still, Lucia Popp does well, and it is good to hear Alain Vanzo again.

The revival of *Pêcheurs de perles* survives pleasingly from 1961, and the three Verdi revivals all have much to offer. *La forza del destino* has Milanov, lovely in her first aria, and di Stefano outstanding and – yes – subtle in his. In *Luisa Miller* Anna Moffo shows what a fine singer she can be. Finally there is the best *Ballo in maschera* of the stereo era. A vintage performance with Leontyne Price and Carlo Bergonzi heading the cast, and a rousing, reassuring end of the season.

1976

Ferrier in Edinburgh

When comparing the great with the good, we commonly say 'worlds apart', and the odd thing is that on analysis the 'worlds' often look more like hair's breadths. So with the two recordings of Kathleen Ferrier singing Schumann's *Frauenliebe und -leben*. The studio recording, known and loved for many years, preserves an exceptionally beautiful performance, yet there is more to the songs, and there was more to the singer. Now Decca release a new album in which we can hear her giving the *Frauenliebe* before an audience, with Bruno Walter as accompanist: a famous occasion this, in the Edinburgh Festival of 1949. And there is no doubt about it; the good performance has become the great. So one makes a detailed comparison between recordings and starts to note phrases in the Edinburgh version that have a special depth or vividness. 'Nur in Demuth' and 'selig nur und traurig sein', for instance, in the second song; surely these are newly vivid, worlds apart from the studio recording. But no, they really are almost identical. Hardly anything of the fifth song ('Helft mir, ihr Schwester') has analysably changed; and if one thought that a comparable passion and intensity in the last phrases of the whole cycle were missed in the studio performance, then again one finds this simply is not so. Yet the impression of greatness and of an essential difference grows with each playing.

One very obvious difference lies in the piano part. John Newmark was a sensitive accompanist and a good pianist; Bruno Walter may have been both of those things, yet that isn't exactly how one would put it. He is an accompanist only in the sense that he is company; he has as much to say as the singer, and he talks out loud and clear. In fact he gives that piano a fair hammering. But how he shapes the melodic phrases, how he feels the life within the placid-looking left-hand writing; how (for instance) he makes the chords tell their story in the link-bars of 'Süsser Freund'. The man has all the strength of the music within him, and of course his forthright release of it communicates its inspiration to the singer. But Ferrier herself is transformed, or transfigured perhaps. So let analytical criticism try again. 'Selig, selig bin ich dann' she sings in the second song: radiant now, though quite serious and unsmiling in the studio. 'Süsser Freund, du blickest mich verwundert an'; ah! now she's speaking to him and we know it because a newly flexible speech rhythm has come into her way with the words. 'An meinem Herzen', turbulent, full-hearted, with a playful contrast to come with the new rhythm of 'du liebe Engel'; the studio version is lighter, merely pretty, and without this emotional perspective. 'Nun hast du mir …' and momentarily she hates the man who has been so heartless as to die, leaving her alone; and she didn't do that in the studio. The differences are still of a hair's breadth in one sense; they depend on the slightest change of volume, or of the quality of a consonant or the shape of a vowel. Worlds apart even so.

Where Ferrier is entirely consistent is in the great beauty of her singing. I would be curious to know how many readers thought that her singing was the subject of the previous paragraph; and they could readily be forgiven, for that is the way in which 'singing' tends to be most commonly discussed. But of course one might just as well have been talking of an actor, or of, shall we say, a recording in which Bruno Walter tried to sing as well as play. This album brings home afresh just what a great *singer* Ferrier was, the voice so very beautiful, its timbre so individual, its control and focus so very fine. Her legato was utterly genuine, accommodating beautifully (for example) the 'turns' in 'Er der herrlichste'. The depth of her tone impresses afresh in the Brahms songs also included in the album, her power of crescendo without distortion of quality or disturbance of vibrato. The recording (which, understandably, is not technically speaking a joy in every respect) catches the firm core of her voice, the bracing freshness that it had in reality, so unlike the overripe sounds that used to come from her early records heard over the radio or on the old gramophones. It catches the nobility, the joy and strength of the woman and artist; and, what is rather different, the genuineness of the *singer*.

Festspiel '74

No doubt a live audience helped in the success of that performance; in both Ferrier and Walter one feels their intense determination to make the music communicate, to reach the hundreds of people sitting there-and-then in front of them. That recording is one of those in which the sense of a live occasion warms the heart and enriches the experience. But I must say that I do not find this an invariable rule by any means. There are people who hold it as something of a first principle that a studio recording will lack a spontaneity and life that are present in performances from the stage or concert platform. And no doubt most record collectors have a certain number of live recordings that are cornerstones of their collection. But I suspect the more generalized, doctrinal claims; I often conclude, frankly, that they come from folk who don't really like records very much, and also that, unforewarned, or unnotified as by the coughing of the audience or the clomping around the stage, the live-performance devotees would be just as likely to find spontaneity and life in a studio recording.

Certainly this quarter I felt that little was gained by recording *Die Meistersinger* live from Bayreuth or *Così fan tutte* from Salzburg. The *Meistersinger*, under Varviso, is not so strongly cast that the performance calls for preservation. I personally would not want to hear a second time the Eva or the Walther, the David, Kothner or Nightwatchman. Anna Reynolds is a fresh-voiced, sprightly Magdalena, Klaus Hirte a strongly projecting, mean-toned Beckmesser, and Hans Sotin a distinguished Pogner – it is good to have the evidence of live recording that his splendidly healthy, resilient singing of Pogner's demanding solo ('Das schöne Fest') shows such impressive stamina. And then there is the keenly anticipated Sachs of Karl Ridderbusch. Of all Wagnerian bass-baritones since Schorr, Ridderbusch has the beauty of voice and humanity of timbre right for this role, and in parts of it he is virtually ideal. His scene with Walther in the Third Act is one of these; the 'Wahn' monologue preceding it is another, with its compassionate pessimism and the noble swelling of affection all beautifully caught in the voice. Occasionally one feels a disappointment; sometimes a more emphatic, less vocal, treatment of a phrase than one had expected of him, sometimes a feeling of rather dull projection as compared with the Pogner or Beckmesser, sometimes a sense that the high passages may be tackled successfully but at the expense of the voice's original depth. But he sings out magnificently in the last scene and of course another liability with the live recording of such an opera is that a singer may well be cautiously husbanding the voice in earlier scenes whereas in a studio recording there would be no need, but, on the contrary, a gain in freedom, and hence most probably in that much-valued spontaneity and life that are supposed to be the mark of a recording from the stage.

The live *Così fan tutte*, on the other hand, reminds us that there are certain kinds of spontaneity and life that it is as well not to have. On the stage, a certain broadening of the trim elegance, an underlining of humour and situation, are perhaps inevitable and may not prevent a discriminative enjoyment. But on record these things seem crude, and they draw one's attention to what is being lost in the way of detailed, disciplined concern for style. Almost any comparison will serve to illustrate the point. For instance, the duet 'Prenderò quel brunettino' for Fiordiligi and Dorabella in Act 2 is fun in the Salzburg performance; there are good touches, and the gaiety of the occasion can be sensed (the occasion, incidentally, was also the eightieth birthday of its conductor, Karl Böhm). But return now to Böhm's 1962 studio recording and we find what is missing among the jollifications of the live one. It is the pointing of dotted notes, the feeling for rhythm, the symmetry of phrasing, as they balance and answer each other, the play of contrasted legato and staccato, the little shiver of excitement in the *fioriture*: worlds apart, though again, in fineness of detail, only a hair's breadth. Then there can be, in a live performance, the sort of excess we find in Ferrando's aria, 'Un'aura amorosa', taken very slowly and almost coming to a standstill before the end. Peter Schreier, the Ferrando, intent on squeezing every possible drop out of the melody, in fact mauls it so that its shape is lost; and we turn with relief from this tenor who is generally reckoned as being one of our best Mozartians to another who I believe had never sung a single role of Mozart before recording this one. Alfredo Kraus, in the earlier Böhm, maintains a genuine *legato*, with a well-focused tone and a disciplined style, and the aria coheres. His is not exactly a *melting* performance; for that one turns to Léopold Simoneau in the long-deleted Karajan recording, making a more than welcome reappearance on the World Record Club label. And this, to my mind, is still *the* performance, not only of the aria but of the opera. Note, for example, in it but not in the relatively unpolished Salzburg performance, how the two women, Schwarzkopf and Nan Merriman, match their voices (as indeed do Schwarzkopf and Christa Ludwig in the HMV Böhm). They are careful to accommodate vibrato and other kinds of personal characteristic so that the duets can be 'played' as by two well-matched instruments. At Salzburg, audiences were lucky to have two such strong and able soloists as Janowitz and Fassbaender, but their voices blend only in the most nominal sense. In solos they are often excellent, Janowitz giving an exquisite account of 'Per pietà', and I'm certainly grateful for the opportunity of hearing this in a live recording, though again one wonders whether a strong influence in the recording studio would not have helped her to work on the final bars which bring a lovely performance to a less than triumphant conclusion. Still, the gramophone is rich in its provision of this opera at the moment, and on the whole all versions are more satisfactory than this one. The Colin Davis performance is stronger in its women than its men; the Solti seems to some listeners rather over-brisk and charmless (I don't find it so, as a playing of the generous highlights record newly issued confirmed). The classic Böhm is full of delight: everything is realized with wit (where the Salzburg performance, despite the delicious appearance of its stage-set as photographed on the album-cover, comes over on record as a less sophisticated comedy altogether). Better still, to my mind, is the old Karajan; right from the start of the *allegro* in the Overture there is a personal touch, sophistication that sparkles, intimacy that is also strong and spirited.

Porgy and Bess

Summertime 1976, and 'the livin'' if not notably easy is at any rate agreeably helped along by the new *Porgy and Bess*. Not merely new, the recording is also the first to present Gershwin's complete score, which it does with a fine declaration of independence: the work, as its conductor Maazel says, was approached not as light opera, negro opera or any other subsection, but simply as opera. The all-negro cast, the Cleveland Orchestra, the clarity and warmth of recorded sound, all make for a quite special experience, as does the work itself. The opening bars tell of a marvellous rhythmic energy, a score worked at with almost that kind of passionate, tireless vitality that one might associate otherwise with Michael Tippett. The two composers do indeed make contact at several points. Gershwin catches the lithe, plaintive tenderness of negro melody as Tippett does in *A Child of our Time*, and in the choruses of the two scenes in Serena's room there is the sense of a mass yearning towards freedom and light; it recalls the wordless choral passage leading into the last spiritual at the end of Tippett's oratorio.

But the latest recording of *A Child of our Time* (it was issued in November of last year and somehow slipped through the retrospective net) moved me profoundly, while *Porgy and Bess*, a little surprisingly, did not quite do that. Why should that be? One always wonders – is it mood, accident, would it another time be the other way round? But whether valid as criticism or only as autobiography, the fact is so. Now both performances are highly disciplined and unsentimental. In Colin Davis's reading of the oratorio there is no melting into that first spiritual, no lingering at the end of it; similarly in *Porgy and Bess* Maazel does not luxuriate in the agonies, the spiritual ecstasies. And yet 'Go down, Moses', slow and noble and muscled by that powerful orchestral counterpoint, came with an intensity and sheer emotional force that was beyond anything in *Porgy*, and so with the whole of Tippett's Part 3. One basic difference, I think, lies not in the technical quality of the writing or the soul behind it, but in the sheer *loudness* of *Porgy*. The recording brought back to mind my first reaction when I saw it on the stage – one of those famous performances of 1952 when Bess was somebody called Leontyne Price. I was impressed, certainly, but also nearly deafened. One's emotional responses to music must be much influenced by rise and fall in the volume of sound. I think, for instance, of the way in which the brooding quietness of 'The world turns on its dark side' works upon the emotions in *A Child of our Time*, or the beneficence of the flute's meditation upon hard cancerous fact; or the quiet rapture of 'The moving waters renew the earth'. It was the absence of this, I think, that did much to limit the emotional effect of *Porgy and Bess* for me.

For many people, a limitation comes through the admixture of 'popular' songs and Broadway-musical choruses such as 'Oh we're leavin' for the Promise Lan'' or 'Oh I can't sit down'. Both are delightful in themselves, and I can't say that they worry me in context at all. The character of Bess and the quality of the last scene are stumbling blocks, I find. But when all is debated and assessed, it remains a very special and valuable opera; and one thing this recording makes quite plain, as Edward Greenfield said in his review, is that opera is the word. For one thing, it needs real opera-singers. Even Sportin' Life is all the better for having a voice, as François Clemmons shows. Crown would be all the better for having more, or rather for using his powerful voice less crudely simply because Crown is a crude character. About Leona Mitchell, I shared EG's misgivings concerning the evenness of her voice-production, exciting and convincing as her performance is. Willard White's Porgy, humane in feeling, generous in tone, is excellent. The whole enterprise has been splendidly carried through on all fronts, and the recording takes its place among the best of recent times.

Floreat Fiorenza

Looking back over the reviews, I seem to have enjoyed the *Capuleti e i Montecchi* rather more as an opera than did Richard Osborne, and the *Norma* as a performance rather less. Caballé's assumption of Norma is courageous, and her performance is at many points delightful to the ear and moving to the emotions; and of course it is a role that notoriously asks for everything and can hardly ever get it. She impresses certain phrases most lovingly upon the memory: 'ed un dolor insieme d'esser lor madre', or, meltingly beautiful, 'così trovava del mio cor la via'. Then in the dark, tragic music of Act 3, 'Teneri figli', she produces the most lovely floating tone that still has depths of feeling. Yet her 'Casta diva' and the recitative before it give only partial satisfaction: there is a feeling of dangerous pressure in loud passages, as though the voice has not more to yield, the high notes losing their absolute steadiness, and even the body of the voice threatened by that sort of chesty underlay which, in the opening recitative, gives her an almost matronly authority. But, more than this, my experience was that at several points in the opera, when a slightly waning interest had to be recalled, it was the singing of the Adalgisa, Fiorenza Cossotto, that brought it back to full attention. Her voice, powerful as it is, is under the firmest control; every note is focused, scrupulously placed and held, and the evenness of tone throughout her extensive range is quite exceptional among Italians. She can soften her naturally bright-edged tone, and she shapes her melodies, such as 'Mira, o Norma', with taste and musicianship. In an earlier recording of *Norma* she sang opposite the ill-starred Elena Suliotis; now worthily partnered, she shines as a pre-eminently fine singer even in this company.

She also appears in the recent recording of *Un ballo in maschera*. The cast is again a distinguished one, but again the strongest and most consistent impression among them all is created by Cossotto in the relatively short role of Ulrica. As in *Norma*, the tenor is Plácido Domingo, and very fine too in both operas, his voice darkly shaded, giving a performance generous in feeling as in sheer opulence of tone. Martina Arroyo sings Amelia, not an especially imaginative portrayal either in characterization or vocal style, but her voice, beautiful in the lower and middle registers, matches Domingo's well. Cappuccilli, as Renato, also seems to lack inner tension, and his big voice is often unattractively used, though he phrases with breadth. The recording is spacious too, and Muti conducts with feeling for the passionate rise and fall of the music. But the one touch of greatness, of magnetism working through a voice and its management, seemed to me to come in the fortune-telling scene, dominated by Cossotto. Her sense of rhythm and understanding of accentuation are invaluable in ensemble, as is the voice, which can make the portentous 'Così scritto è lassù' ring in one's memory for the rest of the opera.

The New Singers

Who are the new singers ? Here we are in the mid-1970s, the prime years of an established top team of operatic artists – Caballé, Freni, Arroyo, Cossotto, Verrett, Domingo, Pavarotti, Milnes, Cappuccilli, Ghiaurov. We still hear from Sutherland and Price, Bergonzi and Gedda (for instance); but essentially the casting of the basic Italian operatic repertory has depended for some five or six years now on the ten names listed above. Five years is time enough for some new singers to have emerged. Who are they?

High on my list of those who, unknown to most of us in 1970, have recorded impressively since then is

Jessye Norman. The great promise of this artist was evident in her first recorded role, the Countess in *Le nozze di Figaro* and she showed the extent of her achievement by meeting the formidable demands of Weber's *Euryanthe*. Her voice now seems to be in full bloom, the tone gorgeous in its richness, its production smooth and even, finely controlled. This we hear in two recordings this quarter; one of Verdi, one of Wagner. She sings in *Il Corsaro*, not suffering at all from comparison with Caballé who has the other soprano role (there is a trio at the end of the opera in which both women are dying for the hero, who then throws himself into the sea). Medora's Romance in Act 1 (sometimes suggesting 'D'amor sull'ali rosee' in *Il trovatore*) is one of the most attractive solos, and Norman's performance the most beautiful; there is a noble body to the tone, a strength within the velvet, a sure mastery of the difficult florid passages over a wide vocal range. The Wagner record exploits a smaller area of the voice, but requires a greater expressive range, and it is here that the principal limitation of her work is felt, especially in comparison with Janet Baker's performance of the *Wesendonk* songs, also issued recently. But in a way this is almost reassuring. She can deepen her interpretative powers with time, whereas time would be unlikely to help repair a misused voice or correct a faulty technique. Her voice is at present a most lovely instrument, and its beauty has never been more striking than in the *Wesendonk* songs. Inclusion, on the reverse side, of Isolde's Liebestod makes one hope that she will not be tempted into too heavy a repertoire (though the singing is exceptionally lovely). Fortunately reassurance comes with Sue Regan's article on Norman (August issue); a young singer who so recognizes the overriding importance of vocal technique and who still goes back to her teacher ('I need another set of ears and as my voice is constantly changing I need constant unbiased advice') is not likely to do anything silly about the music she undertakes.

Let us hope the same is true (I've no reason to think it is not) of that most delightful of 'new' singers, Frederica von Stade. Her solo recital endears itself further with every playing; a marvellously sure stylist, irresistibly idiomatic for instance in the song from Offenbach's *La grande Duchesse*, and achieving a fine intensity of passion and grief in 'D'amour l'ardente flamme'. I enjoyed too her record of solos and duets with Judith Blegen: some exquisite touches in her singing of Chausson's *Chanson perpétuelle*, and an accomplished performance by Blegen of Saint-Saëns's light-hearted charmer, 'Le bonheur est chose légère'.

Another mezzo-soprano who makes a strong, and at times overwhelming impression in a recent recording is Huguette Tourangeau, a majestic Queen Elizabeth in Donizetti's *Maria Stuarda*. Her solo in the First Act astonishes both in the sheer sound of the voice (a superb contralto depth to the low notes and plenty of easy resonance throughout the wide range), the flexibility of her technique, and the authority of her characterization. A splendid opera this, with its finely sustained sextet, and its compassionate feeling throughout. A notable performance too, with Pavarotti carrying that kind of thrill which is the peculiar gift of the Italian tenor, and Sutherland (at 50) often brilliant, sometimes celestial; her voice has loosened a little so that recording catches a beat, but it is still uniquely ample and pure in quality.

The 'new' tenors are, I suppose, headed by José Carreras, who does so well in *Il Corsaro*. He is probably most in line with Bergonzi, and indeed I compared their performances of the solo 'Eccomi prigioniero' in Act 3, finding Carreras (helped by his conductor, which Bergonzi is not) the more subtle and imaginative singer here. A 'fatter' tenor voice is that of Franco Bonisolli, described as 'one of the greatest hopes for the future' on the sleeve-note of *La traviata* from the film made in 1973. His Alfredo, sung to the admirable Violetta of Mirella Freni, is stronger in characterization than in vocal elegance, but it is an unusual voice and we should hear more of him. Perhaps more too of Giacomo Aragall, an earlier Alfredo who seems to have disappeared from the recording studios; and perhaps something of Giorgio Merighi, a vibrant, very Italianate tenor who has been well received at Covent Garden.

But talking of reception at Covent Garden brings to mind the artist most conspicuously absent from this list. I find it extraordinary that in these precious years when the bloom of youth is full on that most lovely voice, the recording studios should have so largely failed to engage Kiri Te Kanawa. As the Countess, Mimì, Micaëla, Maria Grimaldi and Desdemona she has given the loveliest and most appreciated performances I have heard. She should by this time at least have had a solo recital to match von Stade's. And one final plea: when there is such a lack of good baritones, might it not be possible, on one of his visits to the West, to entice Yuri Mazurok into the studios? Written comments on his performances, with such records as we know, suggest that he is probably the best now living.

Lieder: the Great and the Good

In the field of Lieder there are no masters like the old masters. Not so very old, one must hastily add, but both Schwarzkopf and Fischer-Dieskau are now definitely in the ranks of senior artists. DG have reissued the monumental Schubert albums by Fischer-Dieskau and Gerald Moore, the first of them containing 12 records and 344 songs, the second even more. Volume 1 covers the years 1817 to 1828, and I have at present arrived (with enjoyment tainted by a consciousness of virtue) at Side 18 and 1825. Delights inexhaustible, the great variety of Schubert's styles (in his accompaniments, for instance) being one, and the thoroughness and resourcefulness of Fischer-Dieskau's art another. No song, hardly any phrase of any song, finds him (or Gerald Moore, for that matter) uninterested or uninteresting. Occasionally, a soured tone will fall on ungrateful ears, but even then it will probably be a way of pointing to a darker and generally unnoticed element in the song; *Im Abendrot* is an example (Side 17). His vocal range is as remarkable as his command of moods. The songs cover two octaves and a fourth: repeated low Es in *Das*

Abendrot (Side 5) and high As in the entertaining mock-heroics of *Herrn Josef Spaun* (Side 11). Everyone will come away with an immense list of 'finds', wondering why on earth they are not as popular as (say) *Litanei* (Side 4, and sung with never a wrinkle in the smoothness of line) or *Der Musensohn* (Side 13, resilient and unfussed, flanked by the delightful *Im Haine* and a most touching setting of Goethe's *An die Entfernte*). Twenty-two pounds fifty is still a good deal of money but I can think of few uses for it more sure to last a lifetime.

Schwarzkopf's recital is also a precious possession. Her voice is still beautiful – like her lovely appearance on the concert platform it is scrupulously cared for, nothing is slack, and there is a radiance, a kind of glamour that both enchants and tells of standards. In *Widmung*, the first song of the Schumann group, she sings with spring-like freshness; and how beautifully she 'places' the notes in Wolf's *An eine Aeolsharfe*. With this goes an intense absorption in the mood of each song and a rare ability to concentrate a listener's attention. No wonder Eric Sams in his review (March issue) called her the supreme Lieder singer of our time.

Coming now to Janet Baker's Schumann record (she is not exactly an 'old master' though dameship confers a certain seniority), I hope Mr Sams will forgive me if I say that I was mildly disturbed when his review of the *Frauenliebe und -leben* did not mention the Ferrier/Walter performance as one that was so to speak 'in the running'. But no, I returned to it after a second playing of the Baker/Barenboim, and to me that Edinburgh Festival recording remains the most vivid and moving of all. Still, the new one is a great joy. Barenboim has an exact ear for the balancing of a solo melody (in either hand) with its accompaniment and working it in duet with the voice; and in the *Liederkreis*, Op. 39 he is marvellously able to paint in the deep, rich colours of forest and twilight. In the comparison between this and Janet Baker's earlier version, I found the point made by Edward Greenfield in *The Guardian* a fascinating one: that the keys used in the *Frauenliebe* are now higher until you come to Nos. 6 and 7, where the lower keys of the new recording give a maturity and warmth to the maternal songs.

These are great singers and exceptionally fine recordings. There are others that give pleasure, if with less distinction. A thoroughly happy record is Elly Ameling's recent Schubert recital. The programme suits the voice, the emotions extending (but only just) to a bitter sense of loss in *Die Liebe hat gelogen* and *Du liebst mich nicht*: pleasing to know, too, as I have found only very recently, that the voice is if anything even more fresh and bell-like 'in the flesh' than on record. Yet the limits of her art are clear when one comes to her *Frauenliebe und -leben*: there is a wholesome straightforwardness of interpretation, but the bright, spring-like voice is hardly able to convey sufficient depth of feeling; she is much better with Schubert's *Schmetterling* or *Im Haine* on the other side. Then there is Robert Tear's second 'Soirée', following his Chopin-Liszt recital with a delightful Mendelssohn and Weber programme. These seem to me the most satisfying records he has made; there is masterly characterization in his singing of Mendelssohn's *Neue Liebe* and fine work throughout by Philip Ledger as accompanist. Peter Schreier too impresses in his *Schwanengesang*, sung with a grey, haunted tone, finding a unity of feeling in this collection of songs which William Mann, reviewing Fischer-Dieskau's DG recording, cautions us against thinking of as a cycle. But again one returns to the old master, to Fischer-Dieskau in HMV's reissue of his 1963 recording to find a warmth of voice lacking in Schreier, and culminating in a performance of 'Der Doppelgänger' where the thrill of supernatural horror is communicated so much more powerfully for a finer, surer resonance in the high notes of the great climactic phrases.

Boult's Dream of Gerontius

The old master triumphs here too. This is a glowing, intense and passionately charged reading by Sir Adrian; spacious but not sanctimonious, stressing the breadth and strength of melodic line rather than the chromaticism. About Nicolai Gedda's Gerontius I didn't really share Alan Blyth's feeling that he is insufficiently experienced or 'soaked' in the part. I thought, in fact, that as a dramatic and spiritual experience he entered it very fully, while the limit to my enjoyment came from certain features of his voice-production, rather unsteady on some sustained notes, and too drained and other-worldly in his role of Soul in Part 2. Robert Lloyd I thought particularly good in his second appearance, as the Angel of the Agony. The chorus work is fine, and the quality of recording near to ideal. But all of these features are secondary to the overall power of the work itself and Boult's direction – the Prelude to Part 2 lifted gently heavenwards, the Demons' Chorus more musical, and 'Praise to the Holiest' more cohesive than ever before in my experience, and the last pages inspired but not (favourite pejorative word of Aldous Huxley's) 'inspiratory'.

Oxbridge

The English choral tradition derives much strength from cathedrals, parish churches and choral societies, but in the years since the war its standards and leadership have owed more and more to the ancient universities. The Choir of King's College, Cambridge, set standards of sensitivity and musicianship that were far superior to the cathedrals; so, at least, it seemed to me in my own years at Cambridge when the choir was under Boris Ord. 'The Glory of King's' is the title of a recent set which asserts the excellence that seemed in those days to be incomparable. It comes, however, as a well-deserved tribute to the choirmaster who followed Ord, David Willcocks; he softened and sweetened the sound, I think (not entirely a good thing), but also extended the repertoire and made some superb recordings. Several of these are collected in this three-record set, ranging from a very gentle, caressing treatment of Palestrina's *Missa brevis* to Britten's; catching the inspiration of Vaughan Williams's G minor Mass (superb in the 'Et vitam venturi') and the rhythmic exultancy of Byrd's *Haec dies*.

Incidentally a major part of 'the glory of King's' was always their performance of the psalms, and I returned with gratitude to Willcocks's Volume 2 having been much depressed by Volume 3 under his successor, Philip Ledger: far too slow and deliberate, with 'abominable in their wickedness' enunciated like a choir of Daleks.

In the old days, 'the other place' never seemed to me to compete at all, but it is very different now with several excellent offerings from Magdalen under Bernard Rose (a fine recital of early English music recently to hand) and perhaps the most exciting series of choral records now being produced, by the Choir of Christ Church Cathedral under Simon Preston. They have given a second Lassus recital, made up of eight-part motets and the Penitential Psalm 5, a huge work that calls for exceptional staying-power and responsiveness in its singers. And quite superb is their *Israel in Egypt*, the recording which has given the greatest pleasure of all I have heard this quarter: a work that is white-hot in sustained descriptive power and a performance which catches the inspiration with quite exceptional insight.

'Musicke of Sundrie Kindes'

This is the title of a four-record album of Renaissance secular music from 1480 to 1620. Under the direction of Anthony Rooley, The Consort of Musicke give splendid performances, sometimes (as in the 'Cries of Paris' on Side 3) with brilliance, always with life and an almost possessive love for the repertoire. New and delightful pleasures abound, with the fertile creativeness of these years coming to extraordinary fulfilment in Gesualdo; the discords of his madrigal *Mille volte il dir moro* (Side 6) are ecstatically resolved, the harmonies, intervals and developments constantly amazing. I wish Emma Kirkby did not sound so thin and piping in *The Silver Swan*, and I wish that the informative booklet did not involve one in so much turning of pages; but such points are nothing to the rich provision these musicians offer.

There is a great wealth of little-known music in several single records too. A recital of songs by Josquin Desprez presented by Musica Reservata under Michael Morrow has some extraordinary singing, as in the darkly unaccompanied voices sounding almost purely instrumental in *Plaine de deuil*. I enjoyed too the Martin Best Consort's eighteenth-century entertainment called 'The Fine Old Tory Times': wholesome tunes, lively arrangements, engaging lyrics and a good idea.

Another delightful programme is the one devised by Peter Hurford for his Alban Singers, 'Songs of Leisure and Love'. The style of performance comes as a change and a pleasant one after the groups I have just mentioned; they sing with a gentler tone, a more human affection. I see that Denis Arnold criticized their performance of Wilbye's *Draw on, sweet night* as too slow but to me it seemed beautifully sustained, and they caught (as many do not) that lovely phrase 'And whilst thou all in silence' as an exquisite moment. There are also three part-songs by Robert Lucas de Pearsall whom most of us know only at Christmas time for his arrangement of *In dulci jubilo*. He relishes the intertwining of voice parts and the smiling resolution of mild discords: the singers with him. Most winning of all I found the two part-songs by John Gardner, colourful pieces for a virtuoso choir, and well served at St Albans.

Two fine records of choral music from the twentieth century to end with. The first is a recital of music by Edmund Rubbra sung by the St Margaret's Westminster Singers under Richard Hickox; the Masses of 1946 and 1948, the first in English, the second in Latin, are the main works. Both are of great beauty, the Latin Mass more colourful, more mystical, more exploratory in its harmonies; and in each Rubbra seems to show a particular affection for the 'Benedictus', lovely settings both of them. The choir sing with sensitivity and fine tone, occasionally marred by the bass line which tends to be hard-edged yet lacks depth of tone. For the other record we return to Cambridge, for music by Patrick Hadley, a former Professor there. *The Hills*, written in wartime, is a joyously liberated work, one that lets sounds bloom. The start of the third section ('Wedding and after') has such rich, resonant choral writing, unashamedly tuneful, giving full generous space for the melodic ideas to come into full life, that it seems extraordinary this should be a first recording and the work still relatively unfamiliar.

Looking back, I see that I have written an account of almost unspoilt enjoyment. That will never do. Let me add a mention of four records that go into my Black Book: Orff's *De temporum fine comoedia*, Gordon Crosse's *Purgatory*, highlights from Bernstein's Mass, and (with trembling) Stockhausen's *Moments*. They are works which, not liking, I resolve to get to know better – but not yet!

1977

Two Great Dames

'Finally,' says a newspaper report on last night's opera, 'a word about the singers.' Apparently they wore costume and make-up, some of it suitable, some of it not. They acted, some of them better than others. They were (in turn) charming, robust, malevolent and well-nourished. They enunciated words, they had a little trouble with the scenery and conductor, and one of them missed the subtleties of her role though she sang well enough … 'Sang'! Astonishing word, for one would never in such reports gather that singing mattered one way or another. The beauty of a voice, its particular characteristics, its evenness, its freedom, the musical beauty of the singer's singing: these, apparently, are peripheral matters. A lumpy voice or a steady one, a pure voice or a scratchy one – what does it matter as long as their owners get the notes, words and expression right and act up? Well, one answer is that it matters to the public and to the future of opera.

It is in some such context that two recent albums deserve the warmest welcome. They celebrate the art of two great Dames, one of them Nellie Melba, the other Maggie Teyte, and they focus attention inescapably on the singer's singing. We hear two soprano voices that in their prime were of the most lovely purity, and which survived their prime with a firmness and evenness of tone that would be remarkable in a 25-year-old let alone a sexagenarian. They show you what legato means, what a trill and a scale should sound like, how a high note should appear in the air and a wide upward interval be taken in a clean, confident leap. With Dame Maggie there are limitations of interpretative insight; with Dame Nellie there are severe limitations of taste sometimes spoiling the beauty of a note, a phrase, a verse. But the best of these singers is also the best in the art of singing; the essential art, that is, which is concerned with the production of sound.

Brief examples. Melba's poise and evenness in the testing phrases of 'Porgi amor', her scrupulous accuracy that never inhibits brilliance in 'Sempre libera', the perfect trill of 'Caro nome', the bold unforced strength of the high notes in *Ave Maria*, the sheer loveliness of sound and line in *Come back to Erin* which with such modesty (it is a striking characteristic of much of Melba's singing) takes a simple melody straight to the heart. Teyte's unflawed purity in the 'reviens' of Berlioz's *Absence*, the clean, springlike rise to the last note of the phrase 'Et mon coeur s'est levé par ce matin d'été' in Chausson's *Poème*, the magical high notes of pleasantly lilting tunes from *Monsieur Beaucaire* and a show called *By Appointment*. Both artists were capable of conveying feeling (Melba in for instance *Le temps des lilas* or Ophélie's solo, Teyte in Duparc's *Extase* or the vividly 'projected' *Oft in the stilly night*, made in 1941). Both are utterly themselves; immediately recognizable. But above all, both leave us thirsting for more of their sound. It is an example of a deep thirst which the ordinary opera-goer takes to the opera house: a thirst for beautiful singing, by comparison with which the preoccupations of the reviewers are often secondary matters. While these excellent albums enjoy their no doubt all-too-brief life in the catalogue it is greatly to be hoped that they will inspire singers and teachers to reaffirm basic priorities, and the general public to acclaim real singing when they hear it.

Russian Song

Shostakovich's *Seven Poems* of 1967 recorded by Vishnevskaya and Rostropovich form a specially fine part of a valuable album of Russian song. The *Seven Poems* are written for various combinations of voice, piano, violin and cello, often touchingly simple, always with beautifully shaped melodies, and ending with an impassioned invocation to music, 'sovereign of the universe'. The other cycle by Shostakovich, called *Satires*, is harder to enjoy without an understanding of the language, though there is much to admire in the performances. For the rest we have Mussorgsky and Tchaikovsky – an unusually fine selection of Tchaikovsky songs, and the *Sunless* cycle newly moving through the sensitivity of these artists to mood and atmosphere.

Vishnevskaya's singing provides a counter-thesis to the main theme I started with. She does not at all consistently make beautiful sounds, yet there is no doubt that we are hearing a great artist. She catches all the sadness of Tchaikovsky's lonely maiden longing for her lover, or the mistiness of night in

Mussorgsky's *Elegy*, the ghostly 'bayu bai' of Eremushka's lullaby, the desolation of Ophelia in the first song of Shostakovich's cycle. And sometimes she will sing with virtually no flaw in the voice at all: *Mid the din of the ball* is a most lovely piece of pure singing on the Tchaikovsky record.

For a sure and superb mastery of the voice, however, there is Irina Arkhipova, whose recital is of Rachmaninov as well as some of Mussorgsky's *Songs and Dances of Death* and six rather less interesting songs of Tchaikovsky. Great singing in *The Field-Marshall*, with the frowning intensity of battle and the exultant authority of Death who stamps down the earth on the bones of the slain. A regal style in Rachmaninov's *In the silent night*. And a beautifully softened tone, all the edge taken out, and only a gentle warmth left, at the end of *Oh, never sing to me again*. Yet some kind of inner quality, some subtlety and imaginativeness, draws me back, even after this, to the less perfect Vishnevskaya. There is a kind of greatness about her in this recital, and greatness is well known for upsetting critical principles.

Pied Piping

I don't know how many critical preconceptions David Munrow upset; I should think the principal one was the basic notion of what can be accomplished in a single lifetime. His testament includes two new record albums which themselves might represent a very respectable life's achievement; remarkable additions to the catalogue in themselves, doubly honourable when we know them to be among his last. 'Music of the Gothic Era' and 'The Art of the Netherlands' are both of them superbly and joyfully educative albums. Of course there will be those who know it all already or reckon they do; but for the vast majority of music-lovers these records are like the opening-up of a new wing in a great gallery. What shall we stop in front of? Two works of Pérotin, *Viderunt omnes* and *Sederunt principes*, as alike and as different as two Brahms symphonies; *Alle psallite cum luya*, thirteenth-century 'pop' to the extent that its tune will be with you for the next month, and its rhythm insists. *La misnie Fauveline* where the Duplum voice sings about the new girl he fancies and Triplum is displeased with Fauvel for having the cheek to ask Dame Fortune's hand in marriage; Machaut's *Lasse! comment oublieray* with some amazingly poignant harmonies. And in the Netherlands album an inexhaustible wealth of works and styles – the extraordinary mass of sound and syncopation in Antoine Brumel's *Gloria*, the dance rhythm of Isaac's *Agnus Dei* from his *Missa la Bassadanza*, Josquin's austere *De profundis*, the deep sonorities of Ockeghem's *Intemerata Dei*. Above all, perhaps, Jean Mouton's *Nesciens mater*, where the ear is beguiled into a sublime forgetfulness of the miracles of canon and counterpoint that the composer is working.

Of course much is being done in music now to bring these earlier centuries into the range of our appreciation. Another musician doing so with much distinction is Anthony Rooley, whose Consort of Musicke have recently recorded Dowland's *First Books of Songes* and so revealed the full range of a volume of which most of us will have known only part. But even at a time when this is something of a growth industry, David Munrow's contribution was a special one. There can hardly have been a day during the latter years of his life when somebody did not come to a new delight in music because of him. These posthumous albums are a great enrichment of the musical life, and the pied piper will still be among us for at least as long as they are.

Weber

In all those lists made in school-days, when music was so readily assimilated and so confidently appraised and when composers stood in competitive array, favourites to be ranked and enumerated from one to 100 – where stood Carl Maria von Weber? Something like thirty-second, I should think. And there, it is much to be feared, he stayed: acknowledged, approved, but unexplored. Then last year came his centenary-and-a-half (he died in London in 1826, aged 40, beset with ulcers, tubercles and much suffering), and the event has been marked by a supply of records sufficiently concentrated to bring him freshly to life for more listeners than one.

Not for the first time, it is some 'minor' music in an 'unimportant' recording that works the trick. A recital of Weber's songs by Martyn Hill and Christopher Hogwood, with a fine reproduction of a Caspar Friedrich on the sleeve to whet the appetite and attune the mood, brings his individuality into sharp focus. It is the gaiety, impulsiveness, grounded in folk music and growing into art song (subtlety that doesn't sophisticate the straightforward happiness of spirit). And we find it in such songs as *Unbefangenheit*, *Minnelied* or *Die freien Sänger*; *Reigen* ('Round Dance') is another delightful one, giving scope to the surprising resources of the fortepiano in accompaniment. And there is *Die Zeit*, a more serious song, which Martyn Hill (like Robert Tear before him, in that very enjoyable Weber/Mendelssohn 'Soirée') sings with pallid tone, drained of all vibrancy. Not that Hill has a great deal of vibrancy in the first place, and one sometimes wishes for more sheer voice. But the songs suit him; he is nimble, resourceful and humorous and after the yodelling *Mein Schätzerl ist hübsch*, and the 50 seconds concluding *Elfenlied* I feel I want to bang the cymbal and drum-stop of the fortepiano in appreciation.

More important, the appreciation spreads. Opening up DG's reissue of *Der Freischütz* and *Oberon*, I listen with newly interested ears. And both merit their reappearance. Jochum's *Freischütz*, from 1960, still impresses as a warm, joyful performance; if less urgent and insistently serious than Carlos Kleiber's, it has more glow, more romanticism and more joy. Irmgard Seefried, a singer I normally love to hear, is not a really satisfying Agathe, but there is a most accomplished and winning Aennchen in Rita Streich – she makes it worth putting up with the variable Max of Richard Holm and the invariably crude Kaspar of Kurt Böhme. The *Oberon* reissue spares us the spoken dialogue, but does so at the expense of dramatic continuity. Domingo brings a marvellous combination of Italianate golden tone, musical command (in those fearsome runs, for instance) and incisiveness to the part of Huon. And Birgit Nilsson is at her best in the Cavatina of Act 3, a kind of counterpart to Pamina's 'Ach, ich fühl's' in *Die Zauberflöte*, beautifully scored.

Abu Hassan also brings Mozart to mind in association with Weber: a happy entertainment, and sometimes (as in Fatima's arias) quite hauntingly beautiful. The recording dates from 1971, is conducted by Heinz Rogner, and has Ingeborg Hallstein and Peter Schreier as a well-matched Hassan and wife. Still, this is, I would say, a matter of mild enjoyment (I hope that doesn't underrate it), while *Die drei Pintos* is something more. To me it brought the season's most enjoyable evening with the gramophone. Great fascination, of course, lies in the interplay of the composers: Weber, the 'Weaver', woven on Mahler's loom. But above all there is intense and rarely slackening pleasure in the sheer fertility of melodic and rhythmic ideas, in orchestral colours and good-hearted comedy. The Overture itself is a discovery (a perfect introductory tune for a radio or television series, like *Les francs-juges*), and it leads joyfully and briskly into the opening chorus. The Spanish students, despite their la-las, are all very heartily German, and so really, despite the Spanish rhythms, are the solos. There are some gems among them: Clarissa's 'Wonnesüsses Hoffnungstraum' is particularly lovely. And there is a richly sustained, irresistibly spirited finale. A good performance, too, under Gary Bertini, with Prey, Popp and Moll among the soloists, and a quite light but sweet-toned lyric tenor called Heinz Kruse to be noted. The semi-centenary has done its job. It also sends me back to the fine recording of *Euryanthe*, the musical masterpiece among the operas; and it has me already looking forward to the next occasion for celebrating Weber – 1986, and the bicentenary of his birth.

Jochum's Meistersinger

Not everything is to be enjoyed in the version of *Die Meistersinger*, which I nevertheless recommend. This is Jochum's keenly anticipated recording, with Fischer-Dieskau as Sachs and Domingo as Walther. How extraordinary it is that of all the three recent sets not one should have an even passable Eva. Hannelore Bode was the principal weakness of Varviso's cast, and lo and behold she reappeared in the Solti. Jochum has Caterina Ligendza, whose voice is certainly finer than Bode's but is neither fresh nor steady; she is taxed by the higher notes and her timbre hardly ever suggests an Eva. But Jochum's way with the score is so very right, and it places Fischer-Dicskau's distinctive Sachs in a richly human context which is right for it. If one compares versions, it is generally to find much in all three conductors, Solti emphasizing the breadth and majesty of the work, Jochum its radiance. Then compare the three singers in Hans Sachs's final address to the people ('Verachtet mir'). Fischer-Dieskau's is by far the most specific, the most complete in understanding – gaining his understanding from what Wagner wrote (in words and music phrase by phrase), and not from what, in a general sort of way, people *think* he wrote. Norman Bailey (with Solti) sees less and does not sing better. Karl Ridderbusch (with Varviso) has more variety in his singing of this passage than Bailey has, and he sings better than either of the others with beautifully solid, resonant tone. He, I would think, is the best singer of the part since Friedrich Schorr (who remains supreme, as I found once again in these comparisons). As for the three Walthers, well, Domingo may not do everything according to the heart's desire, but he provides the sort of voice that I never thought to hear in this part; the others come nowhere near him, and his mastery of the role is a considerable achievement.

Verdi's Macbeth

The two performances, conducted by Abbado and Muti, both leave us in possession of a masterpiece never really well recorded before. They were issued almost simultaneously (towards the end of last year) and the reviewers naturally spent much of the time making comparisons. I did so too, but have to present what appears to be a minority report, for I marginally preferred the Muti. The chorus is particularly important in this opera, and the Ambrosians with Muti are far better than the Scala Chorus with Abbado. The Ambrosian witches point their *sforzandos*, relish their wool of bat and tongue of viper, are altogether keener to get up to mischief; and the sopranos have no wobblers among them. The Ambrosian assassins also carry on a real dialogue while the Scala singers simply go through the operatic conventions. Muti also supports his chorus with livelier rhythms: the scene of Banquo's murder is a case in point. In the Ballet (to take another example) he obtains much clearer articulation from the New Philharmonia players, and there is greater rhythmic alertness throughout. The production of the opera as drama also seems to me to be more vivid and imaginative. In the Banquet Scene, for example, there is a fine pictorial realization of the drama as the ghost vanishes (strings holding a *pianissimo tremolando*) and we share the horror of the guests. Sherrill Milnes (Muti's Macbeth) presents a man shaken to the depths of his being, and when he proposes a return to the drinking song it is in a voice still pale with the horror of his experience. Piero Cappuccilli, in the Abbado recording, is far too undisturbed in this; and that would be the main force of the comparison throughout. In this Banquet Scene, too, it is Cossotto (with Muti) who gives the more vividly dramatized performance as Lady Macbeth: as she takes up the interrupted 'Brindisi' it is with anxiety in her voice, covered by growing assurance as the song continues. Verrett, with Abbado, is less imaginative here, and excellent as she is in the opera there is no doubt to my mind that Cossotto's is the more suitable voice for the part. Cossotto has a hard brilliance that is entirely in character, and as her voice is a louder one than Verrett's she can sing further from the microphone and gain in the more realistic sense of perspective. On the other hand, there is the superior tone of Domingo and Ghiaurov (both with Abbado) as against Carreras and Raimondi (Muti) in the roles of Macduff and Banquo. I also think that in some important places in the score (the introduction to the Sleepwalking Scene for instance) Abbado captures the mood with more depth of feeling than Muti. And on its own merits, comparisons apart, the Abbado performance stands as a fine achievement. But when an opera comes out 'double', there is, for the critic at least, all the fascinating toil and trouble of comparisons; and mine repeatedly established a preference in this work for Muti.

Troilus and Cressida

The British share in this Shakespearian opera is perhaps just a trifle debatable. But at least we can lay claim to the whole of Walton's *Troilus and Cressida*, which in its revised version has enjoyed (for a modern opera) considerable box-office success this season at Covent Garden and been recorded live from the stage there. In the opera house I loved hearing the music again; it had taken strong root in the mind during the intervening years, and I found this in itself sufficient to ensure an enjoyable evening. But experience of the recording has not been so happy. Of course it is good to have a recording at all, and if taking it live from the current run was the only way of ensuring that the opera should be recorded then all well and good. But the fact of a stage, an audience and so forth does not guarantee a more dramatic or persuasive recording; and in this instance the dry acoustic that seemed to prevail on the stage was a positive hindrance to dramatic conviction. And then the singing. I'm afraid I did not admire Cassilly's Troilus or Gerald English's Pandarus in the theatre; and on record I liked them less. Cassilly's tone is so unlovely, his style so unromantic, his vowels so unpleasing that it is hard to feel any sympathy for the character. And this Pandarus is such a plebeian fellow, without style in his enunciation or grace in his tone (and Peter Pears, who created the role, was the vastly preferable opposite in these respects). Nor do I think Dame Janet Baker really presents the true Cressida. Walton has of course changed the character in transposing the voice-part and giving it to a mezzo. As Magda László sang the role, Cressida was a haunted, vulnerable, tender little creature who needed a Troilus so that she could come alive. The mezzo-soprano voice is so much more 'capable', businesslike, and Dame Janet never suggests a fragility or the element of neurosis. Her outgoing way is surely wrong for the 'inner' mood and manner of 'Slowly it all comes back' and much else. In the Third Act she does catch the pathos and rise to the tragedy with strength and nobility. But the recording as a whole does not seem to me to rise to the occasion; I prefer my memories.

Nesterenko and Shostakovich

I often think that you learn a voice best if you are learning some new music at the same time. Best of all are the occasions when the great composer and the great singer make themselves known simultaneously. Thus I learnt Sarastro's arias from *Die Zauberflöte* and the great bass Plançon together, Elisabeth Schumann came with the Quintet from *Die Meistersinger*, and (to take an instance nearer to what I have in view at present) Boris Godunov's Monologue became a permanent mental possession along with Chaliapin. The trouble is that the opportunities to do this occur less frequently as one gets older, and it may well be that this is one reason why we tend to love the singers of our youth: they introduced us to the music and through the music we met them. Anyway, this quarter brings a fine example. The great score and the great singer introduce each other, and we can learn both at once.

The work is Shostakovich's *Suite on verses by Michelangelo*. A very late composition, written during 1974 and 1975, it gives powerful, chastening expression to the fierce spirit of the poems. 'Truth', 'Love', 'Death' and 'Immortality' are some of their titles; several tell bitterly of the artist's struggles with himself, his work and the ruling powers. Shostakovich reaches out to the depths of them, and his music, from the awesome bleakness of the two trumpets at its opening, through all the sombre painting of the deep strings accompanying the bass voice, is essentially stark and unsettling. Marvellously, though, it is at the same time exhilarating. The musical ideas have such strength, present such contrasts, and are realized with so much beauty as well as authority that the effect is of seriousness without morbidity. Indeed, part of the astonishing strength is that it all ends with a dance and a tinkle of the celeste.

When Robert Layton reviewed the records in May, he said that his account of the music had in the nature of things to be something of an interim report: it takes more time to work through to the particular quality of the greatness one feels sure is there. Similarly, I suppose, one should qualify one's report of the singer, for greatness should be attested over a larger repertoire and a longer time. But on the present showing Evgeny Nesterenko would seem to me to be, as a singer, a bass in line with Chaliapin and Christoff, and nothing less. His voice is strong and firm, a true bass (you can hear the bass 'underlay' in the baritone range), resonant and precise in focus. He sings with that kind of 'follow-through' method which makes the tone instrumental: there is none of the common habit of impairing the legato by pushing or swelling on the individual notes of a phrase. The declamatory phrases are never given the Germanic kind of *sforzando* that mars a proper singing tone; test it, for example, in the eighth song which tells how the sculptor's hard hammer works at the rock, and where Nesterenko produces a tone with firmness and majesty to match. He softens it beautifully too (there were even occasions when just fleetingly that extraordinary record of Chaliapin singing Rubinstein's so-called *Persian Love Song* came to mind). Interpreting with deep feeling, he performs in every way as a great singer would; one can hardly say more.

The recordings are of excellent quality, as is the playing of the Moscow Radio Orchestra under the composer's son. The two-record album also includes the *Six songs to lyrics by English poets*, and (sung by the mezzo-soprano, Irina Bogacheva) the *Six songs to poems by Marina Tsvetayeva*, both of them fine works. Nesterenko himself made a strong first impression in *The Tsar's Bride*. I hope we shall not have to wait long before hearing him again on record, and (is it too much to hope?) perhaps in person.

Comedy

Shostakovich also provides a striking contribution under this heading, again in a first recording. *The Nose* satirizes the middle-class and officialdom, and you may have to be a Russian, and none too squeamish at that, to enjoy the joke; but the score is packed with invention, and again has room for an amazing variety of sounds. The witty percussion intermezzo and the galop are in perhaps the expected idiom, but then how totally unlikely it is that the next scene should be set in Kazan Cathedral with a gorgeous tapestry of rich choral sound. Some of the characters are genuinely comic creations; the situations can be movingly and even nightmarishly vivid; and we are signposted through the libretto by the happy chance that the Russian for 'nose' appears to be 'nos'. There is also the attraction of a masterly, zestful performance (the score insistently risks a shambles). The Moscow Musical Theatre presented the opera in 1974 and the recording is a triumphant proof of the company's achievements, with special credit no doubt due to the conductor, Rozhdestvensky, and to the leading singer, Edward Akhimov, tirelessly resourceful in such a demanding role.

Do the Russians laugh at Gilbert and Sullivan, I wonder? (Do they ever see it? Is it translatable?) I'm afraid that I find a great deal more wit and point in Act 2 of *The Gondoliers* than in the translated libretto of *The Nose*. But what a masterpiece that Second Act is; the Second Act of *Patience* too, for that matter. They have been major sources of enjoyment in recent months, both of them in the reissued sets under Sargent. *Patience* has dear old George Baker, not really in character for Bunthorne but clear in every syllable, Monica Sinclair a superb Lady Jane, and Elsie Morison a pretty Patience (but leaving me dry-eyed in 'Love is a plaintive song' – not so Winifred Lawson whose lovely 78rpm record I was hearing recently). *The Gondoliers* also has excellent playing and a fine Inquisitor in Owen Brannigan, more roundly, weightily in character than D'Oyly Carte's Kenneth Sandford. On the other hand, D'Oyly Carte have a better Casilda in Julia Goss and a much more idiomatic Duke in John Reed. I'm told on all sides, incidentally, how very good *The Grand Duke* is, but have not been able to hear for myself. I can't say that, judging from records, the company appears to be going through a very good patch at present. I felt this in their centenary recording of *Trial by Jury* too, one shining exception being the performance of Michael Raynor who, from Counsel in *Trial*, turns first-rate gondolier, with 'Rising early in the morning' providing the main pleasure of the set.

A new recording of *La Grande Duchesse de Gérolstein* has gone far to unsettle my insular conviction that G&S are really a good deal better than Offenbach. This, certainly, is a delight, with a sparkling performance under Michel Plasson, with Alain Vanzo spry and resonant as the engaging hero, and Régine Crespin cutting a fine figure as the Duchess. But, alas, she doesn't seem to be in her best voice, and it was pleasant to turn to Saga's reissue of an abridged version which has Eugenia Zareska, creamy-voiced, seductive and commanding, in the lead, and which offers a well-packed 73 minutes on one record. *La vie parisienne*, also under Plasson, begins delightfully (in St Lazare station) but has a rather tiresome rigmarole of a story, and in this Crespin's voice is distinctly unattractive.

And so to Johann Strauss. I enjoyed both the Carlos Kleiber and the Böhm *Fledermaus*. Highlights from the Böhm have come out recently with their reminder of Janowitz's glamorous Roselinda and the captivating Adele of Renate Holm. Their excellent counterparts in the Kleiber are Julia Varady (glorious tone and commanding style) and Lucia Popp. Hermann Prey is a romantic Eisenstein, René Kollo a graceless Alfred. Then there is the doubtful attraction of the leery, androgynous Orlofsky of Ivan Rebroff, a sort of cross between Bluebeard, Bluebottle and Old Mother Riley. And *Wiener Blut* was sheer joy. An inexhaustible stock of melodies from the 73-year-old master, a fine performance under Boskovsky, again with the delectable Renate Holm, and a lovely evening with the gramophone.

Back a few years, and we find a less conscious provision of gaiety but no lack of it in Haydn, Mozart and Schubert. Schubert's *Die Zwillingsbruder* with Fischer-Dieskau as twins has a winning freshness that is captured also in a pleasant collection called 'Schubert on Stage'. This includes what is surely one of the most charming meetings in all opera – that of Alfonso and Estrella, sung most pleasantly by Elly Ameling and Claes H. Ahnsjö. He is also one of the tenors in Haydn's *La vera costanza*, the second of the operas in Dorati's projected complete edition. Like *La fedeltà premiata* it deepens in the Second Act, with Jessye Norman singing her arias most beautifully. I found it a little less interesting than the *Fedeltà*, but that, too, is an interim report, for (like Shostakovich, strangely enough) it is just the sort of music that reveals its individuality through repeated listening.

Immediately captivating, however, is a formerly unknown overture by Mozart to an incomplete opera, *Lo sposo deluso*. It is coupled with a not entirely satisfying performance of *Der Schauspieldirektor*. But that overture, with a heavenly slow passage in the middle section, should not be missed.

Gobbi's Return

Italian comedy has been best represented in recent lists by *Gianni Schicchi*, which has also provided a happy choice of opera for the return of Tito Gobbi to the recording studios. The great decade of his recording career was between 1951 with that supreme 'Pari siamo' and 1961, with Iago to Vickers's first Otello. With the 1966 *Nabucco* his voice had started to sound tired, though there was still plenty of life in it, and the 1973 Treasury recital, mostly of earlier recordings, also had some most beautiful and characteristic singing of Italian songs, recorded in 1964, like Ruffo's old favourite *Visione Venezia*. This seemed to write a satisfactory *finis* to his discography. But now he has re-recorded this favourite role of Schicchi which he did so finely in the 1959 performance, itself just recently reissued with the rest of the *Trittico* in a three-record album. The new version finds him with voice darker and drier but still unmistakeably Gobbi. Maazel secures much fine and well-pointed playing from the orchestra, though I think he produces some exaggerated effects too. Plácido Domingo sings Rinuccio with rich tone, but I liked the youthful ring of Carlo del Monte in the earlier HMV set. Of course the old record is still the one to go to for Gobbi's Schicchi, especially as it is now such excellent value in sequence with the other operas. There is a new *Suor Angelica* too, also under Maazel who is marvellously perceptive on orchestral detail. But though Renata Scotto's heart is in the right place, her voice cannot compare for beauty with the Victoria de los Angeles of those days. And Gobbi's Michele, in *Il tabarro*, is a masterpiece of brooding passion. That is a feature of the other role he undertakes in this postscript to his career in the studios: that of old Chin-Fen in Leoni's *L'oracolo*. It is interesting to be able to hear the score of this *verismo* piece which was such a stand-by for Scotti in his declining years. The atmospheric crowd scenes are really very attractive but it seems unable to rise with any strength to the tragedy. The main singing part turns out to be for the bass, sung here by Richard van Allan who I thought began rather badly and ended rather well. For Gobbi himself it is moving to catch again the inimitable tone in a phrase like 'per insultar la miseria' but, as I say, this is a postscript and quite a brief one. For the great artist at his best we must turn to the reissues: to the *Trittico* mentioned above, to Callas's first *Lucia di Lammermoor* (their duets are fine but the recording production is not up to the generally high standard of those days) and, best of all, to the *Simon Boccanegra*, which I rank as one of the most cherished of all operatic recordings.

Some Unenchanted Evenings

The reissue of Gobbi's *Simon Boccanegra* includes as a fill-up a recital by Boris Christoff, another of the supreme artists of the post-war years. Finer still, as a memento of his greatness, is the reissued *Boris Godunov* under Dobrowen, Christoff's first recording of the opera. Many were the delights of playing this again (including that of hearing the young Nicolai Gedda, as mellifluous a Dmitri as one is likely to find). Equally enjoyable was the evening on which I listened to the reissued 1959 *Don Giovanni* under Giulini. With a cast headed by Sutherland and Schwarzkopf, and a sureness of touch in every detail, this presented the opera as it simply has to be: an operatic event of rare distinction, for no other opera (unless *Fidelio*) is so surely killed by mediocrity.

But these, you will note, were the reissues. When we come to the new sets I found again and again that though the recording and the orchestral playing may be of the finest quality, the singing was not. A prime example is *Der fliegende Holländer*. There were times when I wished I could just listen to the orchestral score, for Solti and the Chicago Symphony Orchestra give a glorious account of it. But Norman Bailey's Dutchman, Janis Martin's Senta and René Kollo's Erik seem to me to be vocally quite unlovely. Kollo is at his worst in the lyrical melody 'Mein Herz voll Treue bis zum Sterben', and even Martti Talvela, whose voice is intrinsically such a fine one, is stylistically rough in much of his music. Then we have had a *Nozze di Figaro* under Barenboim, where Fischer-Dieskau and Sir Geraint Evans produce generally so little beauty in the singing of their roles that the whole performance suffers. The women (Harper, Berganza and Blegen) are better, but on the whole the singing is far preferable on the Colin Davis recording and of course the whole opera promptly becomes the joy it should be.

Among the novelties is Meyerbeer's *Le Prophète* and I greatly looked forward to hearing it. The work itself brought several pleasures but the total experience of the opera remained heavily earthbound, again I think principally because the singing was not adequate. McCracken resorts to a kind of bodiless head voice when he wants to sing softly, and his would-be heroic singing for the most part lacks ring and body. Scotto's tone hardens unpleasantly on high notes, and Berthe is a role with many of them. Bastin's tone lacks colour and the veteran Jerome Hines is unsteady. That leaves Marilyn Horne, who ten years ago would have been magnificent (as her solos from the opera were in recital) and who now is still often impressive. But as a whole, the singing does the opera less than justice.

The other opera new to the gramophone brings me to another cause for concern. The work is Donizetti's *Gemma di Vergy* and its star is Montserrat Caballé, who for the most part sings magnificently. The opera has some most lovely passages, with a glorious finale to Act 1. Again and again Caballé performs as the truly great singer. But she nevertheless is the cause for concern. Her records over the last few years have repeatedly provoked the comment 'celestial' when she sings softly, and nothing half so complimentary in loud, high and strenuous passages. Now these account for much of the time in her recent recital record, starting with an alarmingly reckless performance of Lady Macbeth's letter scene, breaking savagely at the change of vocal registers, aspirating the runs and attacking with nothing short of brutality. This may be appropriate to the character, but, speaking for myself, I do not want to hear that character doing violence to one of the most beautiful voices in the world. There is also the *Turandot* solo, which has much that is good about it, but not sufficient to reassure those who, like myself, have read with misgivings of a projected recording of the opera with Caballé in the title-role. The real Turandot voice needs a free ring and resonance about the loud high notes, and it is a role which can be cruelly hard on a voice that is not right for it. I personally sat uneasily through quite a lot of the *Tosca* and thought much of that was too strenuous for the voice. The recording, under Colin Davis, is a triumph for the conductor, producer and engineers, and there are some moving passages including much of the Third Act. Caballé sings a fine 'Vissi d'arte', magical in the last bars. But many are the times when it is all too easy to forget that this is one of the world's most lovely voices, and when, indeed, one becomes apprehensive for its future.

Recitals

The Scarpia of the Davis/Caballé *Tosca* is Ingvar Wixell, who has also a Verdi recital in the lists. He may not be the most convincing of villains but he is certainly one of the best baritones. His voice has beauty and solidity, and his production carries a feeling of natural mastery. 'Il balen' from *Trovatore* is as good a test of the Verdi baritone as any, and Wixell passes it with distinction. The Scarpia of another *Tosca* set, incidentally, is Matteo Manuguerra, and he, dark and vibrant, is a baritone of whom we should hear more. This is a dramatic performance under Rostropovich, but its heroine, Vishnevskaya, is too often hard-toned and uneven. She, however, has a fine recital record of songs by Rachmaninov and Glinka. The Glinka songs must surely have the dullest of piano accompaniments, but the dramatic quality of Vishnevskaya's tone is wholly appropriate in Rachmaninov, and she is able in *Oh never sing to me again* to sustain a fine line with much technical control as well as eloquent expressiveness. A top favourite among all of this year's records is also of Rachmaninov songs. This is the second volume of performances by Söderström and Ashkenazy. It may be that much of the more passionate impulse comes from the pianist, but Söderström sings with the most lovely quality of voice: hear the Shelley setting, for instance, *The little island*, where the voice floats clear and high over the quiet chords of the opening, or the Pushkin *Arion* where the legato is so beautifully preserved. A wonderful record, this.

Among Lieder recitals, Judith Blegen sings her Richard Strauss charmingly in a Strauss/Wolf programme and the last song of all, *Amor*, is also a dazzling display piece. Jessye Norman gives the now standard coupling of *Frauenliebe und -leben* and the *Liederkreis*, Op. 39. With Irwin Gage now playing the accompaniments with something of the free rubato of a Cortot, the singer is able to give a warm, imaginative performance and with much beauty of tone. Dame Janet Baker has a Beethoven/Schubert coupling, finely accompanied by the English Chamber Orchestra under Leppard; an unusually intimate performance of *Ah! perfido* and a rare aria from Schubert's *Lazarus*, sublimely simple in its ending, are among the great attractions here. Finally, one more reissue and another great voice from the past: Kirsten Flagstad sings Sibelius. If sampling, try the first song last (it's far from the best) and perhaps the last first – a setting of *Come away, death* drawing on that superb wealth of rich deep tone. It is in fact (to revert to my opening point) a good record for learning the voice and the music together, pausing occasionally to remake the scarcely credible calculation. For these recordings were made in 1958, and the singer was born in 1895.

1978

Fischer-Dieskau and Lieder

As by some unknown law of physics, the Lieder albums gravitate to the bottom of my in-pile, and for a long time I've wondered why. I love Schubert, and yet here I am carefully bestowing the Hermann Prey cycles where I shan't be likely to come upon them for another month or so. Wolf has always been a favourite composer, right from the years of the old Society albums. So how is it that the third volume of songs by Fischer-Dieskau and Barenboim has remained unopened for weeks on end? Perhaps it is because Eric Sams gave them a somewhat discouraging review – as he did the *Italian Songbook* by Mathis and Schreier, which has also been gathering dust. But of course I really know the reason all the time; and that is, that they are hard work. Each song is a concentrated, self-contained creation. It lasts, say, two minutes, but demands a lot more time than that. You must read the poem and hear the song while following the poem, and then again with your eyes closed, and then again a little while savouring it in silence – but of course the machine has long ago whizzed you on to the next one and the next. The Lied is, in this aspect of the matter, perhaps the branch of music least well suited to habits induced by the long-playing record recital.

In another sense it is ideal for the gramophone in that it is music for the home, for the living room. And this gives rise to one of the complaints Eric Sams had about this new Fischer-Dieskau Wolf album. He found the style of many of the performances quite alien to the true nature of the Lied, which is intimate and restrained. It was often, as he said, as though Fischer-Dieskau and Barenboim had engaged the Royal Albert Hall and felt that the songs must be impressed upon folk in its uttermost recesses. And so it was: *Der Freund*, the two soldier songs, *Der Schreckenberger*, *Der Glücksritter*, all of these on the first side, are rung and pounded out, and there is more *fortissimo* to come on Side 2. With this goes a loss of charm, even in some of the quieter songs. I found (also at the bottom of the pile) the second volume of 'The Art of Hans Hotter' and compared Hotter with Dieskau in *Der Musikant*: the new record is more playful, more fun, but old Hotter has the charm, the smile, the affection and the intimacy. It is a much more lovable performance. The best part of the new album, I thought, came with the group of Robert Reinick poems: not often heard and full of charm, captured often with magical lightness and grace by both of the artists. And of course in the 'big bow-wow' pieces the pounding *fortissimos* might be acceptable in a single song with the space of silence after it; but the record goes round and round and the ears feel bruised.

None the less, complaining about Fischer-Dieskau is never a very lengthy process with me. As often as not, a sudden insight or some sheer beauty of sound flashes upon the mind in mid-complaint; he is constantly stimulating. I wish that were true of the Prey album of three Schubert cycles new to this country. A good *Schwanengesang* rewards patience after a *Winterreise* that comes alive only in the songs from 'Auf dem Flusse' to 'Irrlicht', and a *Schöne Müllerin* with enervated, breathy tone and dull expression. How prosaic and dull-toned, too, are Norman Bailey's 'Songs of Love and Death'. That recital has been highly praised but apart from some remarkable breadth of phrasing in the *Ernste Gesänge* it seemed to me to be quite undistinguished. To return then to Fischer-Dieskau and the new Schumann album is to acknowledge (and warm afresh to) a master. All those changes of mood and colour in *Widmung* and *Die Lotosblume* which evoke no responsiveness in Bailey are sensitively felt in Fischer-Dieskau, who with Christoph Eschenbach as pianist provides a

Lieder album that to me seems inexhaustibly delightful. It should have been right at the top of the pile from the start.

Operatic Scholarship

In three other operas this quarter the centre of interest is textual. The most surprising of them may be *Lucia di Lammermoor*, where most people will have assumed that, while the Mad Scene will be embellished *ad lib.*, the rest is more or less as Donizetti wrote it. Not so, however. The scholar-conductor Jesús López-Cobos has edited the score from the autograph, making, he says, well over a hundred important changes involving orchestration, tempo and so forth and, most interestingly, key. The role of Lucia, he concludes, was written for a dramatic soprano rather than for a high coloratura. And when the high sopranos took it over, as they did immediately, they transposed *down*! The authentic text is now performed with Caballé singing in the original keys, involving no especially high notes, which, one must add, is just as well. Then there is *Boris Godunov* where the composer's own version has been recorded for the first time. Here the difference lies partly in the order of the scenes and, more pervasively, in the nature and details of orchestration and harmony. At the lyrical climax of the Monologue, for instance, Boris does not sing the soaring melody with its high notes, and the harmonies beneath his line are altogether more disturbed and difficult. Martti Talvela, the Boris, is a genuine bass rather than the frequently heard bass-baritone, and the opera ends not with his death but with the plaintive verses of the Simpleton.

For myself, I have to admit to a duller response than I would have expected, hoped for or approved. Textual detail is of fundamental importance, and with so many details affected there should have been some moments of revelation or perhaps a totally new experience. Quite possibly the leisurely tempos weakened the effect of the *Boris*, and maybe the variable adequacy of the casting in *Lucia* (Carreras far outclassing the other men) reduced the impact there. Both are important recordings, but neither, I fancy, is likely to be greatly loved. Nor perhaps is *Leonore*, but this is a different matter and it brings revelations in plenty. The original version of *Fidelio* was already a great score, but Beethoven's censoring pencil went through bars and sometimes pages of most intricately written music. He reshaped a melodic line here, altered an introductory passage there, reconstructed much of the finale and cut mercilessly at unnecessary elaborations. Again the recording does not present an ideal performance (only Ridderbusch as Rocco singing really well), but it still does valuable service. With the finished *Fidelio* in mind, one comes as near to seeing how genius goes to work as one is ever likely to be.

Records of Singing

Permanence can be dull, no doubt. Here today and gone tomorrow, our trifling pleasures can have a savour lacking in all the priceless objects which will lie under glass covers till doomsday in the British Museum. And a quick turnover is certainly good for business. But it was with a sinking heart that I read the words 'Limited Edition' after the announcement of EMI's 'The Record of Singing'. Here surely should be the nucleus of a new and permanent Historic Catalogue. The old HMV catalogues before the war had as an appendage a generous selection of historical recordings that were occasionally added to but never plundered in the annual deletions list. Its existence meant that one could sample the work of the famous artists of earlier times; and this new publication, with its informative, finely illustrated accompanying book, also enabled us to sample, and, as I think everybody who has a copy will have discovered, to savour many quite unexpected delights. A student who cannot lay out £35 on the spot ought to be able to build up a collection of these records one by one. And in 10 or 20 years' time the records should still be there, permanently available, while recital discs devoted to the most important artists should be added to this central collection so as to provide the opportunity for a genuine meeting where 'The Record of Singing' has supplied only an introduction. I expect economics forbid, just as they seem to forbid the proper preservation of much else that is precious in the world. But this is what ought to happen. The first joy in the album itself has been soured somewhat by the gradual realization that so many more of the speeds and pitches are wrong than was at first suspected. But this flaw must not detract disproportionately from the welcome the set deserves and the enjoyment it provides. It contains so much that otherwise cannot be heard at all and so much that is of quite exceptional quality, that it is still worth every penny.

Other recent historical issues also properly belong to a permanent archive. The Wagner celebrations of 1976 were honoured by EMI Electrola who published a ten-record album called 'Singers on the Green Hill'. Available here as a special import, it was reviewed by Alan Blyth in February 1977, but I have only just now completed my pilgrim's progress to Side 20. Of course there are some horrors among the early Wagnerian recordings, but what beauties too. No less than four baritones in turn sing Wolfram's music to perfection (Herbert Janssen, Hans Reinmar, Gerhard Hüsch and Karl Hammes); the great Parsifal of Gotthelf Pistor is there; Emmi Leisner, Karin Branzell, and, most wonderful of all, Ottilie Metzger, bring marvellously sumptuous depths of real contralto tone to the music of Fricka, Waltraute and Erda. Then there have come, in the last few months, three-record albums of two of the best singers who entered the international operatic scene in the 1930s. Tiana Lemnitz is a kind of archetype among sopranos. A certain ideal of womanly gentleness and grace is probably better represented by her voice than by any other. The new album contains the records by which many listeners over here came to know her, in the music of Agathe, Desdemona, Pamima and the Countess in *Figaro*. But it also has much previously unpublished material: recordings made, for example, at the same session as produced that heavenly *Wiegenlied im Sommer* for the Wolf Society (there is a most lovely *Sankt Nepomuks Vorabend*), and in 1948, including possibly the best of all versions of the Elsa/Ortrud duet in *Lohengrin* with Margarete Klose.

Jussi Björling is the other singer whose art is represented in a recent album, and this I reviewed myself last December: just a reminder, though, that it contains some of the extremely rare Swedish recordings from the 1930s, and even from 1929 when he was just 18, a lyric tenor with exceptionally sweet tone and a true legato. And this, too, is part of 'the record of singing' that ought not to pass away. I would settle for a single record in the archive, rather than three. But that one record ought to be there: the Historic Catalogue's Björling or Lemnitz, and available till doomsday.

Schütz and Monteverdi

A critic perpetrates most of his injustices unconsciously, but there is one injustice that has been committed in these columns of mine repeatedly, reluctantly and yet deliberately. One's aim, of course, is to survey, select and discuss, apportioning space and prominence according to value. Yet here immediately comes a dilemma, for my sense of value is not necessarily the same as the next person's; and yet a critical survey must express personal conviction or it is useless. But personal experience in itself involves a dilemma of the judgement, for it sometimes has to weigh a knowledge of enjoyment against a sense of importance. The importance of a big album or a first recording or a historical reissue usually carries the day. But enjoyment is a different matter, and time and time again I have found my own greatest enjoyment to lie not in the big albums at all but in a single disc and a relatively unspectacular one, whose 'importance' relegates it to the second page. Moreover, as often as not it hasn't been made by any celebrated principal of the opera house or soloist from the concert hall, but by a well-trained choir.

So: let right be done! This quarter's joy and true delight came, for me, not half so much in the operas or song albums as in two choral records, one by the Schütz Choir, one by the Monteverdi. Both are delightful because of the quality of the performance, and in both the music deserves to take its place in the rich catalogue of unacknowledged secondary masterpieces. Coming upon Schütz's Motets Nos. 4-8 was, I felt, an experience almost comparable to meeting for the first time Donne's Holy Sonnets. As with Donne, an entirely personal voice speaks out and addresses the listener (God or man) with a sudden, apparently spontaneous urgency. There are the grinding or melting harmonies that have of themselves extraordinary emotional power. Like Donne again, there is also the way of making an opening statement that will seize the attention – *Ego enim inique egi* (No. 6). The development may then involve a sudden quietness and depth('I tasted the sweetness of the fruit, thine was the bitterness of gall'), or perhaps, as in No. 7, modulating with the utmost imaginative simplicity (quite as masterly as any complexity) for the homophonic closing phrase, 'Rex meus et deus meus'. Or it may run to the dancing happiness of the last lines of No. 8 – 'et misericordias tuas in aeternam cantabo'. Whatever it is, there is a mastery of form and technique matched by urgency and individuality of personal utterance.

Roger Norrington's Schütz Choir sings this (and their Consort of solo voices the Monteverdi *Lagrime d'amante* on the reverse side) with much sensitivity. Limitations are imposed by the tone-quality of some of the women singers: in spite of the passionate emphasis in Monteverdi, it remains very English, and in spite of the remarkable control in Schütz, it is still very feminine. Nevertheless, remembering also their achievement in Richard Strauss's motets some years back, I still think they must be one of the best choirs in the country. As surely is John Eliot Gardiner's Monteverdi Choir. Their latest recording is of Handel's *Dixit Dominus*, with *Zadok the Priest* as an extra. Gardiner always brings a freshness of insight to his performances. The slow tempo of *Zadok* is part of a completely fresh reading, the newly meditative style of the prelude giving a quite special effect to the choir's entry. And the distinction of this performance of *Dixit Dominus*, evident in itself, is further clarified by a comparison with the earlier recording from Amsterdam. That received a warm welcome on its appearance, but Gardiner's version has so much more care for detail, so much more imaginative grasping of pictorial effects, as well as the virtues of a firm beat that forbids any of that slight and intermittent 'getting ahead' which so often weakens the vitality of such music as this. The recorded sound is spacious, with altogether more strength and splendour. A joyful record, this, and justly at the head of this quarter's listing.

Enter Obraztsova

At least the celebrated Russian mezzo-soprano has been worthily presented in her western gramophone début. Elena Obraztsova, with whose powerful tones and the praises thereof the opera houses have been ringing, comes before us in a solo recital and as Azucena, one of her best roles, in the new Karajan *Il trovatore*. This recording has its limitations, but it is quite a different thing from the other recent all-star *Trovatore* on Decca. This one has something to say about the music. For instance, there is more *pp* than *ff*; there is a new dreamlike quality in some of it; and much is made of bold contrasts. It will take time to test its validity. Leontyne Price, in vastly better form than in the recent *Requiem* under Solti, gives a performance that is always distinguished ('Tu vedrai' in particular needs to be heard, tense in its mingled joy and anguish). The others have their moments. And Obraztsova certainly makes an impression. The sound is large, forward and challenging. Even so, I can only think that the effect of her voice in the theatre is something notably different from that on records. In the great line of mezzos, for instance, it has not the velvet of Onegin, the warmth of Stignani, the richness of Horne, the firmness of Cossotto (taking all these singers in their prime, as Obraztsova presumably is now). And the recital disc brings out a further limitation best suggested by a contrast with two others, Schumann-Heink and Supervia. For Obraztsova conveys no charm or subtlety of coloration. Her expression is monotonously severe. Her Delilah invokes love's aid and tells of the coming of spring and the opening of her heart in the severe tones of Turandot enunciating her fearful enigmas. Her Carmen is a creature of infinite sameness. Her 'O don fatale' certainly has the magnificence we have read about. But there is a peculiarity about the gramophone: it does not demand so much, and it wants much more.

Music and our time

The music of one's own time can mean less than that of any other, and also much more. Often it talks an unknown language and offers no expressive gesture to help the understanding; but sometimes it speaks one's own tongue as the music of no earlier period can do. So these late works of Shostakovich which have been prominent among new releases over the last few months have 'meant' more to me than anything else. Of course, to talk of music's 'meaning' or its 'language' is in itself a dubious procedure, yet again the quarter's listening enforces the recognition that the music I enjoy most is the music of which (however unsatisfactory the formulation) I say that it 'means' most. And in conjunction with Shostakovich come – forming a curious association – Poulenc and Previn. The Poulenc is his *Figure humaine*, an unaccompanied choral work written in wartime, and the Previn is his music for Stoppard's play *Every Good Boy Deserves Favour*. These, with Shostakovich's Fourteenth Symphony and his Michelangelo Suite, speak, as I say, 'my language' – except of course that it isn't 'mine' but that of an age.

Figure humaine appears in its first recording, and yet it is clearly a major work. The fresh voices of the singers (the Uppsala Academy Chamber Choir conducted by Dan Olof Stenlund) and their feeling for rhythm and texture seem to give it an ideal performance, and coupled with it are the *Four Little Prayers of St Francis* (for men's voices, very moving in their simplicity) and the G major Mass (brighter in the new St John's recording – but compare the 'Sanctus' where the Swedish singers find a special beauty and rightness). The choral writing of the *Figure humaine* is wonderfully inventive in style and flexible in ideas; and with all its tenderness, beauty and vivacity it has a quality that may be more common in Poulenc than I personally have found up to the present – a profound seriousness.

I don't recommend the recording of *Every Good Boy Deserves Favour* in quite the same terms: the play is much more visual than one might think and Previn's music is derivative. Yet that harsh epithet should not be used to dismiss the score, in which music has precisely the function of an extra language, translating, supporting and deepening the meaning of words and actions. As with Poulenc's *Figure humaine* it shows a music of wit and inventiveness now totally serious; and the major composer to whom Previn turns for the language of his most overtly serious pages is Shostakovich.

Shostakovich's last works include the orchestration of Mussorgsky's *Songs and Dances of Death*. Superbly sung by Vishnevskaya, they work upon the listener with an intensified concentration of genius much as I find Shostakovich's orchestration of his own *Suite on verses by Michelangelo* intensifies his original writing of the songs with piano accompaniment. These are now recorded by Shirley-Quirk and Ashkenazy. The performance is a fine one, and the piano accompaniment impresses by its spare austerity. But far more expressive, I find, is the orchestrated version as sung by Nesterenko with the Moscow Radio Orchestra conducted by the composer's son, the power of its language enhanced by association with the Mussorgsky orchestrations and with the Fourteenth Symphony. The Symphony also is given a memorable performance with the Leningrad Chamber Orchestra under Lazar Gozman, and Nesterenko again superb as the bass soloist. The mezzo is Zara Dolukhanova with her rich voice still (1976) in fine condition and with the stylistic mastery of a great artist in full maturity. As for what it expresses, this 'anthology of death', I find some kinship with the poems of Paul Eluard, so finely set in *Figure humaine*, and also with

Stoppard's play, so admirably complemented by Previn's music. In all of them the music of our age speaks to our age about suffering, oppression, death and hope, in language as sure and meaningful as any spoken words can be.

The Ring Rung

The audience at the London Coliseum cheers *The Twilight of the Gods* to the echo at the end of the recorded performance and their applause must by this time have resounded throughout the land if not the world. It is indeed a great achievement on the part of the English National Opera Company and the Peter Moores Foundation that this complete cycle should now be so creditably on record. Yet even at the moment of making such acknowledgements and reading Lord Donaldson's Foreword in the accompanying booklet to this last issue, a mildly querulous voice begins to protest in one's head. Lord Donaldson asks: 'Who would have thought, 20 years ago, that it would be within the bounds of possibility to record the *Ring* in English with none but British singers ... and under a British conductor?'. 'But wait a minute,' says the little voice. 'Twenty years ago maybe. But 50 or 60 years ago there was some vision, not to mention a conductor called Albert Coates and singers like Florence Austral and Tudor Davies, who managed to make 24 double-sided pre-electrical records in English; and I think that if they had known how the gramophone industry was to progress they would have been surprised that an English *Ring* had not come earlier.' My protesting voice continues a little longer in its ungrateful way. 'Was it really a good idea to record "live" from the stage?', it asks, finding quite a lot of it not more but less dramatically vivid than studio recordings. Unhappily I think it also has to be said that Rita Hunter's voice now records much less well than it did four or five years ago in the *Siegfried*, and that Alberto Remedios, who was genuinely distinguished in his singing of that opera, does not quite achieve the same excellence in *The Twilight*. Norman Bailey's Wotan has remained a constant throughout his three operas – intelligent, reliable and authoritative; yet (one can only put it personally) very rarely does he sing with what I can hear as real beauty of tone. The individuality and utter devotion of Reginald Goodall's conducting remain the greatest strength of the cycle (least satisfying, I thought, in the *Rhinegold* and the 'Forging Scene' in *Siegfried*). His speeds allow time for everything to be properly sung, distinctly heard and duly pondered. English-speaking listeners are far more likely to understand the *Ring* in a clear-minded fashion through these recordings than by any other means, and in that they have immense value.

1979

Abbado's Carmen

Opera nights at home with the gramophone should be a special treat. The titles, the casts, the great conductor, the stylish album, they all call to us from the glossy pages of the advertisements, and we promise ourselves a long, uninterrupted evening by the winter fireside enjoying the opulent sounds with a rare sense of well-being and fulfilment. But of course a major opera recording is a large undertaking: there is nearly always a drawback somewhere, and it is not all that often that we find the rich promise of expectations more than partly fulfilled. Two recordings that in recent months have provided totally satisfying evenings are the *Fanciulla del West* under Zubin Mehta and the *Carmen* under Abbado, both from DG and both superb in the quality of recorded sound.

There is no such thing as the definitive *Carmen*. It is a score that responds to many different kinds of approach, and so does the role of Carmen herself. Because she is such a vivid character, and because the centre of critical interest these days appears to lie in opera as drama rather than in opera as itself, there is a tendency to overlook the fact that the part benefits from being well sung. Teresa Berganza sings more scrupulously, I would say, than any Carmen on the complete LP recordings other than Victoria de los Angeles. Like her, Berganza never indulges in a fierce chest voice that is separate from the main body of the tone – a tone, it must be said, that is straight as a die with never the suspicion of a loose, uneven vibration. Thus the Habanera, Séguedille and Chanson bohémienne are all stylish, beautiful pieces of singing; and the characterization takes its lead in the first place from that. Berganza has set out her views on Carmen in a letter to the producer Piero Faggioni, a letter which is included in the accompanying booklet. 'Internal security' is the key-phrase: nothing superficial or sluttish in this girl, no need for exhibitionism and the usual displays of 'Spanish' temperament that are no more truly Spanish than they are truly Carmen. The outcome here involves no dulling of effect, for Berganza has seen with exceptional clarity and independence what it is she wants to do. Though her voice is not an especially powerful instrument, she uses it skilfully so that everything tells; moreover, her Carmen is often most deadly when most quiet ('Au quartier? pour l'appel?', 'Non, tu ne m'aimes pas', 'entre nous tout est fini'). Her charm is more dangerous than los Angeles's; but the challenge, the exercise of will-power and voice are utterly different from that of Callas, whose Carmen is at the other end of the spectrum. 'Internal security' does not need to stage a *tour de force*.

Berganza's strength at the centre of this *Carmen* is matched by Carol Neblett's admirable performance in *La fanciulla del West*. It was good to find that the records conveyed such a faithful impression of the ample, unworn and often beautiful tone that was so gratefully heard in the theatre. Neblett also resists any temptation to exaggerate; she invests the role with unusual dignity. Warmth is there in her personality as well as in her voice; and that voice, with its considerable power and a youthful bloom still upon it, is one of the most exciting to hear rising to the high C. In the recording (and this is not always the case) it is just as it was in the theatre.

The *Carmen* and *Fanciulla* sets have other things in common. The conductors, Abbado and Mehta, draw fine playing from their orchestras and show a strong feeling for the score. The tenor is common to both – Plácido Domingo, a rich-voiced Dick Johnson, the high spot of his performance being not the famous 'Ch'ella mi creda libero' but the autobiographical appeal in Act 2, and his Don José sounding much more effective than it did in the recent Solti recording. Sherrill Milnes also appears in both operas, rather lacking the southern vibrancy desirable for Escamillo, but making a strong impression through presenting Jack Rance as a human being rather than the conventional villain of melodrama. Most important in both recordings, these principals are part of a company. There are no weaknesses among the many small parts; the chorus work is excellent; the performances, in all their fine detail, are a unity. One often hears debate about the merits of opera recorded live from the stage. In both of these recordings we have a performance by companies involved in new stage productions, both of them, in Edinburgh and London, genuinely creative events. The stage is in everybody's mind, but the conditions are right for recording. Such circumstances may well be the best of all.

Tippett and Haydn

John Whiting prefaced his delightful play *A Penny for a Song* with words from the *Book of Wisdom*: 'Let us leave some token of our pleasure in every place, for that is our portion; else get we nothing.' A good motto for a creative artist (and not at all a bad one for a critic), it came persistently to mind during that most intensely enjoyable part of the quarter's listening, the hour spent on Tippett. Philips have issued a Tippett 'sampler' record. The unction of its title ('A Man of our Time') and the eclecticism of its contents (a movement of this and a few minutes of that) may well deter the squeamish; and I know of at least one of my senior colleagues who would not so much be reduced to speechlessness as extended to the extremes of eloquence by the very idea. But I can only report my own portion of pleasure. The bits and pieces include the *Presto* from the First Symphony and the *Rondo* from the First Piano Sonata. There are excerpts from the *Birthday Suite* and *A Child of our Time*; and the second side has 'highlights' from *The Midsummer Marriage*. The profusion of notes and the dancing rhythms express pleasure such as I think no other composer of our time has communicated. As for the sampler, a thing of shreds and patches it no doubt is; but how it renews affection and redirects attention. There must be many who will go from the excerpts to the whole symphony, sonata or oratorio. As for *Midsummer Marriage*, there must also be many to whom the complete opera is difficult of access for one reason or another, and who as record buyers with a limited purse will welcome these highlights rather in the words (if not the spirit) of *The Book of Wisdom*, reflecting 'else get we nothing'.

The one comparable delight this quarter has been Haydn's *The Seasons*. The earlier recording under Colin Davis had certain advantages, but the new one under Dorati is admirable in every respect except the distant, slightly fuzzy sound of the choir, and it is the first to present a completely uncut version. Among the soloists is Ileana Cotrubas, who has in it just the right kind of part to bring out the best qualities in her singing; she is especially charming in the fresh and folk-like air 'Ein Mädchen, das auf Ehre hielt'. In this and other passages one catches the affinity that Robbins Landon mentions with Mozart's

Die Zauberflöte. It is a work of great joy in life, where all creatures turn and praise the creator; where there is a time to hunt and a time to drink, a time for spinning, a time for winter, in life as in the calendar. The freshness of inspiration never flags, and as the last chorus comes to its fine, joyful conclusion, one feels gratitude to another who has 'left some token of his pleasure in every place', a composer for all seasons.

Haydn/Mozart/Beethoven

In a work like *The Seasons*, Haydn is his happiest, best, most natural self. But can as much be said of the operas? This is a good time for taking stock, for three of Haydn's operas have been with us on records long enough to have been to some extent absorbed into the system, and this quarter brings two more. One of them, *Il mondo della luna*, was performed at the Scala Theatre in 1951 in English, when its reviewer in *Opera* wrote that it was clear why Haydn's works for the stage were seldom performed: the composer had little feeling for the medium. The records present an elegant, lightly ironical comedy and an enchanting score. Beginning in laughter, it ends in affection: there is much more humanity in it than an outline of the plot might suggest. The other recent issue, *L'isola disabitata*, is quite different. Its fine overture sets the mood for serious drama, and the leading characters come near to tragedy. It is also much shorter (two records to the normal four). The separate identity of all these operas becomes more apparent with familiarity, and so, certainly, does both the liveliness of musical invention and the excellence of these performances. All under Dorati, the first, *La fedeltà premiata*, came out in 1976; *La vera costanza* followed: and *Orlando Paladino*, probably the most enjoyable of all, appeared in 1977. The recent recordings have fine performances by Arleen Augér, Linda Zoghby, Edith Mathis, Frederica von Stade and the Italian baritone Renato Bruson (who would be found useful in the standard Italian repertoire). From each comes a number of delightful arias, and, although one can quite see that this is what Philips won't want to do, at least for the time being, what would be most welcome would be just a 'sampler' record (a two-record album ideally) of highlights from the Haydn operas as they provided for Tippett on the record discussed earlier. Looking over my notes on all five of them, I see so many items marked with double underlinings and asterisks, and with comments that make me want to go back and hear them again immediately. A well-chosen 'sampler' would, I should think, please the converted and swell their ranks.

Bach's Cantatas

The quarter can probably boast more than an average share of important and keenly awaited operatic recordings, but the primary debt of gratitude, I would say, is due elsewhere. The Munich Bach Choir and Orchestra under their conductor, Karl Richter, have now completed the fifth and last of the projected albums of Bach cantatas grouped so as to cover the whole of the Church Year from the first Sunday in Advent to the 27th after Trinity. Sixty-four cantatas are included, and in them are riches inexhaustible. One might suppose that some time or other, not on Easter Day or Whit Sunday, but, say, on the ninth Sunday after Trinity, Bach might have nodded and produced a piece of routine work without special character. Never, in all of these 64, is there anything of that kind. A more splendid monument to the vitality of the human spirit would be hard to find.

It says much, too, for the vitality of his performers that they have been able to maintain such a fine standard of achievement throughout such a large-scale undertaking. Not that everything is ideal. A tendency in allegro movements to press slightly ahead of the beat momentarily disturbs the joyful confident coursing of the notes. Then, as Nicholas Anderson pointed out in his very full and balanced reviews, the choice of instruments and tempos is sometimes unsatisfactory, and the approach sometimes, in his words, 'a bit lush, a bit too heavy' (contrasting with the Harnoncourt series in this respect). Some of the solo voices could do with more tonal beauty, some with more imagination. But for the most part the orchestral and choral work is admirable, the solo obbligato playing exceptionally fine, and the solo singing both accomplished and committed. Let me give some examples of the soloists' work in the two final volumes with six records in each. Edith Mathis, in freshest voice and with scrupulously accurate intonation, brings radiance of tone and spirit to the 'Lebens Sonne' in No. 180 (*Schmücke dich*) and is sensitive to the penitential character of 'Liebster Gott', with its lamenting oboes, in No. 179 (*Siehe zu*). Júlia Hamari sings 'Weh der Seele' in No. 102 (*Herr, deine Augen sehen*) with compassion, and we welcome her intelligence and reliability again in that most heavenly of alto arias, 'Wie furchtsam wankten' in No. 33 (*Allein zu dir*). Peter Schreier is at his best in No. 148 (*Bringet dem Herrn*) and masters the fiendishly difficult runs of No. 26 (*Ach, wie flüchtig*). Dietrich Fischer-Dieskau's great range of expressive power and technique (including a good trill) passes the tests of No. 27 (*Wer weiss, wie nahe mir mein Ende*), and unfailingly he looks to the heart of each recitative.

But this is no more than to recommend a house by displaying a few bricks. Better perhaps simply to stress the pleasure these sets have provided over the two or three years in which they have been released. Heard in succession as is possible on record, the cantatas exhilarate. Within the formal framework (chorus-recitative-aria-recitative-aria-chorale) the variety is endless: in one a splendour of brass and woodwind, in the next a chorale sung over a sombrely treading bass with soprano and tenor soloists interspersing quasi-recitative; in another the flute and cello intertwine with the soprano voice; and then a recitative blossoms into arioso. And incidentally, if we turn to investigate what Bach was doing for that ninth Sunday after Trinity, the hypothetical occasion of his nodding-off or churning-out, we find him (in No. 105, *Herr, gehe nicht ins Gericht*) writing the most lovely Passion-like introduction for the first chorus, with a sublime passage over a held pedal note before its allegro second half; then a soprano aria with the strings pulsing sadly while the oboe winds a melancholy wreath around the voice; an astonishing bass recitative to follow; a firm, memorable melody for the confident tenor solo; and a chorale. in which the strings comment, still reflective and ending *pianissimo*. No routine that Sunday; simply, as with all the others, a master at work with the full exercise of skill and devotion.

Four Last Songs

In a tribute to Kathleen Ferrier, Benjamin Britten remarked that as a rule (but here was an exception) he took no great pleasure in what people called 'a beautiful voice': too often it was like a pretty face, devoid of character and soul. A most exceptionally beautiful voice among us now is that of Kiri Te Kanawa, and it seems that for some listeners her singing has the kind of limitation that Britten had in mind. Reviewing her recording of Strauss's *Four Last Songs*, Alan Blyth implied some misgivings, while allowing due recognition to conscientious preparation and to the sheer beauty of sound. For myself, coming to it with a great love of both of Elisabeth Schwarzkopf's recordings, I found that the 'sheer beauty of sound', and whatever else was there, brought such intense pleasure that it was unusually hard to get up and start making analytical comparisons. Lovely throughout, the voice provides the ideal sound for phrases like 'wie ein Wunder vor mir', 'Sommer lächelt', 'Und die Seele unbewacht'. The spell of such singing is not to be broken. But of course the great point is that it has not been broken, and it assuredly would have been if its beauty had carried even the whisper of 'heartless', 'soulless', 'unimaginative'. Recall, then, the colourings and modulations of this singing. The first song begins 'In dämmrigen Grüften', and the tone bears the colouring of half-light, just as it will shine out radiantly in 'deine selige Gegenwart' at the conclusion. The repose of 'sehnt sich nach Ruh' in *September* deepens with the intimation of death in *Im Abendrot*: 'es dunkelt schon die Luft' shudders a little with the chill of it. When I compare Schwarzkopf, it is to recognize again the supreme communicativeness of her art as well as the great beauty of voice. But whereas this has hitherto left me with a sense of dissatisfaction in all other recordings of the songs, here it does not. With splendid, sensitive playing by the London Symphony Orchestra under Andrew Davis, well recorded, and coupled with a recital of songs of great and varied beauty, the record survives the comparisons. There is more to it than beauty of sound, but, in any case, the furnishing of such beauty is probably the most important interpretative service a singer has to provide. And – to return to Britten – Browning's Fra Lippo Lippi had views on the subject. Suppose, he says (and I think it won't hurt to quote him as prose), 'you have beauty with no soul at all (I never saw it, put the case the same), if you get simple beauty and nought else, you get about the best thing God invents.' And, as he says, 'that's somewhat'.

Operatic Recommendations

Two other distinguished singers of the younger generation taking part in recent operatic recordings are

Frederica von Stade and Julia Varady. Te Kanawa herself also sings in a performance of *Die Zauberflöte* which, though available to special order only, is worth consideration. Those who love this soprano's art as I do will need no persuasion to listen to her Pamina, and again I have to differ from my colleagues who find a lack of depth in the singing: on the contrary, there seems to me to be a nobility in the enunciation of 'Die Wahrheit, wär sie auch Verbrechen' and the address to Sarastro, and later, in Act 2, a vivid change of expression from despair to hope, such as I do not recall in other performances. Kurt Moll is as good a Sarastro as we have in complete recordings of the opera, and José van Dam for once makes one wish to rename The Speaker The Singer. Edita Gruberová, much in demand now in coloratura roles, has the range and flexibility, but while some notes are firm, others are not. Peter Hofmann lacks grace as Tamino and Philippe Huttenlocher is a vocally inept Papageno. Lombard, as usual, takes things slowly but has a certain amount to say about them. Karajan, of course, has a great deal to say about *Le nozze di Figaro*, which he recorded with an attractive cast including von Stade as Cherubino. A main point is the differentiation of the public and the private. Recitative is usually private in this reading, and mostly goes at a reflective pace and quietly. In concerted passages, 'asides' are made clearly recognizable. It is a performance of marked contrasts, as foreshadowed in the playing of the Overture. The faster tempos are sometimes a little uneasy: one feels aware of the conductor 'moving it on'. But many passages have the special touch: Cherubino's 'Non so più', for example, is completely different from von Stade's earlier recording, the voice caressing and yearning to an accompaniment of gentle murmurs and subdued ardours and excitements. Von Stade is excellent throughout. Figaro and the Count (José van Dam and Tom Krause) sing with fine tone (and we have become accustomed to hearing something else), Cotrubas is a delightful Susanna; but, despite the great praise that greeted her singing of the Countess in Vienna, Tomowa-Sintow's voice records with a rather tremulous sound on too many notes (her 'Porgi amor' bears no comparison with that of Schwarzkopf or Janowitz). It is still a *Figaro* full of life and insight: hearing it is a special event.

There is more Mozart, but it is tempting first to follow the delectable Cherubino in a transformation into Massenet's Cinderella. *Cendrillon* is an opera likely to be known to most listeners only through the solo from Act 3 recorded by von Stade in that glorious first recital, where it already charmed and made one wish for more. In the complete recording this solo is still more vividly sung, with a terrified breathlessness and then a lovely sense of relief in the ringing of the carillon. It is a delightful opera, often exquisitely scored, and investing its heroine with that kind of sadness that finds such an eloquent instrument in von Stade's voice. 'Reste au foyer, petit grillon', 'Adieu, mes souvenirs de joie': such passages remain long in the memory. I could wish that Prince Charming had not been turned into a tenor and that the

Pandolfe (Jules Bastin) had been able to conjure up a more mellifluous tone and elegant style for his part in the touching duet of Act 3. But the recording is still treasurable, partly for the work itself, partly for the spirited and sensitive performance under Julius Rudel, partly for the charm of its heroine.

Julia Varady, whom I mentioned earlier as a singer of special quality, brings distinction to two very different operatic recordings: *Idomeneo* and *Cavalleria rusticana*. In the *Idomeneo*, finely conducted by Böhm she sings the role of Elektra, one in which a hard, unsympathetic voice is usually considered appropriate, a kind of Mozartian version of Verdi's Lady Macbeth. As Varady's performance makes very clear, the music is not written in that way: the cantilena of 'Idol mio, se ritrosi' and the gentleness of that heavenly solo 'Soavi zeffiri' enclosed by the chorus 'Placido è il mar' are just as much a part of the role and character as is the wild and desperate final scene of her madness. The other members of the cast (Mathis, Schreier, Ochman) do some good work, but and often strikingly it is Varady's Elektra and Böhm's fine individual way with the score that distinguish the recording. As for her Santuzza in *Cavalleria Rusticana*, it is in a class of its own. There is Pavarotti, with his splendid resonance and quite a lot of dramatic feeling in both this and *Pagliacci*; there are Freni and Wixell and Cappuccilli; and the maestri Gavazzeni and Patanè riding the old war-horses with spirit and skill. But long after the sound and fury have died down, it is the Santuzza of Julia Varady that stays in the mind.

If the veracity of Italian *verismo* sometimes strikes one as questionable, the reality of Shostakovich's *Lady Macbeth of Mtsensk* carries terrible conviction. The new recording is the original version of *Katerina Ismailova*, the version that so enraged Stalin in 1936 that it was silenced for 27 years and emerged only after much rewriting of score and libretto. A magnificent performance under Rostropovich has Vishnevskaya and Gedda in what must rank with their very finest work on records; Robert Tear, too, contributes a masterly study of the shabby peasant, and only Birgit Finnilä seems unhappily cast, as the flirtations Sonyetka. Certainly one of the great recordings of recent years.

Green and Pleasant

A world away from the desolations of the steppe and the brutalities of Siberia, *Hugh the Drover* is the most English of operas and one of the most joyful. It has always seemed to me an astonishing gap in the British record catalogues (*Gloriana* is another) and hearing it on records after all these years was a moving experience – for, with all its folky simplicity, it is essentially a passionate score. The recording, under Sir Charles Groves, gives much of the expected pleasure; but Robert Tear (fine as he was recently at Covent Garden as Tom Rakewell and brilliantly as he portrays the peasant in the Shostakovich opera) is not right for Hugh. I find it difficult to think whom I would like to hear in the part among present-day tenors (James Johnston used to do it splendidly at old Sadler's Wells): might Robert White be possible, his not very obtrusive American accent being acceptable as a West Country burr?

Also from the heart of English life and tradition come a collection of Vaughan Williams's choral work by several of our best choirs, including King's lovely performance of the *Three Shakespearean Songs*, and a lively anthology by Martin Best called 'William Shakespeare: Ages of Song'. Elizabethan and eighteenth-century settings are followed by a pleasant fantasia, *Sounds and Sweet Ayres*, written for its present performers by Guy Wolfenden. Very English too is the music of Gerald Finzi: *Dies natalis*, sung by Philip Langridge, and the ceremonial ode *For St Cecilia* (LSO and Chorus under Hickox) lift the heart wonderfully well. And I must say I found the heart responding very positively to the part-songs of Parry and Stanford so beautifully recorded by the Halsey Singers. Parry's *Songs of Farewell*, a masterly and moving work of his old age, rise to the great challenge of Donne's 'At the round earth's imagined corners', with resourceful seven-part writing, catching the mystery of 'you whose eyes shall behold God and never taste death's woe'. There is pleasant, elegant material too in the 'Glees from Georgian England' sung by The Scholars, an accomplished group, though with a rather piping soprano who would for continental listeners, I'm afraid, be also recognized as very English. It is also a characteristic of Emma Kirkby, invaluable musician as she is, bringing much that is apt and delightful to the music of Dowland. Anthony Rooley's Consort of Musick add the *Mr Henry Noell Lamentations* with psalms and sacred songs to their admirable recordings of Dowland; but I'm afraid I do find that the unvibrating, rather squeezed vocal tone nags a little.

Dowland's *Sweet, stay awhile* gives its title to a recital by Sir Peter Pears and Julian Bream, one side Elizabethan, the other having Britten's *Songs from the Chinese* and some folk songs. It ends with Essex's nostalgic lute song in *Gloriana*; doubly nostalgic to hear Pears's voice, with its utterly personal but very great beauty, in this music in which we heard his singing in the first performances over 25 years ago. The recital is a fine memento of Sir Peter's singing in this late stage of his career, the voice, both mellow and strong, in better form than in the folk song recording with Osian Ellis a year or so earlier. And, incidentally, like John Coates, also at an advanced age for a singer, he manages his breathing miraculously in *It was a lover and his lass*.

Pears also plays a prominent part in the recordings made from the Benson and Hedges Chamber Music Festival at The Maltings in 1977. Among the riches here is an irresistible performance by the Amadeus of the Minuet and Trio from Schubert's Quartet in B flat. But quite extraordinarily moving is the *Abraham and Isaac Canticle* of Britten, sung by Pears and Baker, with Graham Johnson. The cruel trial of father and son inspired Britten to write some of his most tender, heartfelt music, and the performance catches the inspiration perfectly. Great enjoyment, too, comes with the recent recording of Britten's *Spring Symphony* under Previn. The orchestral tints and choral textures are beautifully caught (hear the start of the Vaughan poem, 'Waters above', or the soft unaccompanied opening of Auden's 'A summer night', for instance). Then, in the last section, there is a magical lift and lilt to the waltz going on under 'Which to prolong, God save our King'. Lovely work; excellent recording.

Sacred Pieces

Thus far the season has been one of almost unclouded enjoyment. Disappointments arrive with three Bach albums. Regensburg's recording of the *St John Passion* suffers from a boxy acoustic, boy treble and alto soloists, an exaggerated *marcato* style in choral runs, and a general sense of doing a neat and tidy, academically respectable job. Best are the short choruses such as those of the nosy gossips who question Peter, and the smug citizens who know all about the law. I have a soft spot for the less academically approved recording by Corboz, and it is strengthened by comparison with this. Then there have been two recent recordings of the *St Matthew Passion*, one by the Bach Choir under Willcocks in English, the other by the Stuttgart choir and orchestra under Rilling. Tear's intelligent and individual way with the narration and Felicity Lott's clear, firm singing of the soprano solos did something to distinguish the English recording, but I found it generally an unmoving performance, with its thin choral sound and its 17 players. Some of the soloists in the Stuttgart recording (Huttenlocher especially) are unsatisfactory, and here again one feels the performance to be the victim of a policy – a sort of brisk, no-nonsense, sweep-away-the-cobwebs approach that is not exactly insensitive or heartless, but not loveable either. Here, as with Regensburg, the dramatic choruses and the intelligent handling of chorales are the best features. But there is something about the *St Matthew Passion* that resists being crammed into a living-room. I began to feel, playing these, that a run-of-the-mill performance in the local church would bring me closer to the great work.

From the New Testament to the Old, and the unedifying tale of Judith, assassin of Holofernes. Young Mozart (then 15) called his piece, *La Betulia liberata*, a sacred oratorio, but despite the lengthy theological argument, taking up pages of the printed libretto, it remains secular in feeling. A second recording comes hard on the heels of the recent one under Vittorio Negri and on the whole it is rather less good. This has Hanna Schwarz as a matronly avenging heroine who returns from the dread deed as from an evening service at church. Birgit Finnilä, with Negri, was too gentle and undramatic for the role, but she is exciting compared with Schwarz: it calls for Dame Janet Baker. The performance under Leopold Hager is all rather mild and leisurely; certainly there is more life in the finale of Negri's recording. The best performance in this new one comes from a South American singer called Margarita Zimmermann as Charis, who seems to have a fine voice with an extensive range and considerable dramatic presence. I hope we may hear more of her.

More enjoyable than these sets have been three single records. Kodály's *Hymn of Zrinyi* and two other choral works have been bravely and successfully tackled by the Brighton Festival Chorus under Laszlo Heltay: fine choral writing, accomplished singing, and, on the second side, some brilliant organ playing by Gillian Weir. The tone of the Brighton choir compares very favourably with that of the American Westminster Choir who sing with Boulez and the New York Philharmonic Orchestra in Wagner's *Das Liebesmahl des Apostels*. This is an astounding work from 1843, massive in concept and full of pre-echoes of later Wagner, especially *Parsifal*; I had the strange experience of listening unsympathetically (strip it of its noise, I thought, and it's really very indifferent music) and admiring in retrospect. There were 1,200 voices, we are told, singing in the original performance; this one really wanted more, so that the disagreeable quality of some of the individual voices could be subsumed. The Chicago choir do much better with Verdi's *Four Sacred Pieces* under Solti. The quiet beauty of these deepens with every hearing, but they could be ruined by a few tremulous voices among the women choristers. None of those here.

Song Recitals

Two by Elly Ameling and two by Janet Baker: a pleasant prospect. Ameling's 'Souvenirs' programme on CBS came as a happy surprise – an extension of her recorded repertoire in all sorts of directions: Rodrigo, Rachmaninov (in Russian), Ives (with high-class chatter, 'We're sitting in the opera house', as though by Groucho's Margaret Dumont), Schoenberg, Purcell (*Music for a while*), and all rounded off with a charming Afrikaans lullaby. How good that this unfailingly well-behaved artist should have the chance to let her hair down, to follow a whim and a personal taste, to be gay and charming outside the normal range of her Lieder and classical repertoire. Even so, it is her usual recording label, Philips, that we have to thank for the excellent series of recitals, now including a Brahms collection, which have brought into the record-year something of the freshness that used to come with Elisabeth Schumann. The Brahms record has a very Schumann-like *Vergebliches Ständchen*, also a not very fulfilling *Von ewiger Liebe*, which Schumann would, I fancy, have left alone. But there are many less familiar songs, beautifully sung: *Agnes*, *Des Liebsten Schwur*, and the sad, still mood of the folk song *Die Trauernde*. As with Schumann, there is depth in the lightness of her tone and touch, witness the quiet profundity of feeling in the concluding *Immer leise*.

Janet Baker's new recital, 'Arie amorose', was I fear, somewhat under-rated by me in my original review. I did say that its pleasures were many, in spite of grumpy misgivings about the accompaniments and even certain features of the singer's style. But play a single item from the collection (such as Domenico Sarri's *Sen corre l'Angelletta*) and one can only conclude that it would be a great pity to miss the record. There is also a most welcome reissue of the Scarlatti-Monteverdi recital originally issued in 1970. This I have always thought of as one of the singer's finest records, giving the essence of what she has to communicate. What was newly impressive on this re-hearing was the richness of Scarlatti's expressiveness in his *Salve regina*, a marvellous composition, with ever-changing styles and moods.

1980

Opera

The gramophone room has virtually been turned into an opera house this quarter. Songs and choral music have not utterly disappeared from the companies' lists, but in proportion to the operatic issues they have been much as are the intervals to the actual performance in the opera house itself, and this retrospect will have to be proportioned likewise.

Prelude: Replete with, and in turn replenishing, the love of music are Mendelssohn's Psalm-settings, essentially cantatas or motets in form. Volume 2 gave such delight that Volume 1 was straight taken down from the shelves, heard again and enjoyed still more. Admirable performances by the Chorus and Orchestra of the Gulbenkian Foundation under Michel Corboz. Whether by some quirk of taste or circumstance, these are the records that have provided the greatest pleasure in a quarter that has been particularly rich in enjoyment.

The Dons

The fame of the Salzburg production of *Don Carlos*, under Karajan, has led to high expectations from the recording, and they are not disappointed. If one came new to this most haunting of Verdi's scores, one would learn to love it through this recording despite the omission of the Fontainebleau scene. Folk of my generation, I dare say, count themselves most lucky in respect of this opera to have learnt it through the best of post-war Verdi revivals at Covent Garden, the Visconti production of 1958, and probably nothing will replace the memory of Gré Brouwenstijn, a most noble and touching Elisabeth, Jon Vickers, then at his very best and finely suited by the role of Carlos, Tito Gobbi and Boris Christoff. And I do not think that those memories are going to be disturbed by the performances on this recording, fine as they are. But if Agnes Baltsa had been the Eboli of that earlier production she would have stood very worthily within the ranks of that unforgettable cast. Her voice, firm and fresh, rings out with splendid fullness in the upper register, and she brings humanity as well as authority to the role. Carreras, too, sings with much feeling, if with not quite the intensity that Vickers (and I'm sure Martinelli before him) brought to the music. He seems to me to be the one, among our three leading 'Italian' tenors, who is at present the most consistently successful in combining emotional involvement and care for a truly even singing line. Cappuccilli gives one of his best performances on record, his tone not instrinsically memorable, I find, but a good manly body of sound and a justly famous breath control. Of the others (Freni,

Ghiaurov, Raimondi, van Dam) much could also be said, as of the conducting and the recorded sound. Of that I have just one complaint, rather similar to what William Chislett had to say about (of all things) Carlo Curley's organ recital, 'that if the softer passages are to be heard at a desirable level some of the louder ones tend to be unsocial'. The orchestral *fortissimos* assault the ear in a way that is often out of proportion to their musical importance.

An over-insistent orchestral presence is sometimes thought of as characterizing Solti's operatic recordings, but it is certainly not so in the new *Don Giovanni*. The playing here is precise and spirited without ever being aggressive. That is one of the set's best features, the other being the Donna Anna of Margaret Price. True, she disappoints in the long run in 'Non mi dir', but otherwise it is an excellent performance, with dramatic conviction and great beauty of tone. The other singers are acceptable, apart from Sylvia Sass who is an inadequate Elvira: her 'Mi tradì' comes perilously close to caricature. The Elvira of the rival *Don Giovanni*, conducted by Lorin Maazel, is Kiri Te Kanawa, and it cannot be said that the opening of 'Mi tradì' finds her at her best either. She is often splendid, however, making much of phrases that frequently go for very little, and in general singing with more projection and character than in her earlier recording under Colin Davis. The Maazel set is seriously weakened by Edda Moser's Anna, and is not helped by the rather hooty sounds produced by Teresa Berganza, miscast as Zerlina, and the pale tone and over-emphatic style that mar much of Kenneth Riegel's Ottavio. On the other hand, the scenes with Giovanni and Leporello are well-paced and vivid, and Ruggiero Raimondi is particularly good in 'Fin ch' han dal vino'.

In these newly recorded versions, however, I would willingly trade both *Don Giovannis* in exchange for *Don Quichotte*. Massenet's opera will be new to most listeners, and to those whose only taste of it has been the Death Scene as recorded by Chaliapin, the vigour and interest of the score will almost certainly come as a pleasant surprise. The excellent recording, with the Suisse Romande Orchestra and Chorus under Kazimierz Kord, is a lively production with effective, unexaggerated performances by Ghiaurov and Bacquier as Quixote and Sancho. Régine Crespin may be a characterful Dulcinea on the stage but her singing does scant justice to the music on record. Otherwise all is fine, and this opera of Massenet's old age emerges as very possibly stronger, more youthful and vigorous than anything else he wrote.

Interlude: From the land of the three great Dons we have a song recital by Montserrat Caballé and a collection of airs from the zarzuelas by José Carreras. The tenor is again in fine voice and sings the attractive melodies with a sure sense of style. Caballé is at her best only in three sweet-sad songs by Granados; in Falla's *Seven Popular Spanish Songs* and still more so in the songs by Turina the voice is all too often unsteady. For a sound full of the warm south, turn rather to the second side of Victoria de los Angeles's live Festival Hall recital of 1964 where a deep voice from the audience comments softly 'Bravo' at the deliciously hummed ending of one of the songs, and where each subsequent item finds the singer's voice in fuller, warmer bloom.

The Ancients

Turning from old Spain to the classical world of Greece and Rome, we have once again the troubles of Titus and Ariadne, and learn of the tortuous developments which eventually cause Xerxes to marry the one who loves him and leave the other free for somebody else. I find it an effort to follow the ins and outs of such plots, and yet the dramatic element in *Serse* is by no means negligible: Handel's opera has, for instance, the contrasted reactions of the characters to adversity prompting a series of beautifully written and effectively juxtaposed arias in the Second Act. Xerxes is sung by Carolyn Watkinson, whose mastery of the runs (as in the Act 2 aria 'Se bramate') is immensely impressive. Malgoire and his orchestra of original instruments give a fine performance, and there is some highly accomplished singing by Anne-Marie Rodde, Barbara Hendricks and Paul Esswood. The new version of *La clemenza di Tito* under Böhm has strong competition from the Colin Davis set. In comparing the singers I found the older set generally preferable. For instance, in Vitellia's opening aria Dame Janet Baker's noble anger in the earlier recording seems preferable to Varady's rather shrewish huff in the new one; and while Varady brings more variety and subtlety of expression to the *allegro* section, Baker is more even on some of the runs. Von Stade and Minton (Davis) have more charm and lightness in their duet than Marga Schiml and Berganza (Böhm); and I find Burrows (Davis) more agreeable to listen to than Schreier (Böhm). But Tito's first aria becomes a different thing under Böhm, whose slower tempo gives it a more thoughtful character, just as the March has greater breadth and the Overture a livelier pointing of the rhythms. Böhm also scores in a comparison of his *Ariadne auf Naxos* from 1970, recently reissued, with the Solti recording made in 1977 and issued the previous month. Böhm shapes more imaginatively, with more light and shade, more affection. His cast was headed by Hildegarde Hillebrecht as Ariadne and Jess Thomas as Bacchus; yet Leontyne Price, with the beauty gone from her tone for much of the time, and René Kollo as Bacchus are also far from ideal in the Solti. And it is interesting to compare the two performances of Tatiana Troyanos who is the Composer in both. Not only was the voice fresher and firmer in the early recording, but the characterization had more life.

No: out of this grouping of the quarter's operas my vote would go to the first recording of what experience may confirm to be a masterpiece of Russian opera, Taneyev's *Oresteia.* First produced in 1895 and never again in the composer's lifetime, it undertakes the massive task of presenting as a single work the three plays of Aeschylus; and, though perhaps two passages fail to meet the challenge, the opera as a whole makes a profound impression. It is richly scored, with particularly fine choral and orchestral writing, and the melodic and emotional impulse rarely flags. A sturdy tenor, Ivan Dubrovin, sings Orestes well; otherwise the singers range from a very competent Clytemnestra to a dreadful Elektra. The Belorussian State Opera and Ballet Theatre, with its conductor Tatyana Kolomyzeva, deserve our gratitude nevertheless. It is a fine work that they have brought to much overdue notice.

Entr'acte: The 'academic' composer of 'decadent' late nineteenth-century Russia makes of his tragedy a joyful affirmation. A notable contrast is afforded by the Soviet composer of genius who makes out of comic material a savagely pessimistic statement. Shostakovich's *Five Romances on texts from 'Krokodil' magazine* and the *Four Verses of Captain Lebyadkin* (the last of his song cycles) are as bitter as any musical works under the sun, and are fittingly coupled with Mussorgsky's *Sunless* cycle and superbly performed by Yevgeny Nesterenko. A contrasting Mussorgsky cycle, *The Nursery*, is included in a delightful recital by Söderström and Ashkenazy. This also has children's songs by Prokofiev and Gretchaninov, while Nesterenko's recital appropriately contains Shostakovich's songs from *King Lear*.

Shakespearian

Making an opera out of any of the major Shakespearian tragedies presents a formidable challenge to librettist as well as composer. A first reaction to Reimann's *Lear* is to remark how very neatly the job has been done. Then of course one has to continue: more than 'neatly', it is imaginative and well pointed (how well, for instance, the music comments, by backward reference to the start of the whole opera, that when Lear stands before his fiendish daughters, 'a poor old man', he has brought himself to this pass initially through his own actions). How moving it may be is another question, and one can only report on first reactions, namely that I was moved only at the point where the voices of Lear and Cordelia combine after the reconciliation. The extremely beautiful singing of Julia Varady makes a great contribution here: it's a very strenuous vocal part, but at least it is meant for singing. About the other parts one may have doubts, but the cast, headed by Fischer-Dieskau, is a strong one. In the allocation of the voices, incidentally, it was surely a mistake to cast sturdy reliable old Kent as a tenor – just as it is hard to see the sense of making a tenor out of 'honest Iago', as he is in Rossini's *Otello*. Not that there is a great deal of Shakespeare about that opera, and not that it necessarily matters. The recording is a fine one and so, with some reservations, is the opera. Occasionally the idiom is too closely associated in our minds with the comic operas (as in part of the first finale in Act 2), but there are many fine numbers: genuine inspiration enters with the Quartet 'Incerta l'anima', placed very much as is the Sextet in *Lucia di Lammermoor*. Then (pleasing in themselves but much more touching in context) the Willow Song and Prayer bring an unadorned, unaffected simplicity of utterance, where all has been brilliance and ornamentation. And what ornamentation! Carreras and von Stade cope wonderfully well; I don't think we have had a full-voiced *spinto* type of tenor singing runs like this since the very early years of the century.

Intermezzo: The third volume of Schumann's songs recorded by Fischer-Dieskau and Eschenbach brings many pleasures and happily completes the valuable series. The artists show their mastery in small things – the *Herbstlied*, for example, which has so many subtle changes of mood in its brief life. New to me were the 'songs' with spoken words, imaginatively written and beautifully performed. It is good too to find Fischer-Dieskau still capable of singing with such sweetness; there is a most lovely performance of *Meine Rose*, infinitely touching in its quiet, sad, sweet return to the words and music of the very opening.

Witches and Other Night Fears

As well as issuing Taneyev's *Oresteia*, DG have brought out *Absalom and Eteri* by his pupil Zakharia Paliashvili. This is a Georgian opera (première 1919) and now has its first recording under Didim Mirzchulava. With its folk idiom and colourful choral and orchestral writing, it is an attractive score, though the most striking piece of melodic invention (and clearly the composer thought so himself as he brings it back in the finale) derives from a few bars in Rachmaninov's song Op. 21 No. 7, *How fair the spot*. As in the *Oresteia*, the standard of the singing is mixed; and so it is again in Tchaikovsky's *The Enchantress*, under Gennady Provatorov. But here too one is grateful for the opportunity of hearing a work which, if not totally successful, has some extremely fine passages. There are delightful choruses early on; indeed, throughout the First Act it seemed impossible to account for the opera's 'honourable fiasco' at its première. The weakness really lies in the last Act (of which Tchaikovsky thought so highly) and in the hocus-pocus of the wizard, with his spell 'that will burn to the bone'. The villain of *Absalom and Eteri* (villainously sung too) produces a poisoned gift, through the magic powers of which the heroine loses her beauty, so that after supping full of these Russian horrors one feels better able to stomach the Witch in *Hänsel und Gretel*. When she is sung by the delightful Söderström, of course, that is not a problem. What is difficult to accept is the aptness of the casting, and in fact I don't. And then in the cast is an erstwhile brilliant Witch, Christa Ludwig, now miscast as the Mother. On the other hand, the children (Cotrubas and von Stade) should certainly be their parents' pride and joy, a charming couple, put to sleep by a particularly charming Sandman, Te Kanawa (*Il nano sabbiolino* or *le petit marchand de sable* – a pleasant acquisition for those who, like me nowadays, learn their foreign languages largely from operatic librettos). I found just a touch of the Sandman's influence elsewhere in the recording: tempos a little slow, orchestral colours a little subdued. Comparisons reinforced the point: the vivid recording and rich orchestral sounds of Solti's version emphasized the mildness of this new one, and Karajan's Overture in the classic recording of 1953 comes to life with much more energy and excitement. There's still much to enjoy in this greatly looked-forward-to recording under Pritchard, but it's all just a little muted.

The fairy-story witch and the Russian wizard are really much more sinister than the Father of Evil himself as he appears in Gounod's *Faust* and Berlioz's *Damnation of Faust*. In the Berlioz he is Fischer-Dieskau, whom we have heard at his best this quarter in the Schumann album, and have here surely at his worst. The notes are badly focused, the vibrations disturbingly uneven, the tone lacking in depth and sonority. Nor are Domingo and Minton completely on form, the tenor sounding less steady than usual (though following with the score I could not see where the charges of inaccuracy, made by some critics, had their basis), and the mezzo rather inclined to squeeze the notes, especially in the 'King of Thule' song. Barenboim conducts a variable performance, favouring slow, relaxed tempos, but sometimes making the sound glow warmly. In his recording, the acoustics help Prêtre to bring out the full warmth of Gounod's score, but he is unaccountably heavy and graceless in the Kermesse Scene. The cast has some of the glamour of an old-time *Faust* (Freni, Domingo, Ghiaurov), but the singing is not really very stylish, and the most pleasing performance is Thomas Allen's as Valentin.

Postlude: I see that in my notes on the Byrd album by the Choir of King's College, Cambridge, the first comment is 'v. gentle & lovely. a blessing at the end of the day!'. Not very analytical, but I know what it meant. One feels it at the end of the opera-quarter too. The homogeneous voices, the quiet, reflective, flowing lines, the stillness. Mind, I see also that criticism was not entirely quiescent: 'only an over-insistence on consonants troubles', the notes say, and there is a savage double-underlining of the 'r' in 'gratia'. Why do we have to have this intrusion? In the echoey building, yes, but in recordings it is tiresome (as, for instance, an explosive 'c' announces the phrase 'cujus regni' in the Creed, cutting through the lovely sound for no special reason). The St John's Choir has (or has had) pronunciation troubles too. Why, for instance, should the trebles tell us in Purcell's *Te Deum* that cherubim and seraphim 'contsinually dso cry'? But, such niggles apart, these are three albums providing very great pleasure: St John's 'Choral Festival', King's Byrd album and 'Festival of King's'. After all the opera singers have been put to rest, try Master Goodman taking his five top Cs in the Allegri *Miserere* in that last album. Could Melba herself have sung them more beautifully? And was she ever, in all her career, given anything quite so beautiful to sing?

Karajan's Pelléas

The only other major recording to make a comparable effect, as a distinctive and unforgettable experience, has been the new *Pelléas et Mélisande* under Karajan. Again one has primarily to state the purely personal fact, for what it is worth, that the opera has never moved me so much either on record or in the theatre. The great beauty of the orchestral playing and the excellence of Michel Glotz's production provide the basic conditions; the appeal of Frederica von Stade's Mélisande provides a particular distinction; but overall there is the inspiration of Karajan's intellect and sensitivity seen here completely at the service of finding out the heart of the music. Thus the first scene blooms more passionately, involves one more in the feelings of credible human beings, and, as there is never a lapse in the extraordinary dreamlike concentration, all else follows on. If any cause for regret suggests itself, it is that the male voices tend to be drawn in, as it were, towards the centre: that is, the Pélleas (Richard Stilwell) is a baritone, not all that sharply differentiated from the Golaud (José van Dam), who in turn is not wholly distinct from the baritonal bass of the Arkel (Ruggero Raimondi). Possibly this contributes to the sense of reality in that the characters lose their 'story-book' identity (the romantic youth, the heavy husband, the sepulchral old king); yet musically there is a loss in coloration. Von Stade, so very girl-like, unoperatic in tone, her voice possessed of so much latent sadness, gives an infinitely touching performance. Of course the recording has to stand the test of time, but surely it will survive as one of the classics of the gramophone.

Messiah and St Matthew Passion

Christopher Hogwood's recording of *Messiah* and Karl Richter's of the *St Matthew Passion* are in some ways poles apart. *Messiah* is presented with the greatest possible care for historical accuracy; the aim is to produce, as near as can be, a performance like the one heard in the Foundling Hospital in 1754. It may be that many listeners who admire what Hogwood has done will find it inconsistent or even impossible to approve of Richter's handling of the *St Matthew Passion*. Richter's Munich Bach Orchestra is not an Academy of Ancient Music, and his feeling for Bach involves him in quite marked and frequent *rallentandos* at cadences, while the tempo of the chorales may vary from line to line. Where Christopher Hogwood, always open-eyed and on his toes, generally favours a bright tempo, Karl Richter sets the prevailing mood of his performance with a massive chorus of lamentation. His speed for this opening, 'Kommt ihr Töchter', is about half that taken by Helmuth Rilling in his recent recording where all is urgency and controlled 'building' of sound; it is also a good deal slower than his own 1959 recording. Once at least the slowness comes perilously close to sentimentality ('Wahrlich, dieser ist Gottes Sohn gewesen'); out of context it would surely seem excessive, and yet what it tells me of is love for the sublime bars and not a desire to make an effect, to produce a *tour de force*. The performance is all love: and if the love finds its expression in a *rubato,* a *rallentando* that raises cries of 'Romantic!', my own feeling is that I would rather have that than an historically authentic performance in which I can feel very little heart at all.

In its quite different way, Hogwood's direction of *Messiah* also expresses love of the music and certainly renews it in the listener. The notes he writes in the accompanying booklet make explicit so many fresh insights, and indeed freshness is everywhere in this recording. The incisive opening, more a march to Calvary than a meditation on Gethsemane; the spring in the step of the first chorus; the vividly pictorial effect of the shortened 'Pastoral Symphony'; the ruthless crack of the scourging motif ... each number deserves its own comment. There is also a marvellous sense of the architecture. We have had several excellent recordings of *Messiah* in recent years, but this is in many ways best of all, and it has its special claim as it follows the 1754 score.

A word about the solo singing in both recordings. Richter has some internationally famous artists, while Hogwood uses a home team of young singers brought up in the study of old music and having similar notions of the kind of vocal sound appropriate to it. I don't always enjoy that sound, I must confess: Paul Elliott's 'Comfort ye', which opens the whole performance, is thin, flat-toned (so that I want to say 'yowly' and wish there was a word in the dictionary to use instead), and it seems to presage ill. But much is beautifully done; and they do make a homogeneous team, almost a school. In Richter's *St Matthew*, Dame Janet Baker is her magnificent best in some of the less grateful arias like 'Können Tränen', and Peter Schreier narrates with a fine feeling for pace and also with remarkably beautiful singing-tone. Clearly I have to modify remarks made not long ago in these columns about the *St Matthew* being a work that belongs in church and resists export to the drawing-room.

Operatic Displeasures

It is perhaps unfair to include Solti's *Fidelio* under this heading, for much of it is excellent. Being the first digital operatic recording to appear, it has its place in gramophone history; the orchestral playing, the ensemble, the vividness of the spoken dialogue, the depth as well as the energy of Solti's reading all make a great impression. But the solo singing is of a different standard. The actual notes on which Hildegard Behrens declaims the word 'Abscheulicher' or those on which Theo Adam exclaims 'Ha, welch' ein Augenblick' are examples of the sort of thing that would never pass in a violinist or cellist but seem to be acceptable if a singer produces them with sufficient dramatic force to enable one to call it characterization. Adam has a kind of barking emphasis that I find quite unacceptable, and Behrens's voice, silvery and ample at the top, hasn't the warmth and depth of tone that her great role needs. The Second Act is better than the first, but here the recording suffers the misfortune of Peter Hofmann's impaired vocal condition: a lack of resonance and lustre diminishes the characterization as well as the music.

The recording remains an important one and I would not part with it. But recent recordings of *Norma*, *Rigoletto*, *Eugene Onegin* and *Werther* have left a taste that effectively kills any appetite for re-sampling. The Scotto/Levine *Norma* leaves an overall impression in which beauty has no part. Going back, one can play passages, especially from Act 2, in which the singing and playing are quite moving. But the total effect is dominated by the hard, clanging drive of Levine's conducting, with its double-quick-march, and by the unsteady, often hard quality of Scotto's higher notes. As for the *Rigoletto*, that is quite simply disqualified, in this age of competition and plenty, by the inadequacy of

Beverly Sills's voice: she sings with feeling and fluency, but the tone is now shallow and unsteady to a quite prohibitive degree. Milnes characterizes most vividly and is in fine voice. Rudel conducts efficiently but without anything like the distinction of Solti in his 1964 recording, recently reissued. The Duke in both recordings is Alfredo Kraus, and I find him distinctly better in the earlier one. Kraus often deserves his reputation as a stylist, but if one tests it by the 'Questa o quella' of this new recording, it does not pass: the legato is poor and the total effect graceless. Again one might say 'characterization'; I simply find spoilt music and second-rate singing. Much the same applies to Kraus's singing of 'Pourquoi me réveiller' in his recent *Werther*: his pathos and passion are much too overt, just as his holding of the loud high note and *diminuendo* at the end of the first verse are excessive and *un*stylish. Or take such a moment as his 'A ce serment restez fidèle! Moi, j'en mourrai, Charlotte': there is surely a call here for self-restraint, but the self-pity is tearful and abject. Domingo is far better and his conductor, Riccardo Chailly, is altogether more sensitive and imaginative than Michel Plasson with Kraus. On the other hand, Domingo's Werther is sung to the totally miscast Charlotte of Eleana Obraztsova. Troyanos (with Kraus), though not ideal because of the rather glamorous 'operatic' associations of the quick vibrato, is certainly preferable. For the recent *Eugene Onegin* there is still less to be said. Nesterenko sings with splendid tone and authority, though without much subtlety, in the relatively limited role of Gremin; Atlantov has plenty of feeling in his Lensky. But Mazurok remains surprisingly lacking in interest, Milashkina is for the most part shrill and tremulous, Mark Ermler conducts a charmless performance, and the recording is dry and hard in sound.

Karajan's Tosca

A certain kind of ideal in the recording of opera is fulfilled in Karajan's new *Tosca*. The Germans probably have a long abstract noun for it – 'seeing-by-hearingness'. Through some extraordinary quality of concentration, the performance so commands attention that all seems dramatically vivid on the mind's stage as though one were watching a producer of genius at work in one of the great opera houses. It is not a matter of the clanking of the chapel door, the cannon from Fort St Angelo, the slamming of Scarpia's window and so forth; it is essentially a matter of the music, as when in the opening it searches, with Angelotti, for the key, and smiles with the entrance of the Sacristan. Nor is it that the music is merely illustrative: its beauty and its brutality constitute the drama, in a sense that goes beyond details of plot, the stage figures and the scenery. One might wonder whether the passage following 'Recondita armonia' or the chords which so meltingly lead into 'Qual occhio al mondo' have ever sounded so beautiful, so affectionate (and through them we know of Cavaradossi's tenderness and depth). Then in Act 2, the hard penetrative insistence of the brass has probably never quite so compellingly told of the physical realities of the police state (and through this we know the ruthless energy of Scarpia's will). The tenderness and the bestiality have perhaps never touched each other more appallingly than here at that moment when Scarpia's announcement of the hiding place, 'nel pozzo del giardino', cuts into that fleeting and lovely interlude of gentleness ('Floria! sei tu') on Cavaradossi's release from the torture-chamber. The characters of Tosca and Scarpia, in this recording, take leave of their stage-representations; no counterpart here to the stagey conventions of the swirling cloak, the rolling eye, the hand to heart. Tosca we see as a fascinating and lovely woman of infinite variety; that is clear in the early part of the love duet; and later ('Ed io venivo a lui') the expression of hurt, noble in its restraint, prepares us for the intense yet aristocratic feeling of the 'Vissi d'arte'. When Scarpia arrives on stage, the authority impresses in a more subtle way than usual. 'Un tal baccano in chiese!' He is shocked; he does not need to raise his voice, for the rebuke and his mere presence have their effect. More of the role than usual is sung quietly – the first solo in Act 2, for instance, is a private utterance, and even when nominally addressing Tosca ('Tosca divina', 'Ed or fra noi') it is as though, incapable of real human relationships, the concern is still with self. In all this it seems irrelevant to speak of Katia Ricciarelli and Ruggero Raimondi: we are involved with Tosca and Scarpia, and with them only as parts of the music-drama, which, as I say, we see as well as hear in this recording. And it is, yes, a certain kind of ideal that is realized here. When I add that it is not quite my own kind of ideal then that is probably more a confession than a criticism. I like, in my ideal Tosca, a greater wealth of voice, of tone, than Ricciarelli has to offer; I like a richer, more vibrantly resonant tone in my Scarpia. And I think that without having read that Carreras had come to the recording sessions straight from Japan we would still have commented that he sounds tired, and that, although his singing of 'O dolci mani' now has a new refinement, his voice in most of the opera sounded a good deal fresher in his earlier recording under Sir Colin Davis. It is a great recording, this new *Tosca*, greater than the sum of its parts: we have come now the full distance from the gramophone's early provisions when *Tosca* as 'Opera at Home' meant innumerable versions of 'Vissi d'arte' and 'E lucevan'. And yet, gratefully accepting the Karajan as one ideal, it's to some of those hackneyed old solo records that I return when trying to give body to another, a different ideal, not as yet fully realized.

1981

Legato

William Mann's remark towards the end of his review in *The Times* of the recent Covent Garden production of *Le nozze di Figaro*, noting that for once legato was the rule and not the exception, lodged in my mind for several reasons, the immediately relevant one being that it chimed in with some of my own thoughts while listening to several of the quarter's records. Can it be true? We get so used to grumbling that legato is a thing of the past, yet we have a *Rigoletto* and an *Aida*, both of them operas open to a noisy, declamatory abuse of the vocal line, and, though they are no doubt less than perfect, it is clear that care for a genuinely smooth, well-bound vocal line has been a prime consideration. But emotional overemphasis is only the most blatant enemy of legato. More insidious are the use of a light aspirate, easing the way from note to note especially during runs, and, equally disruptive, a method which secures clarity in runs by hitting each note separately rather as a pianist might play semi-staccato. Yet lo, here are operas by Handel and Haydn, full of runs that might incite the one abuse or the other, aspirating or hammering, and, behold, legato is again the rule rather than the exception. More insidious still is that method by which the voice is made to swell slightly on each individual note: it is a feature that can become a habit among sensitive singers, but it works against the production of a well-bound phrase, an even line, a true singing tone. In Mozart (or in Monteverdi) it is a common resort, yet here we have operas by both, and once more, by and large, legato is preserved. The gramophone and the voice are not commonly seen as always having made progress step by step together. When the voice begins to show signs of catching up on some of the standards of the past, it deserves, perhaps, a little mild celebration in this column.

Il ritorno d'Ulisse

There was a time during the summer of 1972 when all conversational paths seemed to lead to Glyndebourne. *Il ritorno d'Ulisse in patria*: Monteverdi's opera, Raymond Leppard's realization of the score, Peter Hall's production, Janet Baker as Penelope – and I found myself nowhere near Glyndebourne that year. Then in 1979 it all started up again: 'Have you been … ?', 'Are you going … ?', 'What did you think of … ?'. Frederica von Stade had now taken over the leading role, and the excitement was hard to bear, for again I missed it. One contented oneself with some variant of 'Sour grapes': it couldn't have been that good. But now the recording is with us, gloriously vivid in humanity and splendour, and leaving no doubt that it was every bit 'that good'.

The splendour is there, beyond question, in the manuscript, the bare melodic and bass lines; but for the great scrolls and flourishes of harp and harpsichords, the majesty of organs and solemn brass, we have to thank Leppard. I understand there are those who don't: those who think that there is altogether too much of Leppard in between the bare outlines of Monteverdi (or whoever else may have had a hand in it). Leppard's Monteverdi has the rich decorative splendour of King's College Chapel, and when one is there it seems pointless to spend time wishing one were in the Escorial. Meanwhile this splendid flourishing of imaginative orchestration and dramatic production is matched by forward, unapologetic recorded sound, the voices close but not out of proportion to the instruments, an acoustic rather more sumptuously reverberant than any normally associated with Glyndebourne. The humanity lies in the expressive music for Penelope and Ulysses, sung with noble restraint and sincerity by von Stade and Richard Stilwell. Von Stade has probably never had a role that draws so fully upon her special character as an artist. Her singing of the opening monologue is known to us already through a recent recital, and one remembers how the very first sound of the voice in that performance was so poignant in its expression of dignified suffering. In context it is doubly moving, as after the lively masque-like prologue the drama deepens with those repeated descending scales, Penelope standing so isolated in heroic resolution and controlled longing. 'Torna, torna, deh, torna, Ulisse', most lovely in its quiet enunciation the first time, is repeated with tense, strong tone: an unforgettable point in the monologue. Perhaps most moving of all is the moment towards the end of the opera when Penelope, so long accustomed to self-discipline, allows herself to believe that Ulysses will return ('Creder ciò ch'è desio'). In all of this, the beauties of voice and character are exactly matched – as with some other great operatic performances of the past, the identity is complete.

Punch and Judy

'The fascination of what's difficult' was Yeats's phrase for something he knew more about than most men, and of which at the time of writing he had had more than enough. He said it had dried the sap out of his veins. Without feeling very much more desiccated than usual, I began to reckon that I understood Yeats's mood rather better after this quarter's listening, in which the recordings that impressed most have been the *Chansonnier cordiforme* and *Punch and Judy*. The latter may seem to fall readily enough into the category of difficult (and fascinating) works. About the *Chansonnier* the first difficulty is that it seems easy. It is an unmatched collection of fifteenth-century love songs ('cordiforme' because of the heart-shaped volume in which the songs were compiled), and has now been recorded in an altogether excellent four-record album by Anthony Rooley's Consort of Musicke. The instruments, many of them made specially for the recording, provide delightful accompaniments; the singers fit their voices to the music with quite remarkable resourcefulness and mastery. Each of the songs gives ready pleasure, and none is likely to deter through any harshness or lack of appeal, melodic, harmonic or rhythmic. The difficulty arises when one starts to do more than merely hear. Most of the songs, it appears, are notable among the whole collection for some particular characteristic. One of them is known as the most perfect example of its style, another is closest to folk tradition, another is 'possibly the strangest of all'. Sometimes the special feature that makes it so can be readily appreciated: it may be the almost dizzying intricacy of cross-rhythms, or the particularly sinuous or angular character of the vocal line. But proper appreciation involves the understanding of form, for this is a formal, disciplined craft, and the rules are there, rather like the rules of rhetoric, to be inventively observed. How familiar with this music and its rules does one have to become before being able to respond, for instance, to the delayed appearance of the 'b' section in a *rondeau*, and to the delayed tension which is created when the delayed 'b' section is 'especially distinctive'? How long may it be, indeed, before we recognize its special distinction among 'b' sections in the first place? More unsettling than this, how much must one have heard if one is to appreciate the aptness of two musical settings, the first of a poem which says how good the poet's mistress is, the other telling that he gets nothing from her and will shortly die, when, according to one's first reactions, the settings might musically and emotionally be almost interchangeable? There is a vast wealth of material here, immensely attractive even to the casual ear. The more fascinating it becomes, however, the more aware one is of difficulty – and perhaps, as Yeats says, 'spontaneous joy and natural content' are (at any rate temporarily) forfeit.

With Harrison Birtwistle's *Punch and Judy* difficulties are more apparent, and to that extent probably less intractable. The gramophone has certainly done a real service in this excellent recording under David Atherton (fully worthy of its *Gramophone* Record Award); and, as the librettist Stephen Pruslin says, it is an opera that lends itself especially well to recording. As for the difficulties, some are manufactured and arise only if one is intent on fitting it into some desired mould (psychological or political or philosophical). Others perhaps arise out of words, form (the ritualistic sequence of Morals, Passion Chorales and so forth), multiplicity of intention (it is partly 'an opera on opera'). But I found a greater difficulty, related somehow to 'the fascination of what's difficult' in these other respects. It is briefly this (and it involves heaven knows what problems of logic and aesthetics): the experience of the ideas and concepts, dramatic and musical, is strong, while the experience of the work itself is weak. The fascination of the structure, verbal expression, musical concepts, makes contemplation interesting. But at what stage, I wonder, does the actual sound (as opposed to contemplation of the idea) lead one to care for 'my Punch' or to feel for him and Pretty Polly anything remotely corresponding to what one feels (as the librettist says) for Tamino and Pamina or Florestan and Leonore? At least the gramophone gives the opportunity to find out.

Discovery

Discovery is indeed the keynote this quarter. Hardly any of these quarterly surveys is without a report on some new work, new to the gramophone or new to the listener, but it's rare to come up with a new composer. Peter Aston of the University of East Anglia has done just that in his discovery of the true worth of George Jeffries (*c*1610-1685), organist to Charles I at Oxford, withdrawing to the Northamptonshire village of Weldon and there writing church music which is possibly the most strongly individual of its period; certainly it is among the best. Aston's researches date from several years ago when he came upon a single alto part that looked so extraordinary in its progressions that he felt he must find the rest and track down the composer. 'A Musick Strange' is the title of the record made at the University and introducing Jeffries's church music to the record catalogues. The record title, apt as an introduction, is also the title of a Whitsuntide anthem, a setting of a rather marvellous poem, as is another of the anthems, *Whisper it easily*, and both are works of exceptional beauty. The cross-breeding of English music with the Italian, particularly Monteverdi, produces a notable enrichment in the writing for solo voice (highly accomplished work here by the baritone, Stephen Varcoe); and the composer's earlier experience in secular composition strengthens the dramatic quality of the Easter dialogue, *Heu, me miserum*, which, as Professor Aston points out, anticipates Purcell, and, incidentally, introduces us to a delightful soprano in Yvonne Seymour. The recordings are well done technically, and the presentation is admirable in scholarly thoroughness: certainly one of the records of the year.

From the same period, or a little earlier, come three pleasant and valuable records by the Consort of Musicke. 'Amorous Dialogues' gives one side to the English, one to the Italians. The most striking discovery here I found to be Sigismondo d'India's *Da l'onde del mio pianto*, a lament with poignant harmonies and modulations, requiring of the singer skill in florid work and an extensive downward range, Martyn Hill doing notably well in both respects. Most delightful, no doubt, is an old friend, Monteverdi's *Bel pastor* (interestingly paired with a duller setting by Da Gagliano): charmingly performed, and, while noting that it could be sung with more evident temperament and personality, one has to acknowledge that it is probably none the worse for that. 'Pastoral Dialogues' has a similar arrangement, and again the Italians show themselves more sophisticated and rhythmically interesting than the English. The English side does, however, include what the notes call 'Dowland's great trilogy' (*Sorrow, stay*; *Die not before thy day*; *Mourne, day is with darkness fled*) here in their original form: 'arguably more dramatic', and certainly making clearer the contrapuntal interest though losing something of the sense of personal and private grief when the songs are shared. Emma Kirkby sings sweetly as ever (charming, for instance, in *As I walked forth*) but David Thomas, who does so much so well, spoils quite a lot of his work by aspirating the runs. These two are also among the singers in the remaining record, a collection of songs by William Lawes, most remarkable, perhaps, for the two laments, one on the death of John Tomkins (*Musick, the master of thy art is dead*), the other on his own, by his brother Henry: *Cease, o cease, ye jolly shepherds, for gentle Willy, your lov'd Lawes, is dead*. In their quiet, uncommercial way, such records as these are among the catalogue's best assets.

A splendid addition to the catalogues has also been the recording by John Eliot Gardiner's Monteverdi Choir with the English Baroque players of Handel's *L'Allegro, il Penseroso ed il Moderato*. This is an import into this country and may not have had the wide circulation it deserves: I hope the *Gramophone* Record Award in the choral section may help to promote it. A lovely work, full of delights, even in the 'Moderato' section (words by Charles Jenner, and generally deemed a mistake). Again the soloists sing with admirable accomplishment and grace: not great names (Patrizia Kwella, for instance beautifully clean in her runs and intervals), but all thoroughly good musicians. Gardiner always gives something special to a performance, and here, as ever, there is an unfailing sense of enjoyment, a spring in the step, a delight in this alternation of moods, the contest between which is only nominally settled by Moderato's golden mean.

Sweet reasonableness, which asserts itself here, prevails also in Haydn's hitherto neglected oratorio *Il ritorno di Tobia*. Despite alarming references to Asmodeus and a monster's blood, the story is a homely one, coming to its crisis with what appears to be a matter of the treatment of cataracts, shielding the eyes by the use of a piece of cloth from too sudden exposure to the light – a practical suggestion which it takes the archangel Raphael to make. Dorati's recording with the Brighton Festival Choir and Royal Philharmonic Orchestra introduces a work that is always pleasing and sometimes (notably in Part 2) deeply impressive. Sara's aria, with its group of woodwind players providing a rich obbligato, is one of the finest things in it: there is also a strongly dramatic F minor chorus and an expressive duet for mother and son: these are perhaps the gems. Philip Langridge sings some demanding music with considerable technical skill and good tone until pressed for volume. Benjamin Luxon gives a most touching performance of his sad aria on his blindness ('Invan lo chiedi'). It is good to hear Barbara Hendricks's bright-edged tone, and Della Jones deserves a special welcome: this is her most important recording to date and she brings splendid assurance and authority to her work.

Enterprise

The operatic season has been an enterprising one. I see that readers are up in arms against the duplications of *Aidas*, *Toscas* and best-sellers in general, but in my allocation for opera this quarter *Der Freischütz* is the only one that comes anywhere near the top ten, and I have had to leave for next time Strauss's *Intermezzo* and Dargomizhsky's *The Stone Guest*, neither of them exactly pot-boilers. As for the singers, it is true that Caballé and Freni, Pavarotti and Carreras, Milnes and Ghiaurov are prominent among them. But for those who complain that it's always the same, there are also Behrens and Eva Marton, Vanzo and Siegfried Jerusalem, Dalibor Jedlička and Peter Meven among those singing leading roles. I can't really see much to complain about here.

With one exception, however, all these operas make easy listening; no trouble about 'the fascination of what's difficult' in them. The exception is *From the House of the Dead*, Janáček's last opera, with its masterly adaptation of Dostoyevsky, and its more marvellous concentration and generosity of spirit. Indeed, the opera is a testament of the human spirit and its ability to find love, joy and even beauty in places where the opposites prevail. The recording, the third of the Janáček operas recorded under Mackerras in Vienna, brings out the full warmth and vitality of the score. Jedlička and Ivo Zídek give fine performances, with the veteran Beno Blachut as the Old Prisoner who has probably the most memorable line in the opera. But of course it is essentially a company-opera and no doubt it was this sense of a thoroughly integrated and dedicated company that helped to earn its ***Gramophone*** Record of the Year Award, the second in three years to have gone to this series.

This, in its grim way, is an exhilarating work. The other operas this quarter have their moving qualities also, but basically they are altogether more comfortable. The odd-one-out in period is Korngold's *Violanta*, an extraordinary work of mature feeling and technical assurance by a prodigy of 17. The recording, with the composer's son producing and Marek Janowski conducting, does justice to the very skilful atmospheric writing – that quietly expectant passage, for instance, when the servant enters with candles. Much seems to anticipate *Il tabarro*: the off-stage voices, the night-music, the very shape of the scenario. In the three main roles Walter Berry sings with dignity as the husband, Eva Marton with a fine high C *fortissimo* though not all else quite so impressive as Violanta, and Siegfried Jerusalem provides the best singing as Alfonso, dearly loved of the ladies who when he gets into hot water at last has to plead that he was badly brought up!

There is more than a touch of decadence about the score of *Violanta*, scented and eventually sickly in its love-death as 'flowers fall into the room which is enveloped in a magical red glow'. Back now in the nineteenth century proper, the remaining operas are much more wholesome. Gounod's *Mireille*, for example: it has its sugary, pious death-scene, but the first half of the opera is entirely delightful, alive with happy choruses, unpretentious songs and, at the end of Act 2, an ensemble in which the melodic gift is used with real feeling for the tragic situation. The recording from Toulouse under Michel Plasson has Freni and Vanzo in the leading roles and a good supporting cast led by Bacquier and van Dam. It is good to hear Vanzo again, singing, I thought, with more charm and grace than he brought to his role in *Mignon*. Freni's French pronunciation seems to have improved since *Roméo et Juliette* now on the reissue list and not entirely deserving the upturning of noses that the mere mention of it tends to provoke. The same cannot be said of her voice which is less than steady in the louder passages. Much is well sung, however – the 'Magali' song, for instance, and the plea 'A vos pieds, hélas', coming just before the fine ensemble mentioned above.

Freni also sings in *Guglielmo Tell* and here she is in excellent voice, singing a role that has more to it than one generally reckons. The aria 'Selva opaca' is all we hear in excerpts, but the solo in Act 4, the duets, the part in the beautiful trio for women's voices, and her intervention in the Altdorf scene all add up to a part which is well worth the prima donna's attention. Of course it is regarded as the tenor's opera, almost impossible in the demands it makes upon the high notes. Pavarotti is the marvellous answer to those at any rate: his high notes have the sort of ease which most tenors command on notes just about one tone lower. And then he retains such an ample body of sound in the lower part of the voice too; there is a true heroic quality which makes him suit this role as very few singers in its history can have done. Artistically, the supreme moment is the aria 'O muto asil', and this is very far from its proper supremacy in Pavarotti's performance: both the elegiac feeling and the lyrical sweetness of the aria elude him. In the duet with Tell he is superb, and at least at one point later on he shows the finest side of his art, without any high notes at all – it is the passage starting 'Cari, onesti e dolci accenti' in the Act 2 duet, beautifully poised and phrased, with Freni responding in kind. Milnes's performance, too, I thought full of fine things and always imaginatively and convincingly felt. There is strong support in the smaller roles, and how good it is again to hear two English National Opera singers, Della Jones and John Tomlinson, acquitting themselves so well in this international company. Despite some commonplace passages, the opera makes a deep impression: much gratitude to Riccardo Chailly for an account that brings out so much of both the tenderness and the tension.

Although *Guglielmo Tell* is designated *melodramma tragica*, it has a happy ending (and musically an inspired one), as do my other three operas despite their stresses and strains on the way to it. There is *Der Freischütz*, richly of its period, taking us through the Wolf's Glen which was once upon a time such a delightfully terrifying horror-scene. Nowadays the scene probably stands a better chance on the gramophone than in the theatre; but no, the music isn't really strong enough to produce the old-time *frisson*. It's Agathe's arias that move us most (Hildegarde Behrens often ideal, occasionally unsteady); then the choruses (the Bavarians in fine form); then the orchestral pieces (Kubelík in charge of a thoroughly sympathetic performance). How lucky if in addition there is a Max who can be listened to with pleasure (alas ...), and a Caspar who can sing the notes (and Peter Meven, firm and sonorous, can do a good deal more than that). Then we have *I Puritani*, and to my mind Bellini's best. Muti conducts with great sensitivity, catching the rich romanticism well, and allowing the singers to be creative. Alfredo Kraus is certainly at his very best here, and his widely acknowledged place as by far the best of tenors for many years in this repertoire is confirmed: grace in the arias, triumph in the upper register, and a genuine singer's control of his material (not taking everything from the conductor), all make this as nearly a model performance of this kind of role as any we have in complete recordings. Caballé has moments of ravishing beauty and also brings a creative imagination to bear; I do find the beat and hardness on the higher, louder notes troublesome even so. In this and the final opera, *Stiffelio*, Matteo Manuguerra sings competently and tastefully in the baritone role. *Stiffelio* itself is splendidly vindicated as we hear it now under Gardelli, though I don't think it should drive *Aroldo* back into the vaults either. Comparing performances a little, I thought Caballé in the *Aroldo* recording conducted by Queler made a much lovelier impression (at Queler's slower tempo) than does Sass in the main soprano aria. But Carreras is excellent in the name-part, and Sass herself can be fine (as in the development of the Prayer). The recording is an enterprising conclusion to an enterprising series, and to a quarter's operatic listening that has been full of interest.

Miscellany

And still the discoveries. Louis Nicolas Clérambault (1676-1749) has hitherto been as little known to me as the soprano, Rachel Yaker. But here are both, making promising introductions, in two cantatas, *Orphée* and *Médée*, well recorded on Archiv. From *Medée* the 'Invocation', strikingly solemn and sung with sumptuous tone, makes a strong impression, as does the singer herself, athletic and even-voiced in her runs, warm yet well-defined in tone. I shall look out for her again. How long ago was it that we first said that about Dame Janet Baker? Her recent Liszt recital with Geoffrey Parsons is a fine example of her mature mastery, wonderfully delicate in *S'il est un charmant gazon*, catching the manner of the *mélodie*, bold and intense in *Die Fischerstochter* with movingly restrained, muted passion in its conclusion. *Die Lorelei* becomes a masterpiece of narration; its changing moods and colours merit an essay in themselves. Then the similarly mature mastery of Fischer-Dieskau is evident in the *Three Ballads of François Villon*, an abrasive part of a mixed Debussy recital with Barenboim conducting the Orchestre de Paris. Barbara Hendricks's radiant tone and sensitive shading give great pleasure in *La damoiselle élue*. And – more discovery – there are two choral pieces, student work, well worth bringing to the light of day again, particularly for the relish of the sweet of tooth.

Douce and seemly, Pergolesi's *Stabat mater* is back with us. 'A musical nightmare', Berlioz called it, but he never heard the boys of St John's College, Cambridge, in it: the choral duets are really the great pleasure here, though Felicity Palmer and Alfreda Hodgson bring a lively rhythmic sense and a good stock of trills to their solo parts. Handel's *Utrecht Te Deum and Jubilate*, deliciously, darkly aglow with discord and resolution, then all ablaze with drums and trumpets, thrive in the hands of Simon Preston conducting the Choir of Christ Church Cathedral, Oxford, and the Academy of Ancient Music: a most delightful record, this.

Hugo Wolf Society

I shall remember Easter 1981 as the Hugo Wolf season. Abominable weather did its best to depress the spirits all day long, in spite of which a rare sense of well-being would assert itself at odd times of the grey day, and I would realize that its cause lay in the Hugo Wolf Society box with its thoughtful provision of one record for each evening of the week. A subdued, concentrated joy, the whole experience. Of course many of the recordings – perhaps most of them – were old friends, constant companions indeed. Nearly all of the singers have also been one's familiars over many years. Possibly a listener for whom this was not so would have found the pleasure less keen, though I like to think that in such cases there would be a compensating freshness, a journey of happy discoveries as one meets new singers, new songs or new performances. I didn't this time stop for comparisons with modern performances. They 'play' as it were in one's mind at the same time. Fischer-Dieskau 'plays' in the mind, for instance, spanning phrases which Herbert Janssen, breathing more often, breaks into two or even three. Elisabeth Schwarzkopf also enters the mind, a smiling, vivid presence in playful pieces where Rethberg is no fun and Gerhardt is almost forbidding. Most repeatedly, our present-day accompanists, a host of them, come in and rap old Coenraad V. Bos over the knuckles (feeling apologetic almost directly afterwards as he goes on to play something with unspoilt mastery). More seriously, one does miss the wider range of emotions which modern singers can command in Wolf – irony, bitterness, playfulness; both the greater intimacy and the greater vividness of communication. But when all of that is said, the delight remains intense and lasting. Some of it is due, simply, to the beauty and character of voices. Janssen, Hüsch and Kipnis are the 'regulars', the first as fascinating and individual in timbre and production as the second represents (as it seems to me) good ordinariness raised to an extraordinary degree; and the last, a miracle of sonority, depth and lightness, achieving a softness that has none of that yawning quality that one so often hears when a big voice is made to sing quietly. Among the women, Rethberg's purity, Lemnitz's softness (a cradle of a voice), Ria Ginster's warmth: all are of rare beauty. And then the guest artists – McCormack and Schorr, greatness in their tones however momentarily disconcerting in immediate juxtaposition. Such voices of themselves bring distinction to the recordings. Let me name one song from each of them that is unforgettably at one with the singer: *Alles gingen, Herz, zur Ruh*; *Auf dem grünen Balkon*; *Grenzen der Menschheit*; *Mühvoll komm ich*; *St Nepomuks Vorabend*; *Mir war gesagt, du reisest in die Ferne*; and, of course, *Ganymed* and *Prometheus*. Then, in the later volumes, there comes that more vivid, more specific insight that shows very probably the growing assurance and persuasiveness of Walter Legge with his artists. There are those two astonishing performances by Helge Roswaenge, and in Karl Erb he had a singer who could cast an unbroken spell, as in *An den Schlaf*, or catch the ever-changing moods of a song (humour in the despair) as in *Der verzweifelte Liebhaber*. In some ways most prophetic of developments in post-war years was Martha Fuchs, whose *Neue Liebe*, *Storchenbotschaft* and *Geh', Geliebter* all have the sense of immediacy, of spontaneously developing expression that was clearly what Legge was so much wanting to elicit. I don't think he quite got it from Gerhardt! Yet, back in that first volume, there are treasures too. The authority of *Rat einer Alten*, restraint and maternal anxiety in *Die ihr schwebet*, the responsiveness to atmosphere in the *Ständchen*, the desolation of *Das verlassene Mägdlein* that so pulls at the heart ... no, I wouldn't be without these either!

Schwarzkopf's Last Record

Then, to end as I began, with German song and with a touch of greatness, we have had the sad pleasure of Elisabeth Schwarzkopf's final recording. The voice retains its unshakeable firmness and within the carefully limited range much of its beauty. The control, placing, communication, are all masterly. So lovely is the *Heimweh* (Wolf) that the last line ('Die Augen geh'n mir über') threatens to become true for the listener. Most lovely of all, Wolf's *Das verlassene Mägdlein*, still girl-like in tone, catches the emptiness, the desolate stillness. Brahms's *Mädchenlied* smiles vividly and has that radiance we shall never forget: we, that is, to whom her recitals were for some 30 years red-letter days in the musical calendar, occasions in which the standards progressively established in those Hugo Wolf Society records came to be most scrupulously and completely fulfilled.

Florilegium

'Auch kleine Dinge …'. As Hugo Wolf and Paul Heyse remind us, it is not only the big boxed-sets that give pleasure. This quarter has brought comparatively few of them, but there still has been much to enjoy. It has been very much the season of the single record, rather than the album, and above all one gives thanks for the continuance of that most civilized series, the Florilegium on L'Oiseau-Lyre. Some weeks ago in a London bookshop I heard from upstairs music as of the spheres, and so lifelike was the sound that one felt sure there were two expertly trained, fresh young soprano voices singing Monteverdi in a studio somewhere up above. In fact it was simply Miss Kirkby and Miss Nelson in a programme of 'Duetti da Camera' on L'Oiseau-Lyre. Proximity lends further enchantment; here are perfectly matched voices, precise, sweet and fluent, sensitive to the changing harmonies, intelligent in their treatment of the texts. Only one of the pieces is by Monteverdi himself; the others are by contemporaries including Sigismondo d'India whose writing always seems to be as interesting as his name. Sometimes, as in the Frescobaldi narrative, one feels that a more Italianate, less Roedean tone and manner are wanted, and Ravetto's *Io mi sento morir* should surely be sung by men. But the record is full, as Wolf's song says, of 'the little things that can also delight us', and I suppose that might be applied to the voices themselves: they are not the 'great' voices that fill the opera houses, and they are very English, in the tradition of Elsie Suddaby, Dora Labbette and Margaret Ritchie. That is to say, they are firm, pure and delicate, and unostentatiously put at the service of good music.

Another Monteverdi record with Emma Kirkby as soprano soloist comes from Hyperion and contains sacred music, much of it from the *Selva morale* book of 1640. In the Florilegium series Kirkby usually sings as a member of Anthony Rooley's Consort of Musicke; here she is with The Parley of Instruments, a group directed by Roy Goodman and Peter Holman. Their programme includes three of Monteverdi's six surviving settings of Psalm 110, *Confitebor tibi*, all three being astonishingly individual, and the second of them (for soprano, tenor and two violins) an inspired work of the utmost beauty and inventiveness. The other soloists are Ian Partridge and David Thomas. Again one realizes how much, throughout all these last ten years or so, we have owed to singers like these, and how they have also become practised artists with the skills to deal with virtuoso music we once thought lost to us for lack of ability in our singers.

Others in L'Oiseau-Lyre's Florilegium series have been John Coprario's *Funeral Tears*, seven songs on the death of the Earl of Devonshire (the 'Mountjoy' of *Gloriana*), including 'In darkness let me dwell'; an addition to the Purcell Theatre Music series, with charming pieces for Congreve's *The Double Dealer* and some very decorous un-Bedlamite madness for D'Urfey's *Richmond Heiress*, and Handel's music for *Alceste*, a lost play by Smollett with a marvellously swirling symphony for the arrival of Apollo. The last two records are by the Academy of Ancient Music under Christopher Hogwood, again with Kirkby, Nelson and Thomas among the soloists. I will return to the series later, after mentioning a few other records that have pleased in a similar way. James Tyler's London Early Music Group presents a collection of early sixteenth-century Italian airs and dances on Argo: here I find the dances, with the splendid colours of rebecs, sackbuts and crumhorns, more attractive than the airs sung with a somewhat wearingly unvibrating tone by Paul Elliott – who nevertheless copes well with the high tessitura and sings Josquin Desprez's *Scaramella* with plenty of character. In the Consort of Musicke's 'Madrigals and Wedding Songs for Diana' David Thomas similarly denies his voice natural resonance as he sings Dowland's *Welcome, black night*: it seems to be a doctrine of this school that voices should have the 'flat', non-resonating sound of viols, swelling with a sort of bellows-motion on individual notes, and in darker music flattening further. Personally I don't like it. The madrigals, however, are excellent – including the treatment of darkened harmonies as at 'why weep ye?' in *Hark! all ye lovely saints*, and special moments such as the sense of breadth through strict legato in the 'Long live fair Oriana' of *All creatures now*.

Finally, in this group I most strongly recommend the record of cantatas by Handel, also in L'Oiseau-Lyre's Florilegium series. These are full of delightful things, some of which elsewhere go to words like 'His yoke is easy' and 'All we like sheep'. But most amazing is the *Africa* Cantata (No. 36) for solo bass. With its range from bottom C sharp to high A (sung C and G sharp), its runs and leaps and later on its need for lightness and sustaining power in a high tessitura, this is the kind of virtuoso piece that one might almost have said was impossible for today's singers. Now it has been recorded, remarkably well, too, and not by any of the great names among the basses in gramophone history from Plançon to Pinza and Kipnis to Ghiaurov – but by David Thomas.

Writing Against the Voice

However hard Handel works his singers he gives the impression of being on their side. The twentieth century has evolved a style which (whatever the truth of the matter) usually gives the opposite impression. David del Tredici's *Final Alice* is something of a puzzle in this respect. Perhaps he loves the soprano voice as did Richard Strauss, of whom he puts us quite often in mind; certainly there are passages of an extraordinary, even luscious beauty written for the voice, and Barbara Hendricks sings them ravishingly (here too is a fine example of virtuosity in the modern singer). But there are also fearsomely punishing passages, where the top of the voice is subject to the most frightful demands, usually as the music moves from dream to nightmare. I didn't feel in any way, as Max Harrison said in his review, that all the effort is 'expended to very little real purpose': the effect is curiously disturbing and haunting, I find, and perhaps the love-hate relationship with the voice, if such it is, goes with much else in it that is ambivalent, if not schizophrenic.

In operatic composition the twentieth century has largely set its face against song as inimical to drama. So there is not much song in *Wozzeck*, but much that is anti-song: *Sprechstimme* and whole passages for the 'singer' where beautiful sound is about the last thing wanted. In the new digital recording under Dohnányi, the secondary singers earn gratitude, by and large, for sounding their notes firmly, without wobble. The vocally dreadful roles of Captain and Drum-Major get what I suppose they want, well-defined penetrative tenor quality with no hint of what is ingratiating, lovable or romantic in the tenor voice. Alexander Malta as the Doctor makes us think again, for he sings with rich, even beautiful tone. But the two principals do not; and whereas in eighteenth- or nineteenth-century opera that would normally be fatal, in this it seems not to matter all that much. A Wozzeck who really did sing was Walter Berry and I remember liking his work all the better for it. But Eberhard Waechter in the new version gets through well enough to the dramatic heart of the role, although his voice is sometimes cloudy and in louder passages has developed a marked beat. And Anja Silja, whose singing would surely be found insufferable if this were Mozart (for instance), fits into the general balance of what seems to be required here, for she too dramatizes strongly. So she does in *Erwartung*, also under Dohnányi. Again, my memory is that this can be sung well (meaning by 'singing' the sort of process used in the vocal works of Mozart, for instance): I haven't the record by me, but recall that Helga Pilarczyk did so. Yet the point is that Silja's unsteadiness on high notes and her uneven method of production are not evident disqualifications here any more than the condition of Waechter's voice is in *Wozzeck*, for the composer does not seem to want us to think in terms of 'song' at all. More clearly, she is inadequate in the *Sechs Lieder* of around 1904 which seem to call for a cross between Schwarzkopf and Flagstad. Here the composer is writing *for* the voice, though even these carry more than a hint of the punishment he is going to give it only a few years later in *Erwartung*, a treatment which his pupil Berg metes out with still more ruthlessness in *Wozzeck* and *Lulu*.

1982

John Ward

Postscript. The last Quarterly Retrospect with its appreciation of the Florilegium series on L'Oiseau-Lyre had just gone to press when there arrived one of the finest of all the very fine offerings from that source, again with Anthony Rooley to thank for its provision. I knew some of the madrigals of John Ward (had sung in them even), and was not over-excited to find a two-record album devoted to a composer who had never impressed me as being one of the most individual of the madrigalists. A good many amateur groups will probably have sat round their madrigal tables doing battle with *A satyr* once, caught out by unexpected entries and knotted inextricably by interchanges of upper parts at the repeats. 'And was it worth it?' they may have questioned. Well, in the first place, it becomes a different thing when performed as here: marvellously light-footed and rhythmical. In the second place, this is a four-part madrigal and leaves one quite unprepared for the magnificence of the six-part pieces. Anthony Rooley directs the listener straight to these in his sleeve-note, but I am not sorry that I went dutifully through the records, starting with those in three parts and working towards Parnassus stage by stage. At the summit are eight six-part madrigals, masterpieces of composition, for it is the developed form of the pieces as much as the harmonic and contrapuntal richness that makes a more substantial, a weightier kind of satisfaction than the listener (as opposed to the performer) may usually have gained from madrigals. In the whole vast output of the Elizabethans there may be nothing of the kind to surpass such madrigals as *Oft have I tendered*, *If the deep sighs* and *I have entreated*. Another flower of a rare excellence in the cap of this admirable series.

Welsh Wagner, English Verdi

I missed the Welsh National Opera's production of *Tristan und Isolde*, making the fatal mistake, as I remember, of thinking one could leave it till the second day of booking. The great achievement of, at least, the musical side of the production becomes very apparent in the recording, a performance in which love of the work speaks through all of the playing and much of the singing. Even more than usual, it's a great mistake, I found, to try to 'sample' this performance. Of course one wants to try the flavour of it before the long-promised hours become available to play right through. But random passages are likely to give a particularly misleading impression, especially of Goodall's conducting, where everything is graded with the finest sense of relationships, so that when the great climaxes come they have a strength of almost alarming intensity. Many are the fine things, including (or is this fancy?) a way of 'floating' the earlier part of the Prelude, a suggestion of the boat and the waves such as I can't recall having caught before. Linda Esther Gray's Isolde is surely in the line of the great ones. A lyric-dramatic soprano with a distinctive and personal thrill in the middle of the voice, warm and full in the lower register and generous on high (two fine top Cs in the Love Duet, for instance), she also brings to her singing of the role some of that emotional concentration that seems to have marked the performances of Frida Leider. It is hard on John Mitchinson that the main criticism has to fall on him. Bernard Miles used to have a monologue called *The Truth about Tristan*, but the truth not stated there is that the role in the opera really asks for more than one man can give.

Mitchinson's is a voice with plenty of body in that part of it where most of the music lies; but it lacks ring on top, is not always steady, and never, I think, sounds as a romantic voice. The portrayal is manly, yet in the Third Act this manliness seems to set a limit so that the voice never becomes a receptacle for pain or for the other more extreme emotions. Still, one should be grateful that the music is sung and not barked; and at one point ('Wie sie selig') there is a vocal beauty to match the beauty of the orchestral playing. Anne Wilkens's Brangaene comes through well and it is good to hear Gwynne Howell, who has been singing so well this season at Covent Garden, making a fine thing of King Marke's monologue

The English National Opera's *Traviata* is also something to be proud of, in the precision of the ensemble work and fine quality of orchestral playing under Mackerras, and most of all in the Violetta of Valerie Masterson. I don't like the opera in English (what a namby-pamby fellow Alfredo sounds when his vigorous tune in the cabaletta goes to 'I hate myself; I'm so ashamed', and what old-style English public-school types the Parisians become as they encourage Alfredo with 'That's how to take it! Splendid!') But there are gains too: for instance, the little tiff between Flora and the Marquis suddenly emerges from obscurity, especially when played as spiritedly as here by Della Jones and Denis Dowling. John Brecknock's clean-cut tone is gratefully heard, as is Christian du Plessis's comparative richness, though both have some less welcome characteristics. Masterson is all that her admirers have long proclaimed her to be. She gives a thoroughly admirable performance, both in feeling and in vocal accomplishment, the tone so accurately placed, right in the centre of the note, and no fuss or ostentation of manner at any point. The voice, to my ears, is not quite unalloyed silver; it does not shine with quite the purity of (say) the younger Mirella Freni. The role also calls sometimes for rounder, fuller tone. Yet one is left with no sense of shallowness either of voice or character; on the contrary, the great scene with Germont *père*, the 'Addio del passato' and all of the last Act go to the heart and are probably, in total effect, as touching as any on record.

German and French Song

Among other Lieder records, Sarah Walker's Brahms has its attractions, though I didn't feel the recording quite had the effect, quoted on the sleeve from a press report of a live concert, that she and Vignoles 'lift the curse of High Art off the song recital by sheer gusto'. Perhaps it reinforces the point that record-making is an art in itself. It is something that Hermann Prey too, with all his experience, has not quite mastered. Such a genial character and a vivid personality on stage, he seems curiously unable to communicate gaiety, happiness, affection on record. So in the *Schwanengesang*, recorded live at the Hohenems Schubert Festival of 1978, 'Liebesbotschaft' sounds quite miserable, the 'Ständchen' is unromantic, 'Abschied' is almost stern. On the other hand, exceptionally fine are the more sombre songs such as 'In der Ferne', really sung from the heart, 'Der Atlas' and the climactic 'Der Doppelgänger', very slow and finely controlled. I wondered whether Prey was conceiving the songs as a cycle and whether, to satisfy the imposition of some sort of unity which this would require, the happier songs were consciously being darkened. Another of the major Lieder singers of today, Peter Schreier, has a Richard Strauss recital, in which he shows mastery of many kinds. He sings with intimacy and a rather lovely, silvery *mezza voce* in songs like *Freundliche Vision*. The limitation here is that, as recorded, the voice has a rather pallid, bloodless tone, unsatisfying in, say, *Heimliche Aufforderung*, *Cäcilie* and the climax of *Ständchen*.

Nothing pallid or bloodless, at any rate, about the tone of Jessye Norman. Her *Nuits d'été* has a beauty of sound, deep and dark as the waters in 'Sur les lagunes' and radiant 'parmi la fête étoilée', such as the songs have probably never known before on record. Beautifully lightened are the 'lifting' phrases of 'Spectre de la rose'; and at 'sur l'albâtre où je repose' it is like lying back, not upon alabaster indeed, but on a great velvet pillow. Dissatisfaction enters only at the start and finish; again, curiously (another instance of the disparity between the artist and the person), hardly anything of Jessye Norman's warming smile and personal gaiety comes over in 'Villanelle' or 'L'île inconnue'. The second side, Ravel's *Shéhérazade*, brings the record into comparison with the other recent account, by Frederica von Stade. Both performances gave more enjoyment than I personally have found in this work before (I don't particularly want to have much to do with that poem). But if Norman's recording has a more sensuous luxury of gorgeous tone, von Stade's has more tang, more appetite, more liveliness. The *Chansons madécasses* are also beautifully performed by von Stade, the evening stillness and relaxation of the last song marvellously well caught. A record to go very near the top of the shopping list.

Domingo

Reading the music critics of earlier times has become something of a compulsive hobby of mine over these last few years, and it provokes a variety of reflections about music criticism in the present. Among them one of the most persistent is the prime need in criticism for what I'll call 'celebration'. It is extraordinary how many events that one feels should be written up in letters of gold are passed over with a routine sentence or two, taking their place in the dull catalogue of things. To take an instance from the past, Lotte Lehmann comes and sings her Marschallin again. It was even better than last year or not quite as good, but because it was a regular feature of musical life no more is said; it is passed down the line as something that can be taken for granted. Among the tenors of earlier times, Melchior and Martinelli were outstanding: so our ears tell us as we listen to recordings. But our eyes see precious little celebration of their work among the critics for whom they were, so to speak, part of the furniture. Even Caruso's performances often earned no more than an adjective; even his recordings, while they were still being issued, would win a 'one of his best' or 'not one of his best' award and little more.

It is done all too easily. In this column over the years, some 30 or 40 operatic recordings with Domingo in the cast must have come up for review. His work will have been gratefully acknowledged, sometimes with a certain amount of head-shaking about his doing too much. But whether on top form or somewhere below it, he has sung as only he can sing, and I fear that he has been very largely taken for granted. Listening to his 'Gala Opera Concert' with Giulini it struck me that here he is caught in the fleeting moment of prime. Often hard to put the finger upon, there is nevertheless always a time in a singer's career when all the elements of his art are in their best equilibrium. Domingo has not lost the rich velvety surface of his youthful voice, but we are aware all the time of coming nearer to the strong metal that lies beneath it. In this recital record the velvet and the metal seem ideally in proportion. His style, which has never in my experience been coarse, has sometimes been less than scrupulous and elegant. Here he *is* scrupulous: nothing breaks the line in 'Una furtiva lagrima' or 'O paradis', nothing inhibits the heroism of 'Di quella pira' or the ardour of 'Celeste Aida', yet both have a certain dignity and a care for detail that place them in the small ranks of the genuinely patrician performances. A noble breadth distinguishes his solo from *La Juive* and, if he sounds more comfortable in that than in 'Je crois entendre', it remains something of a wonder that a man who has Otello and Walther von Stolzing in his repertoire can turn with such a degree of mastery to this most testing of arias for the high lyric tenor. The *Lucia di Lammermoor* excerpt similarly has a fine expansiveness, without resorting to lachrymose overt pathos. The *Ernani* finds him, as it were, 'thinking upwards', and just something in the style and restrained intensity recalls Martinelli's old record. Again, there is perfect equilibrium – even, for instance, in the matter of vowel sounds, which, while never naggingly or aggressively open, retain their natural brightness. 'Domingo again', we think as we look at the new record lists. We feel that Domingo, like the poor, we have always with us. But of course we haven't, and certainly a great singer's prime does not last for ever: while it is with us, it calls for a little celebration.

La Gioconda

To revert to the earlier music critics, I wonder what Ernest Newman would have thought of the operatic scene if he were writing now. His comments were often caustic and sometimes almost despairing, but many of the things he complained about have now been improved. And I wonder what difference this would have made to his estimate of the operas themselves. For instance, *La Gioconda* he considered 'despicable', the music 'mostly beneath contempt'. This was when it was given for the last time at Covent Garden, in 1929, and Newman had the advantage of hearing the name-part sung by Rosa Ponselle, whom he admired enormously. Could he, one wonders, have written of the score with the same contempt if he had heard the very careful, almost too refined recording under Bruno Bartoletti? Whatever one may finally think of the opera – and in my opera house the 'Dance of the Hours' would be omitted and the curtain might even go down on the oft-repeated 'Addio' leaving Barnaba to gnash his teeth in the wings – there is far too much in it to be dismissed simply as despicable. The recording brings this out very clearly. The orchestral and choral work is all most carefully tended (the tempos sometimes too slow but at least avoiding any impression of shoddiness). Caballé gives a strongly characterized performance, predictably celestial in the 'Ah! come io t'amo', phrasing 'E un dì leggiadra volavan l'ore' in one, though forcing her rather mean chest voice every now and then. Pavarotti (his arrival less effective than it should be because recorded straight into the microphone) sings imaginatively in 'Cielo e mar' and with distinctive tone throughout. Milnes allows no melodramatic ranting to coarsen his role, Ghiaurov preserves fine legato and definition of tone in the solo that usually sounds wretchedly unmusical, and Baltsa gives her part in the 'L'amo come il fulgor' duet all the passion and fullness of voice it wants, without the vulgar display of chest voice that it so often gets. I cannot quite believe that Newman would come away from this with his heart so entirely full of loathing.

Delius's Idyll

If 'heard melodies are sweet but those unheard are sweeter' perhaps a further proposition might be added to the effect that those half-heard, or over-heard, are sweetest. I remember through the smoke and noise of a public bar once hearing the music of the spheres. It was Monteverdi's *Vespers* and never in all the 20 years since that time, though I have heard the work whole and clear in live performances and on record, has it had quite the magic of that distant fragment of an overheard broadcast on the old BBC Third Programme. Once from the kitchens of a hotel restaurant in the Pyrenees came another fragment on a dim old radio: this time the Transformation Music in *Parsifal*, and again it was as though the heavens opened. More recently, in a place of many noises, a corridor in the BBC's Egton House, London, where Rameau mingles with The Rolling Stones and Mme Caballé, as though in the torments of a hell specially reserved for opera singers, rises to a top C to the accompaniment of Pink Floyd, for once a single record played serenely in the distance, and again it momentarily brought a glimpse of Paradise Garden. It was Delius: there was no mistaking that, even at this distance. Not the 'The walk to the Paradise Garden' as it turned out, but the *Idyll* of 1937, and the voices soaring so ecstatically along the corridor were those of Felicity Lott and Thomas Allen, part of the now famous and prize-winning digital album, 'The Fenby Legend', still up to that time uncaught in my retrospective net. A most lovely work indeed, the *Idyll*, and one among several of comparable beauty (*A Late Lark*, for instance, which Anthony Rolfe Johnson sings with such sweetness). Yet the face-to-face encounter never brought quite the enchantment wrought by that distant music of the accidental over-hearing. Eric Fenby's essay on the record sleeve suggests, moreover, that Delius himself would have known the feeling, for it was so much his own striving, as Fenby says, 'ever to recapture a moment of transcendent bliss experienced in his youth', wanting at once to use words and to dispense with them, to use a precise means to an end which seems to dispel all precision. That is particularly so in the choral writing, in which there are exquisite moments where the words are all lost, obtaining effects which only Delius could have imagined. That Fenby himself, as amanuensis, could have glimpsed the distant music so clearly when it must otherwise have remained shut up darkly in the composer's mind is another wonder, almost as moving in contemplation as the sounds themselves are in the hearing: though more moving than either, as I suggest, is the half-hearing or the overhearing, an unrepeatable moment of delight experienced accidentally in the smoke-filled bar, the casual restaurant, the cacophonous corridor.

Ponselle's Traviata

Then there are the *Traviatas*: two of them, I have to remind readers who do not usually get as far in their ***Gramophone*** as the Historical reviews. Renata Scotto's Violetta once struck me as being possibly the best on record; that was on her old recording originally released in 1963 and reissued on DG. Her voice then was in much finer condition than it is on the new digital version but there are compensations, partly in that her performance remains deeply felt and very touching, and more so in that she is in better company. Alfredo Kraus, a genuinely distinguished Alfredo, sets a high standard in his Act 2 solo; Renato Bruson has the ideal voice and very nearly the ideal style for Germont *père*. Muti's conducting brings much refinement and delicacy, and though the Card Scene is fast and unyielding he also has the strength and sensitivity to concern himself more than most recent conductors with rubato. This is a very complete and textually faithful *Traviata* (cabalettas included, two verses of Violetta's arias, no high notes at the end of arias, etc.); the other is not exactly that. Nor is it exactly, or even remotely, a high-fidelity recording. But again, there are compensations. At her best, Rosa Ponselle brought to the role a beauty of voice that has probably not been equalled this century, and, again at best, an emotional intensity that has not been surpassed. Lawrence Tibbett is, I think, quite simply the finest Germont that I have heard in a complete performance, and their work together in Act 2 ranks with, say, the association of Callas and Gobbi in the 1956 Nile Duet in *Aida*. The conductor, Ettore Panizza, runs away at a *stringendo* and lingers indefinitely with a *più lento*, but there's plenty of life in him. Also, unless one is almost unnaturally immune to such matters, one must surely feel some sense of wonder at listening-in, at this date, to a broadcast from the Metropolitan, New York, in 1935, with the artists so clearly playing to an audience who feel themselves drawn towards the stage, their applause showing their appreciation of being there.

1983

Record of Singing 2

'Enterprise', like 'patriotism', 'law and order', 'paternalist' and 'elitist, has become such a politically-coloured word that one hesitates to use it ('elitist' was struck from my vocabulary several years ago when I learnt that in some quarters that's what it is to prefer the *Jupiter* Symphony to *Yellow Submarine*). All the same, in the business of reissuing old ('historical') records, enterprise is the name of the game. These columns have long celebrated the good work of the Rubini and Pearl labels which for so many years, through the enterprise of their managers and the goodwill of generous collectors, have rescued antique beauty from oblivion. But one always knew that if the EMI giant were to bestir itself we might see some wondrous doings. Impressive tokens of this were the albums devoted to Patti, Melba and Chaliapin, and of course the vast undertaking that brought forth the two volumes of 'The Record of Singing'. More recently there have been several excellent issues, and now in this last quarter especially a major portion of listening-time has been taken up by three weighty offerings from this source, all of them essentially the work of one man.

The re-edited 'Record of Singing, Vol. 1', now issued as 'A Record of Singers Pts. 1 and 2', has been reviewed by the present writer and its background outlined by Alan Blyth ('Here and There', November issue) so I'll say no more about it now except to remark that it is inexhaustible (I have just been back to it to hear that remarkable group of Italian sopranos – de Frate, Teodorini and Torresella – and then on from there you go to the superb Medea Mei-Figner, and there you are listening to the original Lisa of *The Queen of Spades* singing the music Tchaikovsky wrote for her), and to add a word of appreciation about its actual appearance – a window of record labels looking out from the box, with all those designs and colours and names so dear to the collector's heart.

Then there's the new Tauber album ('The Art of Richard Tauber'), of which, at the time of writing, I have yet to see the finished product but which was a great joy when I was writing its notes and again, a few weeks ago, when reviewing it. I can see now the face of an elderly lady of German origin lighting up when I played her that magical 'Gern hab'ich die Frauen geküsst' from *Paganini*. But that is how Tauber is: an inert or unresponsive presence in a room where he is singing is a corpse. There have been countless Tauber reissues, but of all that have come my way this is the one which most does justice to his memory.

The best of good companions in recent weeks, however, has been the Schubert 'Historical Recordings of Lieder (1898-1952)'. This is another of those dream-albums that one thought could never materialize. Ancient treasures are unearthed: Franz Naval's sensitive, lyrical *Der Neugierige* (1902), Plunkett Greene's tireless *Abschied* (1904), Lilli Lehmann unbending happily in *Freudvoll und leidvoll*, Slezak's infinitely gentle *Liebesbotschaft* of 1909. Latter-day riches are released for the first time: Janssen and the *Rosamunde* 'Romanze' suiting each other to perfection, Hotter immense in *Gruppe aus dem Tartarus*, unissued pressings of irresistible Patzak, and Flagstad's *Uber allen Gipfeln*, the title a fitting epitaph for the singer, bringing the whole eight-hour journey to an end. Then there are the exotics, or the folk one hardly expects to find in Schubert: the cavernous, magnificent Sibiriakov of St Petersburg, Ottilie Metzger whom I come to think of as among the few really glorious contraltos on record,

Meta Seinemeyer tragic as a Verdi Leonora in *Gretchen am Spinnrade*, delicate and pure-toned in *Mignon II*, Chaliapin, Schorr, Olczewska, Georges Thill and that wonderful boy in the dramatized *Erlkönig*. The 'regulars' too are magnificently represented, particularly lovely Julia Culp, Karl Erb so totally immersed in the songs, Schwarzkopf and Seefried, Fischer-Dieskau an immediate tightener of concentration. Some are regrettable: Marie Goetze breathing whenever she feels like it in *Litanei*, Ernst Wachter whose low, last 'Glück' in *Der Wanderer* must be one of the funniest notes on record, Sigrid Onegin with glorious voice and somewhat inglorious intonation. But the list of delights is not more than a fraction complete, and of course it involves not merely the singers and the songs as separate entities, but also the opportunities for comparison: five versions of *Erlkönig*, for instance, and 27 of the 106 songs appearing in more than one version. There is also – and here I must end, for there have been other good things this quarter – the absolute joy of hearing these early records in incomparably fine sound. The transfers are completely natural in the quality of sound (full-bodied and clear): you could hardly believe the date of the earliest records (and the very earliest is 1898). I have always said that I don't mind the surface noise of the old 78rpm discs, that the ear simply eliminates it after a very short while; but must admit that it's even better to be so very nearly without it as here. The album (with an excellent booklet, incidentally) is to my mind EMI's great gift to us in 1982 – it came too late for my 'Critics' Choice' this year, but it will not be forgotten next. Nor should the man most responsible for it be forgotten. Though I'm sure he will deprecate any such public acknowledgement, it would be inexcusable not to record my own very great gratitude to Keith Hardwick.

Old Operas for New

Enterprise is probably the key-note of the opera season too: a welcome international collection of works one normally hears of without actually hearing. From the German repertoire comes Lortzing's *Der Wildschütz*. It was interesting to read of Kurt Weill's contempt for this opera, and not surprising, for it presents humanity getting along quite happily with its class-system, and it offers its public a night at the theatre full of cheerful melodies, lively invention, thorough musical craftsmanship and unspoiled good humour; there is no sour, aggressive note in it from beginning to end. The performance goes with zest, Bernhard Klee conducting the finely orchestrated score with full appreciation of its quality. Sotin is in excellent voice and does his big 'Fünftausend Taler' solo with relish and without exaggeration. Mathis, Schreier, Doris Soffel and the attractive voice of Gottfried Hornik are all sources of strength in the cast: I found the whole thing delightful.

The new recording of Rossini's *Mosè in Egitto* brings another page of the musical history books to life, and this is largely thanks to the enterprise of its conductor, Claudio Scimone, whose scholarly championing of the original Italian version revised in 1819 is so happily vindicated. He secures a worthy performance from the Philharmonia Orchestra and for the most part an acceptable one from his soloists. Raimondi's Moses is certainly one of his finest achievements on record: the tessitura suits him well and the sonorous, well-disposed authority of his singing carries him through, despite music which assumes a different kind of training and practice. Nimsgern as Pharoah makes an effective contrast and Ernesto Palacio is so impressive in his range and flexibility that I looked him up in recent numbers of *Opera* – only to find that the reviews I hit upon complained almost unanimously of a colourless voice and lack of power. Richard Osborne liked June Anderson (Elcia) more than I did – and I think that he also found more in the opera than I could do. It seems to me impressive though flawed in conception, movingly beautiful at times (as in the Quintet, the ensemble finale of Act 1, Amaltea's aria, the famous Prayer and the orchestral conclusion). But most of the music hardly comes within hailing distance of the emotions it is supposed to express: the quartet, 'Mi manca la voce', for instance, is mildly sad but with its easy harmony and movement provides nothing like what words and situation require, while the *allegro* which follows (to words such as 'Reason no longer illuminates my soul') would be an acceptable substitute for 'Mi par d'essere con la testa' in *Il barbiere* but is out of its element here.

At times *Ruslan and Ludmilla* too seems not to rise to the occasion – the concerted passage in Act 3, before the appearance of the Finn, ought to be a high spot and isn't quite. Also, the recording, newly issued here, is not, on the whole, up to the standard of the German opera or the Italian. There is plenty of energy in the orchestral playing (the Bolshoi orchestra under Yuri Simonov) and Nesterenko gives a fine performance as Ruslan. But the production is poor, with some crude and inappropriate stereo effects at times and a general lack of stage-atmosphere most of the time. And several of the roles are unpleasingly sung, notably by the sopranos. However, it is good to hear the opera again and to have a touch of distinction whenever Nesterenko sings.

A reissue that is very worthwhile indeed is that of Busoni's *Doktor Faust* conducted by Ferdinand Leitner with Fischer-Dieskau in one of his great roles. He made an immense impression, I remember, singing some excerpts at London's Royal Festival Hall, I think possibly just about the time of this recording (1969), and one can only wonder afresh at the humanity and ruthlessness, authority and vulnerability of his portrayal. The great thing about this renewal of acquaintance, however, was the way the work itself seemed to have grown in stature. The Introduction and Prologues, especially, are gloriously rich and beautiful in sheer sound, while the individuality and inventiveness of the writing become increasingly apparent as time goes by, and they begin to be less overshadowed by the 'establishment' avant-garde which made them seem to be apart from the progressive movement of the times.

Recitals: Opera and Song

The recital by Agnes Baltsa left me with somewhat mixed feelings. The voice is one of the very best we have heard in these last ten years: shining and resonant with the relatively rare quality one would call glamour but for the connotation of falseness. In this record, it is at its most exciting, the range and adaptability most impressive. What a pity therefore that in the Rossini arias so many of the runs (the groups rather than the scales) are aspirated, and that in moving from one aria to another there is only a superficial change of mood. In Lady Macbeth's 'La luce langue', for instance, there is no pallor, everything is healthy; it's only in the last section, regal and determined, that emotion comes through. Oddly, the most imaginative, expressive singing seems to come in the one virtually unknown aria (from Mercadante's *Il giuramente*), and this is certainly one of the high points of the recital.

Lovely voices are not always the most expressive of instruments. On the other hand, there is an awful temptation to carry that remark a stage further and say 'She/he has a lovely voice, *ergo* no expression'. This kind of process has, I believe, sometimes affected the critical rating of Kiri Te Kanawa and, to some extent, Jessye Norman. When two such voices appear on the same record, a kind of musical puritanism comes into play, which says, 'This is too rich a feast; partake with caution.' Te Kanawa's *Les nuits d'été* needs no such caution; it is simply a superlatively fine performance. Norman's *La mort de Cléopâtre* on the reverse side does to some extent obey the suspect rule: the voice is lovely and expressiveness is comparatively lacking. Comparison with Dame Janet Baker enforces the point: more yearning nostalgia in 'Ah! Qu'ils sont loin ces jours', more intensity in 'Il n'est en plus pour moi' and so on – more dramatic projection, less sumptuous richness of voice. But Te Kanawa satisfies richly on both accounts. In 'Villanelle' the light precision, the sharply-pointed ending of verses; in 'Le spectre de la rose' imaginative absorption in the vision, 'Et j'arrive du paradis'; in 'Sur les lagunes' a deeper note of humanity than we have heard in this singer yet; in 'Absence' a confiding intimacy at 'Entre nos coeurs quelle distance'; in 'Au cimetière' the lightness of the shadow that passes in a white veil; in 'L'île inconnue' lilt and charm … And with all of these, the most ravishing beauty of the soprano voice, and (worthy of more detailed comment) sensitive accompaniment.

Such an allowance of voice may well be a luxury in a song recital. It is hardly matched by Edith Mathis in her three-record Schumann album with Christoph Eschenbach: a valuable acquisition even so. Many songs come freshly to view here, some of them included with *Frauenliebe und -leben* on an earlier single disc, but not *Roselein*, for example, or *An den Mond* or *Frühlingslied*, all of them delightful songs and suiting their singer so well. Elly Ameling's Schumann album is the obvious competitor here, and in comparisons I found the honours fairly even, though in *Sonntag* and *Marienwürmchen*, where I'd thought Mathis so good that she could hardly be surpassed, Ameling's more affectionate, less sophisticated approach did prove more likeable still; and (good as Eschenbach is) Jörg Demus, Ameling's accompanist, brings a lightness of touch and a surer way of shaping the phrases, so that it is certainly their version of the *Lieder-album für die Jügend* that I shall be playing most often.

English Choirs and an English Cleric

The Choir of King's College, Cambridge, is still top of the list. The two recent records (among the last under Philip Ledger) are lovely and distinguished as ever. Both of these are of plainsong-based Masses. Palestrina's six-part *Ave Maria* Mass has an especially fine *Sanctus*, with long flowing lines on the first syllable and a splendid 'Pleni sunt caeli' section. The *Agnus Dei* too, with its seventh and eventually eighth voice added, is a marvellously rich soaring sound, perfectly lovely in itself and involving a scarcely detectable intricacy of canons, a perfect example of art concealing art. In Tallis's *Puer natus est nobis* Mass, the cantus firmus is much more prominent, running like a thick rope through the middle. Much is lovely here too (the opening of the *Agnus* and the lulling effect of the 'Dona nobis pacem', for instance) and all is inventive; yet one sometimes wishes to be free of those long, timeless notes in the midst of all. The *Lamentations*, also included on the record, prompts comparison with the earlier 1968 King's recording. The new one has more forward movement, a better sense of the shape and direction of the phrases, though by contrast, I thought the old recording of *Salvator mundi* had rather better attack and was a particularly fine performance.

King's strike me as superior too when compared with Christ Church Cathedral Choir under Simon Preston. Their Purcell album slipped through the net at the time, and now going back to it I find it regularly a shade too deliberate. In *My beloved spake*, for example, the King's recording comes as a relief because they make their effect without pressing the interpretative points so hard. In the new record of Handel's 'Coronation Anthems' with the Westminster Abbey Choir which Preston now conducts in succession to Douglas Guest there is still that slight feeling of a choir strongly disciplined to serve an idea, but not very spontaneously rejoicing. And here again, the King's recording of *The king shall rejoice* conducted by Sir David Willcocks, which I looked out for comparison, goes to a slower tempo, less driven, more naturally happy. I like too, in the King's, Thurston Dart's frisky triplets in the harpsichord continuo, and miss the additional jollity they provided when it comes to the new version. One idea that really does work well is the radical rethinking of the opening of *Zadok the priest*, where the semiquaver arpeggios are subordinated to what is now seen as the real business, which lies with the woodwind and not with the strings at all.

Three attractive madrigal records deserve mention. Best is the Wilbye recital by The Consort of Musicke, whose merits become still clearer through comparisons. One of the best-known madrigals, *Lady, your words do spite me*, was recorded by the Wilbye Consort at a slower tempo and with loss of rhythmic vitality, and by the King's Singers who again cannot quite match the Consort of Musicke in sensitivity to rhythm and structure. The light decorations which I've not heard before are pleasant touches, both in this and in *Sweet honey-sucking bees*. The King's Singers in their record (called 'Sing we and chant it') do particularly well with another (and wonderful) piece of Wilbye's, *Oft have I vowde*, and there are two delightful novelties by Weelkes, *Strike it up tabor* and *Tantara, cryes Mars*. The Tallis Scholars also provide an excellent programme, including the inspired *Sleep, fleshly birth* of Robert Ramsey. I fancy the performances could be more tender in tone and feeling, but they are careful and professional down to the finest detail.

'Rest in soft peace' sing the madrigalists in that little masterpiece of Ramsey's. It is a thought that will have found an echo in the minds of some of our older readers when they learned of the death of Canon John Drummond on August 21st. He reached his century on June 19th, 1981, not long after I visited him at his home in Leicester and listened to his memories of great singers, particularly Caruso, on whom he wrote in this magazine during the 1930s. One record he loved above all. It was Tosti's *Pour un baiser* and hearing it with him on the old wind-up gramophone, one was brought very near to the great voice which he himself heard all those years ago in Plymouth. He remained enthusiastic, bright-eyed and clear-headed; and though his hearing was impaired, he knew those records so well he only had to put the needle down on the disc and the mind heard perfectly. A true collector.

Solti's Nozze di Figaro

'Corriam tutti a festeggiar': (roughly) 'Let's have a party'. So sings everyone at the end of *Le nozze di Figaro*, and at the end of this new recording under Sir Georg Solti they've every right to sing it. A celebration is richly deserved because, although this has been the most consistently well-recorded of all Mozart's operas, there has still usually been some fly in the ointment, 'some stammer in the divine speech'. In operatic recordings how rare it is to find anything else. 'Oh, the XYZ version,' one says in answer to an appeal for a recommendation of a particular opera on record. Then no sooner are the words out than one recalls (in the language of the horror film to which we have recourse on such occasions) 'the ghastly Eva, the frightful Escamillo, the horrendous Musetta'. In this *Figaro* all is well and much is magnificent. I missed Samuel Ramey's Figaro at Covent Garden recently, but shall make a point of hearing the Don Giovanni. If his Figaro on stage was as good as on this recording (and I'm told it was), it must have been admirable in its firmness and body throughout the range, its strong, 'central' tone-quality, and its spirited precision. Thomas Allen, equally firm, sings the Count with plenty of amorous honey in the voice, and with an intelligent mastery of the whole range of feeling in the opening of Act 3. In the finale ensemble it is hard to imagine the Count's lyrical phrases better sung than they are here or to conceive of a more moving reconciliation with the Countess. That has always been one of Dame Kiri Te Kanawa's best roles: I personally have never heard, in the opera house, a Countess to match her. Both arias are not only surpassingly beautiful in tone, but convey with grace and poise the full depth of feeling there in the music. In the Letter Duet it's rather like a mixture of zabaglione on a summer evening and lemon juice on a spring afternoon: beautifully sung all the same. The lemonade here is Lucia Popp, a delicious Susanna in character, and not on this occasion doing too much 'squeezing' (it's not an entirely satisfactory term but I mean the habit of making a crescendo on the individual notes of a phrase). Von Stade's Cherubino completes the delectable trio. She makes an immediate impression; strong and intelligent in recitative; she is also beautifully personal as 'Non so più' turns 'inwards', and she catches the yearning underlay of 'Voi che sapete' to perfection. Kurt Moll, Jane Berbié and Robert Tear make up the trio of troublemakers without overplaying, and, with Yvonne Kenny in the role, Barbarina's appearances are especially welcome. The orchestral playing is alert and sensitive, the chorus fresh-voiced and precise, the recorded sound excellent. So where is the fly in the ointment? There must be one, surely. Perhaps there is something in the very first comment I noted down in the Overture: that it sparkles but doesn't smile. Perhaps a point that I came to feel rather strongly by Act 4 has some justification – that the orchestral sound is too large-scale for Mozart. But this is like standing around in the middle of a great party and looking for something to be miserable about. Much better to join in: *corriam tutti.*

Ricciarelli's Aida

Turning from the new *Tristan und Isolde* to the new *Aida*, one can only wish, for a start, that Margaret Price had been signed up for that too. Ricciarelli, who sings Aida here, came on the international scene some 12 years ago and has taken a position in the first rank of Italian opera singers of her time. But 12 years of hard work tests the basic training and production, and listeners who felt uneasy about these from the start are likely to find their misgivings confirmed by the two latest recordings, the *Turandot* and now this *Aida*. It may be questioned whether the voice is right for either part in the first place (Turandot in power and tessitura, Aida in timbre). There are some loosely focused notes in Act 1, the high As of 'O patria mia' tend to spread, and the beat in her voice contrasts with Domingo's evenness in the octave passages of the final duet. The long phrase with the high C in 'O patria mia' is something of a *tour de force*, yet it's carried on such a thin thread of sound that the potential beauty of the soft singing of the phrase is much reduced. She is often movingly anxious and haunted in expression; there is also authority and intensity. But these qualities, the interpretative and the vocal, should at this stage in her career be at their best point of equilibrium (as they are with Domingo), and it is to be feared that the development of the one seems to signal the beginning of a decline in the other. At any rate, Ricciarelli's appearances are as welcome as the flowers in the spring when they follow those of Obraztsova as Amneris. Here is Amneris the formidable, loud and unlovely, exactly the 'image' of the part which Agnes Baltsa is reported as saying deterred her from ever wanting to sing the role. In the flesh, Obraztsova's singing in the Fourth Act might be exciting by virtue of its power; but on records Baltsa's more refined and more beautifully sung performance is infinitely preferable. And yet, if you don't have this new *Aida* you miss Domingo at the height of his powers, and Abbado conducting a tasteful, affectionately-cared-for performance.

Last Songs and First

Lucia Popp appears a third time this quarter, in Strauss's *Vier letzte Lieder*. As AB said in his review, this is now a highly competitive field, and personal feelings enter into it rather markedly. One is peculiarly liable to become attached to a particular performance. I know, for instance, people who will not renounce their original allegiance to the 1953 Lisa della Casa/Karl Böhm recording, though to me that seems to be sung in a very superficial style. To my mind. Schwarzkopf and Szell in 1966 found so much more and also caught so movingly what is autumnal and death-conscious in the songs. Then came Dame Kiri Te Kanawa with Andrew Davis, and their recording had such beauty and warmth of feeling that my allegiance shifted a little. All of this, I'm aware, reads more like autobiography than criticism, but there it is: one's feelings are personal, and the fact that I was not greatly moved by this new recording may have little basis in objective musical fact. An upper layer of something bright, extrinsic, tinkly and lightly metallic above the main body of the soprano voice is a frequent feature of Popp's voice as recorded in recent years: as Susanna in *Figaro* or Christine in *Intermezzo* it hardly matters, but in this music it does. And then, although she modulates the tone skilfully, it is difficult for this kind of voice to get the deeper colours of phrases such as 'und matt in den sterbendes Gartentraum' in 'September'. On the other hand, there is no lack of warmth and tenderness in 'Im Abendrot' and indeed, both vocally and orchestrally, this is a lovely performance, beautifully recorded too. AB found it 'equal if not superior' to its predecessors; perhaps (stranger things have happened) I shall come to think so too.

Happily, no such comparisons, allegiances and personal conditions enter into dealings with the *Four First Songs* – though that, I have to remember, is not their actual title but the name bestowed on them by EG in a *Guardian* review. These are the young Britten's works from Summer 1928: *Four French Songs*, written at the age of 15, and included in the glorious 'Young Apollo' record on HMV. In all of the pieces here (and all are claimed as World Première Recordings) one feels the exhilaration of an infinitely inventive brain. But these songs, so miraculously assured in sheer technique, are something else: without indulgence, indeed with sophistication, they link Britten back with Ravel, a little with Elgar, even momentarily (perhaps) with Puccini. They are, historically speaking, wonderful achievements, but, quite irrespective of their origins, they are surely lovely contributions to the world of music. Jill Gomez is a happy choice of singer, and the whole record, with the City of Birmingham Orchestra under Simon Rattle, comes as a revelation and a delight.

Ce diabolic chant

In the as-yet-unpublished *Dictionary of Lies* there should be entries under 'I see' and 'I suppose'. The second usually means 'I know there is a general tendency towards this opinion but personally I don't believe a word of it', and the first, nine times out of ten, is a substitute for 'I'm still completely baffled'. I myself do a good deal of seeing and supposing when listening to medieval music, but never have I supposed and seen quite so much as during 'Ce diabolic chant'. This is a collection of what is described as 'the extravagant and complex French songs written by composers of the late fourteenth century' including all the known writing of composers such as Suzay and Jacob de Senleches, about whose work the sleeve-note says: 'No song has a more eloquently expressive melody than *En attendant*, a more delightful interplay of inventive melodic figures than the canonic virelai *La harpe de melodie* or more finely controlled and purposeful syncopations than *Fuions de ci*.' I suppose not. The text of *En attendant* (not one of the most 'extravagant and complex') concludes: 'All these dishes are lavishly served to him who cannot live without hope'. So the melody must somehow (I suppose) be 'eloquently expressive' of that. And the syncopations of *Fuions de ci*, being 'purposeful', must enforce the proposition 'since we have lost our patron, let's leave and go somewhere else': I suppose I see exactly how. No: what seems to me to be wanted is a sort of medieval primer. I want a record (or two, perhaps) with a spoken, teaching commentary: one which takes a few short representative pieces and tells me clearly and precisely how to listen. It is perfectly possible to gain a general kind of enjoyment from medieval music – including 'Ce diabolic chant' – without knowing anything about it at all. But to get further than that you have to appreciate the skills involved. This of itself needs teaching, in a way that cannot satisfactorily be done in the sleeve-notes. More difficult still, because it seems to involve learning a new musical language, is the whole business of the 'expressiveness' of this music. We need an expert and a teacher, an Anthony Hopkins in the field, to take us through a few examples, in which the sound, which may at first seem to be quite indifferent to the text, can be shown, stage by stage, to be related to it. A broadcast or two along these lines is not enough: it needs a record, which can be played repeatedly. Our teacher would probably not begin with the songs in 'Ce diabolic chant' which, incidentally, takes its title from an anonymous *rondeau*: 'If I have lost all that which was my own ... it is because of this devilish song which holds sway in this land … This song is not easily dismissed, for half is lost and yet it is potent …'. I see.

Bach and the Solar Plexus

Listening to music is a strange business, as E. M. Forster illustrated in a memorable chapter. Here am I wishing to understand medieval music analytically, and almost at the same time thinking longingly of a time when Bach was a feeling in the pit of the stomach, a sensation that had nothing to do with appreciation of form, let alone historical authenticity of ways and means. With Joshua Rifkin's recording of the Mass in B minor we have come to the ultimate extreme, the opposite pole to the recording by which I had my own introduction to the great work. With perfect coolness and poise the five solo voices enunciate the opening 'Kyrie eleison', and with admirable clarity and coolness the players on authentic instruments give out the music which, as Tovey said, lies too deep for words. There was little historical authenticity and even less clarity about the old plum-label recording in which Albert Coates conducted full choir and orchestra in that opening 'Kyrie eleison', but my goodness how it stirred the solar plexus; especially if you had never heard it before and were unprepared for that magnificence, those massive pillars of sound, and that meditation no whit less profound because some of its detail was obscured by the old recording, leaving an area of suggestion as in the dim light of a cathedral. Gradually, recording has brought Bach and his Mass into the light. Gradually the forces have been reduced and that which was furry round the edges is made perfectly defined; and never has the definition been sharper, the openness more brightly illuminated, than in Joshua Rifkin's version. It may be doubted whether the 'Christe eleison' has ever danced so graciously, whether the runs in 'bonae voluntatis' have ever sounded so heavenly, whether the 'Cum sancto spiritu' has ever gone at a more exciting *prestissimo* and still with such perfect clarity. And many more than this are the delights of the recording which, in the home, I shall probably play more often than any other. The brain will be satisfied, the spirit will be lifted up; but in the pit of the stomach is the memory of another kind of experience of Bach, and it looks very much as if scholarship has banished it for the foreseeable future in our time at least.

Scholarship, not Joshua Rifkin's this time, but Nikolaus Harnoncourt's, seems to insist on boys' voices for soprano and some alto solos as well as the choral work: a mixture of gain and loss, I find, not wholly satisfactory. Volume 30 of the Cantatas has Nos. 120-23, all but the first being chorale cantatas, and each with its own special delight and interest. No. 120, for instance, reserves what one would expect to be its opening chorus till after the alto solo, richly accompanied by oboes d'amore coupled lovingly in thirds. No. 122 has an unusual Siciliano with soprano and tenor in duet while the alto sings the chorale. No. 123 has a chorus with the 'Send her victorious' motif of Donizetti's *Maria Stuarda* prominent. But such noting of special features is nothing to the deep satisfaction of the whole experience; and it is worth reminding oneself that the boxes in this series also include the scores of the works, a real privilege. A pleasure too is the coupling of the *Coffee* and *Peasant* Cantatas conducted by Neville Marriner. In the first, Aldo Baldin and Dietrich Fischer-Dieskau both feel they have to coarsen their music in order to present it 'in character'; Julia Varady manages to characterize and to sing beautifully, with warmer, fuller tone than we usually hear in this music. Enjoyed also has been the so-called *Easter Oratorio*, the cantata *Kommt, eilet und laufet*, a reissue from 1966 under the young Lorin Maazel. A touch heavy, perhaps, in tempo and style (with an unexpected bass soloist in the mighty Talvela); but the recording survives very well, and the work itself, after a succession of heavenly solos and duets, concludes with a jubilant jig ('Preis und Dank'), a cheerful fugue and a chorale with trumpets triumphant.

That recording came near to the old-style large-scale Bach and, yes, the nervous system was not unaffected. Raymond Leppard, presenting a compromise *St Matthew Passion*, with an orchestra of about 40, a fair-sized chorus, mostly light-voiced soloists and brisk speeds, moves the heart (mine) not at all. His Evangelist, Jon Garrison, might be reading the six o'clock news for all the qualities of spirit and imagination he brings to it. Krisztina Laki gives a most beautiful account of 'Aus Liebe' and its recitative; and the chorales are interestingly phrased. But after the last chorus, feeling dissatisfied, I went to Willcocks and felt better immediately. And then, curious to remind myself what it sounded like 'in the old days', I found Reginald Jacques's 1947 recording: misty recorded sound, not at all misty in performance, this last chorus taken much more slowly and with a *rallentando* that let one know that it was the great *St Matthew Passion* and not just a chorus that was coming to an end. The solar plexus stirs.

Beniamino Gigli

Some of the best of Beniamino Gigli is found in Vol. 3 of HMV's Gigli albums, of which the first offered, as I remember, much better value than the second. This one takes a good wide range, from some of the best of the pre-electricals to the *Ballo in maschera* of 1943. Its 'specialities' are the duets and concerted items (omitting the de Luca duets in favour of the Ruffo) and some representative excerpts from the complete sets. An utterly winning start with the Serenade from Mascagni's *Iris* has him wheedling, charming, honeying, voice and artistry at their best. Soon one has to listen afresh to the final scene from *Lucia di Lammermoor*, where memory retains a kind of caricature (huffing abjectly 'Di chi mai, di chi piangete?', all puffy pathos and aspirates): but of course 'Tu che a Dio' is in reality a most lovely piece of singing, with that climbing 'bel'alma innamorata' lying in the richest part of the voice. Similarly, when it comes to the 'Ingemisco' from Verdi's Requiem. Memory performs its Gigli-imitation with soft-centre head voice, spoilt child's portamento and incorrigible 'E-he-het la-hatronem', etc.; but the reality is not only more beautiful in sheer sound than any of that suggests, but also very positively committed and imaginative. The *Chenier* Improvviso strikes me as curious: it's in pitch but seems (by quality and vowel sounds) to be pitched low. I'd always admired this version (1941), but now it seems to go 'over the top', overemphatic in its declamation (whereas 'Come un bel dì', beautiful at the start, grows in fervour and rings out at the end with a glowing feeling of inspiration). The *Ballo* surely won't do: it's a role which must have a nobility of style that was outside Gigli's scope. But his Pinkerton here is supreme: a thousand incidental touches distinguish it, quite apart from the still incomparably beautiful voice.

A Hang-up

'His hang-up,' said an American critic (he was referring to me), 'is the intrusive "h".' Right: I do loathe it and perhaps, since it seems to offend me more than it does some other listeners, a 'hang-up' it might properly be called. Reading in some back-numbers of ***Gramophone***, I find the reviewer of operatic records in 1939, H. F. Little, commenting that he understood some reputable Italian teachers actually recommended it and taught its use, whereupon it was heartening to find in the next number that the blessed Blanche Marchesi had risen from her sick-bed to denounce it as an abomination. She did not, however, name names and was probably well advised not to for only a few years earlier, in 1934, the tenor Steuart Wilson had taken the BBC and Another to court over a criticism made against him in this respect and had been awarded damages of £2,100. Heaven knows what it would be today and, interesting as it might be to find out how the law stands now, I have no wish personally to put it to the test. I am therefore saying nothing against Francisco Araiza and other members of the cast of the new *Il barbiere di Siviglia*, except to note how this suspensive condition of mine, diagnosed by the American critic, was aggravated while listening to them. There are, of course, all sorts of variants of the 'h' (Chaliapin used to favour the intrusive 'w'), and in this new *Barbiere* the intruder is not normally a heavy aspirate; whatever its precise nature, it is a device for facilitating the articulation of runs with additional clarity and precision. That seems reasonable enough and ultimately, like most hang-ups which afflict us, it is all a matter of taste. But when I play Araiza (whom I have greatly admired in other music) singing 'Ecco ridente in cielo' and then try Luigi Alva in the 1963 Los Angeles/Gui *Barbiere* I have no doubt where my preference lies: Alva used no intrusive 'h' or other 'separation-devices' and the effect of that alone is vastly to enhance or, more properly, to do justice to the elegance, gracefulness and charm of the aria. It may be, however, that Araiza and Marriner, who conducts the new set, are not aiming at grace and elegance but at some more robust effect, for when they come to the Count's second aria and the second verse of it we find it treated as a kind of comedy. Almaviva, emboldened by Rosina's reply to his first verse, puffs out his chest and gives the second verse at a good, ringing *forte*, with again some of the habitual intrusions (for instance, on the word 'tesoro' which thus also gains a more comical flavour). It makes a change, it raises a smile: but it forfeits grace, charm, elegance. If the reader has 'The Record of Singing', Vol. 2 he might like to look out Side 9 and try Fernando Carpi for comparison. If the ancient *Barbiere* with Fernando De Lucia is on the shelves it might be interesting to try the concerted passage 'Fredda ed immobile' for a further comparison. The semiquavers there are sung legato and De Lucia makes magic of the little run on 'da respirar', where in the new set the 'separation-device' is again used. I find it extraordinary, in a performance where the orchestral playing is of such finesse, where the talent of the singers is so exceptional, and where indeed a good deal of the singing (including Araiza's in his brilliant final solo) is so accomplished in so many respects, that this particular stylistic feature should be considered acceptable. But there it is: for many listeners it is clearly of no great importance, and I mention it merely as a cry into the void in case others somewhere out there are 'hung-up' in like fashion.

The Brahms Edition

Perhaps it is fortunate that the two composers, Brahms and Wagner, who have occupied most listening-time this quarter had little interest in florid singing. Nothing, in fact, has marred the enjoyment of all three albums that have come my way out of the eight which constitute DG's magnificent Brahms Edition brought out as, I would imagine, the most enduring contribution to the year's celebrations. The Lieder album is itself a monumental achievement. The great span of composition from Op. 3 to the *Ernste Gesänge*, Op. 121 is not only so vast, but so strong and unflawed, so full of beautiful things to stop before and admire at all points. Viewing them whole, like this, increases one's respect. A typical group in a song recital leaves one warmed by the lyricism, the harmonic comfort, but perhaps feeling that it has been a little too easy, and that Schubert on the one hand and Wolf on the other are more bracing. The 20 sides of the records here show the inexhaustible variety of them, while the great absentees are qualities such as meanness, pretentiousness and aggression. The album is another gem in Fischer-Dieskau's crown too. It is true that you have only to dip into the previous Brahms album to note a thinning-out of the tone, a loss of resonance that tempts the singer to indulge his old habit of overemphasis (yet normally when one looks at the phrase in question and listens again, one sees the justification for the particular treatment, for of course with him everything is particular, nothing generalized). Most of the time he sings with extraordinary beauty of both tone and singing-style (examples: *Wie die Wolke*, Side 2, some of the finest legato; *An eine Aeolsharfe*, Side 3, exquisitely tender; *Wie bist du, meine Königin*, Side 4, the voice such an unbland mingle of ecstasy and pain; *Herbstgefühl*, Side 8, the art at its autumnal maturest; *Es träumte mir*, Side 9, with its sighing, acquiescent ending … but the list could take up all the space at my disposal and still be incomplete). Jessye Norman sings the songs specifically written for a woman to sing, and is always welcome as a gracious presence, lovely, for instance, in *Dein blaues Auge* (Side 10) and *Alte Liebe* (Side 13) with its radiant climax. In that song, Barenboim lingers to most beautiful effect in the postlude: he is as loving and careful in his treatment of the simplest songs as he is incomparably, joyously in command of the big virtuoso pieces, the *Magelone* songs (Sides 5 and 6) being outstanding, the *Ziegeunerlieder* (Side 18) uninhibited but never vulgarized. If an abridged version of the set, a two-record album perhaps, is ever issued, the selector will in the first be confronted with impossible choices, but a place would have to be found for the Op. 91 songs with viola (Side 15), Jessye Norman singing them with surely the kindliest, warmest tone since Ferrier, replacing her own earlier recording, and for the *Ernste Gesänge* (Side 20), where the mastery of both Fischer-Dieskau and Barenboim is matched by their unanimity of feeling over the finest details of score and text.

The Vocal Ensemble album, full of delights, would go third on my shopping-list after the Choral Works by the North German Radio Chorus, Hamburg under Günter Jena. Good fresh voices, admirable balance and intonation are the starting points here, where all these pieces, so affectionately written for the enjoyment of choristers, are sung with a due sense of enjoyment as well as musicianly care. It is good to see, for instance, how the most academic of Brahms's fascinations, his affair with the canon, is so rich and natural in effect. Also, what a sign of grace it is that the academic and ingenious element in him is not allowed to interfere with the simplicity proper to the folk-songs. Any single record compiled from this album must, of course, include the late motets, Opp. 109 and 110 (Side 3), gorgeous in choral sound (Monteverdi assimilated via Schütz), and in the last 'sentence' of Op. 109 a Germanic moderation reasserting its sober warm-heartedness most touchingly. As for the Vocal Ensembles album, I don't think I've ever heard both sets of *Liebeslieder* waltzes go more liltingly and at the same time with a more thoughtful approach (so that No. 3, 'O die Frauen', for instance, includes a touch of gentle 'send-up'). The duets are full of charm as are the *49 Volkslieder*, beautifully done by Mathis and Schreier – taken from their earlier DG album and including (as the more famous Schwarzkopf/Fischer-Dieskau set did not) the pieces for soprano and chorus making up the last seven of the collection. I have not heard the Choral album of major works conducted by Sinopoli but have had, as can be imagined, quite enough to keep me busy and happy: the whole achievement of this Edition, in any case, is not a matter for a single quarter.

The Wagner Year

Also good for a lifetime is the 'Wagner on Record' album, the latest of those compilations by Keith Hardwick in which EMI are making really imaginative use of their great archive, and in which the recorded sound is so good that it will be an extremely well-equipped collector of 78rpm originals who can match the opulence, clarity and naturalness of what is offered here. The earliest recording, from February 1926, is of the Prelude to *Das Rheingold*: how it would rattle the old sound boxes and wear through the freshly sharpened fibre needles, but what astonishing depth of sound now appears and what a splendid crescendo is drawn from the London Symphony Orchestra by that most gratefully-to-be-remembered of Wagnerian conductors, Albert Coates. One of the latest, from 1938, has Furtwängler conducting the Berlin Philharmonic Orchestra in a long-breathed, intense performance of the *Tristan und Isolde* Prelude. There were conductors in those days as well as singers. But what singers! As with most of these collections of old records, it is not always the best known or most expected who give most pleasure. The first voice heard, for instance, is that of Herbert Ernst Groh, a light tenor, who sings the Steerman's Song from *Der fliegende Holländer*, addressing his 'Mädel' in a lover's tone (rare enough) and inflecting the little solo with that quality so uncommon in Wagnerian singing, charm. Emmy Bettendorf, heavenly in the quiet sections of Senta's Ballad, fine and firm throughout; Meta Seinemeyer, with her very personal concentration of tone, a tragic underlay to it, involved as ever, in the *Liebestod*; Austral and Widdop in glorious voice in *Götterdämmerung*: these must come to many listeners, I should think, as exciting discoveries. Rethberg's purity, Lotte Lehmann's radiant personality, the velvet of Janssen's utterly distinctive timbre, the exemplary firmness and evenness of Gerhard Hüsch in *Tannhäuser*: there has been a little tendency recently, priding itself on its healthy scepticism and independence, which protests that there was nothing very special about these people and that our own singers have replaced them perfectly well, but I must say, listening to these records again, that the singers in question can no more be 'replaced' than you can replace any loved, valued and special human being. And when we come to the three who are rightly given the lion's share – Leider, Melchior and Schorr – their singing quite simply has a glory about it. From time to time you can catch them out in their phrasing or their note-values; sometimes you wish this phrase, that note, could have been re-recorded or the whole thing have been less hustled along by the pressures of 'getting it in' on the old disc. But the glory remains; and never, I think, has it shone out with a more clear and powerful light than it does on these transfers.

If the Wagner Year closes on this note it may be well enough, though one has to remark that a high proportion of the best material released in this centenary year has come in the form of reissues. The most glorious of all, possibly, remains to be mentioned. Toscanini's Wagner concerts at New York's Carnegie Hall, broadcast early in 1941, have been reissued in the recent Toscanini series and they are newly astounding. One has scene 3 of *Die Walküre*, another the Prologue and Immolation from *Götterdämmerung*. Helen Traubel is not really a Sieglinde (vocally magnificent in 'Der Männer Sippe' even so), but the 'Starke Scheite' proclaims immediately the authentic Brünnhilde and at certain points, touched by the maestro (and no doubt The Master too) she rises grandly to the occasion. Melchior is marvellously vivid, subtle, tender, impassioned. Toscanini's touch of the divine spark was probably never more gloriously captured on record. The control and restraint are as moving as the attack and climaxes are exciting; in combination they are irresistible. Some performances, fortunately not very many, have the listener feeling a need to jump out of one's seat, do a cartwheel or some other improbable act: it is very hard indeed to sit through this one.

Opera: Affections and Disaffections

I imagine that the impulses I've referred to above – to leap out of one's chair for instance – are not generally found to be too troublesome during performances of Gluck's *Orfeo ed Euridice*. It can be moving, but I have to admit that mostly, taking stock of the situation in the darkness of the opera house or in the silence between records, I realize that I am hardly moved at all. The occasions when the power of the work is genuinely felt may be purely personal: during last year's Glyndebourne production, for example, I experienced it only once, during the passage following 'Che farò', and on the recording once again but in a different place, at the chorus of heroes and heroines in Act 2. On record I have found the total experience moving on two occasions in recent years. One was in the Paris version first released in 1960 and reissued by Philips two years ago with Léopold Simoneau as Orfeo and Hans Rosbaud conducting with a sure sense of style. Memories of that pleasure led me unwarily to open with something like eagerness the box bearing Peter Hofmann's comely photograph. What a mistake! As AB forewarned us, this is not the Paris version at all and, as one should have known, Peter Hofmann would not have been the singer to do it even if it had been. Turgid tempos, thick tone, an unsuitable Amor and a repellent Euridice: I don't know about Orpheus being *aux enfers* but I certainly was. The Glyndebourne version, editorially eclectic, with fine orchestral playing and a distinguished Orfeo in Dame Janet Baker should have righted the balance and provided a moving experience, but, as I say, on the whole it did not as far as this listener was concerned. The rather dry acoustic may have had something to do with it; it's difficult to create atmosphere and set the imagination working in a box. Then the supporting parts, especially the Euridice, again made a shallow, charmless impression. Baker's potent, rapt characterization, immense in the moment of anger turning on Amor who prevents Orfeo's suicide, should have been moving in spite of shortcomings elsewhere. Yet, such are the facts of the personal response, I was not affected by this recording half as much as by the one released some months back giving the Vienna score, with Muti conducting and Baltsa singing Orfeo. Baltsa is by no means so strong, grief-stricken or compassionate as Baker in her portrayal, and though the voice is beautifully clear and fresh it is more inescapably feminine. No: I'm inclined to think that Euridice is more important than one normally supposes, and that a sympathetic Euridice (which they have here in Margaret Marshall) makes a crucial difference. Perhaps too the 'keenest, purest, most nakedly affecting' power of the Vienna version, as Max Loppert says, makes itself felt. And there is also Muti, who has conjured up both the elements, of air and fire, with a stronger feeling of commitment than I could sense in the rival recording.

Of the two early Verdi operas in the recent lists I admired *Nabucco* and enjoyed *I masnadieri* yet neither goes on the shopping-list. *I masnadieri* has imaginative, poetic playing by the Welsh National Opera Orchestra under Bonynge; more sensitive, I thought, than the Gardelli recording, fine as that is (the cello solo in the Prelude is representative, its elegiac tone much better caught). Sadly, I did not hear Sutherland quite as EG did, and found Caballé better dramatically and vocally except in the pathetic fluttering she offers as a trill and in the comparative tameness of her cabaletta. Bonisolli's is a most remarkable voice, with its baritonal notes at one end of the compass and its stock of ringing high Cs at the other, and here he is on best behaviour, careful in his style and persuasive in his feeling. But a return to Bergonzi in the Philips recording is a relief all the same: his tone so clean, his line so shapely. One warms to the opera itself, whereas *Nabucco* seems to me the least loveable of all Verdi's operas. One can admire, nevertheless, and the new recording, sumptuously cast, can leave nobody indifferent. Ghena Dimitrova has magnificent power and command, an awesome sweep over the octaves from high C to low: the tone as well as the volume is so ample, and in 'Anch'io dischiuso un giorno' there is a beauty and grandeur that should not be squandered on too many Abigailles, Turandots and such. Cappuccilli's phenomenal breath-control makes his Prayer ('Deh, perdona') memorable. Nesterenko's concentrated tone is welcome, though he has neither the strong individuality Christoff brought to the part nor Ghiaurov's freer richness. Domingo sings his limited part like a god, with fine legato phrases and fiery declamation. On Sinopoli I reserve judgement: the opera lends itself to the sort of emphatic noisiness, the perpetual punctuation by very uninteresting and very loud chords, that makes me flinch.

Putting the Choir in its Place

One of the stage directions in *Nabucco* tells that the Hebrews are singing 'on the banks of the Euphrates'. It is typical of modern production methods that it should sound as if the Euphrates is a long way off, or that while the orchestra is playing on the near bank the choir is over the other side. This is a fairly recent trend, as is illustrated by the reissue of L'Oiseau-Lyre's 1966 recording of Rameau's *Hippolyte ed Aricie*. The recording, under the late Sir Anthony Lewis and with the young Dame Janet Baker singing a marvellously potent Phèdre, gave great pleasure then and it does so now, whereas my memory of the Malgoire recording was of a milder, less animated kind of enjoyment altogether. Comparing the two, one could see several reasons why – for one thing there is more life in Lewis's conducting. But a striking difference is in the positioning of the chorus: the 1966 chorus is recorded closer and is much more involved in the drama, the effect being more exciting in Act 2 and more satisfying generally. Choirs and places where they sing must, one realizes, pose problems for producers. It is not just a matter of where you place the choir, but where they place themselves, whether in King's College Chapel, for instance, or in Christ Church Cathedral. In the Bach Motets recorded at Christ Church, Oxford, by the choir under Francis Grier the problems have not been happily solved. The acoustic is dry, and this, with the rather unyielding tone-quality cultivated by the choir, nags remorselessly. There is a lack of light and shade, so that in *Jesu, meine Freude*, 'Trotz dem alten Drachen' hasn't the striking effect it usually has because the previous section has not been 'lifted' lightly enough. The choir works hard, heaven knows, but the recording gives no sense of joy in the singing as did the Regensburg Choir for DG, where warmer acoustics assisted the spirit of the thing if slightly at the expense of sharp definition. Recording technicians have long learned to cope with the echo of King's College Chapel, Cambridge, and in the Handel 'Coronation Anthems' the echo actually collaborates to give an appropriate sense of majesty and breadth. Whether Philip Ledger's tempos are not a fraction too broad comes into question if one compares his with Simon Preston's recording. With him, *The King shall rejoice* suggests a jollier kind of beano, Ledger's being possibly more Hanoverian. By contrast, the arrival of choir, drums and trumpets in *Zadok the priest* has an almost barbaric opulence in the King's recording, though the continuation of this tempo into the next movement ('And all the people rejoiced') puts a rather heavy restraining hand upon the festivities. As for the introduction to this most famous of the anthems, Ledger's easy jog robs it of grandeur, Preston doing all sorts of fascinating things with it and letting the people rejoice in quick time. But everybody has his own idea of how this should go. In my young days it was a race to see who could do it fastest, and a few years ago we had John Eliot Gardiner going at a stately *adagio.* Has there ever been a character in history who has attained posthumous fame in quite the manner of this same Zadok? He was probably a wizened little man with pimples; Handel makes him sound as though ten feet high and clothed in splendour.

1984

Gardiner's Messiah

The new *Messiah* will not make me ready to part with several older versions; nor, if it is offered in the spirit of Nicholas Kenyon's note, would it wish to. Many different versions have their own kind of value and authenticity. This one, bound to no single text, gains more than it loses by its 'practical approach', and in style it certainly, as John Eliot Gardiner says, rids the work 'of its Victorian, sanctimonious pomp'. 'In this way,' he adds, 'the Handelian yoke is made easy and his burden light.' One could say as much of most recent recordings, but this one has probably a more joyful spirit and a lighter spring to its step than any of the others. 'And the glory of the Lord' has its triple-time lilt smiling more beguilingly than usual, the Pastoral swings with a gentle cheerfulness, 'The Lord gave the word' has the company of the preachers moving in a splendid, colourful phalanx. There are surprises, such as the quiet, very rhythmical start of 'Hallelujah', the hushed repeat of 'Worthy is the Lamb' and the meditative opening of the 'Amen' chorus. Sometimes the markings show up as too deliberate (the 'pairings' of quavers in 'All we like sheep', the *marcatos* in 'He trusted in God' for instance). Sometimes the light and easy style, with its jaunty effect in the treatment of dotted rhythms, not only gets rid of Victorian sanctimoniousness but what some might refer to as decent reverence as well ('Behold the Lamb of God' as given here should have had a different text). For a few bars only are we allowed to linger and a deeper mood to prevail: 'And the Lord hath laid on Him' consequently makes a particularly deep impression. The orchestra and chorus respond with skill and thoroughness to the highly articulate, detailed conception of the conductor. Of the soloists, the admirable Canadian mezzo-soprano Catherine Robbin deserves gratitude throughout, the Texan bass Robert Hale only intermittently – there is some unattractive tone in 'The people that walked in darkness' and some roughness in 'The trumpet shall sound', but he does well with 'Why do the nations', taken with exhilarating spirit at a formidable pace. Over all shines the pure, well-tutored soprano of Margaret Marshall, a singer of whom we can be justly proud.

Contribution to a Debate

An old-time all-time dispute about singing returned to the correspondence columns this quarter. It was initiated in last September's issue and developed first in the January number. Nutshelled, it goes:

Prosecution: Singers nowadays are not what they used to be.

Defence: Thank heaven.

Mr White, an old persecutor of mine, is, I think, genuinely at a loss to understand how anybody with standards, anyone who is aware of (say) Boninsegna and Battistini, Muzio and Lauri-Volpi, can tolerate, let alone praise, (say) Caballé and Pavarotti. Mr Fagan, defending, is also at a loss. What can these standards be? When he listens to distinguished modern singers they sound perfectly acceptable to him; when he listens to famous old 'uns, they sound ghastly.

Now, the debate, as I say and as everyone knows, is probably as old as civilization. It certainly goes back to Francesco Tosi who complained that 'Italy hears no more such exquisite voices as in times past'. That was in 1723. In its application to recordings the argument is a least as old as this magazine, for some of the earliest correspondence columns were heavy with the indignation of Prosecutor ('We shall not look upon their like again') and Defence ('Indeed, I hope not'). Well, the debate of centuries is not going to be settled by a paragraph in the Quarterly Retrospect, but as its subject has been my familiar spirit for a good many years, always buzzing around the head in one form or another, I thought I would contribute my mite.

The new *Ernani* has done well for itself, on the whole. Its cast is headed by a quartet which, if the Defence is to hold up, should stand comparison with any singers of a similar status in an earlier age. So let us try. At the Metropolitan Opera House in the 1920s, New Yorkers heard a number of revivals, usually with Ponselle and Martinelli, sometimes de Luca in the baritone role, and later with Pinza as Silva: famous names, of course, but equivalent, give or take a little here and there, to the positions held today by Freni, Domingo, Bruson and Ghiaurov. First I take the tenors in their Act 1 aria starting with the recitative 'Mercè, diletti amici'. Domingo sings well and his voice may be less of an acquired taste than Martinelli's. But for the rest, a study of their singing is largely a matter of learning about the music from what Martinelli does with it (1915 recording on Camden, but adjust pitch down slightly; or 'The Record Of Singing', Vol. 2, but turn up the treble). For instance, it is from Martinelli that we learn how the recitative can be expressively rounded off. It is through Martinelli that we become aware of the shape of the solo: the lyrical first section, with its conclusion ('d'amor che mi beò') allowed space and grace to register, then an urgent passage marked *declamato* in contrasting style, followed by the return to the lyrical melody and allowed a traditional cadenza without which the proportions of such an aria are meanly distorted. This feeling for shape is notably absent from the modern recording. On then to Elvira and her famous aria starting at the recitative 'Surta è la notte'. Freni softens pleasantly at the words 'col favellar' but has no *sotto voce*, as marked, at 'ti seguirà'. Her triplets are imprecise (worse the second time), and she does not observe indicated *portandos* to any effect. Ponselle (1924 recording on Camden) first impresses by the sheer nobility of her voice, the contralto depth and then the marvellous delicacy on high soprano staccatos. As with Martinelli, we hear a beautiful rounding of the recitative (the *messa di voce* on 'in core'), with nothing corresponding in Freni. Ponselle does observe the *pianissimo* marking at 'ti seguirà' and she is better on the triplets. But the broadening of tempo and carry-over of the voice in some falling intervals later on is what makes musical magic: and again we find nothing corresponding in Freni. The bass aria 'Infelice' finds Ghiaurov authoritative and sturdy in his legato (no intrusive h's) and he conveys some emotion at 'Ah perchè, perchè'. But Pinza (1929 on Pearl) has not only more beautiful, resonant tone, but provides, first, a more incisive attack in the recitative, a better *piano* start to the aria, and then not merely more feeling throughout, but much more sorrow, much more variety of colouring: it is a master-lesson in style and 'interpretation'. With the baritones the comparison emerges more evenly. The aria 'Oh de' verd' anni' is a good example of the *bel canto* solo, and Bruson is in the tradition which also produced Giuseppe de Luca. Returning to de Luca himself, however (1917 on Camden), we hear a still finer focus and evenness of production and a remarkable dramatic intensity in the recitative.

Now, there is obviously much more one could say. But: what most strikes me in these examples is that if I had been asked 'Who has the *conductor*? the modern singers or the old ones?' I would answer every time 'the old ones'. The singing, purely as singing, is also better. But the interesting point (Mr Fagan asked whether this interest in singing is a mere matter of voice) is that the earlier singers were working in a tradition that shaped the arias, cared for the phrases, saw what depth of expression those phrases held within them. They are altogether subtler. No conductor is named on those early records, whereas the new recording is conspicuously 'under' Muti. He is no doubt a greater conductor than his anonymous predecessors; but they and the long tradition behind them and their singers did a better job as far as the performance of these arias is concerned. Mr White has won that round.

Turn of the Screw

The Turn of the Screw has a flavour all its own, not without its sweetness either. In so far as the orchestral parts contribute to it, the new recording satisfies wonderfully well. The light and air, the subtle underminings of confidence in the 'sweet summer' of Variation 3, such things have clarity and space beyond the scope of the original 1955 recording under Britten. For the flavour imparted by the voices, however, I would certainly go back to the original. In the new recording, under Sir Colin Davis, Helen Donath provides some vivid moments ('No! No! What is it?', 'Died?') and gains depth at certain points ('See what I see, know what I know', 'I am alone'); but Jennifer Vyvyan's voice was permeated, in a quite different way, by the tragically wrought feelings of the Governess, and the very flavour of the opera was caught in her tone. Robert Tear, with Davis, makes a fine, weirdly dangerous thing of the Call, but at two or three points in the role displays devilry which Peter Pears more effectively insinuated. Nor, I would say, are Mrs Grose and Miss Jessel so distinct to the mind's eye as in the earlier recording. The boy, Michael Ginn, does splendidly, but the Flora sings with too mature a fullness (would it be impossible, in a recording at least, to find a young girl to sing the part?). In sum, interested buyers are presented with a dilemma: it's the new version they will want to choose for the playing and the clarity of recorded sound, the old for the singing. So the screw is given yet a further turn.

Music and the Real Horror

Michael Berkeley's oratorio *Or shall we die?* is very much a child of our time, like Tippett's oratorio, which suggests itself as the obvious comparison. Will this new piece, one wonders, survive and grow as *A Child of our Time* has done, still moving us after the modern horror that inspired that work has passed into history? Tippett, in word and music, worked with finer strokes, whereas the new oratorio *accosts* the listener. Its methods may indeed bring diminishing returns, obtaining maximum effect in the first sequence of hearings. That was one misgiving that occurred to me. The other was more quirky and personal, perhaps, in that there arises a protest of a different kind from the one intended by composer and librettist: it is that, however serious, however harsh, music remains a pleasure, and that although I can let music provide me with the pleasure appropriate to, shall we say, a tragedy as dark as *King Lear* or to poems as grim as some of Michelangelo's, I find a resistance to taking pleasure out of the words of that bereaved mother of Hiroshima. This may not be a very logical position, and it may not be strengthened by the fact that I am grateful that Michael Berkeley has chosen to write so beautifully in setting the words. Musically its effect is perhaps comparable to the cry of the woman, 'How shall I cherish my man in such days', leading into the first spiritual in *A Child of our Time*. This and much else in the work I find very moving even though with an uneasy sense of indulgence. The brutal 'rock' in 'Cruelty has a human heart' struck me as saying something pertinent and with considerable effect, but I may have mistaken the intended point of it. The so-called parody of a Victorian Hymn in Section 3 seemed crude and consequently ineffective. But, like Michael Oliver who reviewed it with (as I read him) a somewhat similar kind of questioning and some inner tussle, I do find it daunting and impressive, both as a work and as a recorded performance. As MEO put it, 'it has its heart, and for much of the time its craft, in the right place'.

English Rigoletto

A good *Rigoletto* and a good *Carmen* enter the catalogues, both having interesting backgrounds. The *Rigoletto*, providing the sound but not the sight of Jonathan Miller's production with the English National Opera, exposes some anomalies. The translation penetrates the world of the New York Mafia with idioms such as 'Where's the boss' and 'back at my place', but verbally it is rather like Margaret Rutherford dressed as James Cagney. 'You're more boring than usual' is the worst thing that barman Rigoletto can think of to say to the boss's henchmen; and Ceprano's 'You bastard' has us all looking rather uncomfortable. How can it be otherwise, especially when pronunciation remains far more Oxford or Cardiff than Bronx or Manhattan, and when the party music is not rock 'n' roll or even the foxtrot, but a gavotte or minuet. Never mind: given the nature of the undertaking, the company does it well. They have a clear, true, unfussily accomplished Gilda in Helen Field, and in Arthur Davies a Duke ('boss') with a well-placed lyric tenor, crowning his 'Women abandon us' with a brilliant cadenza and top B. John Rawnsley's Rigoletto is a genuine character creation, and he is scrupulous about such details as the trills with which he taunts Monterone, and the legato of the 'but in my home' ('ma in altr'uom mi cangio') phrase at the end of the monologue. At some important points the role needs an easier lyrical touch and more Italian vibrancy, but it is still a notable achievement. I found reactions to Mark Elder's conducting working rather as in the *Otello* recording but in reverse order. The sense of an imperturbable steady beat weakened the tension of the First Act of *Otello*, whereas in *Rigoletto* it was the last Act that suffered. Listening recently to the reissue of Fischer-Dieskau's *Rigoletto* under Kubelík, I found a good deal more atmosphere in the last Act caught in that 20-year-old recording, while for control of tension Toscanini, recorded in 1944, is still supreme.

1985

Lucia di Lammermoor

Your average music critic in the first half of our century would not have given much for mad Lucy's chances of survival into the second. Yet every new hearing of Donizetti's opera impresses, and so far is it from being, as was commonly thought, a mere vehicle for the prima donna that its identity as a work comes to be as implicit in its opening bars as (shall we say) *Siegfried*, *Pelléas* or *Wozzeck* are in theirs. The new *Lucia di Lammermoor* under Nicola Rescigno works powerfully. The brooding mists of the Prelude, the early reminder in the succession of solos and choruses that this is an opera full of things to look forward to, then the shift from the world of men to the fragile femininity of the harp introducing the Fountain Scene ... in all of this and throughout what follows the recording brought the drama to vivid life in my sitting room at least, so that as the evening progressed the world of the Lammermoors became ever more real and Lucy's fate ever more genuinely (and not just conventionally) tragic.

Of course this is no new revelation. Callas and Sutherland made it clear enough; and in a recording that, so far as her own part in it is concerned, may be more satisfying to think about than to actually hear again, Beverly Sills brought a good deal of psychological insight to the role. Caballé, in the edition of her conductor, López-Cobos, added a reminder that as written there is no need for the soprano to rise to any prodigious heights above the stave or really to do anything particularly showy at all. Edita Gruberová now combines some of the best qualities of all of these. She has much of Sutherland's ease and fullness on high, while drawing a firm line and employing a brighter tone more in the tradition of Toti dal Monte; and she has also much of the penetration and intensity that were among the distinctions of the Callas Lucia. Almost as welcome to me is the purity of tone. She is not always steady and even, but her tone at present has not acquired any of that surface-scratch, that accretion of tinny upper frequencies that very few of today's hard-worked voices seem to be without. For some test cases try 'Regnava nel silenzio', where the line is true and unfussed, and where the coloratura expresses a thrill of horror and the trills a quiver of excitement; or the 'Verranno a te', sweet-toned, heart-felt and again unfussed; or the 'Soffriva nel pianto' in Act 2, its quiet grief genuinely moving through the simple beauty of its melody.

With Gruberová, and no less remarkable, is Alfredo Kraus. Here again he shows that he is still quite the best tenor we have had for decades in this particular part of the operatic repertoire. His verse of 'Verranno a te' recalls Schipa, while his ringing high notes in the Wedding Scene suggest something more like Lauri-Volpi. He is, of course, himself, and that is enough; but the comparisons are ones that come naturally to mind and help to acknowledge his status. Occasionally he will overemphasize, or something less than a fresh, youthful resonance may hint that he is now entitled to the sobriquet 'the veteran'; yet left with the memory of his wonderfully broad phrasing and elegantly cut tone in 'Tu che a Dio', one reflects that he too, like the opera itself, is a survivor.

Opera: More Comparisons

The critics who wrote off *Lucia di Lammermoor* by and large did the same for Verdi's *Macbeth* until the revelation of the Glyndebourne production in 1938. 'Crude, foolish and tawdry' was Neville Cardus's phrase for the impression the opera had created on him a few years previously in Vienna. Since then we have had less and less difficulty about taking it seriously, but I think Edward Greenfield is right in his view that the seriousness and consistency of the score have now been most fully established in the new recording under Sinopoli. Even so, moving about between the three recent versions (Sinopoli's, Abbado on DG and Muti on HMV), I was probably enlightened or simply delighted by each in roughly even proportions. Sinopoli isolates the dramatic moment most effectively (as after the disappearance of the witches, when Macbeth and Banquo are left to their thoughts). But in his recording the witches themselves have less vitality and character than in Muti's, while Sherrill Milnes (with Muti) is much more vividly disturbed by the prophecies than Bruson (Sinopoli). That is so again in the Dagger soliloquy, where Bruson is curiously inert, so that even Cappuccilli (Abbado), with his basically conventional operatic horror, responds better to the many changes, and Milnes gives a more complete acting performance than either. In the prelude to Lady Macbeth's first scene Sinopoli achieves tension best, but both Cossotto (Muti) and Verrett (Abbado) read the letter with stronger imaginative involvement than Maria Zampieri; then when it comes to the invocation-cabaletta ('Vieni t'affretta') Sinopoli gives the liveliest spring to the rhythm, but Cossotto outsings both her rivals. Zampieri I thought too variable: the tubular production is sometimes comical and intonation quite frequently raises questions. On the other hand, it is a distinctive portrayal (I found it difficult, for instance, to think of her in another role) and often, as in the Brindisi, her technique rises wonderfully well to the challenge. In the Refugees Chorus and its Prelude Abbado seemed superior, first in articulation and then in building, phrase by phrase. In the finale to Act 1, like EG in his original review, I found Sinopoli's breadth of tempo to be the answer to an unformed prayer: it's the moment I love most in the opera and I've always felt, without quite knowing how, that it had a tragic, lamenting quality about it that never fully emerged.

Turning now to the new *Der Rosenkavalier* I find myself again treading, like the page to Good King Wenceslas, in the footsteps of EG. Like him, I enjoyed Karajan 2 but on balance preferred the Karajan 1 of 1956. Yes, the orchestral sound in the new recording is warmer and more immediate, the slower tempos luxuriate that little bit more seductively, the waltzes lilt with still more verve. But the people, perhaps with the exception of Baron Ochs, have receded. Moll's fruity low notes come through as part of the character, like an idiosyncrasy of speech. But the Sophie, who was such an inspired piece of last-minute casting in Karajan 1, is now a mere pallid prettiness, and the Marschallin of Tomowa-Sintow, intelligent and mannerly as she is, lacks the generous tone, the heart, and the fun of Schwarzkopf's. The play between the Marschallin and Octavian on Karajan 1 had more spontaneity, more smile. Schwarzkopf's delighted sense of release at 'Quinquin, es ist ein Besuch' lights up with a radiance that never crosses the face of her successor, who equally never lets escape from her the common humanity of Schwarzkopf's 'Wie man nichts packen kann'. The new recording has much in its favour – Agnes Baltsa's shiningly pure voice is an asset throughout, and the great Trio goes beautifully. One might well learn the score from it: but, on balance, it is from the older set that one comes to know the characters.

Anyway, there is room for a new *Der Rosenkavalier*: the September *Gramophone Classical Catalogue* has only two listed. It boasts four *Macbeths* (Sinopoli makes five). But *Die Zauberflöte* … ah, *Zauberflöte* has 13, and now with Sir Colin Davis's long-awaited recording comes a fourteenth. The orchestral playing will stand comparison with any of them, without any overall superiority; the conception provokes thoughtfulness and sympathy; the recorded sound is clear and ample. Of the soloists, Kurt Moll's Sarastro is again outstanding, as it was on the recording under Lombard where the voice was further forward but the accompaniment in the first solo plodding. Serra as Queen of Night is firm and accurate, though less formidable than Gruberová on both Lombard and Haitink and without the cold glitter and harder aggressive bird-like pecking of Karin Ott on Karajan 2. Karajan 1 has the most poetic of the Taminos in Dermota, but Jerusalem with Haitink has more of the needful youth in his voice than Schreier on the Davis. Davis's Papageno, Mikael Melbye, overcharacterizes at the expense of the vocal line: Gerhard Hüsch (1938 with Beecham) is the antidote here. Margaret Price, the Pamina, who should have been the special attraction among singers on the new set, sounds too mature, and though passages like 'Die Wahrheit' and the address to Sarastro are most beautiful, 'Ach, ich fühl's' is not what one hoped it would be. The fourteenth *Die Zauberflöte* – currently available, that is – does not emerge supreme; but perhaps amid such a plethora of comparisons no single version could stand serene and triumphant as the music itself.

Dimitrova

I missed, but heard glowing reports of, Ghena Dimitrova's London début in the concert performance of *La Gioconda*. Impressed but not overjoyed by her Abigaille in *Nabucco*, I went to the Covent Garden *Turandot*, where the cheering from the Amphitheatre almost convinced me that it was the fault of my more privileged but really more restrictive seat that I never once caught a thrill. Here was a full-bodied voice, sturdy, firm, exceptionally ample in range as in volume; and, as the sleeve-note of the new recital record remarks, genuine dramatic sopranos are rare. One limitation may have been that no personal inflexion urged a personal response; but, again, I don't know that one looks for this primarily in a Turandot. The real cause, I think, was something referred to earlier: the presence, above the main body of the voice, of a layer (perhaps it is several layers) of another substance, something which in my private inadequate vocabulary I know as 'tintop', something which at any rate is not purity. It was interesting, therefore, to find it, even with very modified treble controls, clearly audible on her new recital record. Interestingly again, the sleeve-note refers to Dame Eva Turner and the prime of Birgit Nilsson, and places Dimitrova (particularly as Turandot) in the line. But I remember those voices very clearly, and the great quality in both was the bell-like purity of sound, the absence of surface-scratch, 'tintop' or whatever one is to call it. Used quietly, Dimitrova's voice also is pure, and she does in this recital sing some beautiful soft notes and soft phrases: an exquisite example comes at the end of the *Attila* aria. But then, listening once more for some personal touch that would endear the singer of (for instance) the *Adriana Lecouvreur* arias in the memory, I found very little. Something about the stern brow which seems to be part of this singer's vocal 'image' reminded me that she was a pupil of Gina Cigna, and then I also remembered that Cigna had, early in her career, still in the 1920s, recorded those arias. And what an extraordinary comparison they made! So much tenderness, sense of touch, imaginative involvement in the mistress; so little sign of it in the exceptionally endowed pupil. It will be sad if her next recital, for another there must surely be, does not bring a development.

English Song

A first recital I enjoyed greatly was Anne Dawson's on Hyperion: also welcome because it is a 'first' for some of the songs, and they are for the most part lovely things and just what we now want the record companies to give us as additions to our collections. This recital was produced with help from the Finzi Trust, and it is with Finzi that the programme begins: some of the Hardy songs. Hardy wrote in his *Apology* of 1922 that he had to depend on certain 'finely tuned spirits' for 'right note-catching'. Finzi's was such a spirit, and his setting of *I look into my glass* is a small masterpiece. Howard Ferguson's *Discovery* cycle, and then songs by Moeran and Bridge make up the rest of the recital, one in which the young singer shows a real power of communication as well as a fine voice. I hardly dare to say it, after so much on this subject, but I again hear that unwanted upper layer beginning to form. I wonder how high on the list of desirables at the start of a singer's career is the preservation of pure, unworn tone. Personally I'd have it at the top, axiomatic and in capitals.

Elizabeth Harwood, who has preserved her voice remarkably well, also assembles an interesting programme of English song. Delius's

Have you seen but a white lily and *It was a lover and his lass* were new to me (the latter attractive too, but oddly angular and over-sophisticated, I thought); and Bax's *I heard a piper piping* has just the right touch, evocative of the open air and Scotland. New in Graham Trew's recital were the two songs by W. Denis Browne, a composer killed in France in 1915: the haunting stately dance-movement of *To Gratiana dancing and singing* draws one back to it. The chilling, hollow feeling of Humbert Wolfe's *Journey's end* set by Frank Bridge, and the gentle lyricism of Quilter's *Weep you no more, sad fountains* suit the singer well (he has a well-mannered style but one really could do with a bit more body and richness in the tone), and Roger Vignoles plays splendidly. The accompaniments are also a special pleasure on the Vaughan Williams record by Robert Tear and Thomas Allen. These are orchestral (CBSO under Rattle), and never, surely, has *On Wenlock Edge* opened so excitingly or the haze of 'Bredon Hill' shimmered more evocatively. The *Songs of Travel* also gain, particularly the spangled orchestration of that wonderfully romantic page, 'Thick as stars at night', in 'Youth and love'. Thomas Allen is, as always, good to hear, but I felt in both singers something less than a real personal, imaginative involvement. For folk-song arrangements some listeners may well like what Douglas Gamley has done with *The ash grove*, *The Salley Gardens* and others for Dame Kiri Te Kanawa. Those who don't may (like me) be pleased to see the 1962 Pears/Britten folk-song record on the reissue list. Britten's arrangements have no prettiness but, instead, a strange, often pained, kind of passion, and always the touch of genius.

Choral Comparisons

A great choir like that of King's College, Cambridge, tends to retain its identity with remarkably little change though choirmasters come and go. Stephen Cleobury has succeeded Philip Ledger, but it is still Ledger's (and Willcox's, Ord's and I daresay Mann's) choir that sings in his first record with them. This is of Italian renaissance music, Frescobaldi being the best known of the composers, Allegri's *Miserere* the best known of the works; and it's an interesting choice, partly because the music is not central to the King's repertoire and also because it invites a comparison with Cleobury's previous choir of Westminster Cathedral. In their record of the *Miserere* the brighter-toned trebles, the quicker tempo, the stronger shading all contrast with the more passive loveliness of King's. Then, if one plays the first item on the Westminster recital, Palestrina's *Exsultate Deo*, it is to find exactly what has been missing throughout the King's record – an outgoing, bright-edged sound and a sense of presentation. The record suggests too a further comparison with the earlier King's recording of the *Miserere*. This is in English and it is the one in which the treble soloist, Roy Goodman, takes his high Cs in a way that Melba herself would have admired. It also is slightly better shaped and less merely reposeful than this recent performance. All the same, there is much to enjoy on the new record. The Frescobaldi Mass contains a sprightly final *Kyrie* in triple-time dance rhythm, a *Gloria* full of rhythmic surprises, with a marvellous finale from the 'Cum sancto spiritu' onwards. The 'Et in aeternum' section of Ugolini's 12-part *Beata es Virgo Maria* also sets the spirit dancing – and, just as all 'good bits' should do, it comes twice. Meanwhile, there is a new record from Westminster Cathedral itself that goes high on the shopping list: a Victoria recital with two Masses, both of great beauty, the first of them preceded by its 'motto' motet, *O, quam gloriosum*. This also invites comparisons. Try the opening phrase and compare it with the St John's, Cambridge 1970 version. The live hand of Westminster's new choirmaster, David Hill, is seen even in the shaping, the opening-out of the 'O' and the comma observed after it, all giving a sense of wonder. Choirs (like St John's) must have sung it a thousand times and not quite 'visualized' that simply expressive effect which is so clearly implicit in the writing: clearly, that is, once it has been pointed out.

Comparisons, I fear, do not benefit the reissued Monteverdi *Vespers* of 1610 originally reviewed in October 1978. The Collegium Aureum under Segarra has the Montserrat boys, whose distinctive tone always gives something special to a recording. But the opening is dull compared with the John Eliot Gardiner version which has far more splendour, attack and rhythmic life. Then in the 'Dixit Dominus' the Collegium Aureum's rhythms sound sluggish by comparison with Gardiner's subdued excitement and impulsive changes. In the 'Laetatus sum', Gardiner has more interesting continuo work, and the Regensburg recording under Hans-Martin Schneidt, also distinctive in its trebles, has a more solid full choral sound. Regensburg also opens the 'Nisi Dominus' with a fascinating wavelike effect, while Gardiner is splendid in the constant live play of ideas, and Ledger's King's recording is urgent and rich in recorded sound; all eclipse the Collegium Aureum, though the Montserrat boys make a fine effect in 'Pulchra es' and the 'Suscepit Israel' of the Magnificat.

Of the Schumann Requiem the final pages moved me most; a gentle beauty there, a rather quirkily intriguing 'Liber animas', a lively 'Pleni sunt coeli', these urge return to a work which left a somewhat fragmentary impression. The Delius Requiem, originally issued in 1968, will draw me back if only to experience again what is so often a lovely moment in Delius, the first entry of the choir ('Our days here are as one day'). Some later passages are ecstatic too, but I confess to not having caught much of the 'harmonic astringency' claimed by Eric Fenby in his notes. With Harper and Shirley-Quirk at their best, and a fine performance of the *Idyll* (more cohesive, I thought, than the one under Fenby), this is an attractive reissue. Best of all, however, and an essential for the library, is John Rutter's editing and recording of the original, or 1892, version of the Requiem of Fauré. The performance could hardly be bettered, and the 'Pie Jesu' solo by Caroline Ashton is wonderfully pure and boylike. Differences of detail and of overall texture make comparisons with the usual full orchestral version interesting. So far as the early edition is concerned the Rutter recording is likely to remain definitive, though no doubt the time will come when comparisons can be made, for in an age when authenticity is so respected this may well become the standard version.

Chabrier

King for a quarter, here in my listening room where I never thought to see him crowned for more than a pleasant half-hour or so, is Chabrier. King in spite of himself, one might almost add, for he accepted a vast liability when he took on the impossibly involved story and naïve libretto of *Le roi malgré lui*. The 'opérette colossale', as Reynaldo Hahn characterized it, presents I'm sure a hazardous undertaking for the company who would like to revive it on stage, but on record it is sheer delight. Musically it combines something of the sense of a creative individuality, a fine critical ear and a scorn of cliché that draw one to Berlioz, with the gaiety of the *opérette* tradition and the refinement of Ravel. Certainly one can quite see why Ravel himself should have declared that he would sooner have been the composer of this than of *Der Ring des Nibelungen*. Some of the numbers are so good in themselves as individual items, that a first reaction is sheer incredulity that they never became popular in the days of 'the famous aria', 'the celebrated trio' and so forth; then, on reflection, it is understandable that, as with Berlioz or indeed Ravel, some idiosyncrasy of phrase-length or of melodic progression, together with a refusal (on most occasions) to deal in the musical commonplace that might make the number 'catchy', is just the kind of quality that precludes popularity. The waltz in the ballet of Act 2, for instance, goes through all of the well-established routines, yet the conventions are mixed with such wit and kaleidoscopic subtlety that something totally unconventional emerges. Above all, there is the sheer superabundant fertility of the writing. Ideas germinate with such fecundity and all with such joy in creation – and not without tenderness and darker shades among the brightness – that it seems to embody the very spirit of comedy.

In charge of the excellent performance is the admirable Charles Dutoit. Barbara Hendricks, with her soprano of slender, elegant cut, makes a charming heroine. Peter Jeffes's lyric tenor and Gino Quilico's healthy high baritone present just the sort of singing we have had all too little of in French music for many a year. The supporting cast do genuinely support (and never let down); chorus and orchestra lack nothing in discipline, and seem to have caught the general enchantment. I found it all a magical entertainment. *Le roi malgré lui* has, or at any rate deserves, a place right at the centre of the true tradition of musical comedy.

Sibelius's Songs

It was a great refreshment, this totally unexpected boxed-set of five records and something like a 100 songs. The measure of discovery, of course, accounts for much: *Black roses*, with what we used to call *The Tryst* and half-a-dozen others made up the volume of Sibelius's songs for most of us, and even to those who, like myself, were brought up on the Gerald Abraham Symposium and remembered Astra Desmond's contribution on the songs, surprise still came flooding in, for, despite the discriminating enthusiasm of that chapter, it contained quite a lot of apology for the weaker pieces and for certain characteristics such as unpianistic accompaniments. Actually, the piano-writing, odd as it may be in some ways, is one of the attractions of these records. Much must be due to the special touch and feeling for it of Irwin Gage. One can well imagine how the suffocating accompaniment of *Vain hopes* ('Farfäng önskan') could become simply hamfisted (much top-and-bottom, with clouds of pedalling and an almost brutal opposition at times to the voice). Or the masterpieces of Op. 38, with their extraordinary rumblings and wanderings in the bass: in less sensitive hands they could sound like clumsy miscalculations. But there is also some delicious piano writing of a more orthodox kind, some fine passionate Rachmaninov straying into Op. 13, for example. Then the poems: ignorance of the languages brings the bliss of release from judgement upon literary merits, but the translations read well, the sounds are pleasing and not inexpressive to the foreign ear – and then what a change to be concerned with forests, birds and mountains instead of the personal crises of the Germans and the vague gestures of the French. In its varied moods, this unsuspected output refreshes and renews the love of song: for it clearly comes from a man with the love of song in him.

How well, too, they are written for the voice. Some sweep forward with broad phrases mounting to an almost Italianate vocal climax ('Var det en dröm' – *Did I just dream* – is as good to sing, I imagine, as any Puccini or Giordano); some are tender and delicate, others (supremely 'Höstkväll' – *Autumn evening*) intensely dramatic; many call for a bold commitment of character, a few (such as 'Teodora' – *Theodora* – perhaps most striking of all) for a touch of imaginative genius. Tom Krause does wonderfully well, as indeed does Elisabeth Söderström in the relatively few but frequently outstanding songs which fall to her. Krause's voice remains so firm, resonant and beautifully produced, so little changed over the years; and this set surely is the crowning achievement of his career on record to date.

Singers and Kids

Youth, its fun and liveliness certainly but also its passions and pains, is celebrated in *West Side Story* with what can at times be a poignancy that pulls at the heart as nothing else does in the world of the musical and little outside Puccini in opera. Its recording under Bernstein has been long overdue, yet now that it has come I find it faintly (but fatally) disappointing. The cool, leisurely opening is fine; Te Kanawa's Maria is not only a dream so far as the pure singing is concerned but also has more of her own native vitality than perhaps any other of her recordings; and much else (Troyanos's Anita, Kurt Ollmann as to the manner born in 'Cool' for example) is all that could be wished. Carreras turns out to have been a mistake, though one worth making. Some of the tempos (but perhaps one can hardly quarrel over them with the composer) seem too slow. But most seriously: he was right in the first place. A diary note on the 1957 rehearsals is quoted in the booklet: 'I guess we were right not to cast "singers", as anything that sounded more professional would inevitably sound more experienced, and then the "kid" quality would be gone.' It has gone and something of the West Side with it. Bernstein called the original casting 'a perfect example of a disadvantage turned to a virtue'. Here the virtue becomes, partly at any rate, a disadvantage.

Rossini

Perhaps Rossini is, as has been claimed, the most underrated of opera composers. If so, I have to admit to having been one of the underraters, for while enjoying the sparkle of the comedies and seeing some way into the deeper places of *Guillaume Tell* and *Otello*, I have always felt that his was a curiously unfulfilled genius, where the seed of an inspired idea would be nurtured in ground that was shallow in musical terms as it lacked the richer resources of harmony, counterpoint and developed form; probably shallow in emotion too because it so readily resorted to facile rhythms and showy decoration. The recent recording and viewing at Covent Garden of *La donna del lago* did little to change this view. There are charming passages, some of them (the duettino 'Vivere io non potrò' for instance) quite touching; there are also moments, notably Ellen's intervention as the clansmen are about to kill Umberto, where the music 'realizes' the drama. Yet even here, or, say, in a memorable passage ('Crudele sospetto') in the finale of Act 1, the writing still has a certain crudity which makes it only relatively satisfying. *Maometto II* or certainly the First Act of it, impressed me as something different: a genuinely fulfilled work, where originality does not lapse into cliché, where the workmanship is thorough and the drama genuinely living in the score.

On both recordings, the performances are well conducted (*La donna del lago* by Pollini, *Maometto* by Scimone), and the standard of the singing is worth a thought. Both operas contain writing for the voice which only 30 years ago (perhaps less) would have caused the connoisseurs to shake their heads in the sad but somehow gratifying conviction that there was no one nowadays to sing it. Here in these recordings are nine singers, probably none of them with names that will resound through the ages in the history books, yet all well able to cope with the technical difficulties. There are, for instance, three principal tenors, not necessarily displaying the most luscious timbre but all with real voices, a good ring to them, doing work which until quite recent times would have been thought of as belonging to some fabled age of the past, of which Fernando De Lucia was the miraculous survivor on gramophone records (and he would have needed to transpose). Yet now that the revival of facility in such singing is taking place, it seems to occasion very little wonder. As Maometto himself, Samuel Ramey performs in his opening solo runs that involve the sort of fluency very properly admired in early recordings by Pol Plançon and duly lamented as examples of an art lost to the operatic basses of later times. Well, to this extent it seems that some of the lost arts are being rediscovered. A cautious celebration might be in order.

1986

The Opera Season

Drottningholm's *Così fan tutte* may have been as enjoyable *in situ* as the English National Opera's *Julius Caesar* was at the Coliseum, but it does not record so well. For one thing, with a single exception, the roles are under-characterized. The Fiordiligi and Dorabella, in particular, sound too alike, and are not good at acting purely with their voices. The Ferrando and Guglielmo do better in this respect, though (for example) there is nothing infectious about their rather formal laughter in the *ridere* trio. The exception is Carlos Feller, who at the age of 61 suggests with his vivid, mercurial Don Alfonso that the gramophone companies have overlooked a natural recording artist. In fairness to the others it must be said that Don Alfonso has less to be bothered about than they have when confronted with Arnold Oestman's demands for speed. They manage, though there are dizzying passages where sheer wonder at the feat so occupies the mind that other responses are driven out; the exercise thus becomes somewhat self-defeating. An exhilaration in the Overture, a lucidity of orchestral texture throughout, an awareness of well-practised company-work on stage and a considerable sense of achievement in that imaginative aims held with such conviction have been accomplished: these are merits, I would say, of a recording which is not an entirely persuasive advocate of its cause.

A strongly convinced conductor is always likely to be controversial and no operatic conductor of recent times has aroused more determined objection than Giuseppe Sinopoli. Some of these betray a personal animus which diminishes their credibility, the new *Rigoletto* being a case in point. When one thinks how conductors as different as Furtwängler and Karajan, Klemperer and Toscanini, or for that matter, John Eliot Gardiner and Arnold Oestman, stamp their performances with their own individuality, Sinopoli (in this *Rigoletto* at least) seems to deserve praise for expressing his unmistakably individual approach within well-judged limits. Admirable, I would say, is the balance of the sombre and the colourful, of what is tender and vulnerable with the life of show, power and appetite. Though everything, from the spacious treatment of the Prelude, with the tragic sweep of its climactic bars invested with a rare dignity and passion, bears evidence of a fresh and independent reading of the score, the recording does not register as a 'conductor's opera'. Where the singers have character, they are the centre. Gilda becomes the dramatic centrepiece, as in a structural sense she is: Gruberová makes every phrase live and her singing of 'Tutte le feste', with its painful reticence, is probably the most moving point in the performance. The two men, balanced on either side, have less vivid identities: Neil Shicoff a Duke no more nor less sympathetic than his part, Renato Bruson a Rigoletto who rarely makes any particular phrase as it were a personal possession. Such a summary, however, tells nothing about the singing as such; and here the performance has an extra strength, for Gruberová's is one of the most pure, crystalline of high sopranos perhaps even since the youth of Toti dal Monte, Shicoff is firm, true and even throughout his now impressively capable voice and Bruson (though the years and some heavy roles have not left him unscathed) is still recognizably the best exponent of Italian *bel canto* tradition in baritones since de Luca.

In some ways the Welsh National Opera's *Parsifal* is much more of a conductor's recording. Certainly Goodall's individuality is persuasive and insistent. This, for instance, is a performance quite unlike Knappertsbusch's: take the start of Act 2, where Knappertsbusch (Bayreuth 1951) is busily turbulent, while Goodall presents a lumbering, juggernaut menace. Of the singers, the Amfortas is plainly inadequate and though Warren Ellsworth (Parsifal) has a distinctive timbre, so that one feels he should have been remembered by Gurnemanz and the rest between Act 1 and Act 3, he still needs to hold a steadier vocal line. Waltraud Meier is a splendid Kundry till late in Act 2 when the part puts overmuch of a strain on a mezzo-soprano voice. Donald MacIntyre, on the other hand, revises the general notion that Gurnemanz is a role for a deep bass – a Norman Allin or a Gottlob Frick. With the vocal heaviness lifted a little, he becomes a good talker and a companionable human being instead of a moralistic windbag. His traditional role, it seems, has been taken over by commentators on Wagner, as in the accompanying essay called 'A Philosophical Approach to *Parsifal*', which supplies this as an exegesis: 'only by denying the will-to-live, by renouncing the pleasures of this worthless existence, can one attain a genuine lasting serenity, the profound calm of inner fulfilment and peace'. Perhaps that explains the last stultifying ten minutes of nineteenth-century stained glass 'inspirational' religiosity that sends one home longing to have Amfortas's wound reopened since it produced so much better music.

Curiously, the two remaining operas in front of me now are also somewhat diminished by their endings. Gounod's *Roméo et Juliette* is good to meet again, and the recent recording from Toulouse under Michel Plasson presents it convincingly. Catherine Malfitano has the right freshness and is scrupulous in the waltz-song; Alfredo Kraus rings out passionately in 'Ah, lève-toi, soleil' and always sings with character; but this is a great opera for secondary parts, and I thought Gino Quilico's Mercutio outstanding. Strange, though, that a composer who shows himself capable of measuring up to his subject in the opening of the opera, in the graceful melodies of the love music and the grandeur of the ensemble after Tybalt's death, should not rise to the final tragedy.

Then in Respighi's *La fiamma*, so often impressive as music drama, there is another failure to match the requirements of the finale. The idea of the woman standing almost self-accused as the crowd takes up the cry of 'witch' is a powerful one, but after so much that is effective this seems almost perfunctory. As Michael Oliver mentioned in his review, the recording has a flaw in its backward positioning of the chorus (in Act 1 it seems right at first because the chorus are off-stage, but later there is very little difference when they are officially on for what should be a resounding end of Act). The opera had its first European production outside Italy in Budapest before the Second World War, and it is appropriate that the first recording should be made by the Hungarian State Opera. Their singers fill many of the demanding roles very well, though the mother, Eudossia, needs a great Ortrud voice, with the dominant character of a Kostelnicka, and the husband needs … well, Tito Gobbi, just as the heroine, Silvana, is a part made to measure, one would think, for Callas. Ilona Tokody does it well, and it would be good to hear more of the tenor, Peter Kelen. Of the opera itself, too.

Solti's Un ballo in maschera

In 1919 when Destinn, Martinelli and Dinh Gilly appeared at Covent Garden in *Un ballo in maschera* under Beecham, the critics praised the singing but deplored the opera, in which 'genius and ineptitude' went 'cheek by jowl'. It was 'old-fashioned', 'incoherent' and 'dull'. It could not be taken seriously and it failed to carry conviction – but (said *Musical Opinion*) 'who cares a fig for dull convictions when Martinelli is throwing at you treasures of tone in that prodigal fashion?'. How times change. The 1919 revival was seen by its reviewers as virtually the last gasp of a dying operatic tradition. They intimated that the twentieth century, now coming into its own, could smile with sophisticated indulgence and lay the old bones to rest, along with other absurd relics of the nineteenth-century grand manner. In the event, of course, certainly in its second half, the twentieth century has done the exact reverse. *Un ballo in maschera* flourishes, an unquestioned masterpiece, and in wider terms the whole of that 'outmoded' tradition has been largely restored to critical favour, sometimes indeed with a kind of levelling reverence which declines to discriminate between genius and ineptitude at all.

Un ballo in maschera comes to mind in particular because the new recording reveals its greatness even more completely and convincingly than its many admirable predecessors have done. The stumbling block, especially in the theatre but also on record, has previously been the first scene and perhaps the first half of the second; the love music, the library scene and the finale are much more clearly the mature and serious work of genius. Solti on this new recording has 'integrated' the earlier scenes, studying them with a special thoughtfulness and performing them so that they have a more serious effect than I can recall being aware of before.

Even in the Prelude, this thoughtfulness induces a heightened sense of dramatic tension. The lyrical theme now tells of more than love; it has the wistful tenderness of a passion that can never be consummated. The emphatic, semi-staccato counter-theme acquires a sinister aggressiveness. When this reappears as the muttering discontent of conspiracy it gains a more pointful identification, and its presence is felt to cast a shadow over the bright, gay surface of the ensembles. These are taken a little more slowly and reflectively than usual. 'Ogni cura si doni al diletto' loses nothing of its sparkle and energy, but the tempo cautions against too much foot-tapping. Serious things are toward. Again, in the Page's pretty little solo we are made more aware than usual of the meaning of what is sung, the half-playful introduction of the occult. Later, the scene of the fortune-teller is prefaced by chords which here slice forbiddingly through the smiling memory of the light-hearted finale, and the Prelude forbids the usual assumption that the music is mere scene-setting for Ulrica and her cauldron. It directs instead to the real catastrophe which she is to foretell.

Occasionally this seriousness may be overweighted (in Renato's first aria, 'Alla vita', for instance, the solemnity threatens to become turgid), but there is no lack of grace, warmth and pure lyricism. Pavarotti gives heart and soul to his part, which clearly he has restudied. His voice has a marvellously untarnished shine still, and the focus never wavers for a moment. That is not quite so with Bruson who, while retaining the exceptional beauty of tone, has forfeited some of his former sharpness of definition; nor does he really convey the emotions of his great solo. Margaret Price, on the other hand, sings Amelia so well that it revives memories of her Desdemona at Covent Garden a few years ago, and there have been few finer performances in recent times than that. All in all, though I would love to have heard it – indeed, would give almost anything to have done so – I can't easily believe that the cast of 1919 would have been all that much better.

Opera: Light and Comic

For years the local library resolutely shelved *Un ballo in maschera* (perhaps under its English title) amongst 'Light Opera and Musical Comedy'. The Gilbert and Sullivan operas would have been close neighbours. And so far as quality within the general category is concerned, there is nothing better. This I still think, despite the increased familiarity we now have with the Offenbach operettas and enjoyable as these are. *La belle Hélène* especially has been a rich, sumptuous pleasure, full of tunes and musical wit (but classical burlesque deprived of a classically-educated public is like a joke told in a foreign language). To have Jessye Norman in glorious voice and authentic style in the midst is a rare luxury, in which the whole cast rejoices and does its admirable best. The Paris, John Aler, appears to be a lyric tenor of talent and Charles Burles, second tenor here, makes a suitably comic Menelaus. There are blissful moments, when the waltz 'Oui, c'est un rêve' is introduced and when the nostalgic waltz of the first entr'acte (reminiscent of its chromatic cousin in the old film, *Carnet de bal*) reappears, sung by all in the finale of Act 2. Even so, I'm not sure that a fresher, more sustained enjoyment didn't attend the last complete Gilbert and Sullivan that I played. This was a late catching-up on my part with the reissue of the D'Oyly Carte's *Patience* of 1961. Here, too, the wit depends on an assumed background of common knowledge. 'Aesthetic transfiguration', however 'intense and utter', means less now than it did then, and soon no doubt it will be translated in some modern version with reference to the appropriate television archetypes. Meanwhile, here is the Savoyard tradition well preserved – best of all in Donald Adams's Colonel Calverly, brimful of energy and joy in the footlights and also, I thought, in Kenneth Sandford's exceptionally beautiful speaking voice (the kind of spoken legato which disappeared from our theatres long ago).

Donald Adams, of course, is directly in line from Darrell Fancourt who is heard in 'The Hey-Day of Gilbert and Sullivan' where those old albums from the 1920s and 1930s are excerpted, the sounds that used to come to us through an unbelievable sizzle of surface-noise now miraculously freed, dusted down and paraded as new. Not enough of Bertha Lewis is my only grumble. But there's Derek Oldham, with his 'Nency' on his knees and his arm around her 'weest', George Baker an immaculate Lord Chancellor, Leo Sheffield superbly judicial over the question of liquor, and some precious moments of Sir Henry Lytton's wrinkled star-shine, sure and delightful in everything except 'Tit willow'.

His younger and less characterful self turns up in the companion volume 'Gilbert and Sullivan: The Early Records', the merits of which I'm afraid eluded me. I noted that the original Mikado, Richard Temple, trilled on the first syllable of 'billiard balls' and that Grossmith's successor, William Passmore, introduced a staccato falsetto arpeggio into the end of the long-suffering 'Tit willow' (much best when sung gracefully and straight). But it was not till Walter Hyde came along with a splendidly fresh, bright and resonant bit of singing that I found myself exclaiming 'At last!' and that was the end of the record.

Fra Diavolo brought disappointment, *Giuditta* worse. There really is something distasteful about this work of Lehár's and operetta's old age, a decadent going-through-the-motions, with a semblance of youthful power recurring every now and then, but all to a horribly indulgent purpose and effect. The colourful start of scenes holds out some promise, and in the performance (as in the recording of *Diavolo*) there is much to admire in the art of Nicolai Gedda. But I'm afraid that Andrew Lamb and I will never agree about this one: Lehár's 'favourite child' seems to me to be deplorably spoilt and sickly.

A great relief it is then to turn to the two masters of operatic comedy, Mozart and Rossini. The new *La Cenerentola* is especially delightful. It has all the elegance and sparkle of a fine baroque theatre, and this is largely due to the conductor, Gabriele Ferro, who seems to have an unfailing rightness of touch in Rossini. Lucia Valentini Terrani is not quite the ideal Cenerentola on record, as her voice and style (admirable in other respects) have little if any pathos, prettiness, or fragility about them. But she is technically very sound, while her Prince, Francisco Araiza, is on best form and her abominable father, the excellent Enzo Dara, gives a genuine singing performance, achieving his comic effects without recourse to those notably unfunny rolled 'r's and falsetto squawks which passed for so long as the stock-in-trade of the Italian *buffo*.

The new *Die Entführung* from Harnoncourt, and no more to be ignored than Oestman's *Così fan tutte*, is another bringer of life and jollity. Accomplished but (vocally) skinny women detract from the relish of the abduction, but the men are fine; Schreier never better, Wilfried Gamlich an engaging Pedrillo, Matti Salminen an Osmin who is always in richly comic character while still singing scrupulously. The Turkish stuff, specially equipped with original instruments, is very much the music of the *Amadeus*-film Mozart, and the only thing needed for its complete success is applause at the end. Applause is almost written into the score; hearing the silence take its place is like treading on 'the step that isn't there'.

Opera: Grand and Tragic

The Covent Garden audience's enthusiastic applause, and the authentic 'braviss!' cried out on top of it, are welcome and fully justified at the end of the magnificent First Act in Bellini's *I Capuleti e i Montecchi*. I cherish the memory of the performance I attended in March 1984, as the best of its kind since the early years of Sutherland's *Lucia*. Records preserve it faithfully, yet it's relatively easy to overlook what was most lovely and special in the theatre – the flawless purity of those two voices. They were pure crystal, without any metallic upper layer of 'surface-scratch'; Gruberová especially had a clear brilliance and beauty of tone for which records had left me hardly prepared, and Baltsa's resonance had the glow of a fine voice in prime health. The imaginative and emotional power of their singing, together and in their arias, was no less remarkable. The records show that it was indeed as one recalled; they bring back, too, an exquisite moment, long remembered, as Gruberová's voice sounds high above the Quintet in a most beautifully sustained phrase. It was a night at the opera of that increasingly rare kind when the audience simply rejoiced in the beauty – both of sound and sight, as it happened. The recording preserves much.

About the new *Tannhäuser* at best I can summon up (as they say in *Patience*) 'modified rapture'. Haitink conducts with dignity and energy in well-judged proportion and Lucia Popp's Elisabeth brings distinction to whatever she sings, though the coloration is limited and the Greeting needs a fuller body of tone. Klaus König is a stolid Tannhäuser, Bernd Weikl a vocally uneven Wolfram, Waltraud Meier a vocally unseductive Venus and there is an exceptionally unsatisfactory Biterolf. It is left to Kurt Moll and Siegfried Jerusalem (in the secondary role of Walther) to provide the real singing.

Richard Strauss's *Guntram* struck me as a superior *Giuditta*. By that I mean that it's wanting to be a certain kind of work, rich in sensations of a sticky, juicy kind. Lehár had all but lost his natural potency, Strauss was only just finding his (there are a few moments when his true, individual self comes to the fore, as in the climax 'Guntram, ich liebe dich' in Act 2). The performance, under Eve Queler, carries conviction, Ilona Tokody singing creatively, as she did in Respighi's *La fiamma*, Reiner Goldberg in the title-role wanting warmth and richness of tone but being sufficiently youthful, energetic and well-defined to make grumbling look like ingratitude.

Last of the Handel Year

No ingratitude here. *Esther* and *Solomon* round off the centenary celebrations, and I also caught up with the reissue of *Alexander's Feast*. This is under Harnoncourt, and it has in it some of his vices (hammering the first beat of the bar, for instance) and many of his virtues, particularly in the excitements of 'Now strike the golden lyre again'. The Overture reminded me of old Sam Butler's remark that it is 'full of the hurry and bustle of servants going to and fro with plates and dishes'; and I thought how he (SB) would have been astonished by the honour paid to his favourite composer in 1985.

The *Esther*, under Hogwood, vindicates its choice of the 1718 text as being more compact and more dramatic. Its soloists convince rather less. There's Emma Kirkby, very neat but very piping, Patrizia Kwella and Anthony Rolfe Johnson pressing the swell-pedal on individual notes, Paul Elliott with his countertenor type of tenor, Drew Minter with his rather beautiful but feminine-sounding countertenor, David Thomas with his curious mixture of tones, some likeable, some not. This seems to be our new establishment: I do hope their successors are learning the right lessons from them and some others from their predecessors (for instance. I'd like to see the baritones and basses given a good course in the records of Harold Williams).

The *Solomon*, on the other hand, gave virtually unclouded pleasure. Excellent singing here from Carolyn Watkinson, whose contralto tone has nothing hooty or academic about it, whose runs are not eased by aspirating or 'separation' devices, and who does not favour the swell-pedal technique. Nancy Argenta as Solomon's Queen and Barbara Hendricks as Sheba do fine work and have wonderful material in their music. Joan Rodgers and Della Jones make a blest pair of Harlots: well-contrasted voices, both of excellent quality; and it was newly amazing to recall that Beecham omitted the whole episode from his recording, dismissing it with some remark as to its being of inferior quality. John Eliot Gardiner accomplishes exactly what he set out to do – to recapture the 'essential *danciness*' in Handel. I wonder if Samuel Butler would have liked that: it's much in his own spirit of breaking bonds asunder and making burdens light.

The Schütz Centenary

This too has ended worthily. From earlier in the year came the *Musicalische exequien*, sometimes (but misleadingly) called Schütz's 'German Requiem'. The performance from Basle under Hans-Martin Linde is a good deal more imaginative and the recording is richer in sound than the Dresden version which is without brass. An austere distinction gains respect throughout the monumental setting of Psalm No. 119, the work known as Schütz's *Schwanengesang*. The Hilliard Ensemble conducted by Heinz Hennig undertake a formidable task and bring all their customary musicianship to it, but also a whining tone on the tenor line and a somewhat throaty one on the bass. Dignity and authority impress throughout the work, but the moments of pictorial vividness – the staccato putting away of the ungodly, for instance – come as something of a relief. It's really with the *Symphoniae sacrae* (published in Venice), that most of us would prefer to remember 'the father of German music'. A splendid recording has appeared on the Erato label, with the Saqueboutiers de Toulouse under no named conductor but with every sign of Jean-Pierre Canihac having been a leading spirit. The dance-rhythms and intricate rhythmic changes in No. 3 (*In te, Domine, speravi*), the deep sonorities of No. 14 (*Attendite, populi meus*), the cheeky start and comic stateliness of No. 2 (*Exultavit cor meum*): all are delightful, with the impulsive, rich Venetian style given a wholesome injection of Saxon persistence. And just at the time of writing I received the CD version of the motets for double choir by the Regensburg Cathedral: again, astonishing dance-rhythms, a kind of celestial disco.

Choral and Song

The setting of *Lamentations* by Marc-Antoine Charpentier (*Les neuf leçons de ténèbres*) is all too easy to hear in a rather dreamlike way, and when one pulls up, finds the place in the text (not always an easy task) and refocuses attention, it is often to find no detectable expressiveness in the music. The performance under Louis Devos seems well prepared though not all the individual voices give pleasure. The dramatic splendours of Cherubini's *Coronation* Mass provide a contrast and Muti's richly sonorous recording on HMV certainly holds the attention. 'Impressive rather than moving' was Robin Golding's verdict in his review and that seems about right, though there are moments (notably the great soaring phrases of the 'O salutaris hostia') when inspiration takes hold; times too when one can quite see why Cherubini should have found so great an admirer in Beethoven. A less grand and serious side of Beethoven himself appears in his arrangements of Scottish airs sung by Robert White in a collection called 'The Gallant Troubadour'. They are minor works in the whole mighty canon no doubt, but all are distinguished, not least by an apparently infallible instinct for when not to 'arrange'. *The parting kiss* is a gem of an example: a most beautiful, direct, tender melody, and Beethoven treats it with affectionate respect. Robert White is at his best in this, with a gracious, warmly-felt, finely-sustained line. Weber's arrangements on the other side of the record are attractive too – but they have taken a further step into the drawing-room. Beethoven is nearer the cottage and the field.

Unacknowledged Legislators

The unacknowledged legislators of the record industry (I mean that part of it which concerns readers of this magazine) are the scholars. The standard classical repertoire becomes ever more recorded and over-recorded, and what listeners, critics, performers and the companies themselves seek with increasing appetite is something new; or, more accurately, something that is both new and old. Here the scholars call the tune. The editors and annotators, the men of museums, vaults and archives: these are the real sources of musical energy now. They extend our range, so that we are almost as likely to find ourselves buying the new Ockeghem recording as the new Brahms; they remake our musical map so that Sigismondo d'India is as familiar to our tongues as Vincent d'Indy and at least as well worth the discovery. Familiar things are made new, so that a different light is cast on masterpieces so time-honoured as Schubert's *Winterreise* and works so widely loved as Fauré's Requiem. This quarter brings a 'new' Rossini opera; it also makes us realize afresh that we never really knew one of the greatest of operas by Verdi. Without the scholars, the so-called 'classical' music industry would have grown old in its ways. What they bring from the museums renews its youth; and what they restore to life with their pens revitalizes the whole culture.

The DG *Don Carlos* under Abbado presents the five-act version of 1886, with the original French text. That is distinction enough, but it also has, as an appendix, six passages dropped before the first performance of 1867 and either eliminated in revision or recomposed. This, genuinely, is a treasure-trove. The sombre Prelude and chorus of workmen and wives lamenting the long winter and the hardship of war is so germane to the opera and has so much inspiration in it that it surely should be restored to its proper place. In fact, throughout this appendix one's gratitude for it as a bonus is somewhat undercut by a feeling that a great chance has been missed to present all of this extra material in its place in the opera. The chorus (oddly suggestive of the choral dances in *Gloriana*) at the start of the Garden Scene is also much too good to cut; Eboli's solo too, with its reminiscence of the Veil song skilfully worked in. The ballet matters less, though it has its splendour in the Spanish anthem and the magnificent sonority of the finale. The Elisabeth/Eboli duet supplies just what is missing, dramatically and musically, with such a lovely healing melody and (rare in Verdi) the two women's voices in harmony. The deletion of the concerted tribute after Rodrigo's death seems next-to-criminal: a priceless sketch for the 'Lacrymosa' in the Requiem. The finale, with its anathema chorus making the appearance of Charles V so much more effective and with its extra chorus of monks, is again sheer enrichment. The recording has done a great service in providing these items, and it opens the way for another recording to integrate them.

This Abbado set really ought to have been one of the great operatic recordings. It isn't quite that, partly because the orchestra is recorded with an immediacy denied to the voices; partly because the resonant acoustic does well for monastery, palace and prison, but not for park and garden; partly because the French vowels are too often italianized. One interesting point is that it reverses the imbalance of the old Santini mono recording in which Gobbi as Rodrigo and Christoff as Philip were so powerful and distinctive in voice and character that they eclipsed the others. Here Leo Nucci is an unremarkable Rodrigo and Ruggero Raimondi an unmoving Philip. Valentini Terrani sings the Veil song with accomplished fluency but makes relatively little of 'O don fatale', so the lovers, Elisabeth and Carlos, become the focus of sympathy and interest. Ricciarelli, though a little threadbare in her aria, does know the heart of this sad Queen, and Domingo, though he could do with more fire in his defiance of the King, has a nobility of tone and style that makes this rank with his Radamès and his earlier recording of *Don Carlos*, as one of his finest performances on record.

Schreier and Richter

The new *Lucio Silla* is not quite a world première. Its predecessor, made in Salzburg with Leopold Hager conducting a distinguished cast, including Varady, Augér, Mathis and Schreier, is now unavailable, more's the pity; and the opera itself (the astonishing work of a 16-year-old) deserves a place in any self-respecting collection. Live from Brussels, this new recording is just about the noisiest I've ever heard. Even when only two people are on stage a rugby scrum appears to be practising on the boards at their side. Other irritations, such as some unpleasant singing and a booklet full of photographs but bereft of translation or historical note, also help to speed the recording on its journey to the everlasting silence. A reprieve from banishment, however, is secured by the exceptionally beautiful and accomplished singing of Lella Cuberli. Most lovely is the Pamina-like aria 'O del mio padre ombra diletta'; most brilliant the agitato 'Partò, m'affretto'; most moving the exquisitely written 'Fra i pensier'. Cuberli also redeems the recent recording of Rossini's *Tancredi*, just as she is an additional strength in the preferable version, under Ferro. She too is a singer to watch.

If the battery of tramping stage-noises is the bane of live operatic recording, its counterpart in the concert hall is persistent coughing. This afflicts the performance of *Winterreise* by Schreier and Richter at Dresden. Schreier has complete mastery now of all the many subtle things he wants to do. A weird, half-crazed tiredness haunts the voice. The cheerless, empty feeling of 'Einsamkeit', the febrile darting energy of 'Letzte Hoffnung', the numbed resignation of the last two songs remain long in the mind. Oddly (and perhaps mistakenly) I felt that Richter was not the right pianist for this singer. He never makes the piano snarl with the voice or even trudge with the traveller; instead he seeks out the musical beauty of the writing, whereas Schreier works towards the weariness, the fever and the fret. Even so, there are moments of flawless beauty in his singing as in Richter's playing: the heart-easing 'Die Augen schliess ich wieder' would be worth going a long way to hear – but then some of those who actually did make their winter journey that February in Dresden cough and break the dream as surely as the cockcrow does in the song itself.

Compact History

On the very point of opening this month's 'Quarterly' with a fanfare in praise of the Compact Disc, I read my orchestral, chamber and instrumental colleague's misgivings on the subject last month. 'For all the technological improvements of the Compact Disc,' he writes, 'its advent may not be an unmixed blessing.' The rapidity of its development threatens the continuation of the LP and is likely to bring an impoverishment of the catalogues, costs being such as to discourage the production at medium price of recordings outside the 'mainstream' repertoire.

A retro-spectator is nothing if not one who looks backwards. If Robert Layton is anxious about the fate of the LP, I write as one who has never been wholly reconciled to the demise of 78s. Seriously (it seems necessary to add), I believe that certain of the listening habits which 78s encouraged – concentration, a way of 'listening through' to the reality beneath, not accepting recording as a substitute for the reality of live performance, and even the 'rinsing' of the mind in silence after the short side had run its course – were a high price to pay for the clarity and convenience of the LP. Even the habit of listening in fragments ('bleeding chunks' of Wagner and so forth) was not half so pernicious as it was made out to be: the fragments meant a great deal and could be integrated readily and rewardingly when the complete work came to be experienced freshly for the first time. Obviously, there is much more that could be argued on all such issues, but I raise them now because of their relevance in the area that most concerns me; that is, singers and singing.

It is true that manufacturers have started to add some 'historical' issues to the CD catalogues: RL's comments themselves arise out of the Furtwängler centenary albums. The more remote past, however, has always been seen by anyone with a care for the future of singing as being a vital part of the inheritance. Will this be transferred to CD? Over the past decade particularly, EMI have made a magnificent contribution in their Treasury series, with such imaginative productions as the Schubert, Schumann and Brahms song anthologies, 'The Record of Singing' and, most recently, the essentially complete Battistini. Will these eventually appear on CD? Perhaps the large resources of that large company will stretch that far; it is pretty certain that the small companies which have done such pioneering work in the field will not, under present circumstances, be able to put out transfers of early records which, however valuable, can have very limited commercial prospects.

So, looking backwards, one is concerned about the future. My other misgiving is more fundamental. There is scarcely an autobiography of a singer brought up in this century in which the gramophone does not play a part in the stirrings of ambition. Pavarotti tells how his father 'would bring home records of all the great tenors of the day – Gigli, Martinelli, Schipa, Caruso – and would play them over and over'. Pavarotti's father was a baker. Even in our own times I can imagine it might just happen that a baker's son might want to sing 'like that' if Pavarotti were on a recently acquired 78 – 'Pavarotti's Greatest Hits' is not the same thing, there's too much of it and instead of whetting the appetite it satiates it. But the gap widens all the time. I cannot think that the baker's son of today will be fired to become a great singer by father bringing home his complete operas, inevitably known as 'the Karajan this' and 'the Solti that', on CD.

Songs of Toile and Trouble

I wished for the blessings of CD while listening to Esther Lamandier's fascinating and now famous Award-winning 'Chansons de Toile'. Still more, I wished for a cleansing of the aural pollution of our noisy century. With the clear voice in unaccompanied song rising up out of the middle ages, our nice quiet road suddenly seemed to have become a speedway with cars revving up and roaring past, lawn mowers tirelessly a-rattle, and the bass menace of planes taking an eternity over their *crescendo* and *diminuendo.* And all the while the tales of bele Yolande and bele Ysabiaux unwound, verse after verse of courtly gossip imparted with a strange mixture of innocence and artifice. Listening presents its problems, and it was interesting to hear David Fallows on BBC Radio 4's *Kaleidoscope* suggest that there is more than one way of going about it: the dutiful and intelligent way where you cope quite comfortably with a preliminary reading of the modern French translation and then tangle with the early French while the record is playing, or, alternatively, just sitting back and letting it work a dreamy, hypnotic sort of spell. In my case, virtue was rewarded for I did the first with the first side and enjoyed it, the second with Side 2 and pretty soon nodded off.

I'm altogether happier with the pessimism of Thomas Hardy, fortified as it is by a great love for certain aspects of life, and with the sensitive, never overwritten settings by Gerald Finzi. The two-record album on Hyperion has Martyn Hill and Stephen Varcoe singing well, Clifford Benson playing sympathetically throughout, and a collection of songs each of which one would like to linger over. That is rather less true of Arthur Somervell's cycles, *Maud* and *A Shropshire Lad*. They are thoroughly workmanlike, with ideas that shun banality and piano parts that do more than accompany; but the neurosis of Tennyson's narrator eludes the tasteful composer, and his idiom is too comfortable to do justice to Housman. Even so, the recording earns gratitude as do the performances, with David Wilson-Johnson and David Owen Norris coming up once again, as they so reliably do, with something worth bringing to our attention.

For the German song-cycles, which Somervell clearly had in mind when pioneering an English development of the form, we turn this quarter to Schumann and welcome a new singer. Olaf Bär appeared last year at Covent Garden in *Ariadne auf Naxos* but that was one of those occasions when the opera was smothered by production, and his portion of it suffered most; so he perhaps passed without due recognition. A likeable, firm, naturally-produced baritone voice and a sensible, unaffected approach to the music are among his assets; if one thinks of a singer to compare him with it would be Hüsch rather than (in their very different ways) Janssen or Fischer-Dieskau. He sings an admirable *Dichterliebe*, but in the *Liederkreis*, Op. 39 fails to catch the flavour of 'Auf einer Burg' or the fear felt in the innermost heart as night falls in the woods. At 30, he has time to develop the subtleties; the great thing is that so good a singer has been spotted by a major record company in time for us to enjoy his voice while it still has the freshness of youth upon it.

1987

The Tallis Scholars

The best thing to have come along in the last few years, to my mind, is The Tallis Scholars: each record is a joy. This quarter the great delights have been their Josquin and Palestrina. No doubt the singers are handpicked, and their selection is itself a tribute to the fine ear of their director. They are a wonderfully homogeneous and disciplined group, yet sound like a choir of human beings. The ethereal beauty of the high sopranos has all the purity of boy trebles, yet the basic soprano tone is a good, full-bodied sound. The basses are not all baritones and the baritones do not obviously aspire to be tenors; while showing all due sensitivity they retain a genuine bass quality. The tenors are well-defined, not a kind of second-alto line. The presence of some male altos among the women altos does not instantly proclaim itself, but adds seasoning in well-judged proportion. While there is no suspicion of intrusive vibrato, an equally welcome absentee is the unnatural, doctrinally-insistent production of ironed-out, rigidly ruled tone. Nor are their notes the squeezed, bulging sort; nor do they aspirate their runs or tap the notes into place like a row of little separate nails, or, so far as I can tell, indulge in any of the other fashionable bad habits. Far more consistently than in most operatic recordings, there is beautiful singing to be heard here and when it comes to solo work, I'd rather any day hear Alison Stamp sing her phrases with high C in the Allegri *Miserere* than listen to most of the Verdi and Wagner sopranos of the present day.

That, of course is only the start. The deeper pleasure lies in a feeling that each finished performance arises out of a reading that, during the course of rehearsal, everybody has come to see the sense of. Nearly always their performances have caught some special feature of the work. In the Palestrina *Missa brevis* there is a fine caring feeling about the start of the *Kyrie.* In the *Gloria* the forward impulse is maintained to the end as though by an infection of excitement among the singers. Phrase after phrase in the *Credo* has its own, proper, imaginative realisation, culminating in the inspired 'Amen'. The companion-piece, the Mass *Nasce la gioia mia*, makes a fine contrast to the rich splendour of its six-part writing, and the healthy resonance of the voices enjoys a more spacious acoustic. To the Josquin Masses (*Missa Pange lingua* and the oddly named *Missa la sol fa re mi*) the Scholars bring such a perceptive ear for the rhythms that they awaken a new appreciation of the vitality and joy that exist in such things. The 'Osannas' of both Masses have the rhythmic excitement of good jazz. The *La sol* Mass (on the sequence AGFDE) is an astonishing construction, and one where the ingenuity and mastery are not merely technical gratifications, but expressive, their interest being harmonic as well as contrapuntal. Peter Phillips tentatively claims this as a first recording: it is certainly an important addition to the now substantial catalogue of records for which he and his singers have earned our gratitude.

Sinopoli's Forza del destino

Sinopoli has done for *La forza del destino* what Giulini did for *Il trovatore*. There are similar objections about slow tempos, though whereas Giulini's deprived important solos of their fire and brilliance, Sinopoli's principally affect the slower passages, often making them very slow indeed. The great virtue of both these DG recordings is that in them the operas finally come into their artistic kingdom. It was quite common in the 1910s, 1920s and 1930s to write dismissively about them, or with amused admiration as for some freak survivor of an outgrown age. Very gradually came the recognition of depth and value beyond that of simple tunefulness or of crude excitement. But though several complete recordings on LP revealed the operas unmistakably as masterpieces, it was Giulini who finally brought out the nobility of *Il trovatore*, and it is Sinopoli who finally frees *La forza del destino* from the taints of melodramatic convention and musical rum-ti-tum.

He does it partly through his perception of a special quality in the opera, present in the opening of the first scene, a brooding atmosphere, anxious and tentative in mood. The other new set conducted by Muti on EMI, has no corresponding insight. Similarly, with Sinopoli the atmosphere of the soldiers' camp in Act 3, with its gaunt silences and sense of night and distance, forms a potently uneasy background to the emergence of Don Alvaro, where in Muti's recording it is simply a prosaic fact of operatic staging. What we knew of this opera from the old days – the big solos, the duets and set-pieces – is a distortion of its identity: over a large canvas, strange in its seeming irrelevancies, its capricious jollities, figures flare in the darkness, like the stoical advance of Goya's Pilgrimage to San Isidro towards the implacable hostility of Fate. Sinopoli catches this, in the sad beauty of the Pilgrims' prayer, the brave gaiety of the Vivandières, the spinning-out of the final *pianissimo* as though to infinity. Beside this, Muti has to offer simply the restless energy of Fate's aggression, in the face of which human beings strut and fret upon the stage till time runs out and the curtain must fall.

If only this were the whole truth, how easy choice would be. The glowing memory of the singing on these two recordings, however, is outstandingly that of Domingo's Don Alvaro, and he is with Muti. The glory and richness of tone leap out like gold in a mosaic. As sheer singing it is the nearest I can imagine to hearing Caruso. Carreras, with Sinopoli, has developed quite an uncomfortable beat in the voice, and except in the upper register lacks distinction of tone. He, on the other hand, is better at catching the pain, the bitterness that makes me always hear Martinelli in my mind, whether he has actually recorded that particular part of the opera or not. But Carreras's responsiveness and spontaneity are not matched by his partner, Renato Bruson, whereas Domingo's powerful though relatively simple portrayal is offset by the exciting verve of his Don Carlo, Giorgio Zancanaro. Bruson's voice, still beautiful and pure in quality, has lost its firmness; a dull and sometimes tired tone contrasts strikingly with Zancanaro's almost Amato-like resonance and vitality. Indeed, his performance impresses me as having something of that thrill of the old-style Italian baritone that I had rather given up as lost.

On the Sinopoli recording, Rosalind Plowright sings Leonora with full imaginative and emotional involvement, and is in good voice except for what may be a quality which my ears exaggerate, a persistent layer, a patina, of wear or tonal impurity audible above the main body of the sound. This, to my ears, is almost completely absent from the older (but purer) voice of Mirella Freni, Muti's Leonora. She is not completely steady and, without being at all unfeeling, she gives a more conventional performance; but the tone is still, as I hear it, purer, and this I cherish. As the Padre Guardiano, Paata Burchuladze (Sinopoli) is not in his element, but is a great deal preferable to Plishka (Muti). When saying that Domingo provided the outstandingly glowing memory of the singing, I should have qualified this and added that the Preziosilla of Agnes Baltsa (Sinopoli) is unparalleled on record in vitality and vocal purity (there's another voice, like Freni's, that is free of that 'upper layer' that troubles me with Plowright). Strange, but somehow typical, that the two recordings should have an almost equal balance of pros and cons. As Richard Osborne said in his May review: 'if we could selectively combine the two casts then we would indeed have untrammelled pleasure'. As Don Alvaro exclaims in Act 4: 'Destino avverso'.

Elgar Completed

If writing within easy reach of the gramophone and wanting to recapture the music of the past weeks, it would be the last side of Elgar's *King Olaf* that would draw me. This, as Jerrold Northrop Moore writes, is 'a notable first and a notable last' – the first recording of the work, the last major work of Elgar to be recorded. In his commentary he finds the 'grip of real drama lacking' in the final duet – well, perhaps, but that certainly has its compensations in some rapturous music that recalls the remark that English composers of that period found in the large-scale choral works their substitute for opera. This final section includes a trio as excitingly operatic as (say) the trio in *I lombardi* or at the end of *La forza del destino*, intensely emotional in effect and with the voices soaring ecstatically. The emergence of 'As torrents in summer' has a magical unexpectedness, its familiar beauty incalculably enhanced, its *fortissimo* reprise later on being introduced with as sure an operatic instinct as the return of the 'Nessun dorma' melody at the end of *Turandot*. Among the solo voices in this excellent recording, Teresa Cahill must be mentioned: a performance most moving in vocal range and command, that every now and then reminded me of Florence Austral in that wonderful solo from Sullivan's *The Golden Legend*. They used to smile indulgently at such things. There are fewer to do that now.

The Mask of Time

Tippett's *The Mask of Time* is a prodigious creation, and the recording technically and artistically a miracle of the evolutionary process and the Ascent of Man. But as I parade it, mentally, in memory, and re-read notes made while listening and reacting to this teeming, multitudinous procession of ideas in music and word, grasping at the larger concepts behind them, I find myself stepping back from the universal canvas and likely to be reduced to the ultimate banality: 'interesting'. Why not, at very least, 'moving'?

Perhaps a time will come when the text (the libretto) will be acceptable, as some old operatic translation becomes familiar with time, its idiosyncrasies no longer obtrusive; but, meanwhile, they do obtrude. In his Preface, Tippett writes that 'the libretto should not be read as literature', and that the metaphors 'are swallowed up within the music'. But in practical terms they are not 'swallowed up', for here sits the listener, libretto in hand, and there is the voice of Robert Tear declaiming by way of introduction, 'All metaphor, Malachi, stilts and all'. The record album contains a valuable essay by Meirion Bowen, who remarks of this that it 'provides an important clue to an understanding of the work – and *The Mask of Time* is indeed all metaphor'. But just for the moment we are stuck with Malachi. We're happy enough to accept 'all metaphor' (while mildly querying whether it is an appropriate procedure, this identification of 'clues', with the subsequent investigation their existence implies, as in crossword puzzle or detective story). But it's Malachi that obtrudes and won't be 'swallowed up'.

Of course we pass on. That is, we don't stop the record, consult the encyclopaedia, the Old Testament or Malachi Stilt-Jack Yeats; but for that short space the mind has been drawn away from the music, and in a teasing fashion this is to be the representative and pervasive mode of interaction between word and music throughout.

In the final section, the music seeks to express 'the transcendent' by means of an ecstatic choral passage that remains wordless: the great beauty of the writing, as well as its placing as the climax of the work, alone make this 'moving' (as opposed to 'interesting'). But such liberation from the verbal text brings a great sense of release. A casting of clouts, a leap of the unchained, a severing of the bindweed; and further metaphors for Malachi.

Gothic Voices

If Tippett's complexities, musical and verbal, are thought of as being peculiarly modern, an hour or two in the Middle Ages helps to put them in perspective. The excellent Gothic Voices, directed by Christopher Page, have two recent recitals, of which their collection of music for the Knights of the Garter is richly endowed in complexities and highly recommendable too. Called 'The Service of Venus and Mars', it admits other allegiances, opening with a prayer to the Virgin in which three simultaneous texts are set and sung with marvellous vigour and jaunty energy, rejoicing in the syncopations. The long final 'A' of the 'Amen' in a magnificent five-part *Gloria* by Pycard has an elaboration of counterpoint achieving a sustained ecstasy very comparable to the wordless chorus at the end of *The Mask of Time*. Other items have a more recognizable national quality: the carol, *Ther is no rose of such virtu*, for instance, and the harp solo *Le grant pleyer*, an anglicized version of a French piece which is played first. The skill of the writing, the wide range of appeal and the fine natural style of performance ('Deo gratias' sung with such spirit that the victory at Agincourt might have been that day's news) combine to make this a most attractive record. The other fairly recent collection, 'The

Castle of Fair Welcome', comprises courtly songs of the fifteenth century and so provides a supplementary volume to the group's evergreen 'The Garden of Zephirus': also delightful in a gentle way, never tiring the ear with the technical ingenuities and never insisting too much on doctrinal points of performance.

1988

Treasuries

'Critics Choice' last month included a bonus for reviewers: in addition to the usual recommendations we were to suggest, from any period of recording, a candidate for transfer to CD. Surveying the great library of material available, I thought of the almost empty shelf labelled 'Historical' and voted for the wholesale transference of the old HMV No. 2 Catalogue as it stood in 1939. This was the Historical list which at that time we had thought to be sacrosanct: the hand of the deleter touched it not, neither at first did the outbreak of hostilities shake it. Its glory was its singers: Battistini, Caruso, Chaliapin, Destinn … the famous ones and also the less well remembered who were justly celebrated in their time and who still provide many of the critical touchstones (Amato, Boninsegna, Clément, Hempel …). The catalogue also listed instrumentalists such as Paderewski and Sarasate, even composers (Grieg and Saint-Saëns), actors, politicians, comedians. Volume 1 on CD, going alphabetically, would take us from Henry Ainley reciting *Carillon*, with Elgar's music conducted by the composer, to the great baritone, Mattia Battistini whose complete output has already been transferred to LP in one of the most enterprising and resourceful of all in the EMI Treasury series. The suggestion, I may say, was frivolous only in the sense that I assumed it was not very likely to be acted upon. And, yes, if there was a question of whether the whole catalogue was required, I would take it, Gas Shells Bombardment, Adrift on an Ice-Floe, Asquith's Budget Speech and all.

The Treasury series itself, on LP, flourishes. I don't know what commercial success ventures like the Battistini set and the new Spani album are likely to have, but they certainly involve those who are interested in such things in a great debt of gratitude. The name of Hina Spani is not well known over here as she never sang in this country nor, to my knowledge, in the United States, though she was famous in southern Europe and South America throughout the interwar years. I hardly think that anyone could go further than the first band of the new album ('Ma dall'arido stelo divulsa' from *Un ballo in maschera*, recorded in 1927) without recognizing a voice and art of exceptional quality. One always has to guard against excessive claims for the 'old' singers (they did many things wrong, by our standards, and Spani is no exception – hear the uneven triplets in 'Tacea la notte', the next item); but it is a great loss in terms of musical and human experience not to know them, and here, clearly, is a candidate for CD transfer. Earlier in the year we had the Flagstad Wagner album, with a superb newly released Liebestod and those nobly sustained, warmly voiced *Wesendonk* songs with Gerald Moore. Irmgard Seefried's early recordings were another pleasure, especially the Mozart songs, beautifully performed, and always with that touch of independence and individuality that helped to fix her so vividly in the memory years after she had ceased to appear over here. Perhaps something personal and idiosyncratic in the tenor Alessandro Valente justifies his place in the series, not that I personally would share that view, though the rare and finely sung excerpts from Wolf-Ferrari's *Sly* earn gratitude. Joseph Schmidt is another matter: the ringing tone and fluid production, the sheer conviction of his singing (glorious, for instance, in the *Die tote Stadt* solo) and often an exceptional responsiveness to changing mood, all distinguish him. Here too the transfers are exemplary, and the album is another that calls for present purchase, as the Treasury series is not protected from the deletions list and casting into outer darkness.

Another English company still producing fine historical LPs is Pearl. The Martinelli recital recently added to their catalogue contains splendidly natural, clear-cut transfers and the selection is a fine one. The magnificently phrased Edison electrical version of 'Celeste Aida' is included, so too the still more exciting Nile scene with Ponselle. Pearl have also given a lead in the matter of CDs, though I have to admit to wishing it was with some other material. The singer is Alessandro Moreschi, 'the last castrato', *l'angelo di Roma* and so forth, recorded to dismal effect in 1902 and 1904. The solos are grotesque, the choral items truly dreadful, but just every now and again there comes a high note which suggests something of the power and purity for which the castratos were famous. The impressively produced LP collection on their Opal label sold well (and indeed it does provide entertainment of a sort) and now appears on CD. It makes a rather sad sight, sitting there on the Historical shelf alone: or almost alone, for though RCA have released a Caruso CD, a good selection too, it is processed by the Stockham Soundstream computer, which will not be to everyone's liking. Nor can the company take much pride in its presentation (the ugly cover, inadequate notes and, in the last two items, mixed-up dates).

The Callas Commemoration

Here, by contrast, is a chapter of history that has been done full justice on CD. The replaying of so many of Callas's EMI operas in their new form has been one of the great pleasures of the past year. Outstanding among them again emerges *Un ballo in maschera*, and joys beyond expectation (though that was considerable) came from *La bohème*. Both are marvellously complete character-creations by Callas herself, and they take their place among the most satisfying of all the many recordings of these operas. The new issue, Callas live at Amsterdam and Athens, begins so wonderfully, 'Dolce e calmo' (or 'Mild und leise'), with Isolde's *Liebestod* that the rest tend to become, in memory, merely 'the rest'. Yet the *Pirata* recitative, the aria with its many lovely touches including a magically soft, rapidly ascending scale, and the cabaletta totally concentrated in tone and spirit, are also valuable additions. The Verdi arias from 1969 show the voice thinner and more infirm, but such losses are less disabling than may have been feared and the selections are both interestingly and wisely made. Against the *Don Carlos* aria, 'Tu che le vanità', I had noted what at the first time of hearing had seemed a disappointing want of majesty in the launching of the first phrase, but then in Tony Palmer's ITV South Bank Show film on Callas we saw this as absolutely right. Her face and mind work with the emotions of the orchestral prelude and the voice merely enters in continuation, not with the majesty of the prima donna giving notice that she has arrived, but with the suffering of Elisabeth de Valois uttering a heartfelt prayer.

Before and After

In that film we heard much about the importance of Callas not simply as an artist but as an influence. One of the contributors even said 'She brought drama to the opera', enlightening us about events in the early seventeenth century and leaving the impression that drama was absent from the operatic stage throughout the three-and-a-half centuries or thereabouts between Monteverdi and Callas. Granted that much of opera's drama lies in the music and therefore in the singing, the gramophone gives little support to such a notion. In 1929, Hina Spani, for instance, sang with as much care for the drama of the *Ballo in maschera* aria as for its 'pure' vocalization. Flagstad, no great actress, gives an emotionally powerful account of Isolde's Liebestod in the 1948 recording mentioned above, and Callas herself is by no means more dramatic or vivid in it than was Lotte Lehmann in a recording made when Callas was a schoolgirl.

Nor has the post-Callas era invariably seen the dramatic element strengthened. Here, for example, are two operas by Giordano in new issues by CBS. In *Andrea Chenier* we have the magnificent singing of the baritone Giorgio Zancanaro. The timbre, production and, for the most part, the continence of his style in this turbulent music are admirable and give great pleasure even in a comparison with, say, the mighty baritone of Titta Ruffo in the same arias. But Ruffo, in the early years of the century, is the one for the drama. Similarly with the protagonist. José Carreras, whose voice sounds overworked, puts great fervour and dramatic conviction into his performance, but it would be easy to produce a dozen or more recordings of the Improvviso from the pre-Callas era which are at least equally alight with dramatic expressiveness. Eva Marton, the Maddalena, also sings Fedora in the complete recording of that opera. Her part in *Andrea Chenier* is adequate dramatically (though unlovely in quality of voice), but her Fedora strikes me as being distinctly 'pre-Callas', if we're going to allow this sort of classification. In a generalized way the drama is given life in the recording (well conducted by Patanè and, as with *Chenier*, having the rich provision of secondary roles well characterized). But if for one moment, listening to Marton as the heroine, one wonders whether Giordano and his score are to blame for the lack of interest, the answer is to take down the old Gardelli set.

Immediately the heroine becomes a real woman and one capable of inspiring devotion. With the first solo, 'O grandi occhi lucente', we are brought close to a woman of exquisite sensibility with the capacity (as in the phrase 'o schiette labbra') for expressing a rare indrawn beauty of spirit. In that recording Fedora was Magda Olivero, who made her début in 1933. It is in no spirit of detraction from Callas's greatness that one has to say that the talk about eras BC and AC (Before Callas and After) does grave injustice to the many fine operatic artists – and not simply singers – who came before; and that it is more than a little complacent about those who have come after.

The Rare, the Rich and the Redundant

A singer who brings distinction, musical and dramatic, to whatever she does is Julia Varady. She adds excellence to the cast of Spontini's *Olympie* in what I take to be a first recording, though not advertised as such and having a cast-list that on the whole looks better than it sounds. The performance, however, is less important than the score itself and this turns out to have warranted something much better than its century-and-a-half of neglect. If there is anything Italian about it, it is care for the voice. Otherwise it's a matter of German thoroughness, French grandeur and something else French: a sort of unpredictability, a shunning of the obvious, that continued through Berlioz on to Chabrier (with *Le roi malgré lui* in mind) and (*Pénélope*) Fauré. It would be interesting to learn more about the performing edition, which varies from both of the scores known to me and seems open to objection on various grounds except in the point that matters most – the fact that it works.

If *Olympie* is one of the recommended purchases for the quarter, the new *Lohengrin* is certainly another. Though it is not an opera for which I have a great personal liking (too many bars where portentous assurance protects inherent dullness), I would not want to be without it, and with fewer hesitations than Arnold Whittall who had the responsibility of the first review, I would expect this to be the recording most attractive to return to, especially for the energy and rich colouring of the work. To represent Solti as merely an energizing factor is quite wrong, yet when a bustling, scurrying link-passage suddenly sparks you know, as surely as you did with Beecham, where the electricity is being generated. The richness of sound owes something to the modern recording – the stage opens out aurally to its full breadth and height. But it is also due to the regal sonority of the voices. Like AW, I have reservations about Randová and Nimsgern as the wicked ones (he somewhat brutish in his massive power, she having passed the peak of four or five years ago, when she was not merely a good Ortrud but a magnificent one). Unlike AW, I have no welcome for the casting of Fischer-Dieskau as the Herald, a role which calls for a young voice and which makes little use of the special skills that served him so well as Telramund. But Sotin, at his best in Act 1, has one of the finest voices in the world today, and Domingo and Norman are among the most richly endowed of all. Their Love duet becomes the focal point of the drama as never before in my experience. Domingo's Lohengrin is an achievement that deserves all respect and gratitude. The Narration in particular carries a sense of total absorption in its development: a fine piece of vocal sculpture with imaginative workmanship to be enjoyed in its many details.

A durable and timely *Lohengrin* then – well timed also to herald Domingo's scheduled appearances in the role at Covent Garden later this year. If the welcome that greets Muti is relatively muted that is partly because his *Le nozze di Figaro* comes at a moment when it seems unnecessary. Thomas Allen's Figaro is less apt than his Count, and particularly in the First Act the conducting gives little encouragement for the comedy to expand and be its natural self: the two influences together present an unsmiling front (even, for instance, when Allen is allowed a bravura flourish on 'l'aria brillante'). Margaret Price (permitted that most natural and obvious of embellishments, a simple scale back into 'Dove sono') is a movingly dignified Countess, Jorma Hynninen a strongly characterized Count who eschews overemphasis in the German manner. There is much that is good here, and I enjoyed it rather more than Hilary Finch appears to have done. All the same, her verdict is right: that at the present moment this makes one *Figaro* too many.

Lieder

It is good to see Margaret Price taking her place among the leading song recitalists. The position is not easily won, and until fairly recently it seemed as though, however beautiful the sound and thorough the musicianship, that essential quality of communicated insight was not hers. So indeed I still found when comparing her Verdi song recital with that of Klara Takács. Price could delightfully familiarize her listeners with the songs, but it was the Hungarian singer who made them live. Price's Liszt and Richard Strauss programmes are a different matter. The Strauss begins with a charming *All mein Gedanken* and has for a climax a splendidly impulsive account of *Cäcilie*. Liszt has always suited her (her first recording of the *Petrarch Sonnets* was the record that revealed best the quite special quality of her art). Here the voice is not entirely untouched by time and hard use but is still beautiful, and quiet songs like *Die stille Wasserrose* are entirely lovely. For a comparison showing what she does not do quite so well, try Strauss's *Morgen!* in the new Lieder recital by Arleen Augér. This is an attractive record in other respects (a sensitive, privately voiced *Abendempfindung* for instance), though the Wolf *Mignon* songs have less than the needful concentration of tone and feeling.

The two new versions of *Die schöne Müllerin* must both rank high in a highly competitive field. Olaf Bär and Geoffrey Parsons begin too slowly for my liking; I start to get drawn into it, despite the immediate establishment of a relationship with the listener, only with the fifth song, 'Am Feierabend'. The eagerness of 'Ungeduld' helps further to define the personality, and 'Der Müller und der Bach', one of the supreme tests, has a haunted colouring as well as admirable evenness of line. At various points in the cycle one wants to urge 'a little more!' (bitterness in 'Die liebe Farbe', joy in 'Mein', etc.), but there is no lack of interest and always a pleasure to be taken in the companionable voice and wholesome method. With Josef Protschka the method is not always so congenial; pairs of notes are aspirated and every now and then there obtrudes a roughness or a sound which, technical terms eluding me, I have to call a yowl (on 'Sorgen' for instance in 'Morgengrüss' or the 'schau' of 'durchschauert' in 'Pause'). But it remains a highly personal, memorable performance and deserves Alan Blyth's strongly committed advocacy, without which it might well have passed unobserved.

Grave Matters

Like the two *Schönen Müllerinen*, Victoria's Requiem also arrives in rival versions. Both choirs suffer a little from an unblending voice: with The Tallis Scholars it is in the bass line (a rather nagging, overhardened tone); with the Westminster Cathedral Choir it resides somewhere among the trebles (a bright piping voice heard first at the end of the 'Te decet hymnus' and identifiable again ever and anon). Even so, both are excellent recordings, and the work itself benefits from the duplication as each performance presents it in a different light. My preference is for the Westminster Choir, partly because it puts the Requiem, or Matins for the Dead, into its liturgical context and has a more appropriate acoustic. But the principal difference has to do with the style, which allows more tenderness, more humanity: the *Agnus Dei* and the motet *Versa est in luctum* provide examples.

Purcell's 'Anthems for The Chapel Royal' also include grave matters: the *Funeral Sentences*, the separate setting of *Thou knowest, Lord* and a number of penitential anthems, poignant in the intensity of their grieving harmonies. The choir of Trinity College, Cambridge under Richard Marlow add substantially to their reputation in this recording. They begin with the *Benedicite*, strong in rhythm as in full-bodied tone, and end with the great eight-part *Hear my prayer*, skilful in shaping, secure in intonation, sensitive in balance. And what an extraordinary work it is to have come from a young man: as Peter le Huray points out in his notes, all but one of these anthems were written before the age of 25.

What might (but perhaps better not) come to be thought of as the *Cav* and *Pag* of Requiems are paired on a new CD. In sequence, the Duruflé Requiem shows its differences from the Fauré rather more sharply. Unhappily, the Atlanta Symphony Chorus are recorded in the hazy distance, and conductor Robert Shaw's approach to both works makes too much of the comfortable in proportion to the more bracing qualities. Textual interest is provided by use of the Rutter edition of the Fauré (less clear-cut and vital, however, than Rutter's own recording) and, in the Duruflé, replacement of soloists by sections of the choir, thus following the composer's own reported preference. My own preference in that work – which grows in estimation prodigiously with repeated hearings – is for the Corydon Singers, conducted by Matthew Best, recently transferred to CD. This brings out the strength and the colour, dim and gentle much of the time but on occasions flaming gloriously, like the rose window in a great cathedral.

Gardiner

Conductors usually come a good second to singers in these columns (we should not begrudge the singers this small distinction, for the balance is more than restored in general practice). But recent years have seen the emergence of a new kind of conductor, a kind very closely associated with the voice and therefore with the subject of these retrospectives. At first glance, describing them as new might seem to ignore work done without fuss or publicity by generations of able choirmasters. Part of the newness does indeed lie in the publicity, or the new kind of public interest. Another part of it lies in the repertoire and in the forces with which these 'new' conductors of ours choose to work.

The process of cause and effect is not hard to trace. Interest in what most of the world lumps together as 'classical music', finding limited fulfilment in its growth in the present, looks for extensions in the past. The most inviting area for discovery has been in early music, which not so long ago meant music before Bach. What researchers discover one year cries out for performance the next. The performers, almost necessarily small groups of enthusiasts, want to know how to perform this music for which there is often no valid extant tradition. Interest in authentic style increases and more discoveries are made. The process is dynamic in a way that distinguishes it from other spheres of music-making: it calls into being, as the Marxists would say, its individual practitioners. These arise out of the people who would formerly have become cathedral or parish choirmasters, but now they have a special place in the public view, and among them are to be found some few who possess the excellence we call genius. One such, surely, is John Eliot Gardiner. Any future study of conductors and their recordings will need a chapter on him as surely as it will have one on Bruno Walter or Otto Klemperer.

There is nothing here that has not been obvious for several years. Looking back over these notes, I see that in 1975 Gardiner's recording of the Monteverdi *Vespers* drew the comment: 'there is the sense of a man with something special to say about the score'. Now, so many years later, the point is reinforced by a long series of recordings and, as it happens, a clutch of them arrive for review this quarter: Monteverdi's *Orfeo*, Bach's *Christmas Oratorio* and the Mozart Requiem. It was the last that had this listener sitting up (almost jumping up), drawn out of the mood of dutiful acquiescence that an evening's listening to choral records had induced up to that point. There it is: it is the work of a man who – it's clear in the very first bars – 'has something special to say'. The finely moulded Introitus 'Requiem' becomes less a classical lament, more an intense imperative. Again, in the *Kyrie*, the mood is urgent, the choral work electric in concentrated precision. A marvellously live handling of rhythms in the 'Dies irae', exquisite playing in the opening of the 'Recordare' (which seems to have confidence in the power of such beauty to speak tenderly and with depth while being kept, so to speak, on its toes), the processional (*Via crucis*) character of the 'Lacrymosa' ... every movement has its own special, individual quality keenly focused. Where the conductor dares and risks, he does so from insight: the Offertorium, 'Domini Jesu Christe' has never (to my knowledge) sounded like this. Of course, difference for difference's sake is an obvious and unworthy way of gaining attention: but here, I truly believe, it is not that, but rather that rare and precious quality, genuine and valid insight.

No conductor so positive as this is going to please everybody in everything. The *Christmas Oratorio* recording, as Lionel Salter pointed out on BBC Radio 3, suffers from a way of emphasizing the first beat of the bar, designed (nearly always in triple-time music) to set it dancing, but in fact numbing the rhythmic sense, and ultimately likely to drive you mad. The first chorus, the mezzo's 'Bereitet dich, Zion', the 'Füllt mit Danken' and Epiphany choruses are examples. Other choruses ('Ehre sei dir', especially) are exhilarating, and there is some astonishing virtuoso singing by the tenor Hans-Peter Blochwitz. Gardiner seems able to put a face on a choir: a listener never in the mind's eye sees an inert, apathetic expression on the collective 'face'. In *Orfeo* the chorus 'Lasciate i monti', going very fast, made me wonder whether the exhilaration was due to its speed alone, or principally. But no: comparing it with the fine recording conducted by Nigel Rogers one finds that, while in most 'factual' respects (such as tempo) the two performances of the chorus are very alike, in liveliness and enthusiasm Gardiner and his singers are in a different class. It is so throughout *Israel in Egypt*, which slipped through my net when it first appeared on LP. I had greatly admired the Christ Church LP recording under Simon Preston, but in a point-by-point comparison it pales and becomes almost featureless. With Gardiner, how those frogs do jump and all manner of flies are set a-buzzing. To every single movement he brings a special insight and, as only a great conductor can, imparts it to his singers and players who then communicate it to us, with the freshness of a new and personal experience.

Callas at Juilliard

Heard at the opera:

'Wants better singers.'

'Singers? There aren't any.'

'Decent voices; no technique. Want better teachers.'

'Teachers? There aren't any.'

Education is at best a miserable topic of conversation; but talk about the teaching of singing leads straight to Bedlam. As on a special floor of the Tower of Babel, one language is spoken but the words have different meanings for each speaker. There is one right method, but the method is different for each of its advocates, and all the others cause ruin. Recently an interest has developed in masterclasses. These enable the public to keep in touch with a famous artist who would otherwise be lost to view, and they can make good television. When the master allows the pupil to go on without stopping, everybody says how good he (or she) is; when she (or he) interrupts, everyone except the pupil (who presumably went in for it in order to be taught) feels resentful and rather indignant. Illuminating points are often made concerning interpretation; rarely is anything very much said about technique. Method is what we're really curious about ('How is it done?'), but all that part of it goes on behind closed doors.

Now the fleeting moment of instruction gains a kind of permanency: Callas's masterclasses at New York's Juilliard School of Music in 1971 and 1972 appear as part of the commemorative series of recordings, and aspiring Callases can have a lesson whenever they feel like it. But what will they, or we, learn? 'Non mi dir' (*Don Giovanni*) does not provide an auspicious start, opening with Callas's 1953 recording, in which Mozartian poise does not prevail, while, in among many examples of what not to do, the real Callas emerges only in those sighed broken phrases ('il cielo, un giorno') near the end. At the end, Callas congratulates the girl on her improvement, the precise nature of which is not self-evident. A sceptical approach to the whole venture has not yet been discouraged.

But soon comes *Medea*, and now we do begin to learn something. Here the lesson centres on discipline, of several kinds. 'Don't vibrate your voice that much', 'Be absolutely rhythmic', and 'Before you put any passion you have to cold-bloodedly look at the aria'. Part of the lesson is in impersonality and restraint: 'Treat it like it was on a cloud … Very classical – you're working too hard'. Part of the discipline involves an appreciation of form: 'You're making so much out of one note that it's a whole aria put together' – and that is a criticism. There follows a genuine master-demonstration in the recording of 1955.

And afterwards come some more true and valuable masterclasses. A Mimì is advised not to hold back the phrase ending 'le rose': 'it becomes too sugary'. A Butterfly is warned about the whole undertaking: 'It's a heavy piece … like a killer. Be careful'. Eboli is coaxed out of hardness, into grace: 'Play with it, elegantly … More stylish, more elegance'. Charlotte is told: 'You're giving me too much, it's an intimate piece'. Her own attempts at singing are risks taken in the interest of teaching, sometimes sad, sometimes triumphant as when illustrating Rigoletto's 'Cortigiani, vil razza' (and there's a collector's piece). To me she sounds like a good teacher, and the records are for cherishing after all: but principally because they so illuminate her own greatness. We're closer to understanding why it is that she, having influenced and been imitated by so many, is still inimitable. The school-of-Callas tends to aim at ever more outsize effects, vocal and emotional; she, in her best practice and in her own school, appears to have had in view such primary aims as: impersonality, accuracy, non-indulgence, elegance, intimacy, restraint.

A Thanksgiving

I am writing in the season of the bread-and-butter letter. 'After the summer visit, after the seaside picnic, you write a nice letter to the kind people who gave you the lovely things.' It was doubly incumbent on you to write, as I remember, if on earlier occasions you had dropped broad hints to which the present visit or picnic may well have been a response. The January 'Retrospect' for this year contained more than hints; it lamented that, while the CD library was flourishing in most departments, the 'historical' shelf (in which the writer happened to have a particular interest) remained empty. At least, there was one lone occupant, Professor Alessandro Moreschi, last of the castratos, nobly presented on the Opal label: a tragical-comical historical, if you like, but hardly representative. A little too late for that lament to be moderated, came news that the pipelines were full, and indeed the summer has seen them spout forth copiously. Hence the bread-and-butter letter.

One paragraph, usually the second, had to recall some of the 'lovely things' in detail: there was always then the chance that the kind people might come up with more of the same next year. If a little retro-aural snapshot album were drawn from the recent pile of historical issues on the EMI Références label, what sounds, in detail, would we catch? There would be, for instance, the ladies of the Covent Garden chorus of 1937 gamely rising to their B flat as they wish a milennium of life to the already aged Emperor of China who is shortly to be confronted by Dame Eva Turner. Over the orchestra there blazes that high C which, as Walter Legge used to say, would go straight up to the gallery, through the back wall and out into Bow Street. On the same page of the scrapbook, headed '*Turandot* 1937', the Unknown Prince, with a vividly dramatic vocal gesture ('Questo, questo'), comforts the diligently sobbing Liù, and phrases 'il tuo piccolo cuore che non cade' with that breadth and nobility that reveal his identity. For the long-absent Giovanni Martinelli returned to Covent Garden that year and his utterly individual tone is stamped afresh on the memory. At several points in the Riddle scene that voice, normally firm as Turandot's own, quivers with the excited assurance that he has found the answers ('la mia vittoria'). Later still in the evening, after the meditative start to 'Nessun dorma' which the critics so admired, the fire of his singing, the conviction and indeed the surviving shine of the voice, leap as of old in 'Dilegue, o notte'. And the page of the scrapbook turns.

From the Grand Hotel, Milan, on April 11th, 1902, comes the elision of sentences 'cercando io vo, M'ama': an incomparably glorious upper middle voice in the tenor there. Better still to come in November: a natural aristocracy of style and tone ennobling Enrico Caruso's emotion in the famous 'Ridi, Pagliaccio' and, by the side of that in the album, there is the magical *diminuendo* in the *Cavalleria rusticana* Siciliana on 'paradisu' after the finely sustained *forte* of the climax.

Lotte Lehmann, adorable representative of the later generation, stands on the next page. Here is a gallery in itself. Faces in the voice, as vivid as any photographs, follow one another: Leonore's indomitable 'Ich folg' dem innern Triebe', Agathe's starlit appreciation of the 'Nachtigall und Grille', Frau Fluth's arpeggio of spontaneous laughter, Isolde's absorbed reflection of the smile on the face of the dead Tristan. Then, in a special place is the final 'encore' piece in the programme, the song from Lehár's *Eva*. This was timely, for I had recently come upon a review by Spike Hughes of the original issue: 'one to play again and again', he had said. Starting with the speaking voice ('dit et même roucoulé, quel éventail', exclaims André Tubeuf in his note), developing into a waltz, the word 'Komm' breathed out with all the intensity of the invocation to Hope in Beethoven, and a beautifully placed high B: all of it for the album.

Rossini Tenors

Reduced to the singular, that is the title of a recital by the American Rockwell Blake, but if you pulled the phrase out of the air and flung it at a knowledgeable collector or an expert in such matters you would probably get the response 'Oh, you mean Raúl Giménez'. The Argentinian too has a Rossini recital, and this has gained the attention of the 'historical' people, who are usually of the opinion that there is only one Rossini tenor on record, a certain Fernando De Lucia who died in 1925.

Of the two in the current lists, Blake is the more astonishing. His runs are quite extraordinary: for the combination of rapidity, clear articulation, evenness over a two-octave range, they may very well take any prize going. Giménez's fluency is gained with the help of aspirates, and much of his work is spoilt by this. Nevertheless, he has, to my ear, the more attractive voice, and there is more affection in his tones. Blake has a more dramatic style, is brighter-toned and more frankly emotional. We can compare them directly in the *Italiana in Algeri* aria, 'Languir per una bella'. Giménez, one realizes, has a curiously nasal tone and a very pinched, distorted vowel sound on the 'eh' of words like 'tormento' and 'momento'. Blake, one finds, has something that at present is perhaps a 'humanizing' vibrato (giving a sense of passion, full-bloodedness) but which could become a wobble. And neither of them has anything like the graceful, well-drawn line of Cesare Valletti in that number. Returning to Blake, I find much that excites, little that charms. Returning to Giménez, I find charm but a flawed technique in the dependency on aspirates, and a flawed style in the fidgety treatment of the melodic line (in 'Ecco ridente' for instance). Blake's Rossini record is assuredly one for the library, but for Giménez I much prefer the Argentinian songs on another Nimbus CD, a delightful collection with an engagingly personal style in the singing.

1989

Bernstein's Bohème

The black list lengthens. A DG issue enters the Stygian catalogue, inscribed in letters dark as Erebus.

In his review, Michael Oliver concluded that 'Bernstein's *Bohème* is less than *Bohème*'. He prefaced that verdict, however, with the word 'even', having laid most blame on the casting of the singers and the acoustic in which they were recorded. The singing certainly gives limited pleasure and the acoustic limited pain. But what I found a genuine torment was the conducting, which did what I had thought could not be done: neutered the opera, erased its systems, the checks and balances by which its effects are achieved. The acoustic doesn't help, but not so much because it sheds a pitiless white light on the singers (which was MEO's complaint) but because it makes the attic sound as though it has a dome high as St Peter's and renders Christmas Eve noise in the Café Momus almost as hard on the ears as the din of a modern pop-tormented pub. The singers, apart from Hadley and Hampson, give performances of the sort that would attract no attention one way or the other if they were in the place where they belong; but here are a major company and a great conductor promoting them, and one can only say that by such standards the Mimì is uneven in her singing, charmless in her characterization, that the Musetta is charmless and uneven too but also wearingly penetrative, that the Colline is the least persuasive advocate in recent years for the existence of the 'Coat song', and that the Schaunard, a tirelessly facetious life-and-soul-of-the-party, would have been kicked downstairs by the real Bohemians within a few seconds of his arrival.

But all of this is nothing: *Bohème* is virtually indestructible, and I've heard it, loved and been moved by it, with much poorer casts than this. What it will not stand is the touch that turns anything in compound time into a loose kind of hillbilly, that annihilates the fun by slowing it down, that fatigues every *rallentando* by exaggeration and, most deadly of all, seems to be working on the voluptuous and deeply erroneous principle that a pleasure long drawn-out in slow motion is a pleasure intensified. For the first time, in my experience, even the music of Mimì's entrance is rendered impotent, partly because Rodolfo's work-music which precedes it and which should make the contrast, has been a lazy, relaxed little trot, partly because the effect has been pre-empted earlier still by luxuriating in lyrical passages during the all-male scene, and partly because the magical bars themselves are so insisted upon. Those bars, allowed to speak at their natural tempo and in a natural context, come to us not just as representing the tender fragile character of the seamstress, but as initiating the little drama which needs no symbolism to point its meaning and no wider canvas to enforce its universality. And it needs no conductor to pet and seduce it in slow motion. I read somewhere that when it was given in concert-performances the young people of Rome loved it. I'm afraid the old folk down my way found it a pain.

Epic Musical

Show Boat was a rapturous experience up to the interval. Delighted and impressed to find real weight behind it, right from that admonitory first chord; then swinging into the spirit of the thing happily with the choruses – and their lyrics ('On de levee you're too heavy', etc.); melted by von Stade's part in 'Only make-believe', further rejoicing in Bruce Hubbard's 'Ole man river' ... I loved all this. And when it came to 'Fish gotta swim, birds gotta fly' and their many repetitions, they couldn't do what they gotta do too often for me. Then comes the interval, an hour or so away from the gramophone; but, one said to oneself, happily falling into the idiom, 'Can't wait to get back to dat ole *Show Boat*'. First comes the delightful discovery that some of the big tunes still lie ahead: 'Why do I love you' and 'Just my Bill'. But in between those two a little difficulty has arisen. The story has jumped; I suddenly am not sure what everybody is doing or what has happened in the meantime. The libretto doesn't help, and though the booklet contains an account of the plot it is not as clear as it should be in the places where we need assistance. So continuity and momentum are weakened. Never mind, so long as the music maintains its vitality, but now comes a slackening with the music hall sequence. Then, when the story is resumed, the recorded version loses all cohesion: we don't know from the recording that Ravenal has deserted Magnolia, and his eventual return also involves conjecture, recourse to notes and a certain amount of indifference. The musical quality degenerates further in the dances, and the ending, with reprise of 'Ole man river', seems almost perfunctory.

It is not easy to see where the fault lies. Some of it seems to be inherent in the show itself, which underwent so many changes that the textual problems of Shakespeare's bad quartos seem child's play by comparison. But I can't help feeling (as did Andrew Lamb in his November review) that there have been misjudgements in the production of the records. I wonder, frankly, whether buyers will be all that grateful for the third disc, an extensive, scholarly appendage to the work as presented. The one number we're waiting for is 'I still suits me' and (whatever its origins) it deserves to take its place somewhere in the main sequence. Scholarship and entertainment are somewhat at odds here, and my feeling is that the show would have been better served – even better, let's say – if yet another new form had been devised for it, one which took fuller account of the medium in which it was being presented.

Schubert Song: an Inauguration

Scholarship and entertainment combine happily so far in the Hyperion Complete Schubert Song Edition. I should think that Graham Johnson has more ideas in the course of a week than most of us come up with in a lifetime, and he has the energy, initiative and optimism to put them into practice and see them through. The Schubert project bears evidence of his active mind in its basic policy-decisions down to the details of the programmes and the astute written commentaries on each of the songs. His playing of the piano parts is equally illuminating: to take just one example, from the second volume, *Wie Ulfru fischt*, where there is a painter's feeling for perspective, for the foreground, the middle and the back, the intricate play of light and shadow. That second record, with Stephen Varcoe singing watery, fishy songs (but not *Die Forelle*) begins rather tentatively, but develops so as to meet the challenge of *Fahrt zum Hades* and has as perhaps its greatest achievement a most sensitive performance of *Am Bach im Frühling*. Opening the recital with songs about fish-traps, locks and sorting the catch, Varcoe seems rooted to the drawing-room carpet: he's too well mannered and vocally reticent. In the first *Fischerlied* he does produce some full-bodied tone for the last verse, but that only makes us wish he had scaled the whole thing up just a little from the start. He is incisive, and of course unfailingly steady, in *Der Taucher* ('The diver' – the longest of all?). But what an infuriating story it tells, of this king who having lobbed a valuable goblet from a cliff-top into the raging sea suggests that somebody should retrieve it, and then, when one 'herrlische Jüngling' does so, sends him back to do it again, and this time with fatal consequences to the diver. I hope the rest of them pushed the king in after him. No such irreverent thoughts arise during the first recital, where Dame Janet Baker, in fine voice, launches the series and makes us realize what riches lie ahead. And, while on the subject of Schubert, I should say how much I enjoyed Felicity Lott's recital, also with Graham Johnson, which picked the 'pops' and in doing so helped, one hopes, to stimulate a few New Year's resolutions to spend all available pocket-money on forthcoming volumes in the Hyperion series right up to 1997, when the series should be complete.

Ariadne auf Naxos

Rare as a virtuous woman in the view of the Ecclesiast is a perfect opera-set in the opinion of a record critic. The feeling derives from a common experience. How often does the questioner ask 'Do you know what is the best such-and-such?' and the answer is about to come up with 'so-and-so' when a woolly bass, a needly soubrette, an outrageous cut in Act 3 or the poor recording of the chorus arises to stifle anything so simple. Even now, I suppose, it can't quite be done with this present opera: but very nearly, and that twice over. *Ariadne auf Naxos* seems an unlikely case in point (fiendishly difficult in many respects, yet I remember a Guildhall School of Music production not so long ago which presented not merely one cast of youngsters in the fearsome roles but a second on alternate nights). The 1954 Karajan recording has long been a touchstone among all examples of opera on record. Now Masur, with Jessye Norman, Julia Varady and Edita Gruberová arrives, and here equally (on balance) is satisfaction and a delight well beyond that. We know, of course, what is likely to be the stone in the shoe. Bacchus should have been recorded once and for all by Richard Tauber. Helge Roswaenge, Fritz Wunderlich perhaps: Plácido Domingo might be ideal, or for that matter Luciano Pavarotti. But most are hopelessly unromantic; many have that kind of lustreless weight that merely combats the orchestra and survives the arduous half-hour. Neither Rudolf Schock with Karajan nor Paul Frey with Masur can provide a completely self-evident reason for Ariadne's excitement on his arrival, but Schock has a touch of Viennese charm, while Frey's reliable voice is under good control and he conscientiously puts it at the service of the score. For the rest, the three principal women shine brightly, the supporting cast is distinguished, the conducting has unostentatious mastery, and the sound has all the immediacy of a live recording without the drawbacks.

I think the Composer in *Ariadne* is my favourite role in the whole of Richard Strauss. Nobody is likely to supplant Irmgard Seefried – that impulsiveness and fervour, the same sense of a passionate spirit living the part that you find in Lotte Lehmann's Sieglinde. But Varady, in radiant voice, accomplishes marvellously well those mercurial changes from anger to equanimity, vexation with externals to ecstasy in creation. In the old Karajan set Rita Streich's Zerbinetta was girlishly tender, pretty and graceful with the airborne lightness of her great predecessor and teacher, Maria Ivogün. In our own time there has never appeared to be a shortage of sopranos to sing this role that was once considered so impossible: but Gruberová is something quite special. Hers is no soubrette voice, but powerful like a laser beam, its range and technical control exceptional in any company. With her, Zerbinetta (and through her, the spirit of comedy) has a potency equal to that of the romantic Composer and the tragic Ariadne. Humour, intimacy, delicacy, intelligent relish of words, these are all features of a performance that could have contented itself with simple brilliance. In a similar way, Norman might have been content to allow the gorgeous richness of her voice to work its spell, whereas she also presents a woman of deep humanity and heroic aspiration: the richest, most royally coloured of strands in the intricately woven fabric.

Die Walküre: Haitink and Levine

Norman also gives lustre to the new *Walküre* under Levine. When there is so much of Brünnhilde in her voice one may wonder whether Sieglinde can be in it as well. But here her art finds the answer. The voice we hear when Sieglinde enters and finds the strange man lying on her bearskin rug is quite distinct from the tones of Ariadne: lighter, younger, vocally a different character. In the other new *Walküre*, conducted by Haitink on EMI, the Sieglinde is also a great asset, though again one wonders about the rightness of the casting. This is Cheryl Studer, whom I would have thought to be a lovely Eva or Elsa, with the low tessitura and arduous dramatic passages in Sieglinde's music presenting dangers for such a voice. Still, she sings with radiant clarity and is able to make the inspired 'O hehrster Wunder' phrases in Act 3 ring out in a silver that is as pure as Norman's gold. Neither of them catches the terror of Act 2, but they continue to sing scrupulously in it, which is something.

I wish I could warm to the Brünnhildes. With Levine, Hildegard Behrens, with Haitink, Eva Marton; and from each of them, almost equally, I hear a steady note once in a way. Both are at their best in the unaccompanied opening of Brünnhilde's plea. Their sincerity is not in question, and Behrens, as we know, is a subtle artist. But I cannot find in either of these singers the nobility of tone which is the first essential of a Brünnhilde. Nor, while on the subject of the women, can I follow the casting, at this stage of her career, of Christa Ludwig as Fricka in the Levine set: hers was a genuinely noble voice in its time, but this is a role that needs a quality she no longer possesses, and above all the voice must be as firm and steady as the willpower that drives this awesome woman. Waltraud Meier, with Haitink, has not the sumptuous tone of Ludwig in her prime, but the voice is firm and she nags with conviction.

A more than usually human Wotan is on the receiving end: James Morris, fine in both recordings, though like Arnold Whittall I slightly prefer his performance in the Haitink version, where the long expositions in Act 2 are particularly well judged in the balance of speech-rhythm and a satisfying legato. His singing of 'Dein Augen leuchtenden Paar' is touchingly beautiful in both. Gary Lakes (with Levine) is rounder of voice and warmer in the baritonal phrases of Siegmund's music; Reiner Goldberg (Haitink) creates a more vivid character but is vocally a Loge rather than a Siegmund. Kurt Moll (Levine) snarls his observations about the stranger's unpleasing resemblance to his wife, but cannot disguise the fact that it's a comfortable voice full of goodness, while Matti Salminen (Haitink) has the dark menace of a voice absolutely right for Hunding. Vocally, then, the Haitink performance is in several respects preferable; an advantage evened up by the rather more taut playing of the Metropolitan Opera Orchestra under Levine. In the course of making comparisons, I turned once or twice to Solti/Decca, now on mid-price CD with the rest of the cycle: and how he makes you sit up!

Recitals: Fassbaender and Schwarzkopf

After all these 'Yes/but' and 'no/ although' progressions, it is a relief to be able to come out with two unequivocal recommendations. Brigitte Fassbaender's Loewe recital with Cord Garben presents one of the finest voices of our time, a strongly imaginative and individual artist, in a relatively unfamiliar programme. She is a persuasive advocate of Loewe's songs, which have suffered neglect often because of the superiority of settings by Schubert and Schumann. This recital opens with *Meine Ruh ist hin*, and clearly the song is by no means as memorable or profound as Schubert's *Gretchen am Spinnrade*. But Fassbaender makes the most of the subtler touches, with lovely tone and a certain grandeur suggesting the nobility of the girl in her tragedy. In *Uber allen Gipfeln* she sustains the peaceful mood most beautifully, with the last line, 'bald ruhest du auch', repeated in sad stillness. It will have come as a surprise to most of us, I dare say, to find that Loewe also set *Frauenliebe und -leben*: not a masterpiece (too many fill-in chords in the piano part's left hand, and a general lack of excited impulsiveness) but well worth reviving. There is, we discover, an additional poem, the woman now a grandmother giving her valedictory blessing: Schumann did well to omit it, though Loewe's idea of ending with the spoken voice is put to touching effect. He is generally best when simplest, as in the setting of 'An meinem Herzen' as a quiet lullaby, or in the Heine song *Im Traum sah ich die Geliebte*, again sung with the quiet distinction of an artist in her prime.

That too is what Elisabeth Schwarzkopf was in her Carnegie Hall recital of 1956, and one of the most exciting of what I suppose now have to be called historical issues. With George Reeves as her excellent accompanist (a particularly happy way with the Richard Strauss songs), she sings a long programme with encores handed out regularly along the way and ending with that kind of party atmosphere where all is delight and where mutual affection rules between audience and artist, who, in her last song, Handel's *Care selve*, holds them in a trance of sheer love for beauty (a sign of it, especially from this New York audience, is the silence for a moment at the end before the final roar of bravos). She is in freshest voice, and if one cannot add 'with her art at its finest' that is because her art never stopped developing. Each song lives its life in a wonder of imaginative concentration. To pick a few that in some way took me by surprise: *Der Vollmond strahlt* has a most delicate sense of serious appreciation; the Strauss *Wiegenlied* is so affectionate and magical in its *pianissimos*, beautifully judged in crescendo; *Wir haben beide lange Zeit geschwiegen* (Wolf) is a perfect piece of mood-creation; *Der Nussbaum* is kept airborne, always with care for the natural speech-values of the words.

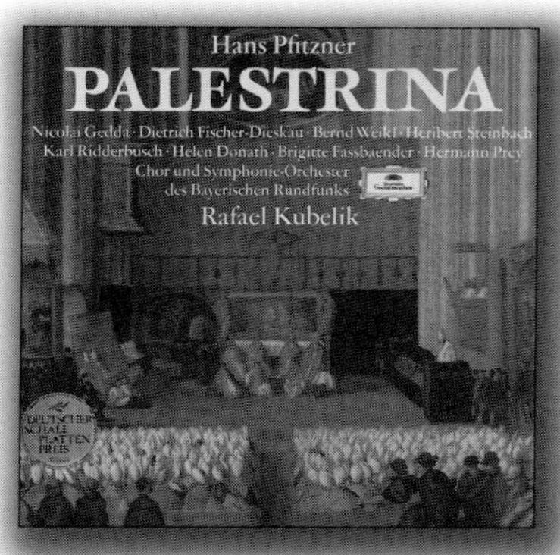

'The Gramophone and the Voice' –
a selection of LPs from JBS's July 1974 Quarterly Retrospect

Photo Decca

Photo DG/Lauterwasser

Singers and pianists:
Kathleen Ferrier and Bruno Walter; Dietrich Fischer-Dieskau and Gerald Moore

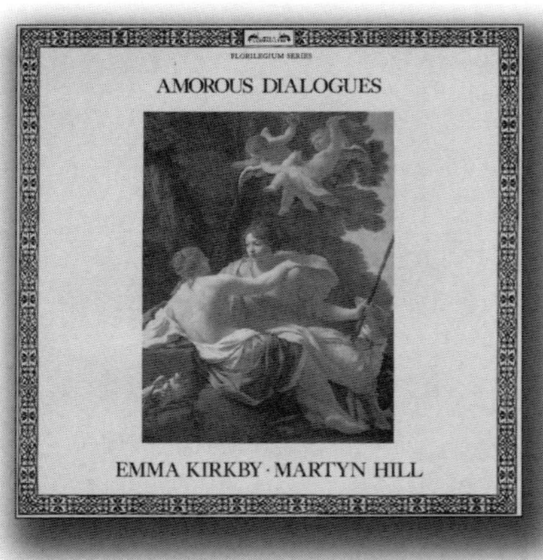

A selection of LPs from the April 1981 Quarterly Retrospect

Dame Elisabeth Schwarzkopf

Photo DG/Lauterwasser

Julia Varady

Photo Decca/Eccles

Photo DG

Renée Fleming • Plácido Domingo

Photo BMG

Giovanni Martinelli as Otello

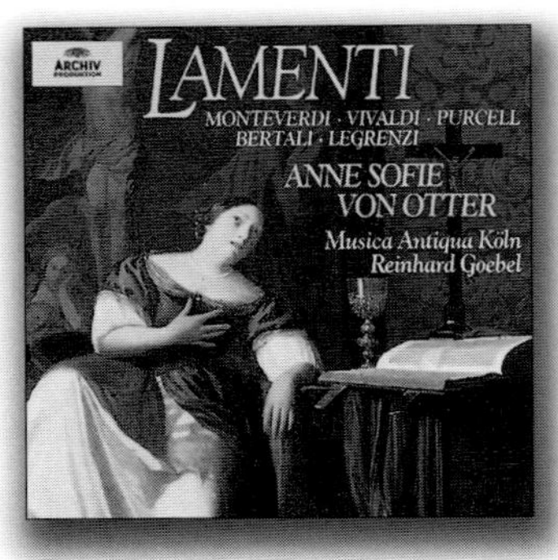

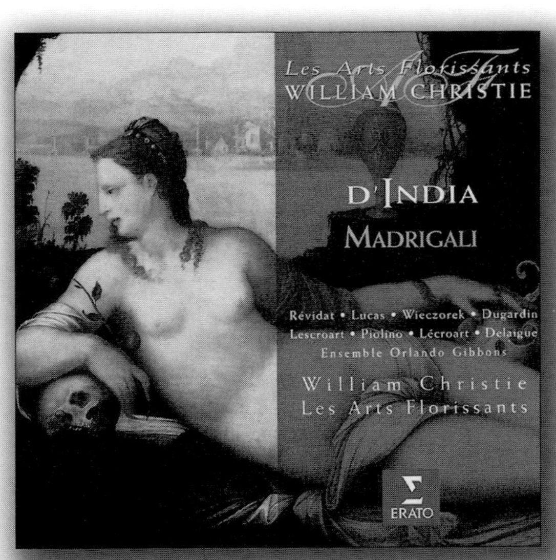

End of an era: a selection of CDs reviewed by JBS in his last Quarterly Retrospect, April 1999, exactly 25 years after his first

Just one caution. The sound is so perfect in definition that hearing it in the living-room gives slightly the impression of looking through inverted opera-glasses: everything is distinct but reduced. Schwarzkopf's voice in recitals was – how to say? – broader, more generous, than what I've just been hearing. Short-sighted people will know how, when you look with unspectacled eyes at a light, it is diffused, covering a wider area; put on your specs and it becomes a narrow, closely defined point or strip of light. It is rather as though the recording has done that; the reality, or the impression it gave in the concert hall, was of the wider, more generous breadth.

Desolate Pleasures

Melancholy entertainment for this year's radiant summer, but the great musical pleasure of the season has lain in three desolate song cycles, one by Frank Martin, the others by Hindemith. Martin's *Der Cornet* sets a diary-like narration by Rilke telling of an ancestor, Christoph, who fought against the Turks in 1663 and died as ensign-bearer in battle. Rilke wrote in 1899, Martin in 1942,but amid all these dates it is other years and another war that come to mind as we listen. 'The pity of war, the pity war distilled' runs like an unstated motif. The pride and the waste ('Was it for this the clay grew tall?'), the cruel intensifying of life's wonder in the shadow of death, the dreadful telegram (as to Wilfred Owen's parents but here a letter to the cornet's mother), all of this turns thoughts towards the Western Front; but the music directs the thoughts more potently still. The male story is told by a female voice, which perhaps deepens the sense of compassion. The orchestration, spare and evocative, is masterly in its reserve and resourcefulness. The fine performance by Marjana Lipovšek and the Austrian Radio Symphony Orchestra under Lothar Zagrosek renders the 23 sections so vividly and with such a wealth of feeling that I can well understand Robert Layton saying that as he listened he forgot that he was also reviewing. For all that, I culled much more vital information about the piece from his review than from the notes provided.

The absence of translations is certainly a fault in the presentation of the Hindemith cycles, and so, as Michael Oliver points out, is the 'far from generous' playing-time of 35 minutes. Still, the two cycles which comprise Op. 23 are sufficiently rare, concentrated and fine in quality to compensate. In both, Gerd Albrecht conducts members of the Berlin Radio Symphony Orchestra, but each has a different contralto soloist, one of whom appears, like Lipovšek, to be a highly distinguished singer. This is Gabriele Schreckenbach, whose noble voice meets in full the demands for a wide range in *Des Todes Tod*. Gabriele Schnaut in *Die junge Magd* sings expressively but with rather bulging, uneven production in louder passages. The cycles share a seriousness that never shuns beauty. The opening of *Die junge Magd* has some of the most lovely writing, and the final song of *Des Todes Tod*, a two-part piece for voice and viola, has a chilly, brooding beauty: naught for your comfort here, but, like Martin's *Der Cornet*, the works impress deeply as discoveries that oblige one to redraw part of one's musical map.

1990

Domingo and Tannhäuser

The new Sinopoli *Tannhäuser* has provided a curious experience, and I'm tempted to write about the recording in terms of the experience, though I suppose one should objectify and depersonalize. Let it be said (and it reads almost like a confession) that I enjoyed it greatly. But it had a swingeing review from Rodney Milnes in the October issue of *Opera*. Why is it that an adverse critique carries so much more weight (in my mind I find it does) than a favourable one? There was Alan Blyth's review in ***Gramophone*** which, with a few reservations, gave approval along lines that broadly coincided with my own. That was no sort of comfort. 'This dreadful recording' Rodney Milnes called it, and he gave roughly 30 good reasons for having nothing to do with it. So out came the score, the preferred Solti, the metronome. Point by point, the 30 were seen not to be wrong. But the final judgement, that annihilating 'dreadful'? All I can report here, simply in terms of experience, is that a week or so later a repeat performance from start to finish brought only slightly less enjoyment than the first time, and I'm not convinced that even that minus degree was accounted for by musical considerations; rather that the initial freshness had gone and a certain amount of critical self-consciousness had set in.

And now, of course, it's almost impossible to 'objectify'. One can offer a few specific points and a few generalizations, but even the selection of specific points is personal. For instance, the first points tested were the speeds of the *Andante maestoso* and *allegro* in the early pages of the Overture, where I found Giuseppe Sinopoli precisely on the metronome markings. Solti, by comparison, makes less of the marked *sostenuto* at the opening, being less concerned with a legato style. Nor does Solti mould the *crescendos* and *decrescendos* as observantly and affectionately as Sinopoli does. Then when the triplets begin, Sinopoli allows them, with advantage, to count for more than the rhythmic/harmonic fill-in which normally appears to be their only purpose. Then take the first points tested in Plácido Domingo's performance, where the comparison is with René Kollo in the Solti recording. First, I listen as critically as I can to Domingo's German, but no, in these opening phrases the vowels, the weighting of syllables, the clarity of enunciation, cause me no disquiet. As to expression, Kollo certainly presents the more interesting, if somewhat whining, character, with a weariness and dissatisfied yearning in the silver-grey tone of his voice, where Domingo in a simpler, more forthright manner tells of his dream and his desire. But here comes a conflict of priorities. There are two small tests of vocal grace in this passage (at the words 'Sommer' and 'verkünde'); Kollo muffs both, Domingo sings them properly. That is a prelude to Tannhäuser's first solo, 'Dir töne Lob', in which Kollo aspirates grossly (not too strong a word), is crudely uneven, and towards the end resorts to a guttural kind of emphasis. Domingo's performance is even and clean, glowing in the beauty of its tone, and ardent in spirit. Now, one critical voice here says 'There is much, much more to *Tannhäuser* than notes' and another says 'Yes indeed, but the notes come first'.

I don't, however, defend the slow speeds that so transform the Tannhäuser/Elisabeth duet in Act 2 (in the E flat section one would never guess *allegretto* to be the marking). Nor does Cheryl Studer's performance satisfy, for though the tone is radiant in Elisabeth's Greeting the expression is not, and her quiet singing sounds less than thoroughly secure. On the positive count, Andreas Schmidt in Act 3 is surely in the great line of Wolframs; Agnes Baltsa's Venus strikes me as being more attractive, not less, for the absence of the more sultry richness often favoured; Domingo rises to the heartfelt cries of 'Erbarm' dich mein' in the ensemble and to the pitiless voice of Rome in the Narration; and Sinopoli brings out the warmth of the score, often with vivid local illumination, as, to take a single example, in the bars before Tannhäuser's 'Zu ihr' in Act 1, when the excitement and glow of the moment are caught (and much more vividly than by Solti) simply by following faithfully and imaginatively the score's directions.

More Opera

More disagreement too, I fear, but a milder, less troublesome one here with Richard Osborne over the Baltsa/Abbado *L'italiana in Algeri*. Again, I seem to have enjoyed more, and the anomaly arises over the fact that memory and written notes made while listening insist on the very quality that RO found most wanting – a sparkle and flair in Claudio Abbado's conducting. What most surprised me was the inclusion of *Il barbiere di Siviglia* among the recordings said to show greater brilliance: for surely the conducting there (like most of the singing) is 'correct' but dull. In *L'italiana* the wit and zest of the Overture are expertly caught (I thought), setting the performance off to a delightful start, and at many points throughout, the conductor's light and lively touch has an effect that is exactly the opposite of that un-lifting *Barbiere*. Complete agreement, however, over the achievement and promise of the tenor, Frank Lopardo, and about the inappropriately resonant acoustic. Also as to the pleasures of the new *Comte Ory* under John Eliot Gardiner, high among them being the performance of the delectable Sumi Jo. It is a highly accomplished cast (John Aler, Gino Quilico and, splendid as the page, Diana Montague), but this new soprano is captivating from the start, an impression which her part in *Un ballo in maschera* deepens. Cecilia Bartoli, the Rosina of the new Decca *Barbiere*, is another singer whose début on record has been particularly auspicious. As her Rossini recital also showed, she has a voice of exceptional quality and range. She is a resourceful artist too, bringing some charmingly personal touches to her 'Una voce poco fa'. William Matteuzzi, the Almaviva, is yet another lyric tenor who has trained conscientiously to cope with Rossini's scales and triplets: it sounds a small voice but precise and graceful, and he acts well. Personally, I could very happily make do with less recitative, and in spite of all its good qualities the recording doesn't quite establish itself as a likely favourite.

Long-term favour seems hardly likely, either, for the new *Così fan tutte* under James Levine. I played it the evening after Abbado's *L'italiana* had so delighted me with its deft, twinkling orchestral work, and here the *fortissimos* came down thick and heavy by comparison. Te Kanawa is lovely as ever; if she doesn't gain attention by expressiveness she does by sheer beauty of sound. It's rather like Domingo as Tannhäuser – and in both instances critical ingratitude is absurd because there are plenty of interpreters but few if any who can sing the notes so beautifully as these two artists, not that their performances are in any way restricted to that function. Marie McLaughlin is one of the few who can begin to rival Dame Kiri, and a Fiordiligi is what she is, not a Despina: Despina has to communicate a sense of fun, and whereas McLaughlin can interpolate a laugh it seems that she can't audibly smile. Ann Murray's tone deteriorates above a *mezzo-forte*: her 'Smanie implacabili' falls most unpleasantly on the ears. Blochwitz's 'Un'aura amorosa' falls sweetly at first but soon becomes insipid; and I cannot think that it was a good idea to follow it, as an appendix at the end of the side, with Guglielmo's 'Non siate ritrosi', which is much better than the solo sung in its place, the abrupt ending of which makes so little sense out of context.

The DG *Un ballo in maschera* will survive no doubt, if only as Karajan's last opera. Vocally it is irradiated by Sumi Jo, who also makes a more sympathetic, positive presence of Oscar as a character than I've known before (the sadness and tenderness of the Page's line in 'E scherzo ed è follia' has surely not been brought out like this?). Josephine Barstow's Amelia, like Leo Nucci's Renato, is vivid and sincere but her tone has become so juddery, and his so loosely focused, that on balance both have to be counted liabilities rather than assets. Domingo again sings so well that it seems ungrateful to ask for more dramatic mobility behind the singing. What fascinates is Karajan's approach which I thought made little sense till about halfway in. Over the First Act he casts a strange dream-like quality ('We are such stuff as dreams are made on'), letting the events contributing to the tragedy move slowly (the first chorus almost frozen in a stillness during which the event is foreseen, as in a Greek chorus). Then it is as though the urgency of Amelia's prelude in Act 2 breaks through the stage gauze into reality, and from there the momentum intensifies towards catastrophe. I'm not quite sure about Karajan's 'going out on a high', as AB puts it (for there are serious weaknesses in the singing), but the performance has a depth, a grandeur, that must be honoured.

Song Recitals

Whatever the qualities are that ensure life after death as a recording artist, they were surely possessed by Lotte Lehmann. The items collected on a disc in RCA's new historical series are taken from the latter half of her career, when she was approaching, or over, 50 years of age (and no less than seven of them were recorded, all on the same day, when she was 62); but there is a largesse, a generosity of tone (never going flabby or wispy) and a gift of the spirit that enrich life whenever they are listened to or called to mind. A wide repertoire adds to the appeal of the recital; the exciting sweep of Cimara's *Canto di primavera* ('Spring song') for a start, then Sadero's Lullaby, *Fà la nana, bambin* and Gounod's setting of Byron's *Maid of Athens*, which Reynaldo Hahn made so much his own that I really thought he had written it. Tauber, Lehmann's colleague in Vienna, belongs to this category of unforgettables too, and I came to take much pleasure in the recent Lieder recital on Pearl, where the Schumann songs are so beautifully shaded and the German *Volkslieder* sung with such a modest exercise of the Tauber charm. But 'came to' has to be inserted, for the record opens with 12 songs from *Winterreise*. Perhaps all copies of these are of poor quality – mine are, and so are the ones used for transfer here. And Mischa Spoliansky plays the piano part with something that might be taken for levity.

For a modern recording of the complete *Winterreise* one is unlikely to do better than with Olaf Bär and Geoffrey Parsons. Again 'there is much, much more than the notes', as we know, but how grateful one is when the notes are as well sung as they are here. There are plenty of interesting features along the journey too – for instance, the way in which the two halves of the verses in 'Gute Nacht' are made to contrast the outer and inner worlds. The overall concept, where feelings intensify from bitterness to anger and then in sheer weariness find a deathly peace, is also persuasive. In Benjamin Luxon's *Schwanengesang* and *Die schöne Müllerin* the steady tone and clear focus such as we hear in Bär's performances are badly needed. But these are rich in insight and vivid with the skills of a practised communicator.

Luxon's work with David Willison is surely as fine a collaboration between singer and pianist as we have had in recent years. Following the memorable Warlock recital they turn to Roger Quilter, where between them they reveal far more in both the voice and piano parts than one probably expected to find there. Luxon's live, intelligent way with words and Willison's finely articulated, sympathetic accompaniments provide a flexibility that may be wanting in the otherwise delightful performance of Quilter's *Three Shakespeare Songs* by Stephen Varcoe. This is of the finely orchestrated version in a programme of English orchestral songs, accompanied by the City of London Sinfonia under Richard Hickox, and I wouldn't have missed it for all the beer in Burton. Butterworth's *Love blows as the wind blows* has a quiet underlying passion; his more familiar *Shropshire Lad* cycle is strengthened by the orchestration; and of a beauty too unspoilt for this world is Finzi's *Let us garlands bring*.

British Choral

In the filling-in of gaps, which has been so much the real growth point in musical life over the past 20 or 30 years (and what happens when they're all filled?), some of the most rewarding of recent work has been that done on the early Tudor composers. Taverner is by now almost as well known and highly rated as Byrd, though we're still in the process of discovery. The *Missa Corona spinea*, with its rich textures, ornate high treble parts and glorious setting of *Sanctus* and 'Benedictus', is beautifully performed by The Sixteen, who also have a programme of motets, anthems and canticles by the Elizabethan William Mundy. He too exploits the treble-virtuosos, to the limits of endurance both for them and the listener, very probably, in his Evening Service. He is an interesting composer, apportioning his talents even-handedly for the simplicity of the new Church and the elaborations of the old: I loved those Amens unfurling streamers of sound at the end of the *Vox Patris caelestis*, perfectly proportioned in the architecture of this cathedral of a motet.

In these I trespass upon the territory of the 'Early Music Retrospect', but it may be well to be reassured from time to time that it is a field in which the non-specialist can also find pleasure. Moving on to the 1900s, which is probably where I belong, I must add a supplement to the section headed Elgar to Walton in my October 'Retrospect': this time it is Parry to Mathias.

Parry figures in 'Great Music from Great Occasions at Westminster Abbey': the Coronation anthem *I was glad* of course, and a performance both thrilling and sensitive. Vaughan Williams's *Festival Te Deum* for the Coronation of George VI is heard live on an excellent Pearl issue which also includes the original recording of the *Serenade to Music* with the 16 famous soloists conducted by Sir Henry Wood and, most important, a hitherto unknown recording of *Dona nobis pacem* from the first broadcast, conducted by the composer in 1936. This is quite exceptionally good in sound (taken from a private acetate) and the performance has the authentic flavour of its period. The *Serenade to Music* in a more casual, though far from careless, modern performance opens an interesting record of three serenades by the New York Virtuosi on ASV. Elgar follows, then Britten. Grayson Hirst sings the *Serenade* for tenor, horn and strings in a way that makes one feel he has been touched by the beauty of the work. His way with the 'Dirge' is probably exaggerated in its portamentos and rather fierce declamatory style, but there is conviction in the independence of approach and it commands attention.

In another recent recording of the *Serenade*, by Anthony Rolfe Johnson with the Scottish National Orchestra under Bryden Thomson, intensity in the 'Dirge' is aided by quickening. An excellent account of the Ben Jonson Hymn ('Queen and huntress') distinguishes the performance, and the dying echoes of the 'Nocturne' are beautifully caught by the players. Britten's first song-cycle, *Quatre chansons françaises* of 1928, makes the record doubly worth having, though *Les illuminations*, sung here by Felicity Lott, has more life and a keener edge to the words in Jill Gomez's recording.

Anthony Rolfe Johnson appears again in the *St Nicholas Cantata* under Matthew Best: a good performance, but what a pity the choir are not recorded closer. It must be almost as difficult as in the *War Requiem* to achieve the right balance, but I don't think it has been brought off here. Very well produced, however, is 'The Hussey Legacy', a tribute to Walter Hussey, Vicar of St Matthew's Church, Northampton and later Dean of Chichester – which includes Britten's *Rejoice in the Lamb*. Very lovely are the Halleluiahs, swinging like a censer, and the fanning out in glowing colours of 'all the instruments of Heaven'. *The Legacy* is sung by the Finzi Singers under Paul Spicer and collects some of the distinguished works commissioned by this 'last great patron of art in the Church of England', as Sir Kenneth Clark called him. Not among those composers, though I imagine he might well have been, is William Mathias whose *Lux aeterna* has now appeared on CD. In construction and provision of forces it has some affinity with the *War Requiem*, and probably presents similar difficulties to recording engineers: admirably coped with here, and, under Sir David Willcocks, a worthy performance of a work strong in conception, rhythm and colour, though less fecund, I would say, in melodic invention.

Muti: Rigoletto and Guglielmo Tell

In the Muti recording of *Rigoletto* the orchestra tends to provide the focal point throughout, but the main disqualification is that the Gilda (Daniela Dessi) and Duke (Vincenzo La Scola) simply do not measure up to the standard of what might legitimately be expected from a recording with the imprimatur of La Scala upon it. The Rigoletto, Giorgio Zancanaro, is another matter: I rate him more highly than AB appears to do, for this is a voice of rare quality and his performance carries conviction (take the monologue as a test, 'O uomini, o natura' having exactly the flash of vividness lacking in Nucci in the new version under Chailly). It is tempting to say that he is as good as his conductor will allow him to be. Perhaps that would be harsh, but I do not warm to Muti's doctrinaire adherence to the letter of the score when the experience of a 100 years or so has confirmed the value of additions such as the cadenza in 'La donna è mobile' and the E flat lead-in to 'Si, vendetta'. The rampaging tempo of 'Cortigiano, vil razza' is no doubt gratifying to the conductor, but probably less so to the singer; and even when he decides to be flexible, in 'E il sol del'anima', there is something subtly wrong about it, a conductor's imposed rubato rather than the natural rubato of singers.

This apparent indifference or hostility to tradition also affects the success of the *Guglielmo Tell* conducted by Muti. Again he tends to see the music from a conductor's point of view rather than a singer's. Natural and even proper, you might say: but how this shows itself in effect (and hence prompts the remark) is that rhythm takes priority over melody. The trio in Act 2 is dominated by the passionate lament of Arnoldo, but Muti's eye goes to the accompaniment where it sees what might be read as a cabaletta-style motor-rhythm, and that is how he takes it, permitting only the slightest *rallentando* at the tenor's mounting 'Oh ciel, mai più lo rivedrò' and so robbing it of half its expressiveness. Equally rigid is the policy at work in Arnoldo's call to arms, when in both verses only the literal length is accorded the high C, which in consequence has the almost comical effect of a vocal bobtail and nothing of the thrill it can produce – and I would have thought is clearly meant to. It is not as though Chris Merritt were short of top Cs; he is in fact quite exceptionally well supplied with high notes and is vastly admired in Italy partly on this account. While admiring much that he does, I can't say that I enjoy it. This is a demanding role in other ways too, and for the intensity of feeling and creative shaping of phrase I generally find myself listening in vain. Zancanaro is a good Tell, but the finest singing comes from Cheryl Studer, who makes of Matilde's scene early in Act 3 the most impressive solo in the opera.

A Season of Britten

Lost in my labyrinth
I'm tired of willing women
My mind beats on
Because it hath no bottom

Ah, you say, a sad case. Poor fellow, poor fellow: he has been too much in the sun. But no. Decca reissued four more of their original sets in May, and I have been too much in the Britten. In the course of four successive evenings *A Midsummer Night's Dream* followed *Death in Venice*, which came after *The Rape of Lucretia*, and *The Turn of the Screw* was first.

We say that the classics are immortal, but it is doubtful whether any later generation quite captures the feelings of a contemporary. Rearranging them in order, we have the years 1946 (RL), 1954 (TS), 1960 (MND), and 1974 (DV): to my generation it's a sizeable portion of one's life, from first to last. And all of these I remember hearing, either live or on the radio, almost as they appeared. Each of them excited a special interest, and all were quick to lodge in the memory. Yet, ungrateful or irreverent as we were, it was the silly bits that trailed around with us, repeating themselves in the mind like some inane catchphrase. It started with *Peter Grimes*: 'Grimes is at his exercise' we would assure friends and relatives, who didn't particularly want to know. Then Lucretia: 'Wake up old woman, warn your mistress,' we urged, as Tarquinius padded along the corridor with dire intent. 'Who is it? Who? Who can it be?' we asked after *The Turn of the Screw*, and though we knew it was only Sir Peter Pears in a ginger wig there was no end to the enquiry. With *A Midsummer Night's Dream* we simulated the breathings of sleep; with *Death in Venice* it was 'Serenissima', the bells, the strawberry-seller, and the hoppety-skippety coyness of 'you no-tice when you're no-ticed'.

And of course the voices: Pears calling to Miles, waking the sleep of the Tiber, peering into the plague-haunted haze of ambiguous Venice; Joan Cross as the curiously accentuated 'old house-*keep*er', Owen Brannigan as Bottom the weaver; the tense, haunted, affectionate voice of Jennifer Vyvyan as the

Governess. No wonder, then, that they take possession, these recordings, in, as Michael Kennedy says at the end of his review, 'triumphant transfers'. Let me refer you to him for further enthusiasm, and pass on to the opera that most conspicuously is not there, and could not be.

Gloriana: the Video

The silliness attributed to that first, Coronation-night audience ('My dear, I didn't dare look at the royal box') evidently did not end with them. There must be an explanation somewhere. Did the executives at Decca catch on to the idiotic reputation of 'Boreana'? Was Britten himself, perhaps, understandably, sick of it after the failure – which, after all, was never a failure with the best part of the critics and public? Whatever the cause, the fact remains that the single most astonishing long-term omission of an opera from the record catalogues has been this one.

Now it appears at last, but only on video cassette. One says 'only', and there is a loss in sound-quality; on the other hand, a very generous recompense comes with the pleasure of seeing, in this excellent filming of the admirable ENO production, an opera which was meant to feast the eyes as well as the ears. Again, it is hardly possible to convey just what *Gloriana* meant to people of my generation who saw it new. Perhaps memory plays tricks, but I remember the Piper sets and costumes as some of the most magical things ever seen in the post-war years at Covent Garden; the solid framework of the later production, however imaginatively used, rather affronted the eyes after that.

The title-role was a great personal triumph for Joan Cross, and there were memorable cameos, such as Edith Coates's pot-pouring housewife and Ina Te Wiata's blind ballad-singer. It surely should have been preserved, certainly in a sound-recording. As it is, we must be thankful for the fine, rich colours of this film, the cameras helping to enhance the sense of space and variety. Sarah Walker remains vivid in the mind's eye, an Elizabeth whose lip will curl with scorn or humour, whose strong heart knows trouble, whose natural dignity is never greater than when she is discovered without wig or robe before the mirror in her dressing-room by the desperate man from Ireland. From the robust, syncopated, fanfare-like opening to the dim, fading notes of the final offstage chorus it is a marvellous score, and surely the most colourful, melodious and varied in Britten's entire operatic output.

Ciboulette

New to me was Reynaldo Hahn's *Ciboulette*, with Mady Mesplé heading the cast. It is perhaps as well to be warned that this is not an operetta to approach with the expectation of a good tune just around every comer. Always there is the delicate suggestion of a tune, a potpourri with the scent of a hundred charming melodies, none of which will do anything quite so commonplace as to be played for all they're worth. A pretty comedy, this, partly rustic, partly of the *beau monde*, with a little laughing love and the restrained nostalgia of an elderly man, dignified in his bearing (and in being sung here by José van Dam) as well as by the open secret of his identity, for he is (or was) Rodolphe, poet of the Latin Quarter years ago, now reticent of his memories but prodigal of sighs as he murmurs 'Ah, la jeunesse!'. Incidentally, Rodolphe (now Monsieur Duparquet) does nothing so vulgar as to whistle Puccini, though the operetta contains a capital parody of Massenet's *Manon* – 'Toi! Vous!', 'Oui, c'est moi! Moi!' exclaim the lovers in delighted melodrama before setting off on their duet 'Te souviens-tu du premier jour à Robinson?'.

Knowing only the famous Aubade, one might expect Lalo's *Le roi d'Ys* to be a similarly charming, light-weight and very French piece. That would be quite the wrong idea, the Aubade merely providing a happy and melodious interlude in a catastrophic story and a score more remarkable for its colouring than for its tunes. The new recording under Armin Jordan does more, on balance, to recommend it than did its predecessors. In casting, much depends on the sisters, Rozenn and Margared. They need to be strongly cast (Frances Alda and Rosa Ponselle at the Metropolitan): in the old Cluytens recording Janine Micheau was too prosaic a Rozenn and in the Dervaux on Le Chant du Monde/ Harmonia Mundi Jane Rhodes was a too strident Margared. Here, Barbara Hendricks has a lovely purity and delicacy of voice and manner, offsetting the deeper, richer tones of Delorès Ziegler. Equally effective is Jordan's insistence on quietness at the right times: the orchestral stillness and Hendricks's tenderness bring out what is genuinely touching in the opera and by contrast make the highly-wrought dramatic element more effective also.

Song Recitals

The Hyperion Schubert Edition gains lustre from its latest volume, the theme of which is night. Anthony Rolfe Johnson is well suited to what one may think of as the Karl Erb repertoire – such songs as *Abendstern*, *Des Fischers Liebesglück* and *Der Knabe in der Wiege*. About the last-named, Graham Johnson notes that in the original key and at not too slow a speed it has the character not so much of a lullaby as of the almost jaunty song of a happy parent. But that is to pick almost at random out of the endlessly illuminating comments that accompany the performances as admirably as he accompanies the singers. *Die Sterne*, one of the most delightful of the songs here, is also heard in an excellent performance by Sarah Walker and Roger Vignoles. Their Schubert recital, fine throughout, carries in at least three songs the special feeling that arises when an artist has been touched afresh by the beauty of the music. As it happens, these too are 'night songs' – *Nachtviolen*, *Im Abendrot* and *Nachtstück* – perhaps *Nacht und Träume* should be added. This closes the recital, with Vignoles playing most beautifully, the vocal line perfectly sustained, and an ideal balance achieved between voice and piano.

Accompanying Peter Schreier in Schumann's *Dichterliebe*, Wolfgang Sawallisch begins with a modified version of the rubato employed by Cortot on the old recording with Charles Panzéra. Here it's more deliberate and self-conscious I would say, but producing a similar sense of a curious kind of uneven, gently staggering gait. At many points in the cycle, this is a performance that runs to extremes of emphasis, pulling-back of tempo, and most especially an underlining of anger, bitterness and overt, almost Werther-like grief. As AB says, it makes very compulsive listening and brings frequent moments of intense revelation. So, yes, it must have a place among 'the best ever', though personally I'm less than happy with it. There's a fine dividing-line, and perhaps one has passed over it even in referring to 'extremes of emphasis' for that comes near to implying overemphasis. I fancy that when my colleague hears a plangent tone I hear something nearer to whining. Whatever it is, it doesn't prevent admiration of much (and generally with Schreier's singing I find more to enjoy live than on record). The first half of the recital concludes with Prokofiev's *Three Children's Songs* and *The Ugly Duckling*; again, I can't quite find a liking, but the achievement is phenomenal.

Christie's Fairy Queen

The ***Gramophone*** Awards are with us again, and for reviewers that usually means catching up on a few important issues that have slipped past. It is a chilling thought that but for the grace of the selectors I would have missed Purcell's *The Fairy Queen*. Most delightful of all incidental music (but always I have to remind myself that it's for *A Midsummer Night's Dream*, despite the Chinese Man and Woman, the Drunken Poet, the swans and six monkeys), it has an inexhaustible range of melody and mood, and when John Eliot Gardiner's recording originally appeared on LP eight years ago one could hardly have imagined that such a skilled, imaginative performance was likely to find a rival, let alone a superior, in the near future. But Les Arts Florissants, William Christie's group fresh from the Aix-en-Provence Festival, have done it: it is better, as Iain Fenlon found when making comparisons for the first review in January. Take, for instance, 'If love's a sweet passion' for which I turned to Gardiner, thinking that Christie was unusually slow (a relaxed, almost languorous tempo quite justified by its context and effect but still a little unexpected): Gardiner's tempo is much the same, but it's a performance almost pestered by refinement, with its over-careful accentuation of the 'pa-', lightening of 'ssion' and so forth.

The new recording has its delicacy too, but also a more forthright, sometimes more risky style, more colour in the instrumentation, a more infectious sense of enjoyment. One can't help noting, too, a slight element of *plus ça change* in the employment of a larger ensemble and of high tenors instead of the voices variously described as countertenor, alto and (in a recent recording) falsetto. Both are welcome, especially as one of the tenors, Jean-Paul Fouchécourt, sounds something like a latter-day Hugues Cuénod. The Mopsa-Coridon duet is a great joy with its 'No no no, no kissing at all' reiterated with posh-prim French-English vowels, and I would dearly love to have heard it at Aix where Nicholas Anderson says it was like 'a couple of civil-servants disagreeing about who left a top-secret document on the photocopier'. One can also well imagine the cool beauty of Lynne Dawson's voice in the Plaint sailing out into the Provençal night air, and the *frisson* which the audience must have experienced, early in the evening, when after the capering of the drunkard the chorus sings

'Let 'em sleep till break of day', putting all human folly and grossness to bed with sublime tolerance and almost unearthly beauty.

Pérotin's Corner

Catching up on the twelfth century was also a pleasure, but a slightly more mixed one. Two of the three records short-listed for the Early Music (Medieval & Renaissance) Award took us back to the age of 'the Lion-hearted King', whose music is the subject of a recital by Gothic Voices, one of the most reliably enjoyable and enlightening groups in the medieval field. Yet, admiring and liking up to a point, I took note of Christopher Page's recognition that it 'takes the listener time to bring the melody into focus and locate its points of tension and release', and ruefully had to acknowledge that this 'important part of the aesthetic experience' was proving elusive.

The lament for the death of Barbarossa (though taken slowly and sung with suitable expression) seemed of itself to be quite a jolly melody, and, unless some satirical point is intended, I find it hard to accept that this doesn't matter and that the objection is covered by admonitions not to judge the art of one period by the criteria of another. There was indeed much to enjoy on the record, such as Margaret Philpot's singing of *Anglia, planctus itera*, but it came as a mild surprise to find, not that David Fallows was enthusiastic but that he was quite *so* enthusiastic ('the best record I have ever reviewed').

Still, from this I can learn; I can't from some of the nonsense surrounding the Pérotin record. This is by the Hilliard Ensemble, whose first sounds have one sitting up and taking a new look at the twelfth century; 'sensational' was the word that came to mind and stayed there though acquiring different meanings and tones-of-voice during the course. It would be wrong, of course it would be wrong, to suggest some kind of cheapness or vulgarity, for this is a scholarly production, and every detail has been carefully, imaginatively worked over and thought about. Yet the immediate reaction (strengthened by a return to David Munrow for comparison) was to feel that they were willing into existence a certain kind of music, a Pérotin who would make connections with modern movements, might even attract a 'sophisticated' listener to (what am I to call it?) very up-market pop. It was interesting then to find this immediate reaction confirmed by Paul Hillier'sbooklet-note which, while containing a certain amount of useful information, took its 'inspirational' tone from some of the most pretentious and (as they stand) meaningless quotations ever gathered into one small space outside 'Pseuds' Corner'. From Thoreau's *Walden* comes: 'All sounds heard at the greatest possible distance produce one and the same effect, a vibration of the universal lyre'. Steve Reich is brought in, as well as gnomic utterances by Stravinsky, Alexandra David-Neal and the ninth-century *Musica Enchiriadis*. We are also told: 'One must know three things if one is to write an organum: how to begin, how to proceed, and how to conclude'. Indeed one must, and in that respect writing an organum is very like making an omelette, going to war or using the photocopier; the fact that the advice comes 'from an anonymous St Martial treatise' hardly makes wisdom out of what I should think must have been tedious commonplace even in the ninth century.

Singers: welcome for five

The five singers before us now are all well established and well deserving of the recital which they have to themselves; for several this is their first on record or at least the first to come to our notice. Two of these five came to me for first review. Cheryl Studer's recital of Italian arias surprised in the first place because of its concentration on the 'coloratura' repertoire. What has haunted the memory and called me back to it is the lyric aria which opens the record, 'Ah, non credea mirarti' from *La sonnambula*. The voice is touchingly beautiful and a fine art is shown in the use of portamento varied with 'straight' intervals; also in the brightening of the tone at the modulation into C major and in the graces of a well-spun trill and a cadenza in which the upper notes are taken easily and without any tendency to harden (contrast the otherwise exquisite Toti dal Monte). Giuseppe Morino's lyric tenor recital is also something that simply must be heard by listeners who are at all interested in such matters. He has some serious faults, but I played again the 'A te, o cara' from *I puritani*, which is surely in the best Italian tradition, elegantly turned, finely schooled and graced with just a slight flicker of the quick vibrato which can so add to the attractiveness and individuality of a voice.

Of the others, the one new to most of us, though well-established in France, is Françoise Pollet. A soprano with a mezzo's warmth and roundness, she sings most beautifully in a repertoire that includes such forgotten things as Gounod's *Cinq Mars* and Saint-Saëns's *Henry VIII*. As in the complete *Les Huguenots* there is some want of ease and a slight loss of quality on the top notes; it is also difficult to inject intensity into such a very comfortable tone. But here is certainly a career to watch with interest, and the recital is one to collect while still available. The contralto Marjana Lipovšek is by now well known over here, and her recital is also something special – for a contralto is what she really is, and that of itself is rare these days. Of course she has the full range of a Verdi mezzo and sings 'O don fatale' without blanching. But the upper notes are not generally of the same fine quality as the lower ones, and the real glory of the voice is heard in the lower tessitura of Azucena's music or of Orfeo's. I also think that, fine artist as she is, she has something to learn about characterizing with the voice for an audience that can use only its ears: her Carmen doesn't seduce or insinuate, and her Dorabella sounds like very much the same person as her Sesto.

Something of the kind might be said about Dmitri Hvorostovsky. His Verdi and Tchaikovsky recital is dramatically convincing as well as being extremely well sung, yet the final impression is that we have been through a series of human experiences and situations but not as though with a sequence of different human-beings. Perhaps it's too much to ask of a first recital that it should be otherwise, and in any case at this stage in a singer's career the singing, as voice and voice-production, matters far more. The voice here is of superlative quality; full-bodied and resonant with great beauty of tone throughout an ample range. It is managed with care for evenness, both within the individual note and in the movement from one to another, and a prime stylistic concern is for breadth of phrase (I can't recall that any of the old masters on record span the phrases of 'Il balen' as he does). Where he will need to exercise restraint, I think, is on the high Fs and Gs where from time to time the vibrations loosen a trifle dangerously (an example is the phrase 'Leonora è mia' in the *Trovatore* recitative). His is still the finest new baritone voice and the most impressive first operatic recital heard on record for some years.

1991

The Mozart centenary

Anniversaries I rather like: they are good for memory and they let you know how the year is getting along. Centenaries are a different matter. They disturb the even flow, the regular rhythm of the year, and in proportion to the status of the subject they can be just a trifle heavy. At times one feels impelled to murmur, as though quoting scripture, that centenaries were made for man and not t'other way round.

The Mozart centenary has still the best part of a year to go before reaching the day itself, but already we are deeply committed. Mozart's death was of course deplorable and ever to be lamented, but, turning over the 23 pages (triple columns) which list recordings of his works in the current *Gramophone Classical Catalogue*, I am not at all convinced that this is any good reason for vastly adding to them. The operas are my immediate concern. The present count up to December 1990 is as follows: *Così fan tutte* (14), *Don Giovanni* (12), *Die Entführung aus dem Serail* (8), *Idomeneo* (5), *Le nozze di Figaro* (14), *Die Zauberflöte* (15). The others (*La clemenza di Tito*, *La finta giardiniera*, *Lucio Silla* and so forth) understandably do less well. Still, it is not only in quantity but in quality also that Mozart has been well served right from the early days of LP when the new singers from the Vienna State Opera made such an impression in the post-war years. New recordings will have to be very good to justify their place in these congested lists.

One that does have some ready justification is the Drottningholm *Don Giovanni* under Arnold Oestman, for its use of period instruments and the fast speeds possible in a period theatre reveal the opera in a new light. Early in the Overture, as the scrawny violins play their wary, scary chromatic figure in the shade of the proportionately enlarged brass and woodwind, they may not delight the ear but they do bring a little *frisson* of the supernatural; dry bones in the charnel-house shifting under the glare of those portentous chords. There are many places (in both of Zerlina's arias for instance) where the orchestration gains a new flavour, partly through tone-colour, partly through the rebalancing of forces; and always the entrance of brass and timpani has enhanced effect, a flash of scarlet and gold with at times the effective addition of blackness. Dramatic cohesion is another gain, and the confidential, sometimes whispered recitative suits the scale of performance. The solo singing indeed tends to be too confidential with not enough sense of projection or use of full voice. Della Jones, who as Elvira is so clean and assured in all passages of technical difficulty, seems less than her full self because of this intimacy, and Arleen Auger, lovely in 'Non mi dir', seems unable or unwilling to put an edge to the voice, so that Donna Anna remains a gracious but somewhat insubstantial presence. Håkan Hagegård, whisper-singing Don Giovanni's Serenade and lightweight in his drinking-song, makes only a slight impression, and the Ottavio, Nico van der Meel, drifts insubstantially in and out of the performance, so that the zest of Gilles Cachemaille's Leporello is trebly welcome. Excellent, though, are the Zerlina and Masetto, Barbara Bonney and Bryn Terfel, whose voice has real flesh and blood in it, bringing Masetto up into the front-line of the principals.

So, some gratitude is due there. Very mixed feelings, however, pursue the two *Così fan tuttes* – it was Spike Hughes who used to get so cross when people spoke of 'Così' but it's a convenience, and he, sadly, is no longer here to complain, so: the two *Cosìs*. The second, which I heard first, is under Sir Neville Marriner and has been widely admired. There is certainly much to enjoy, with Anne Sofie von Otter and Thomas Allen especially well paired as Dorabella and Guglielmo, though Karita Mattila has some uneasy moments as Fiordiligi and José van Dam needs to give a bit more edge to his Alfonso. More seriously (and I am differing here somewhat from AB's view of it as well-paced) there is a tendency to find a particularly lovely, reflective passage and try to make it lovelier still by taking it particularly slowly (slowly, that is, in relation to the norms of tempo set for the rest). 'Soave sia il vento', 'Un aura amorosa', 'Sento, o Dio', 'Il core vi dono' and 'Volgi a me pietoso' are instances where this long-drawn-out treatment does not, in my view, serve a good purpose at all. But if misgivings arise here, they are nothing compared to the curses, 'not loud but deep' as Macbeth says, that accompanied my playing of the Barenboim set. A ponderous start, no life in the *allegro*, no fun in the trio, an old-sounding Guglielmo, an unpolished Alfonso, an ill-matched pair of girls, a wrongly cast Despina (the excellent Joan Rodgers, who sings admirably but is now much more a Fiordiligi than a Despina), an intolerably funereal tempo for 'Sento, o Dio', a disproportionately fast *presto* in the finale … No, it is exactly this kind of recording which let us trust the Mozart centenary will not bring forth.

Records and the whole truth

They don't tell us all, these records of ours, and certainly they tell less than collectors, critics and historians would like to think. With singers whom we never heard in the flesh we are often on comfortable, secure terms: there's a purity about the relationship too, for on record the essence of their art is filtered, free from the ill-chances of history, personality or looks. With those whom we are currently hearing in the opera house and concert hall there are complications, adjustments to be made as we listen to their records. Sometimes the sound coming from the speakers is different, and sometimes (so attuned our ears have become) we hear 'in the flesh' with a kind of superimposed awareness of what the singing would be like as recorded sound. Still, these things are manageable. Where I find difficulty, and one that disturbs, is with singers whose live voices were once part of the fabric of living, and whom I hear now only on record. It's rather like the photograph kept for remembrance; after a while the person has become the photograph. The singer's physical presence (including the living voice) grows dimmer; the record-image gets brighter. I can't say that I like the process.

Of all improbable singers, Elisabeth Schwarzkopf is the one who now brings all this to mind: 'improbable' because she was such a gifted, natural and prolific recording artist that her performances, live and recorded, seemed to be one and the same thing. The whole of Schwarzkopf, you would say, is there on the record. The six recent birthday issues almost persuade that this is so after all, for the riches are inexhaustible … the Mozart songs with Gieseking accompanying, Gieseking's own songs, the incomparable Donna Elvira, the deeper-toned 1965 Schubert Lieder, the Wolf (exquisite *Die Bekehrte*, *Mignon*, *Philine*), the Johann II and Richard Strauss (a fine proud Czárdás from *Die Fledermaus*, an infinitely tender *Meinem Kinde*), the encores (delightful Wolf-Ferrari and deeply, unexpectedly moving, her own favourite, *Danny Boy*). They are timely restoratives.

For 30 years, Schwarzkopf, heard live and mostly in London's Royal Festival Hall (which she never liked), stood before us and seemed to me to embody the great traditions of European singing more fully and enduringly than any other singer then before the public. But absence, which is supposed to make the heart grow fonder, really gives the mind a chance for reappraisal. It is quite possible to borrow other people's ears for a while, and, with them, Schwarzkopf's characterizations – Gretel, Marschallin, Fiordiligi, Eva – could be made to sound like assumptions; grief and gaiety in the Lieder could be no more than dressing in black or spring-colours for the occasion; modifications of vowel-sounds, infinitesimal twinges of intonation, could become features of a vocal caricature; and occasionally something hard in tone or expression would affect the perception of voice-character. Insidiously some such process has attended those ten years of absence: the birthday issues have not merely checked but reversed it. Not that everything on these is equally welcome: the *adagio Der Nussbaum* is an example of a 'policy' decision about interpretation, surely to be abandoned; the *Four Last Songs* with Karajan fall somewhere between the studio performances with Otto Ackermann and George Szell but are (to my ears) less satisfying than either. The six CDs nevertheless remain treasured possessions, and strongly support the opinion expressed earlier of Schwarzkopf's place in the tradition. What they do not do is tell us all: in some elusive way they alter the image. There are gains, perhaps, as well as losses, but if I make an effort I can still close my eyes, look beyond the record-image, beyond the photograph, and catch the artist as she was, standing before us: and that is something more.

Enescu's Oedipe

The lending and borrowing of ears are of course among the main functions and purposes of written criticism, and the loan of Lionel Salter's from London and Andrew Porter's from New York has been particularly helpful in listening to this masterpiece of Enescu's. The Monte Carlo performance under Lawrence Foster is a triumph for the participants as well as for the opera itself, with José van Dam's singing of the exhausting title-role standing as one of the most notable achievements of his distinguished career. Barbara Hendricks, Brigitte Fassbaender, Marjana Lipovšek, John Aler, Nicolai Gedda, Gino Quilico and Gabriel Bacquier would make a formidable team for any vocal seven-a-side; worth mention too is Jean-Philippe Courtis as the Theban Watchman.

And a musical masterpiece is what the opera surely is, though the booklet-writer's description of it as 'a supreme masterpiece in the history of opera' raises some objections. The timing, the feeling for climax, strikes me as weak. For instance, the happiness and sweetness of the opening having contrasted effectively with the gloomy prelude, tension is then dissipated in dances and reiterations of the good hopes already established, so that Tiresias's 'Hélas!', which signposts the way to tragedy, has missed its moment. The cries of 'Douleur!', heightening the drama, should intensify the music. In opera this is the place for an ensemble in which everybody's feelings can find lyrical expression; but the music doesn't flower, relapses instead into a more declamatory style, and the operatic opportunity has passed. This kind of thing occurs at several key-points, and what is operatically successful in the score has more to do with the creation of atmosphere. There is something of the cantata about it; something intractable too in the four-act layout. Sophocles and Stravinsky (*Oedipus Rex*), with their dramatic concentration, just about manage to avoid questions ('Do you mean to say that in all those years of his reign and his married life Oedipus learnt nothing about how his predecessor met his end?' and more of the same tiresome commonsensical kind); but when the drama is spread out, with realistic family settings, it forfeits something in sheer credibility. It then becomes essential that the hero's character and development should be musically vivid, distinctive and compelling as (say) Godunov's or Grimes's; and, as far as I can make out, it is not.

Opera

Nielsen's *Saul and David* has a more secure contact with the stage, but it is curious how both Nielsen and Enescu renounce or neglect or fail to perceive the moment of emotional climax when it arrives. In *Oedipe* it is surely the point when, after the horrors, the pain, the rejection by his people, young Antigone comes to her father's side and accompanies him into exile. In Nielsen's opera it should be the reconciliation of David and Saul in Act 3: 'See, he opens his arms', and David's 'King, my father' – but, whether out of reticence, or some lack of dramatic instinct, the moment goes by, not without feeling, but certainly not with the power it could have had (compare, for instance, the recognition of father and daughter in *Simon Boccanegra*). Still, it is a great pleasure to meet the work on record again. In most respects the new recording improves on its predecessor of 1972. Neeme Järvi conducts a more urgent, detailed performance than Horenstein's, and though Aage Haugland as Saul hasn't quite the keen projection and charisma of Christoff (Horenstein) in the role – or, one suspects, his share of the microphone – he and the others carry conviction and sound all the better for being in the original language. The member of the Horenstein cast I really missed was Söderström: Tina Kiberg (Järvi) lacks the fresh, girlish tone that Mikal needs and which Söderström brought to the part.

It is extraordinary, in this context, how sure Beethoven's stage-instincts proved to be in *Fidelio*. The new recording makes that very clear, if ever it was in question, and in those moments I want to call 'sacred' – the orchestral bars at the start of the quartet, the chords and first sounds of the Prisoners' chorus, Florestan's gratitude for the gift of water – the emotion is conveyed with no false touch. In his review, Edward Greenfield sees Bernard Haitink in this as nearer to Klemperer than to Karajan or Bernstein; comparison of their respective accounts of the Overture, attracts me towards Haitink, for if Klemperer with the Philharmonia has the majesty and power (the more vivid orchestral colours too), Haitink here has the impulsiveness, excitement, mystery, the rustle of spring, the dancing life in the veins. Jessye Norman's vivid Leonore has rare beauty of tone, marvellously well controlled too so as not to overpower Marzelline in the quartet, and technically very able in the great solo. Kurt Moll, as ever, is an excellent Rocco – except for his loud entry on that inconsiderately written high first note of his – and Ekkehard Wlaschiha is an outstanding Pizarro. Reiner Goldberg's dry, rasping tone testifies to the quality of dungeon life and so might be acceptable if it were fortified by some inner fire or subtlety. He is not good, but EG puts the bleak question 'who else could Philips readily have chosen?', and it must be said that answers do not come like ten lambs a-leaping.

At least EMI, or La Scala rather, should have been able to find somebody better equipped than Ferruccio Furlanetto to sing Procida in *I vespri siciliani* under Riccardo Muti. No one, not even La Scala, can pick and choose over their Arrigo (Domingo has said it is as exhausting a role as Otello) and Chris Merritt carries it through with his customary stamina and supply of high notes, and with more spirit than he brought to his Arnoldo in *Guglielmo Tell*: he seems even to be picking up something of the frothy late-Pertile manner, which at least puts some life into his performance. But Giorgio Zancanaro is fine and Cheryl Studer excellent: at times she sounds like a more imaginative Elisabeth Rethberg (in her prime), and compliments cannot go much higher than that.

Incidentally, Studer's coloratura recital has met with some severe criticism both in this country and in France where, apparently, it ranks among the discs which in the second half of the century have caused the critic most consternation. As it had been among the records in my last year's 'Critics' Choice' I thought I had better go back and listen again. The principal gain was to hear and appreciate afresh performances in which an exceptionally beautiful voice is skilfully and feelingly used. It seems that the absence of a tenor in 'Sempre libera' has given offence, his phrases being played as an instrumental solo instead. Consulting my original notes I see a comment at this point 'Better!'. Consternation redoubled! But allow for a moment that Verdi might have written it that way. Would we not then say 'What genius! As the orchestra recalls Alfredo's affirmation of love, Verdi shows us the innermost thought which Violetta is repressing.' And what would we say about the interfering dolt who brought the tenor back to sing outside her window in crude physical presence?

Three more operas in brief now. To enjoy *La sonnambula* you must like the somnambulist. In the new recording she is Lucia Aliberti: fluent, showing signs of the Callas influence, and (I found) unappealing in tone and personality. John Aler's Elvino is worth hearing, Jésus López-Cobos conducts sensitively, but it's a vacuous opera, better kept to the 'highlights' records. *Samson et Dalila*, by contrast, has rarely sounded more substantial and well-packed than it does under Sir Colin Davis, who almost persuades us there is something of Berlioz in it. Baltsa, content to be merely bland in Act 1, gains conviction from 'Amour, viens aider'; her tone has a fine shiny resonance, but she seems (with frequency enough for it to become slightly alarming) to have some trouble with the C in the middle of the stave. Carreras's vocal troubles are more extensive but could be passed over, under the circumstances, if he had managed to capture some real exultancy in his 'Arrêtez' (overemphasis is made to serve instead) and to infuse grief into the tone from the start of the lament. I agree with Alan Blyth on the depressing qualities of Estes and Burchuladze and on the excellence of the chorus. From a little farther back, in November, I share EG's delight in the new *Hänsel und Gretel*. To his reservation over Eva Lind's Dew Fairy, I would add a question-mark concerning the Sandman of Barbara Hendricks who omits the little upward sweeps at the end of phrases (is there some textual doubt about their authenticity perhaps?). I also have to confess to a grumpy reaction to Anne Sofie von Otter's 'playing-children' voice: she uses it in some of her Mahler songs too, and the objection is partly that it's irritating and partly that children aren't like that.

Songs of Gurre and summer nights

One distinction of the new *Gurrelieder* is that the Waldemar sounds like a lover. Who have we had previously? Paul Althouse, Herbert Schachtschneider, Alexander Young, Jess Thomas, James McCraken. None of them, as I remember, combined the strength and the poetry, the heroic and the lyrical. There are times when Siegfried Jerusalem sounds taxed: the protesting cries of Part 2

(‘Herrgott, weisst du, was du tatest’) try him at their loudest and highest. But he is magically romantic in ‘So tanzen die Engel’ and meltingly tender in ‘Du wunderliche Tove’. Tove herself is Susan Dunn, who doesn’t quite have the radiance of spirit, but the tone is both ample and beautiful. Then we have Fassbaender’s Wood Dove, sorrow etched into her voice as it was in Dame Janet Baker’s when she sang the part. And Hotter as the Speaker – a touchingly affectionate, excited performance, not using the bass in his voice at all. And oh that last chorus, the ecstatic summation of all romanticism. I haven’t compared this version, under Riccardo Chailly, with others, but felt there was no need to – which usually means that all is well.

Equally, the *Nuits d’été* with five singers, John Eliot Gardiner conducting, provoked no desire to look further. A delicious lightness in the ‘Villanelle’, delicate spinning of that fine orchestral web at the start of ‘Le spectre de la rose’, a welcome frankness of emotion by Gilles Cachemaille in ‘Sur les lagunes’, a tender privacy of utterance by Diana Montague in ‘L’absence’, the ghostly tone of the pale dove singing among the yews caught to perfection by Howard Crook in ‘Au cimetière’, and a lovely out-of-bed freshness in ‘L’île inconnue’. That, as they say, for starters; manifold delights also in the rest of the programme.

Gardiner: Beethoven and Brahms

There is a joke going round that the organizers of the various annual record awards are thinking of instituting a John Eliot Gardiner Award. It is a joke because (of course) they are not. And its point is that Gardiner is now recording so much and so well and in such a wide repertoire that if he goes on expanding his activities at the present rate he is quite likely to come up as the winner of all the available award categories, with the possible exception of Solo Vocal.

This quarter has seen the issue of two works, Beethoven’s *Missa solemnis* and Brahms’s *German Requiem*, where he has changed the whole discographical map. The great Mass has certainly had some wonderful performances before now, but all the recordings are flawed in one way or another – the best of the three Toscaninis, from 1940, is still by modern standards primitive as a recording, the earlier and better of the Bernsteins gives the soloists too much prominence and has some trembly sopranos among the chorus, Klemperer on EMI is stodgy in the fugues, has an uneven quartet of soloists, and so forth. Gardiner has, I do believe, everything. Soloists, choir and orchestra, recording-balance, clarity without coldness: all the resources and conditions are fine. What then emerges is a performance which has control and abandon, delicacy and grandeur, restraint and recklessness, serenity and that necessary degree of fine madness. The forces are thinned (36 in the choir, orchestra of 60) and perhaps, brought up on the weightier sound, one sometimes misses some old Albert Hall-style opulence. But no: this is the performance to turn to.

The Brahms *German Requiem* gains in every conceivable way, but is immediately distinguished among recordings because Gardiner, quite exceptionally among conductors of this work, concludes that Brahms knew what was best for his own music when he set his metronome markings. Hardly anyone, for a start, seems to think that he can possibly have meant the first movement to go at crotchet=80. Bruno Walter did, and gained accordingly, and now Gardiner does. Similarly with the 'funeral' march (in 3/4), 'Denn alles Fleisch', it is not uncommon to find conductors (Levine and Barenboim for example) who for 60 read 50. The result, or a result, has been that so many listeners, like Gardiner himself at an impressionable age, have found it 'lugubrious and pompous, the German equivalent of Victoriana'. Mind, it should be added that Gardiner himself does not always follow the metronome marking: the opening section of the third movement, for instance, is notably faster, but then I've not found any conductor who believes in the very slow beat Brahms seems to have wanted here. As Lionel Salter says in his review, Rodney Gilfry, the baritone soloist, is 'a real find': a voice of excellent quality, just occasionally recalling the young Hermann Prey, and clearly a sensitive musician. Also it should be noted that, good as Gardiner's introductory notes are in the booklet, his article in the April issue is better still: an invaluable commentary on the performance and its background. Perhaps he should have an award for that too.

1992

Pavarotti's Otello

'Forget all the hype. Forget the larger-than-life figure of outdoor events, listen to the sincere and serious musician captured here as Otello.' Alan Blyth's wise, and warm, words at the start of his review do exactly the right and needful job of clearance: a whole clutter of prejudices, reporters' tittle-tattle, irrelevancies and partisanship has to be swept aside so that one can hear this new *Otello* for what it is. First, it is a great enrichment of our *Otello*-scape. That is, through all the notable tenors who have sung the whole role or part of it on record there is none that sounds like Pavarotti: his voice is completely his own and the voice itself is the great contribution, the extender of perceptions. It is still marvellously well produced, crystal-clear in timbre, utterly devoid of lumps and wrinkles in texture, unforced even in the most strenuous moments and modulating without any constriction when softer, gentler tones are called for. Moreover, it is put scrupulously to the service of the music. Nothing is exaggerated, self-advertising or cheaply 'effective'. And dramatically: certainly he has a great deal of the part inside him now in these first concert performances; even if no more evolves, a lot of Otello is already living a full life here, not simply in the great solos such as the Monologue and Death scene but in individual phrases, the new tenderness in 'la mia dolce Desdemona', the pained moral dizziness of 'credo leale è Desdemona e credo che non lo sia', the terrible abandon in 'E il ciel non ha più fulmini?'.

Now this is not of course the whole story, but I have another *Otello* to listen to and report on before this 'Quarterly' is through, and if previous listenings are anything to go by I fancy that what Pavarotti has not discovered yet will be found there. For the moment let's leave him and turn to other features of the recording. Solti's conducting, for instance. This I found surprising, for many of the anticipated excitements were not forthcoming, while the loveliness of quiet and tender passages gave unexpected pleasure. The bridge-passage leading into the Love duet, for instance, has surely never been more beautifully played, and the generous *rallentando* allowed in the 'Ave Maria' has the touch of personal affection that is so often pharasaically stigmatized as self-indulgent. Yet the storm in the opening seemed all too well-behaved, too controlled and steady in pressure to have real danger in it, and in Act 3 the fanfare seemed merely splendid, almost with a little jauntiness, rather than suggesting the tension, the dreadful straining of Otello's nerves in this ceremonial, and the need for outward order when he is consumed with inner turmoil. Still, at all times there is superb orchestral playing, and outstanding choral work too.

But what, oh what, can one say of Leo Nucci's Iago? AB's 'disappointing' and Manuela Hochterhoff's 'at-least-one-size-too-small' are surely mild comments on a performance which vocally is the very opposite of Pavarotti's – loose in focus, frequently rough and uneven, sometimes lifting to notes, sometimes going over the top both in pitch and dramatic gesture. Most of these faults and a few more are exemplified in the Credo. I differ from AB in not hearing Rolfe Johnson as 'a pleasantly lyrical Cassio' but, like him, enjoyed Kavrakos's Ludovico. And then there is Dame Kiri, whose Desdemona is *dolce* indeed. In this role her singing is remarkably little touched by the advancing years, unless to add warmth of feeling; and in the last Act she comes as near to the heavenly as we have any right to expect in this world.

The other Otello

Keeping the best till last, I have reserved the Metropolitan Opera's *Otello* of 1938 till a time when it could be played again immediately before writing, for the memory of a recording to which one has been insanely devoted for more than 20 years cannot always be trusted. Now that I have heard it again I can hardly trust myself to write. It is, how shall we say, a knockout. The conductor is Ettore Panizza who was Toscanini's assistant at La Scala and his successor in the Italian repertoire at the Metropolitan. He unleashes the most tempestuous of storms, one in which there is real danger for it might at any time run amok; he puts the vast forces of the Met orchestra and chorus through the *allegro vivace* chorus at a *presto* which rivals any Oestman or Norrington with their chosen few in Mozart. He expands and contracts with the singers; and if he doesn't always do what Verdi says in print he has inherited a tradition that knows Verdi from the inside. He leads the performance of an opera which the house had not heard for 34 years, and the excitement of that great score bursting upon a new generation is felt throughout.

Giovanni Martinelli, with the company since 1913, had kept the title-role back till he felt right for it and until it could crown (and to some extent revive) a worthy career. But that says nothing. He very probably did not have the voice for it but his portrayal, as it comes to us on record (there are at least four live performances from the Met) is one of the most intense and vivid of all operatic performances known to me. More, much more, could be said (including points at which he starts where Pavarotti leaves off). The Iago, Lawrence Tibbett, is also supreme, unless in modern times rivalled by Gobbi. Elisabeth Rethberg, at one time voted the world's most perfect singer, is just past being that, but is still a distinguished Desdemona. The recording of course is crackly (taken from a broadcast and made privately for Tibbett, I understand), but for the most part it is astonishingly vivid. It is also complementary to the new recording, which earns admiration, gives pleasure, is sometimes quite deeply moving, while this one blazes. Come to think of it, that was AB's word too. 'A blazing night at the Met' he said. And not extinguished yet.

The Sound of History

With varying degrees of sympathy and exasperation, faithful readers of these notes will have observed that, as far as recorded sound is concerned, technical matters are given a wide berth. Frequency-responses, curves, ambisonics and roll-offs are not to be met with here; if anything is 'digital' it will be 'dexterity' or its like rather than 'remastering'. A KHz has never consorted with a mere Hz in these chaste columns, and polypropylene capacitors are not on the menu. Still, this is only a way we non-scientists have of contriving to sound superior to these mysteries by means of a cultivated ironical detachment, and I now wish I had the scientific knowledge to analyse what it is I find so nasty in several recent transfers of old recordings on to CD, the immediate cause being EMI's 'Wagner Singing on Record'.

This is a highly desirable four-disc set, comparable to the Mozart 'Introuvables', but potentially attractive to a wider public because it draws exclusively on the electrical period of recording covering those years (roughly 1925 to 1955) when most of the great Wagnerian singers of the century were active. Alan Blyth reviewed it enthusiastically, in the same month welcoming the 1936-7 *Tristan und Isolde* from Covent Garden with Kirsten Flagstad and Lauritz Melchior, another of the treasures of time, the restoration of which puts us greatly in EMI's debt. The Wagner anthology is packed with fine things, and normally one would use this limited space to select a few of them for appreciative comment – a superb Gerhard Hüsch, for instance, in *Tannhäuser*, and the rare and fascinating Dutchman of Arthur Endrèze. But, though I played the discs in the 'kindest' possible way, I found that the sound-quality repeatedly distracted attention from the very thing it was supposed to illuminate, the performance itself. In his review, AB noted Maria Müller's 'Dich, teure Halle' at the start of the second disc as being subject to distortion, and in a more general comment wrote that 'the voices sometimes have an uncomfortable edge'. That is certainly true, but instruments also (the violins in the duet which follows, the oboe in the Good Friday Music for instance) have a bright, hard, acid quality that gnaws away at the pleasure of listening. Long before I was conscious of this as a recurrent complaint, let alone any notion that it might become a main theme in writing, my notes were sprinkled with 'v. clear but rather harsh transfer … bright aggressive edge … excessively harsh in trumpets as well as voice … v. toppy … transfer getting v. harsh … now getting hard, gritty recorded sound'. All of that (I find, looking over the notes) is before the second disc.

Now this may be, if you like, the vice of a great virtue, that of bringing out with ever greater clarity all that is on the original recording. Regularly in these transfers the singers' consonants (for example) are more forward, the 's' and 't' sounds sharper than before. With that comes a more vivid picture of the artist as actor-with-the-voice: Frida Leider's 'Ich sah das Kind', for example, is remarkably a face-to-face encounter. Also, when the sound is good, as in the *Meistersinger* Quintet, the greatly loved recording gains from the clarity which separates the strands. Even so, one comes back to transfers such as those of Melchior's *Tristan* solos admirably forward and clear, but becoming coarse and simply unpleasant as recorded sound, though the performances themselves are eminently treasurable.

This set (and hence the point of highlighting the matter) represents a trend: it is something noticed for a long time, namely that the makers of 'historic' transfers have a very natural inclination to want the old recordings to sound as much like modern ones as possible, with the result that at worst they do sound like modern recordings – but bad ones. That itself is symptomatic of a larger tendency concerning sound recording and reproduction. If the Editor will indulge me in the matter I will tell two stories, not irrelevant to these quarterly retrospects concerned with 'the gramophone and the voice'. One: in company with some others who spend much time professionally listening to records, or producing them, I sat and heard a recording by a famous soprano of the present day played on presumably tip-top equipment set up by the firm that produced the disc. The voice, in which every tiny idiosyncrasy was remorselessly exposed, had its pure singing-tone almost constantly overlaid by a kind of patina, a rattle of glinting 'surface-scratch' – which of course the recording and its reproduction hadn't invented, but which (as I knew because I had heard the singer quite recently) had been brought out far beyond its proportionate place in the total 'image' of the voice as heard in the flesh. Nobody present objected, possibly because this was not the subject under discussion. But my fear is that this is what is regarded and accepted now as 'good' recording: good for the orchestra and therefore good for the voice. And the second story is this. When 'the men', decorators, etc., move in, they bring the radio with them. This decorator's radio was a trial anyway, but worse because excruciatingly off-centre in the tuning. Surreptitiously I tuned it in so that the noise was at any rate not grossly distorted. But the adjustment was soon detected, with disapproval.'You don't want to do that,' he explained. 'Expensive radio that is. Spoils the hi-fi that does.'

Siegfried: Haitink and Levine

Here are two recordings of *Siegfried*, one of them highly distinguished. The first, under James Levine, has to be heard; very probably has to be had. Yet one may wonder whether it is possible to recommend either of these versions when one has the title-role sung by a tenor whose Wagnerian repertoire in an ideal world would probably stop at Lohengrin, and the other has a Siegfried who in a well-cast *Ring* cycle would be singing Loge. Unfortunately, it is the Levine recording that has the Loge/Siegfried (Reiner Goldberg), while the less interesting Bernard Haitink has at least the Lohengrin, Siegfried Jerusalem. It is true that Jerusalem has sung Siegfried to considerable acclaim at Bayreuth, but on recordings he sounds merely pleasant: in itself, no doubt, something to be thankful for, but he commands little of that exuberantly healthy ring that is needful throughout the Siegfried voice and especially at the top. It may also be that Goldberg's Siegfried has been accounted a success on stage, but on record the voice-character is utterly miscast: there's a dryness, a surface-rasp, a littleness. However regrettable the fact (and however unlikeable the word), Siegfried does need sheer vocal bulk.

The question of *Heldentenor* apart, we are not in an ideal world as far as most of the other principal singers are concerned either. The Wanderer, James Morris, is common to both versions, and that must be another sign of the times. He is one of those singers who, in my own experience and opinion, gives notably more satisfaction in the theatre than on disc. The recorded voice too often sounds to me, not crudely unsteady, but not really firm or even; and there is something, not throaty, but not quite satisfyingly open and forthright in certain of his vowel sounds. Listening to the Wanderer's part in both of these recordings brings a frustration that is only in part due to the singer (who does much very well, particularly in his clean, resourceful way with the taxing upper notes). More at fault is the recording balance, which in both versions relegates the voice too severely in favour of the orchestra. It may be said that this reflects the natural balance, the sound as it would be heard from a seat in the opera house. But that won't do. In the theatre we use our eyes, and focus upon the characters on stage: our eyes bring the character and the sound of the voice forward in the balance of our attention. On disc the studio producer must be our eyes and ensure that the singers come well forward so that they are the focus of the drama here as they are in the opera house. The noble music written for Wotan in this opera demands that he himself – that is, on disc, the voice of Wotan – should be right in the foreground. Here, in both of these recordings, he is merely part of the aural scenery.

But that scenery has infinite richness of orchestral sound in the Levine version. Just to deal briefly with the other singers first (for they are part of it too), the one role which is sung as in an ideal world is Ekkehard Wlaschiha's Alberich, and that is with Levine; also Levine's Brünnhilde, Hildegard Behrens, is preferable in every way to Haitink's, Eva Marton, and, though Behrens had (in my view) limited success in the DG recordings of *Die Walküre* and *Götterdämmerung*, the *Siegfried* Brünnhilde suits her present vocal condition very well, for its tessitura calls upon the best part of her voice and her imagination feeds happily on the awakening. But it is the orchestral playing, and the response to a special pictorial quality in the conductor's vision of detail, that are of supreme value in Levine's recording. Almost any point would serve as illustration: the very opening, for instance, where the brass menaces and it is as though dim shapes lumber in darkness – Haitink, by comparison, captures less tension and fear, less of a jumpy, nervous atmosphere that has one peering into the gloom, aware of shadows that might at any moment pitch and pounce.

Siegfried 1937

Among the terrors of childhood was the earwig, which, having gained entrance through its favourite channel, would travel ceaselessly along the corridors of the brain and send you mad. In adult life the earwig has been replaced by Wagner (or sometimes Bach). Wagner is a terror for taking possession through a single phrase or harmonic sequence, and then spiralling, banished for a moment while you give your mind to tying up a shoelace, then back he comes with forces recruited from the memory-bank, which is where he has been during his brief and wily absence. Like Amfortas's wound which never stops bleeding, the chromatics of *Parsifal* and *Tristan* twist and turn throughout eternity: Kirsten Flagstad could never go to bed after a performance of *Tristan* but would knit or play Patience for hours before the music began to leave her alone. You go out for a drink with your neighbour and all the time a voice sings within (for this is what it was on this most recent occasion): 'Wache, erwache, du Wala! Erwache!'. Your neighbour does not know that that is what your mind is repeating to itself throughout his discourse; but such is the truth. Wagner, the mighty earwig, is taking vengeance for having been switched off in the middle of the Third Act of his *Siegfried*.

The voice of Wotan the Wanderer in this instance was that of Friedrich Schorr, which may have had something to do with it, for I don't recall that on the previous encounter with *Siegfried* (which was a double one, involving the two new recordings under, respectively, Haitink/EMI and Levine/DG) there was any comparable need for exorcism. Wotan then in both versions had been James Morris, who on record, good as he is (and he's better in the flesh), had produced no thrill, none of that rapture of recognition affirming that voice-and-music are indeed godlike. Schorr did produce just such a thrill: that is, from the very first sound of him, in his interview with Mime, the beauty of voice and scrupulous evenness of production worked with the broad phrases of Wagner's music to embody a nobility in which one could exult. This is so, even though the year of the recording is 1937, when Schorr was probably just past his best. Nevertheless it still stands, even though the recording is technically appalling, from the Metropolitan, New York, made from one of the broadcast Saturday matinees in the series, currently appearing on the Music & Arts label. Alan Blyth reviewed it with, I think, feelings like my own, for he wrote that the thrill of the performance rendered contingent annoyances of 'click and crackle', 'dim moments' and 'grievous cuts' virtually null and void. In fact he went a little further than I would have done in praising. It is that which draws me to comment further now, for I fear an initial disillusionment, or at any rate bewilderment. Surveying the marvellous cast of this performance, AB said: 'Because it is his opera, pride of place must go to Melchior.' Lauritz Melchior was, of course, the pre-eminent *Heldentenor* of his time and probably, as most are coming to accept, of the century. But a listener without prior knowledge of him might well conclude that, in the first scene at least, he does no real singing at all.

The conductor, Artur Bodanzky, may be the culprit: from Siegfried's entry he goes at a great pace, and when he sees *sehr schnell* in the score it is like a bit of speeded-up film, and utterly unsingable. But Melchior and he aid and abet each other. So far from the singer trying to pull back, Melchior seems to be urging forward, with everything enunciated at the rate of rapid speech and with the absolute minimum of opportunity left for singing on the vowel. Listeners who can compare his studio performance recorded with Heger conducting in 1927 will hear how what was then a fast-moving, lively and natural exercise in a thoroughly musical kind of speech-sing has become a scramble. In some degree, this tendency of Melchior's not to give notes their full singing-value is present throughout that afternoon's performance. My feeling is that by this stage in his career, Melchior's grasp of these roles he had sung so often, and in which he had almost the monopoly, was increasingly applied to the verbal text (which he renders fluently, expressively and with an unexpected admixture of humour); and I wonder how often he refreshed his memory of the minims, the dotted crotchets, the full value of the notes in the vocal score.

Fassbaender's Schwanengesang

If one asks what modern singer has the power or the knack of generating excitement – that is, not just pleasure, admiration, but a thrill, a racing of the blood, a sense of momentary exposure to the divine fire – there might be many names to consider, but for myself, pre-eminently and unhesitatingly, I would name Brigitte Fassbaender. There has always been a strength and striking individuality about her, but in the last ten years or so her art has been that of a mastersinger in the full glory of achievement. Her *Schwanengesang* with Aribert Reimann is, I should think, of all song recordings one of those in which it is least possible to lose concentration at any point from first note to last. It is typical of the vigour of her musical personality that what she and her partner offer is a newly thought-out re-ordering of the songs: that of itself concentrates the mind. But essentially it is the magnetic quality of expressiveness and of the voice itself: its power to catch the depth of foreboding and anguish in 'Kriegers Ahnung', the adventurous spirit of 'Abschied', the haunted intensity of 'Am Meer'. 'Am Meer', 'Ihr Bild', 'Die Stadt', 'Der Doppelgänger', 'Der Atlas', in that order, bring the collection to an end, working together as a final movement of surely incomparable tragic concentration and might. I can't think of another woman singer (even Gerhardt or Lehmann) who could have brought this off as Fassbaender does.

Spoken

It is not often that the spoken word concerns us in these columns. Occasionally composers use a narrator, as Stravinsky and Cocteau did in *Oedipus Rex*, or as Vaughan Williams did in his *Song of Thanksgiving*, performed movingly though less sonorously than of yore by Sir John Gielgud in a fine recording under Matthew Best. Occasionally, incidental music is recorded in its dramatic context, as is Mendelssohn's *A Midsummer Night's Dream* score under Jeffrey Tate on a two-disc set: and in this, Shakespeare's play or a generous portion of it is spoken in the most lacklustre fashion by members of the Peter Hall Company. As it happened, and it truly was by chance and not design, I then played Copland's *Lincoln Portrait* conducted by Wyn Morris with narration by (as she was then) the Rt Hon Margaret Thatcher. I played it out of mild curiosity and with some hopes of amusement: but by comparison with that deadpan Titania, that golf-club bore of a Theseus, that inept Puck and those humourless rustics, this speaking (despite repetitious cadences and unintentional ironies) might have been by Dame Sybil or Dame Edith, not to mention Dame Edna.

1993

Chérubin

The great delight of this quarter has been Massenet's *Chérubin*. I really think it is his masterpiece. The charming, subtle undertaking has been achieved to perfection. The whole concept, the story, the libretto, the musical idiom, all are so happily inventive, lit from within by wit and affection. The score is quicksilver, magically nimble in spirit and technique. It might just be that the original cast (Garden, Renaud, Carré, Cavalieri) gave a better performance at Monte-Carlo in 1903, and it is always possible that a preferable recording lies ahead with goodness knows what superlative artists of the future, but this present issue will do very well for the time being.

Frederica von Stade sings the title-role, with grace in the introductory minute-long minuet-like song ('Nous danserons'), with fine adolescent gallantry when honour is at stake, with ardour in the love music and a touchingly restrained pathos when it seems for a while that this seventeenth birthday of Cherubino's may be his last. Cherubino, doing well in the army, has gained his commission; but his days of philandering are by no means over and from his mansion in Seville he bids fair to rival the town's (and Mozart's) still more celebrated lover, Don Juan. At present he is enamoured of the great dancer, L'Ensoleillad (June Anderson), but still has a fondness for little Nina (Dawn Upshaw), who is hopelessly in love with him. If vocal charms could settle the matter, Nina would win. Upshaw sings enchantingly and preserves the simple generosity of character with warmth and delicacy. Anderson, in the more brilliant role, begins to show some deterioration in the upper range, though she still gives an accomplished performance and has some heavenly music to sing. The other main character is called the Philosopher, Cherubino's tutor, wryly observant, wise and good-natured. Samuel Ramey, ideally firm and clean in his singing, presents a somewhat formal personality where we really want the touch of a French Don Alfonso.

Still, the hero of this event is not any member of the cast, nor yet the excellent Munich orchestra or their conductor Pinchas Steinberg, but Massenet himself. The Overture immediately proclaims him to be on top form, with its trilling expectancy in the first bars, its pace and gaiety, one good tune after another, all sparkle and lightness at one point, blissfully romantic the next. And this opera – as is not always the case – fully lives up to the promise of its Overture. Its success raises several questions. One is how well we can reckon to know Massenet, even after so remarkable an extension to the general familiarity as the last two decades have brought (only this quarter another 'unknown' opera, his *Cléopâtre*, has resurfaced on Koch Schwann; no masterpiece but well worth the revival).

Another question is whether it is not time for a reappraisal. At any rate, *Chérubin* strengthens a conviction that Massenet's misfortune was that the operatic taste of his time committed him so largely to the production of tragedies, while his gifts lay elsewhere. He is best when happy and when sad about lost happiness. *Chérubin* gives him ideal scope and finds him at his most assured and mature, the full master of his craft. At the very least it stands in relation to the rest of his work as *Gianni Schicchi* does to the rest of Puccini's; but this recording has left me with the distinct impression that in a general revaluation of Massenet it should go right to the top as being the most finely-wrought, joyfully creative work in his output: or perhaps we should say in the whole of his output known to the general public to date.

The opera season

With the French school well represented by *Chérubin* and to a lesser extent *Cléopâtre*, we turn to the Russian. The three cards are here again ('Troika! semyorka! tuz!' – 'Three! seven! ace!' making a significant addition to the opera-goer's stock of Useful Russian, otherwise restricted to 'ya lyublyu tyebya' – 'I love you' – and lugubrious exclamations concerning God and death). *The Queen of Spades* gains probably its best modern recording in the new one under Seiji Ozawa. I never managed to enjoy the Emil Tchakarov Sony Classical recording quite as much as AB did, so perhaps the pleasure in this has been disproportionately heightened. But *The Queen of Spades* is one of those operas in which one must feel from the start that its special nature is caught in the performance: the yearning, the lurking passions. The Prelude here bodes well. Then there is strong casting in the Yeletsky and Tomsky (Dmitri Hvorostovsky and Sergei Leiferkus), and something to look forward to in the Countess of Maureen Forrester (the voice still rich, the manner in her great scene affectionate in dreamy reminiscence, then horribly vivid in death). So much depends on the Herman. Vladimir Atlantov is now a subtler artist than he was when he made the Philips recording under Mark Ermler, and his voice can still be thrillingly full-bodied yet tense. He lacks the refinement of some of the early Russians, and he has not the full measure of neurosis with which the Glyndebourne Herman, Yuri Marusin, so transfixed his audiences (but how would all that neurotic flattening sound on record, I wonder?).

It is still a distinguished and compelling performance. The main trouble with the set lies in the beat which plagues Mirella Freni's voice in crucial passages such as the despairing phrases of her duet with Herman in the last Act. In many ways her Lisa is a great achievement, and there have been many younger singers who have been quite as unsteady and not half as pure in tone; but her ageing voice is an ever-present threat to the credibility of the character as a young woman, and to the beauty of her music.

Freni's part in this opera, however, is a liability of quite a different, and minor, order compared with that presented by Eva Marton in *Götterdämmerung*. This marks the completion of the cycle under Haitink: often satisfying, rarely exciting. Fine singing comes from Jard van Nes as the First Norn, Thomas Hampson as Gunther, Marjana Lipovšek as Waltraute, and most essentially from Siegfried Jerusalem, who lacks only that extra degree of weight and thrust to meet the full demands of the 'mature hero', the Siegfried of this opera. John Tomlinson is a Hagen in the Ludwig Weber mould, putting to good use his 'great gunmetal voice' (Walter Legge on Weber): yet every now and then a note bulges or otherwise loses shape, as for instance does the first syllable of 'neiden' in Hagen's second phrase. That is the kind of thing that has been not an incidental but a regular feature of Theo Adam's singing, yet he too makes a valuable contribution with his keenly characterized, brightly projected Alberich. The Brünnhilde, however, is crucial. Marton has the power and energy for the part, and that is much; but for steadiness in the emission of sound, for beauty of tone, sensitivity of nuance, I find it profitless to hope. There were moments in Marton's singing of Minnie in the new *La fanciulla del West* which yielded something positive to report. From this great role in *Götterdämmerung* I gained only tribulation, with the sole glimmer of a supposition that this powerful singer may shortly have recorded her complete repertoire.

A singer who has been recording for the past 35 years or so and who on present showing is welcome to return as often as he chooses is Rolando Panerai. On the other hand, if he should decide to draw the line below it now, then his career on records will have been worthily crowned by the *Falstaff* he recorded in 1991 under Sir Colin Davis with Julia Kaufmann as a particularly lovely Nanetta and the whole cast doing well. Davis gives a ripe, generous and unexaggerated account of the score, and Panerai not only characterizes with his customary vitality but his singing is still that of a genuine exponent of the art (his 'Vado a farmi bello' warms the cockles like a good sherris sack).

In *Luisa Miller* the heartening factor is the appearance of a genuine, and genuinely distinguished, Verdi baritone in Vladimir Chernov. He makes a fine impression from the start, but 'Sacra la scelta' proclaims an excellence comparable to that of Renato Bruson when, a good many years ago now, we first heard him in the part. I couldn't respond to the supposed appeal of Aprile Millo in the title-role; she deals creditably with technical difficulties, but neither voice nor temperament seems happily suited. Domingo's Rodolfo has been here before and it would have been interesting to have heard somebody else, say Neil Shicoff, in the part. But what a magnificent orchestra Levine now conducts at the Metropolitan; something of the Toscanini touch makes itself felt in the assurance, discipline and virtuosity of their playing.

Mass and oratorio

Two of the greatest Masses have returned to the lists, and Bach's B minor is in duplicate, with the Leipzig and Dresden forces under Peter Schreier and Richard Hickox conducting the Collegium Musicum 90. Schreier's is fine when he leaves his editing pencil at home and stops marking points. The short-long, staccato-legato policy, the 'pairing' of quavers in the *Kyrie* fugue-subject, the staccato semiquavers of the 'Christe', the staccato instrumental bass in the second *Kyrie*: points which if less insistently made would be quite happily assimilated become fussily obtrusive. Comparison with Hickox demonstrates: he too has a phrasing-policy and knows all about the effectiveness of the short-long, but such points are observed lightly, incidentals in a performance which has a seemingly natural grace and which carries complete conviction. Particularly happy is the lightness of texture, as in the 'Laudamus te', taken fast though with graceful easings of the tempo and with the bass minimally weighted so that the number becomes an arabesque joyfully untrammelled in its energy. The solo work is unfailingly good, and it is remarkable that Stephen Varcoe can cope so successfully with his two arias, so different in character that they normally seem to call for two singers.

The Beethoven Masses both came to me for first review, so I ought probably to canvas the opinion of a colleague for the 'Retrospect'. I shall in fact be curious to discover what is the general view, particularly about the *Missa solemnis*. 'The most luxurious *Missa solemnis* of our time' was the proud announcement: critics have a knee-jerk reaction to this sort of thing. Many a record has been the victim of its own hype, and it would be a great pity if that were to happen in this instance. The line-up of soloists (Cheryl Studer, Jessye Norman, Domingo, Kurt Moll) is a provocation in itself; Levine is in charge in the Grosses Festspielhaus at Salzburg … No, one can see that it will come under suspicion, particularly in these days when the tendency is all towards the 'thinner and leaner' sound in Beethoven as in Mozart and Haydn.

I played the 'Christe' again the other day, tremendously moved by the inspiration of both writing and performance, in which the great voices, the full chorus and orchestra produce a sound which might indeed be called operatic – except that it comes from an opera of such sublimity as has never yet been penned, unless by Beethoven himself in the ensembles of *Fidelio*. I hope the general verdict on this recording will be as enthusiastic as mine, but if not I shall remain unrepentant.

The King's Consort's *Judas Maccabaeus* also proves its worth, though hopes that a tenor with the splendid name of Jamie McDougall might be the new Walter Widdop are not fulfilled. In one respect, at least, and that from the very point at which comparison can begin, his 'Sound an alarm' improves on the Yorkshire tenor's famous record of 1929. Knowing the Widdop version from early days and never pausing to think about it properly, I always mentally construed the opening line of the recitative as involving some archaic transitive use of the verb 'to go': 'My arms against this Gorgias will I go'. But of course when McDougall sings 'My arms!' as an imperative, pausing and then stating his intentions towards 'this Gorgias', he makes much better sense of it. Throughout, he gives a performance in which youth, clarity and intelligence are on his side. But the heroic quality of voice is not there: we miss it, for instance, in 'How vain is man', the B-section of which shows up also a certain unevenness of production. All the same, skill and conviction go far to carry the day, and there is good solo work by the resident team (Emma Kirkby, Catherine Denley, James Bowman and Michael George), the combined forces giving a fine account of this most dramatic and tightly-knit of Handel's oratorios, a reading at present without rival in the catalogue.

Mendelssohn's *Elijah* is presently available in four complete recordings, two of which are in German, and, with this new release, two in English. Sir Neville Marriner with the orchestra and chorus of St Martin in the Fields can be relied on to give a sensitive, well-prepared performance, and the presence of Thomas Allen in the title-role is likely to ensure that this version has a head-on start over its rival. That has Willard White as the prophet, with the London Symphony Chorus and Orchestra under Hickox. For some reason it escaped attention in these columns, so a few comparisons might be in order now.

The opening tells much. In those wonderfully dramatic first bars Elijah stands, nobly dominant, a presence to remain in the mind's eye throughout the Overture and the first part of the oratorio until his reappearance in confrontation with Ahab. Allen's voice is perfectly focused, where White's is notably less so; but White makes the stronger impression because he is given his rightful place, which is the dominant one, while Allen, in the recording balance, is a figure comparatively distant. This remains so throughout. There is also the question of character, for while Allen sings with the utmost beauty and is in this respect by far the best of Elijahs on record, at least since Harold Williams, he is nevertheless too much the normal decent citizen; White with looser vibrancy and less distinction of phrasing, has more of the Old Testament about him, more capacity for ruthlessness. In the fugal Overture, Hickox gives an ominous, cautiously probing feel to the subject in a more imaginative reading than Marriner's, which is merely businesslike but also more sharply recorded. In the chorus 'Yet doth the Lord see it not' Marriner's singers impress with their alertness; in the first of the Baal choruses, Hickox goes for breadth and grandeur, while Marriner's Baalites are brisker, more tidily cheerful but not therefore more apt.

In the first of the tenor solos, Anthony Rolfe Johnson (with Marriner) is mild-mannered, and though he sings the opening words of 'If with all your hearts' with a decent legato, by 'ye shall ever truly find me' he is back to his bad old way of treating each note to a tiny but tiresome crescendo. Arthur Davies, with Hickox, sings with better tone and shows rather more urgency in the recitative, but still hasn't the fervour or stylistic quality that we want to hear. There is not space to go further, and the result is inconclusive. The new version is tidier, better defined, but there is not a great deal of imagination, and the relatively backward placing of Elijah himself is regrettable. I wonder what Gardiner would make of it. And I long to hear Bryn Terfel sing the part; with perhaps Joan Rodgers for the soprano.

Choral and song

Thomas Allen makes a second appearance this quarter, in a Wolf recital which impresses me as the best Lieder record he has made. The programme is divided between Mörike and Goethe settings, with surely unsurpassed performances by both himself and Geoffrey Parsons of *Verborgenheit*, *An die Geliebte*, *Heimweh* and *Anakreons Grab*: the satirical 'drink' songs, too, are virtuoso pieces done with uninhibited relish and consummate skill. Brigitte Fassbaender's Liszt is strong as ever in character, and highlights the interesting matter of a song's existence in two or more versions, opting here for the pithiest and most concentrated. Hvorostovsky makes a similarly personal choice of Russian folk-songs in what is probably his most enjoyable recital to date: some most lovely singing, with a specially haunting magic in the two unaccompanied songs. A Spanish song recital by Patricia Rozario finds her better suited to the milder and more melancholy songs of Rodrigo than to the *Maja dolorosa* of Granados or the smouldering *Polo* of Falla. Better value here are the reissues of Spanish songs by Teresa Berganza, Dame Kiri Te Kanawa, Marilyn Horne and Pilar Lorengar (with Alicia de Larrocha) on Decca or, better still, Berganza with piano and guitar accompaniments in a historical anthology on DG.

A fascinating choral record is the *Lamentatio Jeremiae prophetae* of Krenek. The ingenuity of the part-writing, with its canons and one prize 'crab' canon, sometimes distracts attention from its expressiveness; one also marvels constantly at the Netherlands Chamber Choir, who seem utterly undaunted by this work which Krenek himself appears to have entertained no expectation of ever hearing in performance.

Among English choral composers it is good to see some less familiar names in the lists: Bernard Stevens's fine Mass for double choir (1939) makes an admirable companion piece for Howells's *Mass in the Dorian Mode* (Finzi Singers on Chandos), and Kenneth Leighton challenges close attention in the anthology of his church music by St Paul's Cathedral Choir. Lastly, a recital on Nimbus, 'The Sound of St John's', serves for an affectionate and grateful farewell to George Guest, whose 120 recordings have been a source of unfailing pleasure throughout what amounts to the complete working lifetime of many of our readers – and indeed of at least one of our writers.

The finest hour

'When the Quintet was finished [it was the Schubert C major] I sat back in my chair and solemnly asked myself if in all the years during which I had been absorbed by the gramophone I had ever fully appreciated its magical influence upon the mind until that moment.'

'That moment' arrived on Monday, September 12th, 1938, and the solemn self-questioning was conducted by our first Editor, Compton Mackenzie (not yet knighted) in time for his Editorial in the October issue. I have recently been looking over some old numbers of that period, finding much that acted as a sombrely congenial accompaniment to my own more gloomy feelings about the times we live in. On that evening in 1938 the Editor had listened to a relay of Hitler's Nuremberg speech and had prepared to go to bed 'weighed down by the appalling certainty of another world war from which those of us who came through it alive would live on in a death-in-life of civilisation'. At that time and for the next few years Sir Compton Mackenzie would frequently enlarge his editorial scope, arraigning the BBC ('ignominious and contemptible collapse'), the Sunday papers (one editor 'intended by nature to look after a sewage-farm'), the Chamberlain cabinet in general and the Chancellor in particular ('amiable and esurient and harassed little man') in particular. But after all these exacerbations and the depressing effect of 'the news', foreign and domestic, music would bring relief, and that particular night, instead of going to bed with echoes of Nuremberg rumbling fearfully in his mind, he turned to his records and took out the Schubert Quintet.

Of our time

Again to a background of 'news' (Bosnia, Somalia, Angola and the commonplace horrors nearer home), which that day bade fair to rival September 1938 in respect of appalling certainties in the mind, I played Tippett's *A Child of Our Time*. This was the Hickox recording, which came not long after the composer's own. 'The world turns on its dark side': the oratorio's opening chorus, and indeed all that was to follow, seemed dreadfully familiar ('pogroms in the east ... a war of starvation ... Let them starve in No Man's Land'). So it may have been that that accounted for, at the very least, a considerable part of the emotion. Some months before, the slightly earlier recording had scarcely moved me at all; not, at any rate, as I was hoping it would. The tempos seemed too slow, even if they were the composer's, and the soloists (who would have been the composer's choice too, especially the soprano Faye Robinson who has distinguished herself in association with his work in the past) seemed tonally unsympathetic. But the Hickox, that Sunday: it worked its spell, restored, relieved, acted just as the Schubert did upon our then-Editor with 'a magical influence upon the mind', and particularly upon the emotional part of it.

I wonder to what extent any objectively-based perception of the one recording's superiority over the other would account for the difference in effect. Certainly the soprano soloist here (Cynthia Haymon) brings greater beauty of voice; and that is important, for there are moments in this work (most of all as her first solo leads into the first spiritual) when the sheer sound of a pure, freely floated soprano voice can be infinitely moving. Damon Evans too, though hardly a candidate for the vocal beauty-prize, has the right young-man tone for his 'have no money for my bread' solo. The chorus dramatize well (hate in 'Away with them!') and they have the rhythm (of 'Nobody knows', for instance) as though in their bones.

So objective criteria could be established. But there remains the fact that in the power which music, and music on record, has over us is much that goes beyond the factors spelt out in our reviews. Even the purest, least programmatic music takes us in the context of the rest of our lives – and 'the news'. Tippett's emotion becomes overwhelming in the spirituals, diatonic and in a sense 'easy': but only because they have been, so to speak, worked for. The Schubert Quintet would not have been the music to move Sir Compton, as it did that night, if it too did not sometimes 'turn on its dark side'.

John Rutter's excellent 'Fancies' with the Cambridge Singers and the City of London Sinfonia, one of the most attractive choral records in recent months, could not have served, I think, because its charm and manifold delights have no pain in them. Maxwell Davies's *Solstice of Light* does serve, partly because it also admits a 'heart of darkness' (and, incidentally, what a challenge to the choristers of King's College, Cambridge, and how they rise to it!). It also comes, like Tippett's work, from a sensibility that knows the troubles of our times ('that the last ice age may not cover us'). Even Schnittke's *Choir Concerto*, so extraordinary in its sustained evocation of an age-old tradition, makes its beauty moving, at least partly, because one knows the conditions, the times, that inspired it. I come back to our first Editor's feeling of blessedness in the post-Nuremberg depression: it is at just such a time that one most values the record collection, and after a late-night playing can go to bed feeling blessed despite the worst that tomorrow's newspapers will bring.

Six recitals

Blyth is right again: Fischer-Dieskau's latest (and last) recorded *Winterreise* does not make one eager to linger and savour. The acoustic is an immediate deterrent, yet the partnership with Murray Perahia is a distinguished one and there is always hope of revelation. Instead, it is sad to find that the individuality which amounted to genius is now taking more and more the stamp of waywardness and eccentricity. I had not realized that the recording is the soundtrack of a video, but that explains much: notable too that the singer's art on the concert platform is becoming increasingly visual, so that last time I heard him live, the comparison which came to mind was not with another singer but with the Olivier of late years.

Very different is the work of Andreas Schmidt, a pupil of Fischer-Dieskau's, in *Die schöne Müllerin*. Again, I agree entirely with AB, who says 'Practically everything is bland' (just for variety's sake, however, a difference of opinion might be mentioned concerning the earlier Schmidt/Jansen DG *Winterreise* which AB called successful and I thought premature). The low keys used here are a disadvantage – not so much in the voice as the piano – even so, arousing speculation about the murky depths in 'Dankgesang an dem Bach', perhaps pictorial and ironically prophetic. But the singing catches little of the poet's character, whether in the excitement of 'Mein' or the suffering in 'Trockne Blumen'; 'Die liebe Farbe' brings no pain into the voice, 'Die böse Farbe' no real anger, only a manly forthrightness. In another sense, of course, the singing is first rate – in the production of finely textured sound, and that after all is worth a *Danksagung* in itself.

A further thanksgiving – and at last one without niggles and qualifications – greets Barbara Bonney's Mendelssohn recital. The voice has a freshness that ideally suits these songs of spring and bouquets, gentle moonlight and pretty sentiments. The charm of manner matches too: never merely arch or empty-headed in its prettiness, and always going as far as the songs themselves permit. Very occasionally they venture. *Die Nonne*, with its pre-echo of Brahms (*Vor dem Fenster* and one of the *Liebeslieder*), ventures at least as far as poignancy; *Nachtlied*, this time leading back to Schubert, has less than usual of formularized expression and goes deeper in feeling. But they have to be taken for what they are, and songs such as the *Frühlingslied* ('Durch den Wald') and *Neue Liebe* are quite simply delightful, both in themselves and in these performances.

A voice of comparable purity and warmer colouring is that of the fine lyric soprano, expert in the Russian repertoire, Joan Rodgers. It is a vibrant voice too, capable in itself of a dramatic intensity which should do good service in this Tchaikovsky recital with Roger Vignoles. Up to a point, it does: in the deeply-felt *Not a word, o my friend* for instance, and then in the radiant cries of happiness at the end of *It was in the early spring*. Yet, while JW in his review found her singing 'occasionally a little too near to operatic declamation', I rather wished for less restraint, or at any rate for that sense of passion smouldering away deep in the soul. In *At the ball*, for instance, it was hard to catch the love-sickness in the lonely hours of the night. After *None but the lonely heart* I took out an old record of Nina Koshetz, beautifully reproduced on Nimbus's 'party' record, and though perhaps there is something of old-style, silent-screen 'glamour' about it, there is also more temperament, freedom and boldness, and not taken to excess. The other difference is how much more immediate and personal the 1922 recording of the singer is: this present recital, with its very forward recording of the piano, left me frustrated of the immediacy of communication that these of all songs call for in a sense of face-to-face encounter with the singer.

As for Cecilia Bartoli's recital of so-called *arie antiche*, memory for a moment tricked me into a notion that it was a video I had seen, so vivid was the encounter. If any readers are still wavering about this one, they can hardly have read Hilary Finch's review, and much the best I can do now is to urge them to look it up.

Mind, if by any chance Bartoli herself should be listening to the remaining recital under present consideration, she might ponder the advantages of the legato rather than what Italians euphemistically call the 'articulated' style of singing runs. Catherine Bott has a great many florid passages to negotiate in her recital of seventeenth-century 'Mad Songs' and they are both smooth and sound, yet perfectly well 'articulated' (unless one has lorries in mind). Anyway, it is a splendid record, in which Purcell can claim by no means a monopoly of the masterpieces: John Weldon, John Eccles and 'Anon' have their inspired moments too.

Entartete Musik

Approval of fair play and abhorrence of Goebbels are great points in favour of the Entartete Musik series enterprisingly inaugurated and imaginatively produced by Decca. Even so, the two major operas have presented difficulties. With *Jonny spielt auf* it is a matter of intentions. That whole argument of course is fraught, for who can know what a composer's intentions are, even if he spells them out so that at least there is no mistaking what he thinks they are? But if Krenek, in juxtaposing the old world and the new, by means of 'classical' music and jazz, intends to suggest the moribund condition of the one and the liberating freshness of the other (as seems to be the case), he surely fails. The trouble lies not with the European, 'classical' side (that's moribund enough); it's the jazz, which is hopeless. To do its work in the fable, the jazz really needs to be authentic. It should have an effect like that of the rock music from Moscow I heard on the radio this morning. It appals me to think that this is what freedom should mean, but to this generation of young people clearly it does: it disowns formality, and asserts, if you like (which I don't), the human animal, while symphony concerts and balalaika songs are tagged with the old regime. 'That's my Jonny! What a fiddler!' exclaims Yvonne, the maid, in words that might be part of an improbable pop lyric. But 'my Jonny' is never musically established: his fiddling has nothing of New Orleans about it, and later his banjo song is a feeble thing, the orchestra offering a bit of synthetic Prokofiev. Moreover, in this recording, Jonny has little of the vocal personality needed to justify Yvonne's enthusiasm. Photographs suggest that Krister St Hill may be a lively, perhaps charismatic, personality on stage, but his voice here (and that's all we have) belongs to the other side in the juxtaposition: 'classically' trained and really rather dull.

As a whole, the recording and performance deserve gratitude, little as this account may seem to suggest it. The opera is one we have all read about in the history books, and its nature may come as a surprise. Michael Oliver speaks for most of us, I daresay, when he writes in his review: 'I was expecting period fun; *Jonny spielt auf* is a good deal more than that'. It is indeed, which is what makes one take it seriously as a work of art. As a performance, despite the limitation noted above and another in the somewhat inexpressive Max of Heinz Kruse, it seems fine, particularly well played (under Lothar Zagrosek) and well produced (by Michael Haas). There is also some glorious singing by the Anita, Alessandra Marc. So many sopranos tax credulity when they play a world-famous prima donna: this one really is a voice in ten thousand.

Still, I'd recommend it (the opera, as opposed to Marc's singing) ultimately as a curiosity, distinctive and interesting but hardly as part of what you might think of as the 'active' half of one's collection (as opposed to the records on the shelves, lying there for use this year, next year, sometime, never).

Das Wunder der Heliane may exercise more of a pull, may come down for replaying rather more often. But no: it's like the appeal of a rumoured orgy (you feel that this must be where the good time's at), and when all the pounding and heaving, the silky ecstasies and auto-intoxication are over, you come away with nothing much more positive than regret for all this expense of impotent energy and with a renewed taste for the effortless power of Mozart and Verdi, and indeed for the economy of means in Puccini, whose audience Korngold might superficially seem to attract.

Again, I wouldn't want to suggest that the whole thing (work, performance, recording) is a write-off. There are passages which are not couched in the clichés of simulated ecstasy. Although the singers are given apparently glamorous opportunities, the best writing is orchestral, and the Prelude to Act 3 makes rich, colourful sound out of good material. The chorus which follows struck me as the finest music in the opera and that is something I shall certainly want to hear again. Anna Tomowa-Sintow's singing, too: it would have been still better a few years earlier, but the gleaming tone and aristocracy of style give a keenly appreciated pleasure.

Curiously, though, and regretfully, my feeling is that the re-emergence of these operas has essentially served to confirm their rejection. Not (obviously) on the idiotic and pernicious grounds of race or subject-matter, but, because of their musical and other artistic qualities, I at present would conclude that 'decadent' is indeed what they are.

Byzantium

Still more difficulties here. Michael Oliver cautions very aptly when he refers to 'the half-century-long tradition of expressing doubts about each of Tippett's new works as they have appeared', but, try as I may, I cannot see this as a good setting of Yeats's poem. 'This' is the work for soprano and orchestra written by Sir Michael Tippett for the Chicago Symphony Orchestra and given first performances under Solti in April 1991 (the event made headlines because of Jessye Norman's withdrawal). The poem is one I know well enough, probably with a bit of prompting, to say by heart, and at no point in listening to Tippett's setting have I found an 'Ah!' of recognition or of affirmation or enlightenment rise in the mind. Possibly at 'a starlit or a moonlit dome' it was so, but then I think it was because of the reminiscence of Sosostris's music in *The Midsummer Marriage*. Instead, a certain irritation arises at the way in which the sense, the meaning, of the poem is arrested by what seems to be the inevitable 'picture-writing' at phrases such as 'the winding path' or single words like 'bird' and 'crow'. It's a sort of doodling, or a cartoon's balloon of notes coming out of the word's mouth. More fundamental than that, although the music follows the words clearly enough, I find I can't hear the poem's development in the music. And then of course (for this is relatively frivolous) there is the objection tentatively raised by MEO when he asks 'isn't the incessant (and hair-raisingly difficult) intensity of the soprano line rather exhaustingly unrelieved?'. Faye Robinson copes heroically with the difficulties, and it is perhaps ungracious to mention the tinkle of tone-wear or of tonal impurity which modern recording catches so mercilessly. To tell the truth, I found myself wishing that Tippett's long preoccupation with Yeats's *Byzantium* had resulted not in a word-setting at all, but in an orchestral tone-poem.

Life with an Idiot, and others

Schnittke's *Life with an Idiot* is another hard listen. Briefly, it tells the story of Man ('I') and Wife who, compelled to adopt an idiot, choose Vova ('significantly' Lenin's nickname), who at first is utterly silent (and indeed says nothing but 'Ekh' throughout the opera), who then turns unpleasant, then very unpleasant, then (like Orton's entertaining Mr Sloane, if less entertainingly) 'sleeps' in turn with husband and wife, who, when neglected, complains once too often so he decapitates her with the secateurs. Up to a point, the musical expression compels acceptance as serious farce: the cruel contortions inflicted upon the voices are part of a savage-compassionate, earnest-humorous mind that has created a musical language to serve an extra-musical purpose. The concentration that characterizes Act 1 is dissipated about halfway through Act 2, but that may be the fault of the libretto. The profundity of Victor Erofeyev's story seems, according to the writer of the accompanying essay, to be widely accepted as wonderful in proportion to the number of ways in which it can be interpreted (at times, the notes seem as surreal as the opera). I don't know: it's usually possible to make a universal allegory out of anything if you try hard enough. Schnittke's score is another matter. All honour to the Amsterdam cast and Rostropovich's work with his musicians that they could achieve such a convincing result. Dale Duesing and Teresa Ringholz particularly can claim a mighty achievement – and when they discover the cost to their voices perhaps they will send the bill to the composer.

At least Górecki's writing for the bass soloist in his *Beatus vir* is not lethal: just a trifle inconsiderate. In a fine recording with the Czech Philharmonic Chorus and Orchestra under John Nelson, Nikita Storojev sings the solo part with impressively resonant tone. Michael Stewart is surely right in his view that there is insufficient material for a work of half-an-hour's length, and right too about the misery and despondency: rarely has an expression of hope ('spero') sounded quite so pessimistic. Still, the slow processional crescendo and the 'breathing' chord-sequence remain memorable, as does the

Old Polish Music for orchestra coupled with it.

If the time:material ratio were applied to Tavener's *Mary of Egypt*, that also might look a little thin, but a sense of timelessness is perhaps part of the fabric, as is the drone on F. A quite lovely performance is given by Patricia Rozario, the low range of her voice heard as it rarely has been, revealing a surprisingly deep contralto quality able to make itself heard easily and effectively in the absence of accompaniment. But there is a lot of vocal role-swapping here, so that the baritone Zossima (Stephen Varcoe) sings, early in Act 3, as something very near a tenor, and one of the weirdest sounds ever recorded is that of 'Voice', which consultation of the cast-list reveals to astonished eyes as being sung by a woman, Chloe Goodchild. This is 'An Icon in Music and Dance', a mystical work in which an element of mystery is only right and proper. But mysteries associated with the oft-repeated information that 'The ways to salvation are more than one' (and later 'are YET more than one') include the Voice's extraordinary pronunciation ('the' sometimes coming out as something like 'theowr') and a mild puzzlement as to how this particular fable is supposed to illustrate the variety of 'ways', when both, as shown here, seem to involve time in obedience, self-sacrifice and humility exercised over a long period spent in the desert.

Choral Pleasures

At the head of any list this quarter must come the *Venetian Vespers*, assembled by Paul McCreesh as a reconstruction of a putative celebration at St Mark's in 1643, and performed magnificently by his Gabrieli Consort and Players. Iain Fenlon saluted it as 'an heroic achievement of the highest possible order', and all that I would like to add is a word of admiration for the singers, among whom the falsettists (the term used), David Hurley and Timothy Wilson, perform some of the most delightful work in duet I've ever heard. Also, what a splendid composer Giovanni Rogatti was: his *Dixit Dominus*, with its 'conquassabit capita' sounding almost alarmingly as if it means business, is marvellously varied and energetic, and the *Nisi Dominus* has a lulling motion one would like to think he caught from the gentle lapping of waters in some nice quiet part of watery Venice or over on the islands.

I thought the excellent Netherlands Chamber Choir under Ton Koopman slightly spoilt its Bach Motets by over-accentuation, particularly of paired notes, much too deliberate and insistent in *Komm, Jesu, komm*. Excellent, however, are the Advent Cantatas recorded by the Monteverdi Choir and English Baroque Soloists under Gardiner. I won't say more except in appreciation of Olaf Bär's singing of the wonderful 'stand at the door and knock' solo in *Nun komm der Heiden Heiland I* and to welcome the forward placing of the choir. On Mozart's *Coronation* Mass a difference of opinion with SS has to be registered, for I thoroughly enjoyed the King's, Cambridge reissue which he thought a relatively poor piece of work, while I didn't greatly like the new Hogwood which he loved. It's partly a matter of speeds, so that to my mind Hogwood's *Kyrie* is dulled by the slightly slower tempo, while his *Credo* (though a full minute less than the King's timing) sounded somewhat rushed. SS found Margaret Marshall disappointing, whereas I thought her on splendid form and better suited to this music than Emma Kirkby, whose merely pretty tone and habitual swelling on individual notes limit enjoyment. Also, rather as with Koopman's Bach, I thought Hogwood insisted too much, over-accentuating, and, in the 'Osanna', overdriving.

Perhaps some listeners will find Roger Norrington's Brahms *German Requiem* overdriven. It is certainly fast compared with what we are used to, but, for one thing, is nearer to the score's directions (Robert Pascall's notes deal well with this) and, for another, it lifts the heart. I even like the fugues at this speed (Lionel Salter rather drew the line at them): the C major fugue particularly has all sorts of merry devices set rejoicing. Bär sings coolly but beautifully; Lynne Dawson isn't ethereal in her solo, but her clearly defined tone is ideal for this performance. It seems likely now that in the future, when the evening comes and one of those promptings arises making one say 'Tonight I'll have the Brahms Requiem', the Hickox, probably the best among the sort one's been brought up to, will alternate with this of Norrington's.

The two Verdi Requiem recordings on BMG's current lists will probably not alternate with comparable frequency, though both have good points. The new one, under Sir Colin Davis, gains from a well-considered refinement in choral and orchestral work, while the new reissue from 1977 under Solti brings more excitement and sense of occasion. An overbright top obtrudes sometimes in the sound of the Solti, and the Davis is curiously remote: the volume never seems loud enough until it is too loud. It is good to hear Dennis O'Neill shading-off his phrases in the 'Ingemisco', and in the Solti it is almost startling to recognize the voice of Dame Janet Baker and to feel the intensity with which her individuality presses upon the music.

Operatic mixed pleasures

In opera this quarter, Verdi has meant first and foremost *Don Carlo*. The new recording under Levine gives Alan Blyth, as its reviewer, a pleasure which I shared only up to a point. The Metropolitan Opera Orchestra play magnificently, as they seem always to do for Levine on record. He, in turn, faithfully seeks out the heart, the agonized beauty, of the score. But his Carlo, William Sylvester, gives the impression of a tenor without temperament: a firm voice, a decent legato, but he after all is the centre of it and he has some intensely emotional music; you cannot have a Carlo who is emotionally a cipher. As far as recording is concerned, the Philip (Ferruccio Furlanetto) is utterly miscast. Samuel Ramey, who would have been a very acceptable Philip, is miscast as the Inquisitor: he has the wrong voice-character, lacking the ponderous blackness and depth to match those trombones and double-basses. The women, Aprile Millo and

Dolora Zajick, certainly have fine voices and do some things particularly well, but are at any moment liable to slip out of focus, or complete firmness, and various crucial moments (Elisabeth's brief prayer after the banishment of her confidante is an instance) pass without imaginative concentration. The baritone Vladimir Chernov remains, a most beautifully textured voice and an artist in his use of it. But generally I found that there was too much which gave only partial satisfaction for the recording to provide great pleasure as a whole.

Two other Italian opera sets that proved disappointing were the *Pagliacci* under Muti and *Manon Lescaut* under Maazel. The Puccini opera, like *Don Carlo*, has an excellent baritone in the cast, this time Gino Quilico. But the Manon, Nina Rautio, appealing in the tragic second half, lacks charm in the first, while the Des Grieux, Peter Dvorsky, is as inexpressive as it is possible to be in such a role. Best is the playing of the Intermezzo. Similarly, in *Pagliacci* the principal distinction of the set among its many rivals is the playing of the Philadelphia Orchestra. Pavarotti has not developed the part of Canio much since his 1978 recording, and if Muti has developed his reading of the score it is a matter of the-same-only-more-so. Daniela Dessi, her voice uneven, misses points all along the line as Nedda, Juan Pons is vocally an unpolished Tonio, Paolo Coni insufficiently young-sounding to make an effective contrast as Silvio. The chorus are too far back in their important numbers, and in this drama of the play and its players the concert performance provides little evidence of a producing hand.

Saint-Saëns fares better. He has one opera which is making (to the best of my knowledge) its recording début, and his operatic masterpiece receives something like full justice on record at last. *Henry VIII* is well worth hearing, even in this flawed recording (see LS's review). It doesn't quite rise, musically, to the big moments, and often seems to be on the verge of something deeper and more memorable without quite getting there; yet the score is rich in ideas and colourful achievement. The mezzo, Lucile Vignon, as Anne Boleyn, sings beautifully.

Samson et Dalila, impresses, I think, more favourably than ever before on record, and that right from the start, where the deep, reiterated grindings of slavery, and the chorus, with a fine-spun web of lamentation, the throb of the orchestra's basses beneath it, suggests here something that is not so remote from the *St Matthew Passion*. The orchestra is that of the Bastille Opéra in Paris, the conductor Myung-Whun Chung, and it is a performance that has the refinement of a genuine insight. Waltraud Meier has not a voluptuous voice, but it's good and serviceable, and the characterization (shades of her Kundry, perhaps) is one of the strongest. Domingo, surely, is a marvel. Just at the stage (and in the role) where he might be expected to be getting deeper, thicker, more baritonal, he asserts unequivocally his tenor's identity. There is plenty of steel and brightness; he sings with great lyrical beauty in the Act 2 duet; and his feeling for the role, if not inspired like Jon Vickers, still carries him far.

Gloriana

And so there she sits, *Gloriana*, enthroned upon the shelves at last. The great gain brings a tiny loss, for she has been such a reliable, useful travelling companion, ready to be produced out of the Grumbly Book at a moment's notice. 'What should be recorded that hasn't been?' 'Oh, *Gloriana*.' 'Isn't it extraordinary: yet another *Figaro*, *Tosca*, *Ring* cycle, when we haven't a single ...' '... *Gloriana*.' And now we do have *Gloriana*, there on the shelves, ready to be heard, the last of Britten's operas to find a place there.

It has of course been available for some time on video, where Colin Graham's production is freed from the confines of the stage by camera work which suggests space and atmosphere, rich in detail of movement and facial expression as in colour and pageantry. The filmed performance is also a fine one musically, under Mark Elder, and with Sarah Walker both regal and human in the title-role. The quality of recorded sound, especially an edginess in the voices, limits the pleasure of listening, but it remains one of the most treasurable of videos. The new recording under Sir Charles Mackerras now brings what we have for so long wanted: not merely something to fill a glaring gap in the Britten *oeuvre*, which the record industry in general and Decca in particular have otherwise served so well, but also to do broad and belated justice to a masterpiece.

For that is what it is. From that first opening flash of brass, with its common chords uncommonly colliding in a syncopation that unites the two Elizabethan ages, right to the loving final reiteration of the *Greenleaves* tune, the voices dropping out one by one as the brilliant past fades into darkness and silence, every page of the score teems with the invention of a mind working at fullest, happiest stretch. The objections of even the more thoughtful among its original detractors were mistaken. The Norwich scene, for example, was held to weaken the dramatic integrity: an episode aside from the main development, a dilution therefore, an artistic compromise dictated by the 'occasional' demands of the commission. But here is the Queen among her subjects, an essential element in the depicting of Gloriana, the brightness and beauty of the Elizabethan age set against the darker side which is to come. The recording shows everything to have its place in a work of fine proportions, its episodes firmly placed within a skilfully balanced structure.

If there were many recording to choose from, I daresay this performance would not rank as outstanding. Josephine Barstow's Elizabeth hasn't quite the full-toned firmness which the part ideally wants, but everything is well-considered and there is colour and character in her lower notes ('Anger would be too strong' in the first scene's finale, for instance). Philip Langridge catches the ardent, chafing spirit of Essex well, and Alan Opie's Cecil is gratefully heard, here as on the video. Amid many good performances in the smaller roles, the one flash of vocal splendour occurs right at the start with Bryn Terfel as Henry Cuffe. He also projects in a way that I rather missed in the recording as a whole: the singers, and particularly the Queen, are not so forward and immediate in sound as one might have wished. Still, the set fulfils a long-held wish, and does so with a standard of achievement at least as high as anything we could realistically have anticipated.

1994

Rossini

We have rather got into the habit of talking about 'the Rossini revival', but revivals are flighty things, here today, gone tomorrow, and by now it would probably not tempt Providence too sorely if we were to speak of 'the Rossini establishment'. Anyway, there is no aspect of singing, and singing on record, that has developed so spectacularly over the last 20 years as that associated with the unfailing supply of Rossini operas, cast, without too much difficulty or glaring inadequacy it seems from the broad ranks of young singers (a few 'stars' among them) trained to perform what used to be thought of as the unperformable.

Of course it has not come about all at once, and the pioneering days of the Callas/Serafin, Sutherland/Bonynge explorations in early nineteenth-century opera were not the start either. But for the last few years it has become a matter of no special remark if the month brings forth its Rossini opera, live or studio-recorded, with singers who take it as all part of the day's work that they should sprint repeatedly over a two-octave range in scales, triplets and *gruppetti*, aware that anything they sing may be taken down on somebody's tape-recorder and used in evidence against them.

The three recordings in front of me now are studio versions, but I'm sceptical of the scepticism that sometimes comes into play automatically at this point; and I would not be so if experience had shown that singers fail to bring off 'in the flesh' feats they have performed on record. Discrepancies of several kinds arise, most frequently in the matter of anticipated volume, but over matters of technique (accuracy of runs, breadth of phrasing and so forth) singers' work (comparing live performances and those released on record) has generally proved to be remarkably consistent. As far as the principals heard here are concerned – Cecilia Bartoli, Jennifer Larmore, Susanne Mentzer, William Matteuzzi, Jerry Hadley, Raúl Giménez, Alessandro Corbelli, Thomas Hampson, Hakån Hagegård, Samuel Ramey, Enzo Dara, Bruno Praticò – and as far as my own experience of them goes, I would say that the records in no way flatter their technical skills. On the contrary, a characteristic of technique which will be assimilated without trouble by a normally critical listener in the opera house often obtrudes disproportionately in the 'close-up' exposure of recording. For instance, 'in the flesh' Larmore has habitually produced well-articulated florid singing that has preserved evenness of flow, which to my mind is essential if the technique in such things is to be acceptable. When her recorded Rosina in *Il barbiere di Siviglia* is played at what I would consider a kindly level (kind to the ears and the singer) the impression conforms; but with such highly analytical equipment or method of playback as is supposed nowadays to be our pride and joy, we are brought unnaturally face to face with the singers and hear a more obtrusive 'separation' technique in the scales and so forth than is evident in the theatre. Where 'truth' lies in all this may be endlessly debatable, but the spotlight-glare of much modern recording and reproduction, so far from enabling singers to 'get away with' the products of an inadequate technique, exposes them to relentless scrutiny just at the time when interest and taste have turned most favourably towards the music that tests it so rigorously.

Rossini, Verdi, Puccini

The *Barbiere* which has Larmore as its Rosina is a sprightly, graceful, wittily pointed performance under Jesús López-Cobos. I like it (overall) as well as any version in the catalogue, and its nervy, eager style contrasts with the more carefully measured pacing of Gianluigi Gelmetti in a rival version. Gelmetti contributes an introductory essay in which he disparages the use of 'sparkling', 'effervescent', 'light' and 'amusing' as definitive terms for Rossini; which of course does not mean that he thinks Rossini isn't sparkling, etc., just that he is more than that, and Gelmetti's recording, while seeking out the heart, is often joyously light in texture and funny in detail. It is also complete where López-Cobos makes small cuts (but has the advantage of a two-disc set over three). I can't share Richard Osborne's preference for Jerry Hadley (Gelmetti) over Giménez (López-Cobos) in 'Se il mio nome'. It's true that he sings softly and intimately, introducing an apt feeling of improvisation, but the song itself suffers. In the second verse, moreover, there is surely some questionable intonation. Giménez preserves the melody while still being imaginative in his shading, with a lovely touch on the word 'costante'. There is also relish in Hagegård's bright-toned Figaro (López-Cobos), given more freedom to enjoy himself than Hampson (Gelmetti), who is bound (it would seem) by Gelmetti's determination in 'Largo al factotum' to keep the pace steady. Anyway, both sets are fascinating.

A point of change in orchestral style (in Rossini as with Handel) has been a lightening of the bass. This is so in the new *La Cenerentola* as well as the two *Il barbiere* recordings. With Riccardo Chailly and the Bologna Teatro Communale Chorus and Orchestra at the height of their form, *La Cenerentola* has also the great asset of the leading Italian mezzo-soprano of the age, Bartoli, in the title-role. 'Vocal gold', of course, is the immediate reaction to the first sound of that voice in the song which Cinderella appears to sing at all times while doing the housework: it gets on her sisters' nerves but, for us, with a voice like that she could sing it all day. Again, recording exposes her 'separation' technique in runs. It no longer amounts to blatant aspirating and she sometimes preserves entire the kind of legato method that I much prefer (and which, incidentally, is demonstrated by the Alcidoro, Michele Pertusi), but it remains a tiresome feature of otherwise lovely singing. In refulgence of tone and very slightly in the tenderness of her portrayal, I think she surpasses Berganza in the 1971 Abbado recording, which RO prefers. In other points of comparison, I found Chailly a good deal more fun in the Overture (instrument calling to instrument in the very spirit of comedy), and the new tenor, Matteuzzi, appreciably more stylish and better equipped than Luigi Alva (at that date) in 'Si, ritrovarla'. Certainly the Bartoli/Chailly version is my *Cinderella* for Christmas 1993.

Composers in Person

Love of the music is certainly a quality one might expect to be evident in a performance with the composer taking part; and it is remarkable how rarely his presence is betrayed by any over-emotional or otherwise self-indulgent expression. Four discs in EMI's Composers in Person series include some vocal music and, in all, five composers are involved as accompanists, with one, Lehár, as conductor. Suppose one didn't know, I doubt whether the unique affinity with the music would be proclaimed by a touch on the piano or an especially idiomatic use of the baton. Much more likely to make itself felt is a special aptness in the singer, who is also likely to be of the composer's own choice and in some famous instances to be particularly close.

The Poulenc/Bernac, Britten/Pears disc is the obvious example. The music so exactly suits the voices that the first comment of an unknowing listener could well be 'but it might have been written for him'. Both of the singers are heard in their early years, Pierre Bernac in the *Chansons gaillardes* recordings of 1936, when his voice, slim-toned and athletic, was much more nearly beautiful. Sir Peter Pears in the *Michelangelo Sonnets* (1942) sounds very youthful, the tone rather unkindly attenuated in the dry studio, gaining much more in body with *The Holy Sonnets of John Donne* five years later. Bernac, drier and harder at a *forte* in later years, sings with a finely restrained sad sweetness in 'C' (*Deux poèmes de Louis Aragon*) and in everything finds a masterly answer to all those tricky problems of tessitura Poulenc has thrown in his way.

With a similar sureness, though in how different a style, Lehár wrote for Richard Tauber. Unhappily in this collection it is the Tauber recordings that (with the exception of 'Kann es möglich sein' from *Der Land des Lächelns*) give least pleasure to the ear as transfers: they are, however, in the company of some stunningly good ones of Esther Réthy from the 1940s. Maria Barrientos singing for Falla in 1928 and 1930 gives limited delight (best in the lullaby), but Ninon Vallin is delicious in some songs of Nin, especially the 'Malagueña' (*Cantos populares españolas*).

Best of these, certainly my own favourite, is the Medtner record. It opens joyfully with the *Russian Round Dance* played in duet with Benno Moiseiwitsch. Then among the piano solos there are some magical recordings from 1936, with a winningly personal rubato not explicitly suggested in the score – it is in such things that these records can be invaluable. The vocal items are supplied by Oda Slobodskaya (always commanding attention), Tatiana Makushina (rather thin and worn) and Elisabeth Schwarzkopf, superb in her understanding of what is wanted and, here in 1950, a gift from the gods in the flawless beauty of her voice.

A personal selection

If it's a matter of what has moved me over the past months – lit up the morning, stoked up the fire in the evening – then a curiously assorted list emerges, no rhyme or reason to it. A sudden joy in the sound of mixed voices, of subtly crafted lines, pleasure and pain intermingled, and all with the special thrill of an inspired director's hand behind the performances, arose out of a reissue in Decca's Serenata series. This is a collection of madrigals by Monteverdi and Gesualdo; the date of recording is 1969; the very discreet organ accompaniment is played by one Andrew Davis; and the Monteverdi Choir is conducted by one John Eliot Gardiner. Could it have been his first recording? Among the first, certainly. And what freshness and beauty there is in the performances, revealing what riches of expressive composition (as of course we know perfectly well in theory, but realize in fact only when performances of such insight and care come before us). Then there is the young Jussi Björling (I said this was a curiously assorted list) singing his 'Ah, si ben mio' like an angel ('Sei tu dal cielo disceso?' – 'Have you come down from heaven?' – Leonora asks in another part of the opera) in the *Trovatore* of his Covent Garden début in 1939. And another reissue striking hard into the very centre of the emotional system, Vaughan Williams's *Riders to the Sea*: a fine performance under Meredith Davies, with Helen Watts singing the role of the grieving mother most movingly. Hearing it again made me wonder whether there exists another opera to match this one-acter in the concentrated unity of its score; and indeed whether in all opera there is any more powerful musical-dramatic point than that at which at the very height of the tragedy the predominant minor tonality resolves into major. With the death of her last son, the old woman has nothing more to lose: 'They are all gone now, and there isn't anything more the sea can do to me.'

Two other reissues, while we are in this line of country, also warmed the January evenings, both having had enthusiastic first reviews by Alan Blyth. *The Dream of Gerontius* is a triumph of a transfer, the excellent work of Andrew Walter and Paul Baily. It preserves the first complete recording, which for many listeners is still the favourite. Sir Malcolm Sargent at his best, the Liverpool Philharmonic at theirs; the Huddersfield Choral Society, numbers apparently depleted at the end of the war in 1945 but hardly sounding it (what they do show, rarely to be heard nowadays, is a line of 'real' basses). About Heddle Nash's Gerontius, AB writes that it was 'the most famous ... of his and perhaps any day ... unrivalled in its conviction and inwardness.' Alec Robertson, ***Gramophone***'s original reviewer, was enthusiastic but not quite ecstatic about both Nash and Gladys Ripley: 'the spiritual awe with which the greatest interpreters filled these two parts is just missing. But only just.' He, presumably, could recall the Gerontius of John Coates and Gervase Elwes. It's interesting, though, that the phrase he chooses to pinpoint 'a certain spiritual quality' lacking is 'Novissima hora est', the very one in which Nash for us (certainly for myself) seems most sublime.

Britten's *Rape of Lucretia*, or the two-thirds of it coupled with excerpts from *Peter Grimes*, is the other outstanding retrieval from the 1940s. The *Grimes* passages (1948) show Sir Peter Pears very clearly as he was at that time (his later recordings so often incited objections that this was almost a caricature of what one heard 'in the flesh'). Joan Cross, slightly past her best as a singer, is still the Ellen Orford I hear when rehearsing the phrases inwardly (overlaid perhaps by memories of Heather Harper). She (Joan Cross) is also well heard as the Female Chorus in Lucretia, and Pears of course unforgettable as her male partner, with Nancy Evans strong in voice and character as the heroine. But it is what might be thought of as 'the supporting cast' that so constantly delights – that ruthless, insinuative quality that Denis Dowling got into his voice for Junius, and the delicious serving-duo of Margaret Ritchie and Flora Nielsen. That and Sir Reginald Goodall's conducting, so strong and incisive.

Busoni double-bill

Among the new releases, freshest to the lists is the coupling on Virgin Classics of Busoni's *Arlecchino* with his *Turandot*. These are more than acceptable performances from the Opéra de Lyon under Kent Nagano (I have not heard the separate *Turandot* on Capriccio), and a great virtue of the issue is that, presenting the two operas together, it brings a somewhat elusive composer into sharper focus. Not that *Arlecchino* can ever be pinned down: 'less than a challenge and more than a jest', in its creator's words, its 'meaning' could produce endless exercise for the disciples of 'concept opera'. Most of us will find occupation enough in the score, which is a proportionately intriguing mixture of brisk busy-ness, lyricism, allusion and parody.

The *Turandot* has an irrelevant interest, which remains an interest even so. By comparison with Puccini's, this is a chaste score, animated much more by the energy of comedy than by the designs of grand-theatre. At rare moments the spirits of the two composers conjoin: one such is at the exultation in Prince Kalaf's refusal to pack up and go home. Busoni has no Liù (not a figure for comedy) and he has, of course, no 'Nessun dorma'. Yet he is not short of tunes (one of them, astonishingly enough, is *Greensleeves*), and melodic inventiveness is in fact one of the score's delights. Again, though not remotely suggesting an operatic counterpart to the mammoth spectacle of the silent-film epics (and Puccini is not entirely beyond that), there is a certain expansiveness in Busoni too. The final ensemble with its song and dance and the laughter of eunuchs has also a Beethovenian largesse: a lovely energy of freedom and generosity. The Turandot, Mechtild Gessendorf, has a clear bright voice and an authoritative manner; the Kalaf, Stefan Dahlberg, is a very adequate tenor; Anne-Marie Rodde in a surprise piece of casting as the Queen Mother is still firm of voice but now thin and edgy. The set remains one of the most delightful and enterprising of recent times.

Voice and orchestra: then and now

There is a type of eye-drop which, shortly after application, sends the room dark: the effect is only temporary but it can be mildly alarming if one has not been forewarned. It often seems to me, as I play modern operatic recordings, that some kind of aural counterpart is at work, except that here it is more or less permanent. But of course the analogy is far from exact, for the aural Pilocarpine is much more selective. Unerringly, it leaves the orchestra alone and goes for the stage. It's the voices that are distanced, the characters that grow dim and recede. In the orchestra pit the lights are on, so that those triplets in the viola part have never been better illuminated, and the clarinet's *sforzando* positively glares. Over the head of the players and their ever-evident conductor, the singers can certainly be discerned, though sometimes as from the wrong end of a telescope. And sometimes they appear to be lurking in the wings or, by some clever illusion, to be singing off-stage altogether.

However, this quarter I took an evening off. After a sequence of nights with the new *Boris*, the new *Così*, *Rape* and *Screw*, it seemed permissible to settle down to the old *Faust*. This is Gounod's *Faust* in English, or at least in the English of Henry Fothergill Chorley sung in the refined accents favoured by the British National Opera Company in 1929. The recording in its original form has been consigned by the *Faust*-surveyor in *Opera on Record* (Hutchinson: 1979) to 'the more bizarre footnotes in the history of the phonograph'. But for me it worked like a spell.

Everything was a joy, Chorley and all. The Dutton transfer is splendid, full-bodied and natural. The orchestral playing has point and zest, Beecham no doubt having made his lively enthusiasm for the old work felt, though I can't in all honesty claim to detect any slackening when for a few items Clarence Raybould takes over. Then there is the singing itself. Well, one can quite see that the tone and pronunciation ('Be main the delaight', 'that darrling child') in conjunction with the funny words ('Pray, sir, conclude the canticle so well begun') may appear at this date not unamusing. The sopranos are so very ladylike that they might almost come from the erstwhile D'Oyly Carte. But listen to Doris Vane's Siébel. She sings both solos admirably, and her high notes (A and then B) in the Garden scene are taken with a cleanness and aplomb that any international prima donna might envy.

Miriam Licette, the Marguerite, so clearly has the Melba tradition behind her, with a well-schooled Jewel song and unforced power of projection in the Church scene and Trio. Harold Williams sings his (transposed) 'Even bravest hearts' with a legato worthy of its original, Santley. Heddle Nash is a Faust with manners, a lyric tenor of fine accomplishment who never compromises the standards of a genuine *bel canto* method. And then there is Robert Easton. Even Alan Blyth, in his appreciative review, seems to feel it necessary to be a little apologetic about him and his Mephistopheles. Yet what character there is in his singing. The quick vibrato is less omnipresent and caricaturable than I had remembered it, but when it flickers ('So, captain, lie you there on your last bed of glo-o-o-ory') with that dark dramatic relish, I must say my heart goes out to those days when voices like his and the young Lauri-Volpi's and Supervia's were not squeezed dry of their individuality, everything being flattened down to satisfy a standard vibrancy-requirement (or lack of it).

Above all, there was the pleasure in this recording of having the stage well-lit, the characters there as vivid presences, the voices caught as from the best seat in the house; and I cannot believe that it is only with an opera as 'old-fashioned' as *Faust* that the benefits of such a procedure can be unguiltily enjoyed.

Russian opera and some singers

In their prime we do seem to be catching some excellent Russian singers, even some tenors. The recent *Queen of Spades* has an impressive Herman in Gegam Grigorian and *Boris Godunov* has Sergei Larin, quite the best Grigory (or Dmitri) that I can recall having heard in complete performances either on record or on stage. He has the sweetness of tone and youthful ring associated with some of the best Russian tenors in the past. Nor does he lack anything in expressiveness, his first scene being particularly strong in its mixture of anxiety, striving and excited determination. Grigorian's role is, of course, the more formidable, but where most who undertake it meet up pretty well to the formidable challenge, few in modern times have sung it so well, with a lover's voice where needful and with a ring in it that rejects the coarsened, uncovered 'big' sound. Otherwise, the star of the Tchaikovsky is Vladimir Chernov. This superb baritone, well known as he is to record collectors on account of his part in the Sony Classical Metropolitan Opera *Don Carlo*, *Luisa Miller* and *Il trovatore*, should by now have been presented on his own merits in at least two solo recitals, one of Italian opera, one of Russian. A similar recommendation can be offered in respect of the magnificent Elena Zaremba, Hostess in *Boris Godunov* and worth a good deal more. The Boris himself, Anatoly Kotcherga, is another discovery: a real bass, good at communicating the weariness of soul, and vivid in hallucination.

Both of these are orchestra-first recordings. With the *Boris* I find myself at least partly reconciled because, under Abbado, the Berlin Philharmonic play with a beauty that is constantly seeking out the lyrical heart of the score: I don't think I have ever heard its melodies flow with such fecundity, irrigating what can sometimes seem an essentially hard, brutal, wintry score. But here the Pilocarpine is instantly at work. Not the remotest chance of finding oneself swept up in the turbulence of the crowd, or feeling the anger of the officers, the menace of their whips. Boris's solo – where on stage he is the object of all eyes – passes dimly, just as, later, dramatically powerful entrances in the Nursery scene and the Boyars' Council go for nothing. The effect is of something closer to oratorio than to opera. Greatly, too, as the musical beauty of the performance is to be valued, there does seem to be a certain impersonality. The singers may have been allowed as much freedom as they required or was considered good for them, yet, in Samuel Ramey's Pimen for example, there is a literalism, a correctness that works against the life of the music. Repeatedly it comes down to those two notable modern absences: rubato and portamento.

These are also the great absentees in Olga Borodina's otherwise delightful Tchaikovsky song recital. She is another of the gifted, well-trained singers who have come from Russia in recent years, a lyrical mezzo-soprano not exceptionally opulent in tone or volume but pure in quality and firm in definition. She impressed most recently at London's Queen Elizabeth Hall this last February, ending (as an encore) with the song *Again, as before, alone*, which also concludes the recital on disc. In the hall it was even finer, for the almost disembodied ghost-voice of the lamenting first line carried perfectly, its pallor and desolation immensely affecting.

Here, too, the songs are given with conviction and sympathy; plenty of character also in the work of the pianist, Larissa Gergieva. Yet almost immediately – certainly by the second song – one is searching for something that isn't there, the missing ingredient, that gives a performance more than an adjudicator's good marks, and in fact from many adjudicators might earn black marks and a reprimand. However, in so far as the missing element can be pinpointed, it is the inability or unwillingness to bring that caressing touch to a melody that the well-judged portamento can afford, and the adherence to a discipline which frowns upon those hesitations, small forward impulses, momentary lingerings, which can come about only with a more permissive attitude towards rubato.

Song recitals

Greatness of course is rare, almost by definition, but occasionally it comes our way and we know, with as much certainty as is ever possible concerning such things, that a new 'classic' recording has arrived. So it is with the *Winterreise* of Peter Schreier and András Schiff. It is hard to disentangle the strands here; perhaps quite unnecessary too. In so far as one can separately extract a purely musical pleasure, that is there in the habitually enlightening work of the pianist. Of course, we have heard perhaps half-a-dozen players who have brought such insight and appreciation to the work that they are part of our inheritance, and never to be forgotten. Nevertheless, Schiff does make us forget, or at least feel no need of any other. The balancing of parts within the piano writing (melody and accompaniment, legato and staccato, but that's only the beginning of it) is superfine. Schreier's voice still has exceptional purity, and great technical difficulties are overcome with a mastery that seems to concentrate attention on other matters entirely, subtle in emotional force. Everything tells, yet it is perhaps as far into the cycle as 'Einsamkeit' before the feelings which have been working almost unrecognized cumulate in something explicitly tragic: 'Ach, das die Luft so ruhig', the lines which AB picked on as so haunting in their utterance, and all from then on, are at the very heart of the matter. A little test is that the sweetness of 'Täuschung' seems almost unbearable. And there are many details. For instance, the holding of 'keiner' in 'Wasserflut': it brings back, for once, Elena Gerhardt's responsiveness to the changing harmonies in the piano part, and that, nearly always, has been something listened for in vain.

Incidentally, the singer in a performance of *Winterreise* which was one of the most memorable in my experience, given in London earlier this year, was the young tenor Ian Bostridge, and it is good to see that he has been brought into the Hyperion Schubert Song Edition as a participant in the 1815 Schubertiad, subject of the latest volume. He records well, a voice with a face, sensitive to modulations, preserving a firm line. John Mark Ainsley is the other tenor, singing with great accomplishment in *Die erste Liebe*. There's another *Täuschung* (D230) here, sung by Patricia Rozario, and subject of a characteristic *aperçu* in Graham Johnson's written notes: the clarity and tessitura suggest purity, the chromaticism betokens deception.

Sawallisch's Meistersinger

The new *Meistersinger* has come just – but only just – in time for it to be heard and included in this quarter's retrospect. As it happens, the purpose of these second reviews may in this instance be better served by the restricting circumstances because there is no possibility of making comparisons, which anyway were made very thoroughly and pointedly by Alan Blyth in the August issue. Reading him after listening to the set straight through, I felt the probable justice in the way in which his comparisons detracted from a whole-hearted enjoyment and so to some extent from the possibility of giving more than a 'sensible' recommendation (the kind that acknowledges a recording's merits but cannot quite stamp it with the approving seal of a personal favourite). Of course, even without making comparisons on the spot, one is still mentally placing a performance in relation to others, so it would not be true to say that my report will be entirely on the basis of – what to call it? – simple as opposed to compound listening. Still, it may be reassuring to readers who have a feeling that this is a *Meistersinger* they would enjoy but wonder whether they ought to.

I did enjoy it, and greatly. 'Well,' you might say, 'it's an enchanting opera, one of the most enjoyable, especially for home-listening, when you can take your time about it, follow the score or libretto, and make pictures in your mind instead of being distracted by some bright idea of the producer's.' Yes, but it is usually not long before a singer's wobble or surface-scratch intrudes upon this idyll, and here it soon becomes blissfully apparent that there is going to be none of that. The Eva and Walther von Stolzing, first to be heard, are, wonder of wonders, young-sounding, with firm voices, gracefully produced, lyrically used. The Magdalene sounds fresh and plausibly a suitable girlfriend for David, who himself has a sprightly, well-focused but not obtrusively penetrative voice. A fine Pogner, scrupulous in legato and in the preservation of a genuinely singing bass-tone, and a Beckmesser who, if no joy to the ears, is not vocally a clown: these complete the principals save for the Hans Sachs who in Act 1 always remains an uncertain quantity.

It is time to put names to these sketches. Cheryl Studer presents Eva as a quick-witted young woman, independent enough to make a spirited elopement if driven to it. Ben Heppner, probably the most interesting of tenors to have arrived on the scene in the last few years, is a Walther who combines warmth of tone with dignity of bearing. The Magdalene and David are Cornelia Kallisch and Deon van der Walt, both vivid and idiomatic. Kurt Moll, movingly solicitous as Pogner, and Siegfried Lorenz just disagreeable enough without becoming simply a nuisance, throw into relief the many-featured character of Bernd Weikl's Sachs, wry in his humour, cunning in his methods, optimist and pessimist, the noble commoner, the commonsense philosopher. And, as AB remarked, a successor may well be to hand in René Pape, the Nightwatchman.

The occasional disappointment (Studer's notes at the very start and near the finish of the Quintet, for instance), the inevitable limitation (such as a want of even resonance in the upper part of Weikl's voice), the subtler, more personal intuition that the security of performance is dampening the zest (for example of Heppner's Walther): these are also part of the experience, even without the involvement of comparisons. But to balance against these is a quality in Sawallisch's way with the score that to my mind makes this *Meistersinger* a special one. It has the tenderness, the depth, the colour and other of the necessary attributes, but it also dances. There is a nimble play of musical wit – the wit of joyously achieved counterpoint, of thematic cross-reference that is no deliberated presentation of the visiting-card but a mercurial flash of intelligence. These, to be sure, are Wagner's, but it is Sawallisch's distinction to bring them right to the fore. And with this performance, more than any other that came to mind while listening, it seems the most natural thing in the world that Wagner should take to the waltz or to the nonchalance of that figure which accompanies Beckmesser's gleeful deal with Sachs in Act 3.

Hugh the Drover

How marvellous it would be if one could now turn to Vaughan Williams's opera of village life and see (or hear) in it a kind of English *Meistersinger*! The glorious and tragic truth, I think, is that it might almost have been something of that sort had the inspiration of the First Act survived and been fortified in a substantial Second and Third. As it is, the story takes such feeble, not to say daft, turns, that one can almost hear the composer losing faith, bar by bar. After the night-music, Prelude to Act 2, the best that comes to him is by way of reminiscence, from earlier in the opera or (briefly and possibly not reminiscence but first intimation) of his own *The lark ascending* which he was working on in the same period. Act 1 remains an impassioned and special creation, and for that alone the new recording was eagerly awaited.

The 1978 version on EMI disappointed partly because of the miscasting of Robert Tear in the name-part. Hugh needs a romantic, heroic and credibly open-air voice. Tudor Davies was the original, and many readers, I am sure, will remember James Johnston as being ideally suited in the 1950s at Sadler's Wells. The casting in this new recording of Bonaventura Bottone is certainly more appropriate than it may look and indeed more apt than most of the relatively obvious possible choices that come to mind. But he needs a sturdier body of tone in the middle register; Bottone's strong suit is his upper range (how splendidly he rang out the professional tenor Alfred's top notes in *Die Fledermaus* at Covent Garden) and here there is little call upon it. This is good likeable singing, but miniature and refined where the call is for strength and fire, two of the qualities Hugh celebrates in his famous Song of the Road. The opera is well performed, even so, with Rebecca Evans singing most beautifully as Mary and Matthew Best's Corydon forces on top form.

Choral wonders

Two choral records have given pleasure in which pleasure-in-mystery has been a constituent. The Mass and motets of Cipriano de Rore, heard in a recital by The Tallis Scholars revives an old puzzle. What is this music that reveals its secrets to the eye? The ear, even when trained and informed, can hardly follow all these canons, this foreshortening of cantus firmus, this 'parody' of its given reference. Yet somehow, out of the slow churning, the intertwining of dark, barely discernible strands, in the motet *Infelix ego* we have something of which its scholar-conductor, Peter Phillips, can write in terms of emotional experience: it creates 'an unforgettable mood of doubt and self-questioning'. My 'doubt and self-questioning' lie in the uncertainty as to whether I have genuinely caught that mood, whether indeed it is there to be caught, whether it can be more than a dark deep sea of undulating sound, and then a thing of technical mystery the true and wonderful nature of which is open only to the scholar-musician's eye.

With John Tavener the doubt is rather the other way round. The ear takes it in, and because of the strangeness of sound (which includes simplicity, itself almost a bewildering stranger in the music of this century) the ear is held. But so much is aural sensation or (as in the rising pitch of *The Lament of the Mother of God*) the application of pattern or formula. The enjoyment seems to lie partly in a free-ranging movement of the mind, supported by the music but passing all too readily beyond it.

Anyway, returning to *terra firma*: of almost equal wonder to me is the performance of these things. I listened first to The Sixteen in *Ikon of Light*, marvelling at the assurance and the beauty of texture. But then, turning from these expert adult professionals to the Choir of Winchester Cathedral ('Thunder entered Her'), One finds choirboys facing the challenges of *Hymns of Paradise* and giving a stunning performance of quite comparable accomplishment. The record is one of which David Hill and his choristers can be justly proud.

1995

Chung's Otello

The new *Otello* makes a crackling start with the energies of storm and victory, then knuckles an implacable way forward with the bonehard voice of its Iago, strikes gold in its Otello and wears the white flower of a blameless lyric soprano for its Desdemona. Act 2 makes especially poignant the contrasts of masculine-feminine, sweet content and the mines of sulphur. Its conductor, Myung-Whun Chung, is a strong presence. He shapes and paces expertly, but most of all he observes. This is a score where nothing is there without a purpose. A rest with a pause marked over it is an unwritten stage direction, as a metrically short line may be in Shakespeare. 'Pause', says the score, meaning 'lengthen the silence', before Iago's suggestion to Cassio

'Pregala tu': Desdemona's intercession on Cassio's behalf is vital to Iago's scheme and he wants the advice to sink in (as Verdi wants it to register with the audience – nothing like a silence for gaining attention). This is the kind of detail very sharply and profitably observed in this performance. So, though something protests within one at the headlong pace of the Act's final duet ('Si, pel ciel'), first, we note that the score sanctions such unchecked movement, and, second, that Verdi knew his Shakespeare:

> Like to the Pontick sea,
> Whose icy current and compulsive course
> Ne'er feels retiring ebb, but keeps due on
> To the Propontic and the Hellespont …

Then, sadly, something goes wrong with Act 3. I think the fault (if fault it be) lies with Plácido Domingo, but wonder whether Chung may not also have insisted on some literalism that limits his scope. Of course, if one has just stressed the purposefulness of detail in a score, it is inconsistent to ask for a non-literal reading in certain places (but rather be inconsistent, in my view, than doctrinaire). Otello's final outburst ('Anima mia') surely needs some declamatory freedom from the printed note: there are several other examples, including the famous monotone of 'Dio, mi potevi scagliar', where the reciting notes should surely be pitched as written but just as surely it works against expressiveness if the voice is rigidly confined ('la croce crudel d'angosce e d'onte'). Domingo seems to be loath to leave the singing-note and the singing-tone even when Verdi seems to want him to: 'voce soffocata' in the monologue, and 'terribile' at 'la sposa d'Otello'. Nor in this performance does he allow irony and bitterness to colour (or discolour) his voice in the 'Dio ti giocondi' duet.

Act 4 is fine again, but something essential has been lost. It is a pity, in this otherwise very special recording (which I would still most certainly want to have). Cheryl Studer and Sergei Leiferkus are absolutely first-rate; Ramon Vargas is an exceptionally good Cassio and the bass, Ildebrando d'Arcangelo, also a name to remember (quite apart from being notably hard to forget). There is much more to be said. But on.

Parsifal and Salome

Richard Osborne's review of the *Otello* has not reached me at the time of writing, but Alan Blyth gave *Parsifal* a right drubbing. This has James Levine in sunset-and-evening-star vein ('such a tide as, moving, seems asleep'), and in this opera following the score does not always help concentration (having stayed on one page for an eternity, one ventures to look ahead, only to meet with more *sehr langsam*). But this *Parsifal* of Levine's is inordinately slow.

Perhaps that of itself disqualifies the set from recommendation, and certainly there were other matters over which my reactions coincided very largely with Alan Blyth's (such as James Morris's Amfortas, an old-style bank manager with a touch of the old lumbago). Yet I can't quite follow him in other things. The Transformation music, for example, becomes, in his view, 'a piece of orchestral exhibitionism': other conductors, he says, such as Karajan and Knappertsbusch, have it 'integrated into a total view of the work'. I had no such feeling on first playing, and going back to both Levine and Knappertsbusch (in 1951 on Teldec) again am still unable to locate anything which would pinpoint the objection or substantiate the comparison. The slow speed of Levine is 'integrated' with his other slow speeds (it would be different if he made a special point of spacing-out these particular pages). Granted the slow tempo and the more 'analytical' modern recording (so that one listens to the various parts of the orchestra more consciously), I can't find anything here other than fine playing of an inspired passage.

More seriously, I think AB underrates Domingo. 'A serious drawback' is the general verdict, the only virtues allowed him being 'his customary intelligence and steady tone'. But the tone is more than merely steady: it is of rare, and in this context (as in *Die Frau ohne Schatten*) super-rare, quality. The phrasing is said to be 'often wooden', but this too I find hard to follow as, in the first place, the role is not one which provides much in the way of options for phrasing, and then, when I return to the solo in Act 2 ('Amfortas! die Wunde!') to make comparisons with Windgassen in the Knappertsbusch Bayreuth recording, the phrasing turns out to be identical. Then, it is said that 'the text seems to mean little or nothing to him' (not saying a great deal for 'his customary intelligence'): but again, when I go through that same solo, the difference seems to lie much more in the superior quality of Domingo's singing (fine as Windgassen is) than in any evidence of a failure on his part to understand the text. At certain points (the cries of 'Klage' for instance, or the change of mood at 'Und ich, der Thor') Domingo even strikes me as the more expressive and vivid.

About Jessye Norman's Kundry I'm in half-agreement. That it is 'a part that lies ideally for her soprano shading to mezzo' makes for some extraordinarily beautiful singing especially in the sensuous enticements of Act 2. But there is no wildness, no terror. Both Domingo and Norman bring the precious gift of a great voice to the performance, but to my mind there is a good deal more of Parsifal in Domingo than of Kundry in Norman.

Even so, there is more of Kundry in her than there is of Salome. Here it is not so much a matter of characterization as of voice-character. The voice of Salome needs to be young, silvery, innocent: that is how the grossness of will and act is felt as so utterly appalling. The mezzo element is as wrong in Salome as it is right in Kundry. More important is the top, which Norman still commands triumphantly but without the silvery, youthful ease which, in their different ways and at the time of their recordings, both Behrens and Nilsson in the early 1960s had, and Ljungberg and Welitsch when they recorded the final solo. Norman is well in character when Salome exercises her authority or sheer will-power; also in the 'matt' tone of 'Ach! ich habe deinen Mund geküsst'; and sometimes she is so lovely in tone ('Du warst schön', for instance) that we listen with perfect contentment.

Ozawa and the Staatskapelle Dresden are responsible for much fine work, though I daresay David Nice is right when he says that it ought to 'raise hackles' more than it does.

Tenors: supply and outlook

In *Salome* the pitiful role of Narraboth is sung by Richard Leech, broad of phrase, firm of tone, resonant and lyrical: it is hard to believe the part has ever been heard to better advantage. Here is an excellent tenor, and one who needs a recital record to bring him more sharply into focus.

In Russian opera, *Mazeppa* reintroduces Sergei Larin, the outstanding Grigory (Dmitri) of the Abbado/Sony Classical *Boris Godunov*. Here he has the role of Andrei, which may have started life in the librettist's mind as the opera's 'token tenor' but is certainly more than that by the time Tchaikovsky has finished with him: his aria in the last Act, a plea for death and oblivion, has more of the composer in it, I think, than any other solo in the opera, and Larin sings it superbly. As DN points out in his review, Gorchakova fails to colour her voice expressively or to catch the haunted, other-worldly tone which is necessary if the lullaby at the end of the opera is to have its due effect. In other respects she sings magnificently, as does Leiferkus in the title-role. The historical material would have suited Mussorgsky better than Tchaikovsky, but the score is a masterly piece of work and this a fine recording.

Of the lighter type of Italian tenor there appears to be no great lack – Rossini and Donizetti operas keep appearing, not, in general, to be disgraced by their tenors. One who might be brought in more regularly is Ramon Vargas. He made a promising recital record for Claves, but since then has been cast in secondary roles: Edmond in *Manon Lescaut* (to Pavarotti's Des Grieux) and now Cassio in the new *Otello*. He distinguishes himself in both, as he does as Fenton in the new *Falstaff* under Riccardo Muti. In all of his contributions we become aware of a quite beautiful voice, and in the little aria of Act 3 he shows himself an artist, phrasing and shading with taste and skill. The Nannetta, Maureen O'Flynn, and Quickly, Bernadette Manca di Nissa, also catch the attention – but, as AB says, Juan Pons's Falstaff wants 'face' and a chuckle. Fine ensemble, fine playing, some magic in the night music in Windsor Forest, but nobody listening without prior knowledge would guess that Falstaff himself is one of the great comic characters of the stage.

Most promising of the younger tenors is probably Roberto Alagna. His Roméo in Gounod's opera triumphed recently at Covent Garden, and his performance of the cavatina was the most delightful singing by a lyric tenor that I can recall having heard in the house since the young Pavarotti appeared in *La fille du Régiment* and *La sonnambula*. On disc he is an admirable Rinuccio in *Gianni Schicchi*. This is in the *Trittico* (Puccini's three one-act operas) conducted by Bruno Bartoletti, with Mirella Freni in the three leading soprano roles. It does not work well, that triple-casting; recordings are always merciless in their exposure of wobble, and though Freni sings with feeling and often still beautiful tone, the unsteadiness or ever-present threat of it, constantly erodes the pleasure of listening. For myself the great revelation of that set came with the other tenor, the Luigi of *Il tabarro*, Giuseppe Giacomini. Here is a singer who had never impressed me strongly, one way or another, either on record or in the theatre; but it is five or six years since I heard him last, and have now to conclude that he has developed almost beyond recognition. His is a voice of very distinctive timbre, dark, rich and strong; perhaps a little throaty in production, but most striking and apt in his 'Hai ben ragione' solo. I have been assured that this is indeed the very same voice as was heard recently at Covent Garden in *Turandot*, so let us hope good use can be made of it for recordings while it is still in this condition.

Songs: mostly Schumann and Poulenc

At least there is no neglect of Bryn Terfel in what must be his vocal prime. The Schubert recital shows him also as an artist, one who has the imaginative strength for a wholly convincing *Gruppe aus dem Tartarus* and then the scrupulous legato and ability to work effectively within a deliberately restricted range of volume and dynamics in *Litanei*. The grace and lightness for *Das Fischermädchen* go impressively with the large-scale *Erlkönig* and its frightening characterization of a particularly repulsive child-molester. A smile is missing in *Der Musensohn* and *An Silvia*, as is what for short will have to be called a spiritual quality in (for instance) *Ganymed* and *Wandrers Nachtlied*. But it is a memorable record and must enhance still further the status of this highly individual, versatile and gifted singer.

A striking contrast is presented by Christoph Prégardien in his new recital especially in its last section, devoted to the Heine poems set by Schubert in *Schwanengesang*. If 'spiritual' was a word in the right area for what was missing with Terfel, it is very much what is dominant in Prégardien. He is a singer with several voices: a gentle lyric tenor with silvery upper notes, a baritone with more body than one might have thought, and the possessor, or exponent, of a kind of 'yowl' which is not a particularly pleasant sound in itself but can be mightily expressive (an example is the last syllable of 'mein eigne Gestalt' in 'Der Doppelgänger'). With his pianist, Andreas Staier, on an 1823 fortepiano, he is at his finest in the haunted world of 'Ihr Bild' and 'Die Stadt'. Singer and pianist are also subtle and highly individual in their Mendelssohn (in *Auf Flügeln des Gesanges* the voice concentrating on sense and communication, the dreamy flow of the song provided by its harplike accompaniment).

They also perform Schumann's *Dichterliebe* (the programme is a collection of Heine settings), fixing the character as a poor troubled creature, unstable, perhaps manic-depressive, and yet (again perhaps) ultimately finding a reserve of strength, whether in life or in death. Such speculations hardly arise out of another recent recording of the cycle, by Thomas Hampson with Geoffrey Parsons: most lovely singing here, with each song cared for and felt, yet, in the unjust way of these things, not very memorable. The recital, recorded in Edinburgh, includes *An die ferne Geliebte* (again a bit too easygoing), some settings of Burns in German translation and (best, I think) the six Songs, Op. 48 of Grieg. Two other Schumann cycles figure in the lists. Dame Margaret Price sings *Frauenliebe und -leben* with touching expressiveness, eager and affectionate, till the start of the last song, which must shock: fine, though, after that. The *Liederkreis*, Op. 39 is sung by Fassbaender with ever-responsive tone – desolate, tender, predatory. In some of the songs ('Zwielicht' for instance) the tension of suppressed unease is at odds with the complaisance of the slow tempo; unlike the recent *Schöne Magelone* recording, where she is magnificent, the pianist, Elisabeth Leonskaja, brings an unexpectedly dull touch. There's Brahms in this recital too, including the *Vier ernste Gesänge*, but these often inspired artists seem not to get through to the songs as they did the *Magelone*.

Very little of anything 'gets through' in the Poulenc song recital by Cathérine Dubosc and Gilles Cachemaille. Dubosc's 'innocent' voice is all very well for a start, but then one realizes that this is it. The baritone is less boring, but his development as a singer seems to me disappointing: he appears to have encouraged the upper rather than the lower part of his voice, which is where the colour lies. Something, of course, does get through: the special pleasure of the writing for piano, here in the hands of Pascal Rogé. Changing hands now for those of Graham Johnson, with Felicity Lott in radiant voice, the composer is much better served by 'Homage à Francis Poulenc' on Forlane. Not everything suits; *Banalités* and *La Dame de Monte-Carlo* need to forgo some refinement or, in a different sense, perhaps to refine further (Patrick O'Connor quotes Bernac on the 'touch of coarseness' in the first and Poulenc on the *Tosca* element in the second). But there are many delights here, in the Cocteau and Ronsard settings for instance; and *Tel jour, telle nuit*, in which I imagine the soprano voice meets problems more easily solved by high baritone or tenor, culminates in a most moving performance of 'Nous avons fait la nuit'.

Miscellany

Best for a sweet tooth: Sumi Jo's 'Carnaval'. PO'C said that it was like being in a French pâtisserie shop with all the delectables on show, but as most of my more reprehensible dreams seem nowanights to have just such a setting, I'm not unduly perturbed. The song from Messager's *Madame Chrysanthème* is the one to choose first.

A note now on my review of Amanda Roocroft's EMI recital. The only dissenting voice I heard from was that of a reader who in a sincere and courteous letter wrote that he had enjoyed the record greatly ('experiencing the *frisson* that an amateur like me has to substitute for technical analysis') and was 'disappointed and rather saddened that [I] chose to drop a somewhat wet blanket over the recital'. Well, the sadness and disappointment were mine too.

Finally, a postscript on the point raised in reviewing the Vienna State

Opera, Vol. 1, in which I affirmed that the Radamès of 1934, said to be Lauri-Volpi, was Aureliano Pertile. The expert on Pertile is Paul Morby, to whom, without a word, nudge or hint by way of preparation, I played the excerpt. Puzzlement (it clearly wasn't Lauri-Volpi): replay: a sudden rigidity, tension, concentration: and a cry: 'It's Pertile!' This is actually of some importance, for as far as we know, brief and unsatisfying as it is, the recording is the only one of Pertile ('il tenore di Toscanini') heard live. Mr Morby wrote to Professor Deutsch in Vienna and received a facsimile of the night's programme: Radamès ... Signor Lauri-Volpi. But it's Pertile. We can only assume that Lauri-Volpi was indisposed and Pertile called in. It would be good to know what other people think ... and, more important, if anybody happens to know.

Choral records have been absent from these columns for too long, and I hope to make amends in April; also to say a few words in favour of *The Wreckers* and Conifer's recent première recording.

The Alagna debate

'Quis custodiet ...?' or 'Who shall criticize the critics?' 'Everybody' is one answer; but there are also experts, real experts, in every field, who query, chivvy and harangue those of us who, in a professional capacity, exercise such knowledge and judgement as we have, usually over a larger field than we can hold in perpetual view. Generally, we answer the queries, consign harangues to the wheelie-bin, and do our best to welcome the chivvying because it helps to keep us up to the mark. I used to have a regular chivvier. He is dead now, but for several years no praise of mine for a 'modern' singer would pass without a letter demanding instant resignation and wanting to know what had become of standards. His own standards were set by singers of a certain type and active within a certain period; all since then were known as 'the present lot'. He was rather like the late Colin Shreve whom I once tackled on the subject. 'Don't you like *any* modern singers?' 'Well, who for instance?' 'Victoria de los Angeles?' (this was *circa* 1955) 'No!' 'Schwarzkopf?' 'NO!' 'What about Callas?' 'Isn't it a tragedy!'

Now, in recent years it has seemed that modern singers find much more tolerance among those who take their standards from the remoter past. So, in the previous 'Quarterly Retrospect', when briefly surveying a few likely-looking tenors, with Roberto Alagna in the lead, I reckoned (but perhaps too easily) to speak for a consensus. A thoughtful letter arrived, more chivvy than harangue, more query than chivvy, and the name of the writer was the same as that of my chivvier deceased!

In the 'Retrospect' I had mentioned Alagna's success at Covent Garden in Gounod's *Roméo et Juliette*, and especially his fine performance of the cavatina. My correspondent had also heard him, though at a later performance, 'a frustrating one': 'fine voice,' he concluded, 'excellent French, but of what I would call a pure vocal line hardly a trace'. In 'Salut, tombeau' he compared Paul Franz (*c*1910) and found in him an instant and immense superiority. As to Alagna, he 'could sing with the requisite taste and refinement if he so wished,' but 'indiscriminate praise will not help him to improve.'

So I open this quarter's 'Retrospect' with a 'Prespect', if that is the word. Alagna will certainly be recording again before long. When the next disc of this very gifted tenor arrives, it will be heard eagerly, and high among the desiderata will be refinement, taste and a pure vocal line. I have to say that I thought he had these qualities in abundance. I also thought of Edmond Clément: Alagna seemed that good. So let us hope.

Singers: the younger generation

Hope for the future of singing is of course greatly strengthened when each quarter brings a crop of new (or newish) voices that give present pleasure and promise of more to come. Let me extract eight of them with the intention of returning later to their respective recordings. Renée Fleming emerges as a fully-fledged prima donna in Rossini's *Armida*: a lyric-dramatic coloratura soprano, nobility in her tone, a small but colourful element of close-knit vibrato, a substantial lower register, brilliant fluency in passagework and a command of expression that is her own and not a reflection of Callas. Lorna Anderson and Rebecca Evans: light sopranos, with the freshness and purity of youth in their voices, the one a notable addition to Graham Johnson's singers in his Schubert series (also in the Britten folk-songs), the other a charming Josephine in *HMS Pinafore* and, before that, an equally lovely Mary in *Hugh the Drover*. A British contralto making a well-earned début is Hilary Summers, heard in a moderately successful *Messiah* under Stephen Cleobury: a voice of fine quality, with a character that should prove useful well beyond the oratorio repertoire.

Deborah Voigt, Cassandra in *Les Troyens*, and vocally the best female singer in it (as Gino Quilico is the best male): her variety of expression seems limited, but the tone, with its firmness and beauty, is surely exceptional. Two tenors come into view: Janez Lotrič in a Naxos duet recital I reviewed enthusiastically in February, and to which I will not revert, and Gregory Kunde, best of the bevy of tenors in *Armida*, fearless on high and capable of both sweetness and brilliance. Finally, the baritone Boje Skovhus, who in addition to being a captivating Danilo in *Die lustige Witwe* under John Eliot Gardiner, has a Lieder recital which is certainly among the choice records of the quarter: a high, robust voice most sensitively used and a genuine individuality of character: no hint of an imitation Fischer-Dieskau.

All of these, in my view, are welcome to the fold, and I had rather rejoice in them prematurely than miss out on these precious years when their voices are still young and fresh.

Trojans and Wreckers

How the heart leaps at the opening of *Les Troyens*: nothing so exciting except possibly (by connection or coincidence?) the very start of *King Priam*. The new recording under

Charles Dutoit brings out marvellously well the detail of Berlioz's orchestration, and the conductor's firm, purposeful control is bracingly evident. As usual, one wishes the chorus were balanced more forwardly as in the 1969 Philips version under Sir Colin Davis. I wish, too, that Voigt's excellent singing (see above) were matched by stronger characterization: this Cassandra is far too placid about her prospects ('no marrying for me, no joyful hymns'), and her final vision of calamity lacks the despairing frustration of the unheeded prophetess. It is a noble and beautiful voice even so, and I'd rather hear it than the less even and less well focused sound of Davis's Berit Lindholm, more intense in expression though she be.

Gino Quilico as Choroebus is excellent, his 'Reviens à toi' probably the best piece of singing in the whole performance. And all goes well, the gorgeous orchestral textures illuminated, the playing totally admirable in its precision and sound-quality. Yet the two principals, the Dido and Aeneas, do present problems. Gary Lakes, in some ways 'school of Vickers', has nothing like the ring and body of his predecessor, and he seems to have no top, so that the climax of his entry and the high C of his great solo are muffed (Jon Vickers also is far from ideal, but he has much stronger resources for 'Inutiles regrets'). Edward Greenfield pointed to the love music of Act 3 as showing Lakes to good advantage in comparison with Vickers, who, he says, 'trumpets out at a full *forte* through even the gentlest, most intimate passages'. I fancy Vickers's 'full *forte*' was capable of causing greater havoc than this, but he is certainly less than elegant. Lakes, moreover, joins his Dido in the 'O nuit d'ivresse' to make a nocturne almost as light and airy as the Italian love-birds in *Don Pasquale*. But then, Dutoit's conception of this is very different from Davis's, as the speeds alone indicate (Davis 5'18", Dutoit 3'51").

There remains the Dido of Françoise Pollet, not helped, it must be said, by the lack of prominence and presence given her in the recording of her entry: the spotlight should be trained on her, as it was upon Josephine Veasey in the Davis set. At each comparison, in fact, I was pleased to go back to Veasey, who simply emerges as the better singer, firmer in the 'grip' of her less velvety but still very beautiful tone and much better schooled in the unity of her voice, the blending of registers.

So, *Les Troyens* I enjoyed a little less than EG, Dame Ethel Smythe's *The Wreckers* a little more than Michael Oliver. The odd thing is that I quite agree with his criticisms, which are more analytically submitted than I could have made them, which perhaps accounts for the difference. In listening, I felt always that a local strength held the interest even though a structural flaw ran, perhaps, through the whole piece. And also (it is as though there are three layers to this), behind the pervasive flaws I felt there survived a strong creative and compassionate impulse, so that the attempt, if not the accomplishment, availed. It is true that there is a failure of melodic invention, and that was probably indicative of the 'drying' of this musical genius. Yet *The Wreckers* never loses interest.

In the recording (a Prom performance from London's Royal Albert Hall) two important elements are missing which affect the success of the work itself. The two leading parts are miscast: a stronger tenor than Justin Lavender is needed for Mark (John Coates – who sang in the first performance – after all, was a Wagnerian), and Ann-Marie Owens has neither the opulence of tone nor the charismatic vocal personality for Thirza (a part intended for Emma Calvé). The secondary roles, sung by Judith Howarth, David Wilson-Johnson, Peter Sidhom and others, are extremely well taken, and that helps to secure a welcome for this set. The real trouble is the restricted power and lack of presence of the chorus. Ronald Crichton's memories of the revival in London at Sadler's Wells (telling how the chorus sang 'fit to burst' or to 'awaken the dead') recalled my own memories of the chorus there in *Peter Grimes*, and one knew exactly what he meant. That, the emotional impact of the chorus as a character in the opera, is what is missing in the recording; given its presence I still think *The Wreckers* could earn a sturdy place in the repertoire.

Operatic Allsorts

The viability of *Sadko* as opera will, I imagine, be less sceptically viewed after the success of Philips's new recording. Admittedly, the pace seems slow in Act 1 after the magical swing of the sea in the Prelude; but it quickens soon enough, and from the Third Act onwards all is delight. Valery Gergiev with his Kirov forces does full justice to Rimsky's wonderful orchestration, and there is some excellent singing, Vladimir Galusin's interesting, somewhat baritonal, tenor in the lead.

Of *Armida*'s six tenors, Gregory Kunde, the Rinaldo, is appropriately the best, but the level of performance is high throughout, with enthusiastic audience testimony from Pesaro and a major triumph for Renée Fleming. The plentiful supply of tenors for Rossini, alas, is offset by their scarcity in Wagner. Siegfried Jerusalem, no youngster (35 in fact) even at his début as a singer in 1975, still seems to be the best we have, and his Lohengrin has both lyricism and thrust. With Cheryl Studer in lovely voice and well suited to her role, and Waltraud Meier an opulent, charismatic Ortrud, Abbado conducts a sympathetic and often splendid account. In fact, this *Lohengrin* would be a clear winner were it not for the Telramund, Hartmut Welker, whose production is uneven, his tone lacking the firm incisiveness so much needed for the part, and whose public manner belies the reputation of a 'noble man', which is what the community believes him to be.

The latest in the series of Entartete Musik operas is Viktor Ullmann's *Der Kaiser von Atlantis. Die lustige Witwe* and *HMS Pinafore* also go into this paragraph, and I wonder whether that is hideous to contemplate: an affront to the heroic spirit and hellish circumstances in which Ullmann wrote. I dearly hope not, for his game with Death as a character ('der Gärtner Tod') and his creation of beauty and comedy in the face of Death-as-reality is the very opposite of a killjoy. The work is a little masterpiece irrespective of its origins; with those in mind, it is moving, inspiring and dreadful. The performance under Lothar Zagrosek surely does it justice, and Iris Vermillion's singing of Ullmann's three Hölderlin settings is most beautiful. And I don't think he would object to joining company with *HMS Pinafore*, which is a little masterpiece too, sailing in fine style with Sir Charles Mackerras at the helm and as good a crew as ever aboard her (Rebecca Evans, Felicity Palmer, Michael Schade, Thomas Allen, Richard Suart and the veteran Donald Adams). But what a *Widow*! *Die lustige Witwe*, about which Andrew Lamb wrote with no exaggeration, calling it the kind of operetta recording that comes 'once in a lifetime if one is lucky', is a concentrated delight. Gardiner's flair never seems to desert him, and (as he makes one realize afresh) neither does Lehár's. All the cast (Cheryl Studer, Barbara Bonney, Rainer Trost, Boje Skovhus, Bryn Terfel) appear to have felt the touch of the magic wand, and the whole production goes ahead under the same spell.

In Recital

At the head of this list comes Cecilia Bartoli's 'Mozart Portraits', which is a brilliant example of the art of the chameleon-recitalist: becoming the character in mood, voice and 'face'. It is exactly what so many well-sung, conscientiously prepared recitals are not; and there is a world of difference. Fiordiligi in determined mood ('Come scoglio') is one thing, in humility ('Per pietà') another. She is still one identifiable human being in both, and quite distinct from her maid-servant, Despina, whose aria comes next in the programme. Similarly, Countess Almaviva has an identity faithfully embodied by this singer, who transforms herself dextrously into a natural Susanna. So it continues throughout. The 'h's are regrettable in *Exsultate, jubilate*, but again there is a wonderfully vivid change of mood from the slow movement to the 'Alleluia'.

Next is Boje Skovhus. With Helmut Deutsch, a superb accompanist, he gives what is virtually a Wolf recital, confining itself to settings of Eichendorff and ending with four songs by Korngold. The young Danish baritone sings like a master. A clear, high-lying voice (able to invest *Verschwiegene Liebe* with the sweetness and ease remembered from Schlusnus), and a fine phrase-by-phrase responsiveness that does not fuss the unity of the song out of existence: these are two of the qualities. He has many others, and we must hope for a chance to hear him over here in person before long.

It would be good to hear Uwe Heilmann in recital too. His *Die schöne Müllerin* with James Levine irked Alan Blyth, and understandably so, for it runs too readily to extremes. Yet it has its interest and achievements, which are partly the result of these. For instance, Levine whacks out the jolly-jolly diddle-diddles of 'Das Wandern' with hefty hands (though he varies skilfully too); but rarely has the distant murmur of the brook drifted into hearing-range with more delicacy than at the start of the 'Wohin?' which follows. Heilmann exploits the reserves of his fine voice, though it is a pity they should include a near falsetto tone all too convenient for soft passages. But here's the dilemma: should one see in these cycles (*Winterreise* also) a distinct non-Schubert character, an objective character creation, and, if so, should one uncritically sympathise with him? I don't. Or certainly I don't in this version of the character.

Yet, turning to the 'straight' characterization of Håkan Hagegård in the *Müllerin* or Thomas Allen in *Winterreise* I can't say that I find that very satisfying either. These make their way by fine, scrupulous singing and a general appropriateness of mood: but there is something beyond, a tension, a spirituality, perhaps a neurosis, that they don't catch and which cries out for incorporation.

The songs incorporated into the new volume of the Schubert Edition are more straightforward in their requirements. This is a second Schubertiad, of 1815, some of them part-songs, mostly quite short, with the 'Ossian' poem *Cronnan* as the masterpiece with a strange, rather haunting pre-echo of the *Unfinished* Symphony in its opening. Of the four singers, Simon Keenlyside and Lorna Anderson give greatest pleasure as singers, though all (Jamie MacDougall and Catherine Wyn-Rogers are the others) impress as intelligent artists. Anderson, as mentioned earlier, goes straight into the list of 'whom to look out for'. She, with MacDougall again, and with Graham Johnson as pianist, sings also in the complete Britten folk-song arrangements. She seems to have a genuine feeling for folk-song, and *O can ye sew cushions* and *Il est quelq'un sur terre* are especially delightful. Occasionally, and despite the obvious differences, I seem to hear an echo of Dame Janet Baker (in *Early one morning* for instance) and there is a similar kind of boldness in the surprisingly full-bodied *Ca' the yowes to the nowes*.

King's Ransom

With Vol. 11, the Anthems and Services of Purcell are completed, and Robert King and his Consort can look back in approval. The last record has at least one of the greatest, *Praise the Lord O my soul*, with its sublime opening symphony and its brief *brindisi* in celebration of 'wine that maketh glad the heart of man'. This issue really belongs to the 'Early Music Retrospect', but I want to signal appreciation of the work of its soloists throughout the series. Michael George, singing John Gostling's music, accepted the greatest challenge, but for all of them technique has been severely tested. In his 'Valete' note, Robert King himself makes a special point of expressing gratitude to the solo trebles and the 'super-choir' of hand-picked boys from the cathedrals. It is very appropriate that he should dedicate the whole venture to 'the noble Cathedral tradition', the furtherance of which is so vital to the continuing musical life cherished by readers of this magazine. The Purcell series has been a regular and welcome companion now for almost three years. Put the 11 volumes in one scale and all the rest of the records heard this quarter into the other, and I would be hard-pressed to know which to take.

Disc v. video

Disc versus video: as far as I can recall, it is not a debate which has had an airing in these quarterly notes, and I am not intending now to do more than touch upon it. But, in his review of the recent *Prince Igor*, David Nice suggested Decca's video of the Covent Garden production as a useful source of reference in the process of making up one's mind about the changed order of the Acts. The new version, with the Kirov company under Valery Gergiev, puts the Polovtsian Act (normally the Second) straight after the Prologue, the former First Act becoming the new Act 2. It is an alteration that has been responsibly made, on good scholarly grounds, and much can be said for it. The opera has widely recognized dramatic faults, and the simple transposition of scenes remedies one of them. In its more serious character, *Prince Igor* is 'about' the consequences of war, a concern that is now sustained without interruption. Thus (for instance) the scene of riotous debauchery in Galitsky's camp has effect not as a bit of jolly barbarism of the kind people euphemistically call Rabelaisian, but as the first of those consequences, and so more akin to the Shakespearian drama of disorder.

From the video, however, I returned to the discs and to a different question, namely why it was that for myself (unlike the reviewer) the recording had succeeded only in an incomplete sort of way; and the answer seems to lie with a point that certainly has been raised time enough, one would have thought, in these retrospects – that of 'presence', or lack of it, in the recorded voices.

In fact it was this, quite as much as the reordering, that sent me to the video in the first place. In general, the balance in video-sound favours voices over orchestra, and it does so here. Very much as expected, the characters came to life in the video, not because they were visible but because they were heard more vividly. The irony is that a forward placing of voices is far less essential in opera on film than it is on disc. Video, like a stage production, brings the characters to the forefront of attention, whereas sound-recording has to compensate, deliberately, for the absence of sight. It was something perfectly well understood by record producers such as Legge and Culshaw. Since their time the essential dramatic force of operatic recordings has been repeatedly and increasingly weakened because the characters (that is, the voices) have been accorded a place which in purely aural terms may be comparable to their position on stage, but which makes insufficient allowance for the audio-visual function sound-recording must accept if it is to fulfil the dramatic needs of opera.

Further matters arise. DN's review refers to Covent Garden's production as 'loosely directed', and it seems that with that phrase he has disposed of it. But there is also a question of where you think the centre of an operatic performance lies. Of course we know that modern orthodoxy, as represented by the balance of attention in reviews of operatic performances on stage, has it that at the centre (of power and of interest) stands the producer or director. My memory of that Covent Garden performance, on stage as on video, is that central to the experience was the superb work of three principal singers. The role of Kontchakovna was sung by Elena Zaremba whose contralto has a rare and rich quality perfectly attuned to the sensuous world of the Polovtsian seduction. Anna Tomowa-Sintow, magnificent simply as a woman, charged Yaroslavna's arias with thrillingly impassioned vibrancy, her voice (no longer young) still under masterly control. Sergei Leiferkus concentrated his tone so firmly that his singing would have had compelling intensity even if it had been shaded less expressively. My point is that drama works through character, and in opera the characters are voices. The quality of a voice may be crucial.

Returning to the new recording, I very happily find musical value and interest, but dramatic validity ultimately depends on the quality of the voice-characters and the effectiveness of their presentation in the recording. Mikhail Kit, with his rather ponderous, dutiful bass-baritone, lacks thrust and resonance in the upper notes and forfeits conviction as a fiery, charismatic figure: a dully responsible fellow rather than an inspiring leader, which is Igor's essential character. Olga Borodina, fine singer as she is, wants the luxurious richness, the seductive coloration, the silken legato, that will embody the magic of Kontchakovna's exotic appeal. Galina Gorchakova, whom I take to be one of the supremely gifted singers of our time, has apparently not yet learnt to infuse her beautiful voice with the pain of loss and yearning; so the voice-character of Yaroslavna is not there. But even if these (and the other principals) had fulfilled the heart's desire, the recording would still not have allowed them the central immediate presence which is an opera's right. Still less does it allow sufficient presence to the chorus, who, as we are always being reminded, constitute a principal 'character' in Russian opera. Such reordering as that involved in the act-sequence here is the kind of thing our operatic world deals with very successfully; I wish a reordering of priorities in staging, recorded sound and critical approach could be achieved as effectively.

Hickox's Troilus and Cressida

Here, too, we have a triumph of scholarship, intelligence, musicianship and application. The textual problems of Walton's score find a most happy solution. Opera North have in this production an achievement that merits a proud place in their company's history as surely as it does in that of the opera itself. The recorded performance also reflects credit on all concerned, and the inevitable 'but' is one which I am very loath to start upon. Again, it has to do with voice-character and recording of voice.

After a first affectionately intent listening, I went back, briefly, to the extracts conducted by the composer in 1955, playing Cressida's 'Slowly it all comes back'. Musically, perhaps, there was not much to choose; but for the voice and the drama, there was all the difference between seeing a character on stage in general-purpose lighting as for rehearsal and then seeing her lit for performance. Two factors are involved. One is that Elisabeth Schwarzkopf (in the Walton excerpts) presents more distinctly the voice-character of this girl haunted by shadows, repression, longing and revulsion: the realized complexity is altogether richer, more individual. The other is that even if Judith Howarth (in the complete recording) had a comparable richness of voice and expression, she could not have brought it to such a face-to-face encounter because the recording (fine in all other respects) does not provide that kind of spotlight.

Howarth is a lovely singer and she earns much gratitude in this, her first major undertaking as yet in opera on record. But (again these buts) I'm puzzled. A prominent feature of the announcements and advertisements has been what is called the restoration of the score 'for dramatic soprano'. Schwarzkopf, for whom the part was written, was not a dramatic soprano, nor was Magda László who created it; and neither is Howarth. Curiously, the very notion of 'dramatic soprano' is at odds with the character, whose vulnerability calls for a very special kind of lyric soprano – at one time in her career I fancy Ileana Cotrubas could have been right (and it is then up to the conductor to keep his orchestra down when necessary, more so than Hickox does). I wonder whether the responsibilities of the 'dramatic soprano' did not weigh too heavily with Howarth, so that she lost (or didn't have) the concept of fragility that makes Cressida's tragedy her own and not a generalized operatic tragedy.

Meanwhile, Arthur Davies is a splendid Troilus and Alan Opie a distinguished Diomede. Nigel Robson's Pandarus, I think, is a respectable weakness: one respects his good singing and his determination not to 'do a Pears', but the result (in the recording even more than on stage) is that a flavour is lost, and there are times when his voice could almost be that of Troilus. None of which, may I add, should deter purchase of what is certainly one of the most welcome operatic issues of the decade: an opera which surely, in this new edition, has the capacity to attract audiences that have taken *Peter Grimes* to their hearts as they have the operas of Puccini.

Requiem for a Venerable Critic

No publication seems to be complete these days without its Readers' Competition and comic strip, so perhaps it is time these 'Quarterly Retrospects' were brought up to date. It is unfortunate that the writer cannot draw to save his life and lacks the wherewithal to offer glittering prizes. He will, in fact, give the answer in paragraph 3, and readers are on their honour not to look. The question is: To what recent recording is the venerable critic now listening?

In the first of four cartoons, Venerable Critic is seen with score on knee and beatific expression of pleasurable expectation on face. The artist's skill makes it clear that a new CD is about to be played, volume control having been adjusted, cushions having been plumped up and everything in order. Cartoon No. 2 shows Ven. Crit. leaning forward rather plaintively, perhaps cupping his ancient ear. The artist's skill is such that we see a *pianissimo* marking on the first page of the vocal score, while from somewhere at the back of the speakers comes a barely audible murmur. No. 3 shows Ven. Crit. adjusting volume. Artistic skill shows that he has turned the volume up several notches and, having also started the disc afresh, is about to resume seat with only a very slightly modified expression of former beatific expectation. The fourth and final drawing sports a number of those wavy lines by which the skilful cartoonist can intimate that V. C., settee, cushions, vocal score and surroundings are in paroxysm. The record player and speakers rock like cataclysmic washing-machines. The walls, pummelled from without by frantic neighbours, are collapsing inwards.

One clue to the answer may be found on page 26 of the August issue in which one of the soloists in this recording is reported as saying 'I think we achieved something really unusual'. Another is in the conductor's notes on the recording where he quotes the composer's view that 'for the work to be heard properly it needed to be performed in a large space – a big church or theatre but not in … rooms in which "one can get neither a *piano* nor a full-bodied *forte*".' The answer is, of course, Verdi's Requiem, the conductor John Eliot Gardiner, the recording a 'trail-blazing' one on Philips.

I wonder where the people who make these records think that the majority of people who buy them live. It is also a wonder if the anomaly inherent in Gardiner's quotation from Verdi did not make itself at once apparent: 'rooms' are deemed unsuitable places for the Requiem, which needs extremes of loudness and softness, and these, having been attained, are then crowded back into 'rooms'. It is all part of the philosophy of recording as substitute-listening. Records are for domestic listening, and most music-lovers are sophisticated enough not to want to pretend that they live in the Royal Albert Hall or St Paul's Cathedral. Besides, when it comes to this particular piece of music, most music-lovers, I would have thought, are not confirmed or deepened in their love of it through experiencing the relatively crude sensations of dynamic extremes.

1996

Alagna, Heppner, Caruso et al

A story is going the rounds to the effect that in a recent recording session, the solo recitalist (a singer) was advised to reduce rubato to the minimum so as to facilitate the editing – the combination of 'takes' for the finished product. It helps, you see, if the tempo is strict and steady.

Perhaps that explains what is wrong with a lot of modern recitals on record. For example, the quarter brings two operatic tenors to special notice: Roberto Alagna and Ben Heppner. Both are outstanding among the singers of their generation, proving their worth in already substantial stage careers and now joining the exclusive ranks of tenors deemed eligible for recruitment to the international 'star' casts of major operatic recording projects. Each now has a solo recital to his credit and, on the whole, 'credit' is the word. The programmes comprise, between them, much of what might be ranked as the Tenors' Top Ten, at least within the French and Italian repertoire; after all, that is what people want to hear them sing, and, since to some extent they are being presented for popular assessment and acceptance, the well-known excerpts provide grounds for a relatively confident and fair judgement. They sing (with some exceptions) music that is well-suited to them, Alagna with the lighter voice and style, Heppner the more dramatic. Both have fine, distinctive voices. They produce their tone with care for quality and steadiness; they respect the traditional principles, one of which is the prime importance of legato, the 'binding' of notes to make an even line, or steady flow; and they do nothing that is cheap or unmusical.

Nor when it comes to comparison with the Old Masters do the newcomers show up badly: on the contrary, they establish themselves very firmly as worthy successors. Even so, something is lacking, and my feeling is that it is not so much in themselves as in modern conditions and expectations. For instance, Alagna opens with Edgardo's solo in the last Act of *Lucia di Lammermoor*, Heppner with Marcello's lament, 'Testa adorata', in the *La bohème* of Leoncavallo. The first suggests comparison with McCormack (1910), the second with Caruso (1911). The difference in rhythmic freedom (or rubato) is surprisingly slight in degree, yet the effect of that slight difference is just as surprisingly great. It works, however, in conjunction with the other, and probably more important, missing ingredient in the modern versions, namely the portamento, the curving of a note towards the next, the musical counterpart of a caress, a gesture of affection. Hear, for instance, how McCormack rounds off the aria's first sentence ('su quello') or Caruso warms to a tenderer kind of life the words 'tornerai' and 'manine'. A superiority in the moderns is found with their phrasing, which is broader and smoother in the sense that they take fewer breaths; yet the real smoothness of phrase at the start of 'Fra poco a me ricovero' is found in McCormack because his production is more scrupulously even, and Caruso's breath taken in the phrase 'e che sul cor non mi terrò mai più' (sung by Heppner in a single breath) has its compensation in Caruso's broadening, with *tenuto* and *rallentando*, in the last three words, preparing with grace and feeling for the opening of the song itself.

Those are of course minutiae, and it might be objected that the process of spotting them is commonly called nitpicking. But these particular points are but a few in just the first of the solos in these hour-long recitals. Broader contrasts could certainly be made, such as the rigidity of tempo in Heppner's *Luisa Miller* aria compared to early tenors such as De Lucia, Anselmi and Bonci, or the formality of manner in Alagna's 'Asile héréditaire' and 'La donna è mobile' compared (respectively) with Tamagno or Martinelli and Gigli or Lauri-Volpi. There is excellent material in these modern tenors, and their best singing (as in Heppner's 'O souverain, ô juge' or Alagna's 'Giunto sul passo estremo') will itself serve as a touchstone in future comparisons. But the element of fantasy in such singers should be encouraged, not held always in suspicious check; and two of the principal means by which the personal feelings and imagination of singers in such music can find expression are those which modern practice so persistently represses, rubato and portamento.

DS-T

While writing this I have learnt of the death of Desmond Shawe-Taylor who contributed this 'Quarterly Retrospect' from 1951 till July 1973. By example (and not in any formal sense) he was my teacher, though with his fastidious taste and passion for accuracy he set an impossibly high standard. A writer normally has some particular reader in mind. He can hardly have thought it, but I habitually wrote for him, and it is comforting to know that some habits are so deeply ingrained that it takes more than a death to change them.

Diary of a Retrospectator

Perhaps not the most exciting of quarters, and, anyway, time for a change. People say: 'Do you chaps spend all your time listening to records? Well, you must. And that Quarterly of yours. I mean, "*Quarterly*" they call it, but I bet it's year's-end to year's-end. Must be. Stands to reason. Music all day long, all the year round. I couldn't stand it, me. I'd go mad. And I tell you what – I wouldn't want to hear another note of music ever again. Not ever. I tell you. Honest.'

Well, I have from time to time heard speculations along these lines. I thought it might be of interest, just once, and in this relatively becalmed season, to run a retrospective diary. If I can decipher my own jottings, written purely as an *aide-mémoire* and pastime, I might be able to marry them up with the record-notes, and so help to satisfy the speculators. Then, if anybody really is concerned about this unresting labour of the revolving year, they may find comfort in the old adage that a change is as good as a rest.

November 6th, 1995 Finish and post 'Quarterly'. Hurrah! Statistics: 18 sets and singles covered. 26 left over, some because wouldn't fit, a few because first review as yet unpublished: Schumann *Das Paradies und die Peri* (Sinopoli), Berlioz, *L'enfance du Christ* (Best), Poulenc 'Secular Choral Music' (Wood). Memo: await Dec. Gram. Meanwhile *dolce far niente*.

November 10th Gram comes. No misprints.

Revisions: read with admiration Lionel Salter's Poulenc review. Go back for comparisons with The Sixteen. Renewed pleasure in the New London Chamber Choir's mastery, and particularly their gaiety in the charming *Chansons françaises*. But in *Figure humaine* The Sixteen are better: contrasts more effectively defined, words more sharply pointed, an extra degree of assurance and unanimity in chording, and then in 'Liberté' (the final movement, and a terrible fitness-test for even the most expert choral group) there's a finer-textured sound in The Sixteen and a more purposeful drive towards that blazing final chord. In several tracks of the London choir's recital, an occasional fault of blend among the men's voices obtrudes, yet they're extremely neat in the men-only *Chanson à boire*. Like LS's note that the Harvard Glee Club, the dedicatees, were prevented from singing it, Prohibition being in full force.

Glad to find Joan Chissell liked the new *Das Paradies und die Peri*, and that she disapproved of Florence Quivar's 'vibrato'. Julie Faulkner, the principal soprano here, is often so lovely a singer that it irks to find her infected by the syllabic swell-pedal method: not regularly and to only a mild degree, but the practice can so easily become habitual and the most insidious disrupter of legato. Meanwhile, what a fertile score, and how, especially in its generous finale, the live performance catches fire.

The Berlioz *L'enfance* too: a new wonder of a score on each hearing, and rarely more impressive than here with the Corydon forces under Matthew Best. LS finds John Aler (the tenor narrator) disappointing, with 'fast vibrato' and weak lower-register. The 'vibrato' puzzles – I hadn't noted it and think I would have done (having a liking for a fast vibrato, which is nowadays a rarity). Play again, and do hear to some extent differently, but not as 'fast vibrato': rather as the beginnings, almost the first faint warnings, of that loosening of the vibrations which befalls the great majority of singers (unfortunately).

But emphatic agreement on the excellence of Alastair Miles's Herod – perhaps his most impressive recorded performance to date. Notes and queries: what a very warm, human, characterization of Herod this is! Is the brisk pace and businesslike manner of the shepherds' chorus part of Best's declared campaign against the sanctimonious? And (theological) why don't the angels warn *all* parents with first-born?

November 12th Hyperion and Chandos send (my best suppliers). Play Graham Johnson's Schubert Vol. 24. How does he do it? The 48-hour day. The booklet alone is a month's work. If ever I feel I've noticed something (e.g. the *Waldstein* connection at the end of *Schwager Kronos*) he's been there first. Exc. essay on Goethe: observes that it's through music that most of us know him at all! Superb Keenlyside.

This 'Goethe Schubertiad' has four singers, of whom the baritone Simon Keenlyside is outstanding. Timbre and texture are the prime distinctions, Michael George sounding very lumpy by comparison and John Mark Ainsley tending to lose quality at a *forte*. Christine Schäfer interests. They refrained from giving her *Schäfers Klagelied* (which comes first), but she follows with *An Mignon* where, perhaps aptly, an innocent, slightly gawky girl voice pipes up, then sounds very different (and better) in the mezzo tessitura of *Der Gott und die Bajadere*, the child-voice (a boy treble this time) returning for the 'dramatized' *Erlkönig*, and then sounding exquisite, and presumably her natural self, in the *So lasst mich scheinen* fragment. Fine too is *Ganymed*, but this is altogether a very special performance. Graham Johnson gives it – hard to say – almost a balletic movement. Pointing the left-hand to make a clear, elegant, rhythmic figure, he keeps it dancing through its various developments (and in this performance the stages of the journey are newly clarified) till singer and pianist reach the broad downward stroking of the 'alliebender Vater' where, curiously (or so I thought at first) exact time is preserved, the eventual *rallentando* restricted to the delicate final bars where, like a porcelain figure in motion, the piano reaches the end of its elegant dance. The whole record is priceless. And who (for instance) could have expected such a wonderful addition to the choral repertoire as the third setting of *Gesang der Geister über den Wassern?* Eugene Asti's completion (or restoration) presents us with a masterpiece – and this is its first recording.

November 25th EMI send Roocroft Mozart and contemps. Dismayed to find still don't enjoy, but not the 'sameness' this time – the voice itself. Glad haven't this for first review. I did have first review of Amanda Roocroft's previous recital, and, while welcoming the record as providing just the kind of opportunity for a young British singer one has always wanted them to have, I found it disappointing principally on account of the limited capacity it revealed for characterization and expression. Its successor marks progress in these respects (though I see AB recommends that she should find 'a good interpretative coach, if such a thing still exists'); but the voice, surely, has been overdriven, for the very first impression it makes (in *Alma grande e nobil core*) is of a tone which is neither beautiful nor entirely firm. Better quality comes with softening, and the character here is proud and vengeful so one mustn't judge too soon, and indeed a kind of suspended judgement prevails for a while. The aria 'Se il padre perdei' from *Idomeneo* gives unalloyed pleasure, but then it also enforces the main point, for here the voice is under no pressure of range and volume and can be its best, most natural and effective self. Throughout the recital the technique copes admirably with a most challenging programme, and I do find a much stronger infusion of meaning, so that, for example, Donna Elvira's unhappiness is vividly characterized. But there seems to be a real deterioration of tone, especially (as usual) on upper notes sung loudly; and comparison with Fiordiligi's 'Ei parte' solo as sung by her in the Gardiner *Così fan tutte* shows the voice to have been then in distinctly finer condition.

[There follow days of 'historical' listening not related to reviews, then a joyful week devoted to recordings by Schwarzkopf.]

December 19th Lovely morning with Dennis Noble! And last night many furtive tears over the once despised plum labels Catley, Booth *et al.* And Dutton do it again!

Ah, the internecine strife, the near-ends to beautiful friendships, in days of old! The few of us who were interested in operatic records during school-days in wartime were a close band of brothers till it came to the burning issue: plum-label opera in English versus red-label Italian (or, very occasionally, German, French or Russian). Against my Marcella Sembrich they would range their puny Gwen Catley, and confront the mighty Martinelli with their skinny Webster Booth. But now the old battle-cries rally no troops, and all I find is that a pleasure deferred is a pleasure enhanced. 'Stars of English Opera' has Catley's 'Dearest name' (*Rigoletto*), close-miked but faultlessly clean and well-schooled. Booth contributes 'O vision entrancing' (*Esmeralda*), and he's not Tom Burke: never mind, clean-cut and well-mannered. Janet Howe, Gladys Ripley, John Hargreaves, Redvers Llewellyn: names once so familiar and their memories well served in these solos. Outstanding among them all, Oscar Natzke is on magnificent form as Falstaff in *The Merry Wives of Windsor*. And Dennis Noble's Rossini Figaro, a fellow of infinite resource, is a great delight, as is the disc devoted to him also on Dutton reviewed by myself in this present issue. The star of stars, it must be said, is the Dutton Labs and their transfer-work: clear and bright but mercifully free of the harshness and aggressive 'top' that disfigure so many.

December 20th After yesterday's pleasure in plums try the English *Barber*. Slightly wish hadn't.

That last diary-note tells an autobiographical truth that is not necessarily a critical judgement. There's much to be said for this performance, of *The Barber of Seville*, in English, and featuring singers who must certainly be as good as their predecessors from the 1940s. Della Jones, Bruce Ford and Alan Opie pit wits against Andrew Shore (Bartolo) and Peter Rose (Basilio): all bringing life and soul, good technique and scrupulous musicianship to the task. Gabriele Bellini conducts the English National Opera Orchestra with spirit and refinement. The new translation, by Amanda and Anthony Holden, is a happy one ('Not a dull moment, life is all action/Job-satisfaction is what I enjoy' sings the factotum). So the failure to enjoy must have been a failure indeed. Or (my notes hint something along these lines) could it be that the English, so well articulated, its sense so energetically enacted, has the deadly virtue of revealing a triviality from which the Italian allows us a degree of escape? That's not a thought I would expect Richard Osborne to share, and I can't quite follow him in his own objections to opera in translation. A loss is inevitable, that's true, but quite often there's compensation in the increased naturalness and understanding which singers can bring to texts in their native language.

December 30th William [No. 3 nephew] comes to stay. *Belshazzar* good and loud voted tops. Says Terfel best singer he has ever heard 'in the flesh'. Some Delius also: incredibly lovely for about five minutes then we both tend to nod.

The last admission draws a well-deserved rebuke from Jonathan Swain's review which reports being 'never less than riveted by Mackerras and his team'. In fact, my notes tell of fairly well-riveted enjoyment after all, though (incidentally) also of disappointment over the baritone's 'Oh, honey' entry, which can be magical and here (with Daniel Washington) is wobbly and unappealing. Always, in both *Appalachia* and *Song of the High Hills*, there is unfailing magic at the sound of distant voices with the first entry of the chorus. As for *Belshazzar's Feast*, provided it's not heard too often, the effect is infallible: as exciting now as when first heard. The Bournemouth Symphony Orchestra and Chorus do excellent work under Andrew Litton (with credit to David Hill for the fine standard of choral accomplishment). Bryn Terfel, just slightly less well focused than usual at the start, has, as ever, something special to add. The role of the soloist becomes so much more significant with him. In the first section ('If I forget thee') he is a man among his people, their voice, with Terfel's carrying a rare personal conviction; in the 'shopping-list' the items are relished, visualized each in turn (a softening as the glance moves from 'gold' to 'silver', a smoothness for 'marble', a mystery of oriental wonder in 'cinnamon, odours and ointments');

then in the weird narrative of the portentous graffiti Terfel sees it all so vividly that the skin crawls.

January 3rd, 1996 Last night the New Year as would like it to go on: delight in CD 1 of Blow's anthems: this a.m. CD 2.

David Hill is again to be thanked: his Winchester Cathedral Choir is singing wonderfully well these days, and the collection of John Blow's anthems (all with English texts, so not including *Salvator mundi*) makes one of the richest of all contributions to the excellent English Orpheus series. *Cry aloud and spare not* struck me as the supreme masterpiece here, with its sustained intensity, creative care for form, and dramatic use of voices. A great joy too is *Blessed is the man*, with a generous provision of 'step triple' rhythms to please the King (who would beat time to it). This, of all the quarter's records so far, is the one I shall most regularly come back to.

January 6th Play 'The Red Cockatoo' at last (good title though the song itself lasts only 0'39"). Curiously (perhaps because of yesterday's John Blow) enjoyed the realizations most (Humfrey, Croft). Slightly wish hadn't heard the rave reactions (and 'better-than-Pears') first; but fine. Ian Bostridge records extremely well, and one can listen more objectively than in live recitals where the appearance, that of a gangling sixth-former, to some extent colours the response (not necessarily a matter of favourably or unfavourably but of attitude and a kind of involuntary relativism). He's an excellent singer of Britten's songs, skilful in the technical problems of movement in and out of the head-voice, and with all the musicianship to make the formidable difficulties of his Donne settings sound like second nature. In quiet passages he sometimes reminds one of the young Ian Partridge, though with reserves of voice and emotional intensity that reach beyond. Graham Johnson plays with all the command of a virtuoso: the purely technical side of his art tends to go unmentioned. And, as noted earlier, Britten's 'realizations', particularly of the two songs by Pelham Humfrey, earn special gratitude.

January 9th Tippett day yesterday with *Priam* morning, *Heart's Assurance* (Ainsley) evening. And the previously unheard (why?) *Divertimento on Sellinger's Round* went round and round three times running. *Sellinger's Round*, a sort of Elizabethan barn dance, is treated to some exhilarating variations; delightful too is the *Little Music for String Orchestra* (1946). But the main item on this disc is *The Heart's Assurance* with the piano part orchestrated by Meirion Bowen. Compare it with the original (Martyn Hill/Graham Johnson), and I find it welcome. With piano, the cycle remains a concert-piece (one's aware of the pianist's busy fingers); orchestra-led, it moves more evocatively into the world of *Midsummer Marriage*. With *King Priam* the reissue of the original recording under David Atherton brought exactly the heightened enjoyment and sense of comprehension which Michael Oliver celebrates in his review. At each new hearing, new passages become memorable (though still a sag of interest in the goddesses episode), and the old, rather indignant, feeling of surprise at the opera's length begins to wane. I still find Norman Bailey makes a dull old stick of Priam (what would Terfel do with it?), and Yvonne Minton remains the outstanding voice among the soloists.

[Another ten days with 'historicals' and several releases not yet reviewed; also the beginnings of familiar misgivings that nothing has arrived from major companies.]

January 25th PolyGram have sent von Otter and Gorchakova. 'Quarterly' deadline the 6th.

Anne Sofie von Otter in Mozart and Haydn proved disappointing. A characteristic noted when she sang Purcell not long ago in London is her increasing use of the swell-pedal method on individual notes referred to previously; in the Mozart songs especially she fusses the melody almost out of existence (contrast Schwarzkopf whose performances of these things lack nothing in expression but preserve the singing-line faultlessly and catch the spirit of them with an essential simplicity of style). AB writes that some of the performances here are 'more than a little over-interpreted and mannered almost to the point of caricature', and in my own notes I see (of the desperation of Haydn's Ariadne) 'sometimes near-parody'. Best, I thought, was the last: Haydn's *The Spirit's Song* where the mood is beautifully caught and the pallid tone entirely apt.

Galina Gorchakova also pairs composers for her recital. Verdi and Tchaikovsky go well together, and this wonderful singer has much to offer in both. The voice is of rare quality, firm and powerful, exciting at both extremes of the range (rich, Ponselle-like low notes and a full-bodied high C), and sufficiently supple in movement to make a good showing in the cabaletta of 'Tacea la notte' (*Il trovatore*). In some of her recordings (her famous role in *The Fiery Angel* included) she has shown limitations in the ability to convey feeling through sound alone. But here she never forgets who the character is and what her emotions are, so that Desdemona's prayer is still tinged with the anxiety of the cry following the Willow Song, and Tatyana's Letter mingles hope and fear, tranquility and excitement in exact proportions. Intonation troubles a little in *Otello* and *Aida*, and she has difficulty in 'floating' a soft high note; but in the Tchaikovsky group and *La forza del destino*, especially, there is some glorious singing.

February 1st Deadline approaches. Nothing comes. SOS EMI for long-ordered *Hérodiade*: swift action promised. But now CD player won't revolve. *Factum est silentium*.

February 2nd Trudge miles with CD player – instantaneous cure! Play the Sony *Hérodiade*: mixed feelings, superb Domingo in Jean's aria. Wait for EMI.

February 3rd No *Hérodiade*. Play, and rather glory in, *Trovatore* Salzburg 1962.

The transfer is one of those harsh, 'brilliant' jobs I dislike intensely. Poor Leontyne Price! But I loved it in spite of all. Karajan is in some ways quirky, Corelli likewise, but both are quite uncommonly inspired. Crude in some respects, Corelli is movingly caring in others – his 'Il presagio funesto' passage puts him right up with the masters. The whole performance (and recording) is open to criticism, but I found it immensely exciting. It has the spark and flare of real insight; and a performance that catches the authentic thrill of *Il trovatore* with such conviction is one to take on board.

February 4th No *Hérodiade*. Start writing.

February 6th Finish 'Quarterly'. Hurrah! Statistics: 17 sets and singles covered, 18 left over.

February 7th *Hérodiade* arrives.

Opera in English

That English opera existed before *Peter Grimes* is something we all know, but what many still doubt is whether anything worthwhile was created between it and the first masterpiece of all, *Dido and Aeneas*. This grows in estimation year by year, and its viability for production on television testifies to its accredited power to reach an audience beyond the specialized public that exists for what is still commonly designated 'early music'. In this instance, the specialists may well have watched with some impatience, making a mental note that sound alone might have been preferable. With the recording this becomes possible, and a fine piece of sound-production it is. As to performance, that too has fine features, including the presence of the chorus as a vivid collective character. The main liability is in fact the 'star', the Dido of Maria Ewing, gusty at a *forte* and careless over consonants. The language in itself – even the famous banks of Nile which harbour the deceitful crocodile – troubles us very little. So does the stylized poetic diction of Arne's *Artaxerxes*. This first recording, under Roy Goodman, with reconstructions by Peter Holman, presents what might have been a founding work in a genuine national school of opera. The score and libretto match well; the drama moves forward at a well-gauged pace (more clearly a work for the theatre than are Handel's operas). In fact the limited effectiveness now is due largely to inept casting, for Christopher Robson can never persuade us that he is the hero any more that Ian Partridge will pass as the double-dyed villain.

Tosca in English might seem a more doubtful proposition, more dubious (for instance) than the *Barber of Seville* which preceded it in the current Chandos series. Personally I find it better: to hear the comedy unfold in such clear English was to be confronted, for much of the time, with what could seem irredeemable triviality, whereas the melodrama can be given in English with very little of the expected embarrassment. One thing I do question is the inevitable preferability of a natural, spoken idiom. 'And this is the man who terrorised the whole of Rome' is too natural, too prosaic, for its context. Angelotti's 'Ha! I have baulked them. Dread imagination made me quake with uncalled-for perturbation' was a famous object for derision in the old translation; yet sung, it is surprisingly less comical than the natural-seeming 'Ah! Here is safety. I'm in such a panic'. Opera, as has been observed time enough, defies common sense.

About the *Tosca* recording the principal distinction, praised also by EG, is David Parry's conducting. He brings an approach that seems to have enquired afresh into things (rests, key-changes and so forth) that have been taken for granted over the best part of a century. Dennis O'Neill and Gregory Yurisich sing and characterize effectively, but Jane Eaglen's Tosca is one-dimensional, wanting in tenderness, cajolery, charm.

A Vote for Auber

How, then, do you decide between a *Traviata* and a *Peter Grimes*, *Hérodiade* and *The Fiery Angel*? 'Easy', say some, who would follow their own preference and scarcely hesitate. But I am thinking of the dilemma we find ourselves in, every summertime (when the living should be easy) and we, as adjudicators for the ***Gramophone*** Awards, have to make these impossible choices between one thing good of its kind against another equally good of its rather different kind – all subsumed, however, under the heading 'Opera'. I did the unforgivable thing and voted for *Le domino noir*.

Unforgivable? Well, perhaps that is a bit harsh: after all, the piece is amusing, tuneful, delightful, extremely well done in this recording and a rarity. Still … against those serious masterpieces? Against *The Fiery Angel*, for instance? But this is a column in which Truth will out. I don't like *The Fiery Angel*: its music commands admiration without affection, and its scenario I find repellent. *Grimes* then, or *Traviata*?. But the new *Grimes* is one I could not recommend in preference to the original, and the *Traviata*, desirable as it is for the Violetta of Angela Gheorghiu, has (to my mind) an unattractive Alfredo and a more seriously flawed Germont. Come to that, the leading roles in *The Fiery Angel*, superbly sung as they are here by Galina Gorchakova and Sergei Leiferkus, struck me as less inwardly and imaginatively characterized than by the less richly endowed Renata and Ruprecht of the earlier version under Järvi. So it's back to *Le domino noir*, which, as previously noted, is 'amusing, tuneful, delightful' and so forth.

Delight, melody, amusement – I cannot think that they are such frivolous or trivial gifts for a work to possess, certainly not when in such abundance as in Auber's absurd sparkler. Absurd it no doubt is (though scarcely more so than *The Fiery Angel*), but every improbable twist in the story brings a new reason for the world to smile and lilt away to a charming waltz or foot-tapping tutti. Such things are no good unless supplied in equal measure with spontaneous verve and polished civility. This is a score *qui sait se conduire*: one melody follows another, but without ostentation or the sticky self-indulgence of latterday Viennese operetta. As for the performance, that too is delightful, with Sumi Jo and Bruce Ford as the bewilderingly parted lovers brought together at last. Richard Bonynge conducts the English Chamber Orchestra with relish and Decca have made a first-class job of the recording. There was also the delight of a happy surprise, for I can't say that Auber has hitherto filled my soul with any great confidence. And now here he is, with a light-hearted masterpiece … and my vote.

Britten and the Tenors

Somewhat reluctantly, the mind reverts to what it had recently concluded was a dead issue – the predominant influence of Pears upon tenors singing Britten in these later years. With the younger generation as represented by Ian Bostridge and John Mark Ainsley, the direct aural image of Pears's singing does seem to have faded; and yet, of itself, that is a consideration only skin-deep, for Britten has incorporated Pears into his writing. To sing the pieces successfully, a tenor has to adapt his technique, particularly in the matter of an ever-ready movement in and out of head-voice. It is of course partly in the English tradition (tenors admired by Pears such as Steuart Wilson and Eric Greene probably showed him the way), and so it comes more naturally than it would to an Italian (though Gigli could slip in and out easily enough). The immediate point is that Philip Langridge and even John Mark Ainsley, independent artists both, still take on the Pears-tincture when they sing Britten. It seems to be inevitable. Occasionally a tenor from a different background, Jerry Hadley for instance, tries his hand and it is interesting to see how he will be caught between his own method (which makes him sound rigid) and the felt need to adapt and become at least demi-Pears. What I really want to hear, and still believe would be just about possible, is the *Michelangelo* cycle undertaken by an Italian, a Valletti or Bergonzi perhaps.

Ainsley singing *Les illuminations*, *Nocturne* and the *Serenade* for tenor, horn and strings, is like a singer cast in a stage-role, for which he duly adapts. Most especially in the Rimbaud cycle there is some unwritten instruction towards adopting a voice-character, not one with the strict evenness of vibrato he would try to preserve for Handel, and with a weird vocal 'make-up' that would not do for (say) Vaughan Williams or Quilter. He achieves this transformation wonderfully well, most elegantly, for instance, in 'Phrase' and 'Being beauteous'; but one is aware of it throughout as an assumption, a role, whereas with Pears it was (or seemed to be) himself.

Langridge comes up most intractably against the Pears-voice in the *Michelangelo Sonnets*, and to some extent in *Winter Words* ('The Choirmaster's Burial' brings awareness of an awkward tessitura). But somehow he conquers it with a prodigious effort of soul and physique in the Donne settings. He, Langridge (and perhaps we've been slow to realize it), is a singer of rare, intense inner conviction who can make whatever he sings sound like … well, not to cast the net too wide, like a sermon by Dr Donne. He colours, so that in the first sonnet black, red and white are vivid identities. In the third ('O might these sighs and tears') he takes the harmonic pain on that very word into his tone, and 'What griefs my heart did rent' is not 'interpretation', but reality. The bold attack of 'Oh, to vex me', the fearless outgoing *portamentos* of 'Tears in his eyes … Blood fills his frowns', and the ethereal 'much pleasure' (in 'Death, be not proud') have a kind of crazed inspiration. Altogether, with Steuart Bedford's masterly playing, this is an inspired performance. Possibly Ferrier in Mahler, Pears in Schubert and Britten, Baker in some dramatic monologue ... but otherwise it is hard to think of British singing in our time which has achieved this degree of imaginative intensity.

Yet, turning to the *Canticles*, I think, and cannot help thinking, of an absurdity: of Dudley Moore's parody in *Beyond the Fringe*, which, originally of the folk-songs, spreads wider. *My beloved is mine*, I can't help finding, is funny.

Langridge does magnificently, with a passion in 'For I was flax and he was flames of fire' such as I have never heard: but the whole thing, the high 'off-key' voice, the spiritual sublimation of what will translate so readily into common human experience, so stirs an undercurrent of satire that the whole performance (a fine one, from its frank passion to the enervated, post-coital sleepy voice of the conclusion) risks its dignity. Thus bedevilled by irreverence, I found the *Abraham and Isaac Canticle*, for the first time, almost insufferable: that Britten should put his sublime halo upon this cruel story was bad enough. And practically all that followed on the record, including the irritating mannerism (or is it something more?) of repetitions in *The Journey of the Magi* and *The Death of Si Narcissus*, suffered rejection.

Happily, Britten's fortunes, never long in abeyance around here, revive with *The Rescue of Penelope*, music written for the radio play by Edward Sackville-West. A succession of exhilarated ideas suggests the store awaiting birth in that brain, pregnant as it was in 1943; and the coupling with *Phaedra* (finely sung by Lorraine Hunt) movingly conjoins youthful brilliance and mature mastery.

Herr May's Vienna

One of the most exciting and valuable of all historical projects on record has been brought to its triumphant conclusion with the twenty-fourth volume of 'The Vienna State Opera Live' on Koch. It dates back in origin to 1933 when the archivist Hermann May was given permission to record, as best he could, snatches from the evening's performance – rather as at the very start of gramophone history Lionel Mapleson had caught those extraordinary moments from the stage of the Metropolitan, New York, in the age of the De Reszkes. May's efforts of course have the advantage of the electrical process, and he was no doubt better positioned; but the sound is still primitive enough, beset with wow and various kinds of surface noise. Modern technicians have 'restored' the originals, and often the results are marvellously clean and vivid. At their best, the recordings are like a thrillingly open door on to a stage of which we never thought to catch a glimpse, and yet there on it, present to our ears (and sometimes, we could almost swear, to our eyes) are long-loved singers from the past, heard with all the characteristics we know so well from studio recordings and others for which the exigencies of those days normally gave little scope.

The experiment covered many historical nights, premières, guest appearances, special performances of Strauss conducted by Strauss, and even Lehár by Lehár. It continued into the 1940s, and some of the recordings here are not fragments salvaged by May's apparatus but proud professional jobs with techniques developed in wartime. The array of conductors alone is impressive – Furtwängler, Knappertsbusch, Krauss, Walter, Weingartner, Böhm and so forth. Singers whom we came to know after the war – Seefried, Dermota, Hotter for example – are here in their youthful prime. Some we hardly knew at all, such as the tenor Todor Mazaroff, become familiar; others, like the young Björling, make a brilliant début, or, like Toti Dal Monte, are uniquely recorded on stage. But it is the sudden face-to-face encounters with some of the great Viennese singers of the 1920s and 1930s that is most thrilling. Try, for instance, Vol. 12 where for brief but precious moments Lehmann, Schumann, Jeritza and Schorr are vivid presences, with some superb singing by the visiting Helge Roswaenge.

It would not, I think, be true to say that the general level of performance is shown to be that of some fabled golden age. A lot of singing is recorded here, in these 24 volumes, much of it of indifferent quality. Often the very things for which we listen in performances from the past – the care for singing as singing – are those most conspicuously neglected, while a noisy clamour of 'acting' voices seems to be the rule. Nor is it possible (at least I do not find it so) always to recognize the work of some famous and now venerated figure at the podium. But when all that has been said, there remain these priceless moments: suddenly the open door and the unforgettable glimpse. As a document, the series is of monumental importance; as a musical experience there are dreary stretches, frustrations of bad sound and sudden fades or cut-offs, disappointments as expectations of some artist are unfulfilled; but then (you can never tell when it will happen) the thrill, and with it an impulse to shower blessings on the long defunct head of Herr May and on all those who have supported the present work of restoration.

1997

Martin and La Jeune France

On the face of it, nothing could make more outrageous demands upon choral singers than the *Epithalame* of André Jolivet or the *Cinq Rechants* of Messiaen, yet these are not, so to speak, gross assaults on the voice but rather like a field-day for top athletes trained to the highest pitch of perfection. The Sixteen are just such a group of singers, and they can take up the challenge with such easy virtuosity that they seem able to devote their energies to the higher pursuits of sensitivity, imagination and expressiveness. This collection of theirs, entitled 'La Jeune France' (it includes a third work, *Le cantique des cantiques* by Jean-Yves Daniel-Lesur, a rich and attractive piece of writing too), makes a marvellous recital, in fact one of the great choral records.

That is delightful entertainment, but Frank Martin's *In terra pax* is something more. Like Gerald Finzi in this, Martin quietly and steadily deepens and strengthens his appeal as the years go by. Matthias Bamert conducts the London Philharmonic Orchestra and Brighton Festival Chorus in a fine performance coupled with the orchestral suite *Les quatre éléments*, a musician's offering to Ansermet on his eightieth birthday but possessing a core of seriousness that extends it beyond the limits of a technical exercise. The 'little oratorio', as he called it, begins in disquiet, but develops in inspired confidence. With his Mass for Double Choir this is the music that has made the deepest impression over the present quarter.

Song: Hahn, Schubert and Wolf

It is strange (and thank heaven for it) how composers grow and shrivel in the mind. A few years ago I would not have given much for Reynaldo Hahn's chances of survival over the course of a two-CD recital. But he has done it. Hyperion's French Song series has again the inestimable benefit of Graham Johnson's mind and hands (the pen is his instrument almost as much as the piano), and the four singers contribute delightfully. To extract a few plums at random: *Si mes vers avaient des ailes*, written (I keep forgetting and marvelling at this afresh) at the age of 13, with heavenly *pianissimo* top A from Dame Felicity Lott; *Offrande*, the mezzo Susan Bickley catching to perfection the love-drugged sleepiness of its conclusion; 'Lidia', one of the *Etudes Latines*, for tenor (Ian Bostridge) and a magically distanced, wordless chorus; *A Chloris*, with the Bach-like bass, and Stephen Varcoe singing like a veritable monsieur, all discreet charm.

Johnson stays with us, as accompanist and guide, for Vol. 26 of the Schubert Song Edition. Subtitled 'An 1826 Schubertiad', it includes the Wilhelm Meister setting from that year and several of the best-known songs of all, *An Silvia?* among them. On this, the insert-notes observe: 'The left-hand figurations are those of a born comedian, a jazz bass player before his time, expert in cheeky interjections which add that essential ingredient of "swing" to a hit, and which render him as much of a soloist as the singer.' Similarly the notes in this series are part of the purchase as much as the record itself. Occasionally I find I am muttering away like some thicko in the back row of the sixth-form complaining that the teacher is 'reading too much into it'. I can't quite (for instance) penetrate to those 'two surfaces' ('the right hand harmonies are scrunched together as two surfaces') in *Totengräberweise*. Never mind.

With the ever increasing availability of competitive versions, fringe-benefits such as cover-presentation, texts and translations but most especially the background notes count for more in record-buying. Graham Johnson's notes have set an exceptionally high standard and have also gone to the very limit in manageable length – the new format, welcomed by Alan Blyth, accommodating the booklet without having to squeeze it through those wretched sideslips, is more than timely. But generally it is not musicological profundity or encyclopaedic omniscience that we need so much as relevance: relevance, that is, to the particular recording and (for example) its playing-order. It is extraordinary, and frustrating, to find that the essay on Wolf's *Italienisches Liederbuch* in the recording by Dawn Upshaw, Olaf Bär and Helmut Deutsch fails to follow or comment on the ordering of the songs arrived at by Bär and Deutsch for this performance: it is a major point of interest, and the principles involved need elucidating. Objections arise: for instance, how does 'Ich esse nur mein Brot' (No. 34) fit into the sequence here, and how come 'Was soll der Zorn' (No. 32), referring to 'this rage', follows a song (No. 37) which has been no more than affectionately sad? The performances themselves are fine, though Upshaw's more pert, wide-eyed little-miss affectations hardly endear themselves.

Choral: the Real Mastersingers

At least one of this quarter's records has not yet reached the shelves, remaining at hand for shared and private listening over several weeks. This is the *Vespro della beata Vergine* of the astonishing Johann Rosenmüller. The seventeenth-century Saxon master became (so the notes say) so envied by the Italians that, when in their country, he went in fear of his life. Very understandable, on both sides. It is the work of a man whose mind overflows with musical ideas: one of the liveliest, most inventive works of its century. And it has lain mute all this time, joyfully revived by the Cantus Cölln under Konrad Junghänel, here to remain, I should trust, *in saecula saeculorum*.

Another masterly group of singers is the Ensemble Vocale Européen; and a choral record scarcely less treasurable than the Rosenmüller is their performance of *Israelis Brünnlein* ('The Fountains of Israel') by Johann Schein, described as a sacred madrigal. Again the richness and variety of invention seem infinite; likewise the expectations of continued pleasure. The Sixteen's recording of the Byrd five-part Mass pales somewhat by comparison with the recent version from Winchester under David Hill, a more responsive performance, better at the rhythms, more specific throughout, and blest with excellent trebles. The trebles of New College, Oxford, also have reason to feel pleased with themselves, having contributed nobly to the success of their best-selling 'Agnus Dei'. That kind of chart-scaling future may not lie ahead for the attractively captioned 'Nordic Light' recital – 'marvellously sung musical wallpaper', Guy Rickards called it. Still, there is scarcely a better choir to be heard than the Danish National Radio's; and it could just be that enthusiasm for the choral arrangement of Barber's *Adagio* (as an *Agnus Dei*) extends to Thomas Beck's arrangement of Grieg's 'Spring', the second and more famous of his *Elegiac Melodies* for strings.

EMI's Centenary

The centenary of HMV/EMI cannot go unnoticed in these columns devoted to the gramophone and the voice. Though the dog is supposedly listening to his master, the voice coming through that horn was always (by association) Caruso's or Melba's, just possibly Patti's or even Tamagno's. A noble history and a whole lot of affection are involved. To this day the heart still responds to those initials 'HMV' as perhaps to no other in the world of commerce. 'EMI' stirs no such feeling.

The handsomely boxed Centenary Edition of 11 discs, with its treasure stored in envelopes brightly regal as the red-label celebrity records of old, recalls to mind and ear a century of voices, individual and unforgettable (most of them): singers whose names have illuminated these pages ever since our founding and voice-loving Editor, Compton Mackenzie, wrote the first 'Quarterly Retrospect' in 1923. In those days Caruso's death was a recent event, and Mackenzie wrote, with emotion, to the effect that, thanks to records, somewhere in the world and sometime every day, someone would hear that voice and say 'There was a singer!'. Playing through the first of these discs, somebody will surely say it again having come to Caruso's 'Vesti la giubba' of 1902 on track 6. The reproduction is startlingly vivid, and there before us is that incomparable voice, full-bodied in recitative, soft and sweet at the start of the *arioso*, thrilling in quality, power and breadth at the climax. Almost more wonderfully, it presents, from those earliest days, as truly and compellingly as anything made in our own time, the entire emotional being, doubly impressive because Caruso himself sings with such dignity and restraint.

Then, a few tracks further on, with arrival at the year 1903, suddenly leaping out after the piano's introductory clangour, resounds the voice which in Compton Mackenzie's time they used to say the gramophone had been unable to capture. If only they could have heard this 'Esultate' reproduced as it is here! The 'take' chosen is not one of those published in the old Historical Catalogue's series devoted to Tamagno's records, perhaps being thought at the time too powerful and so subject to distortion and wear. It rings now with such penetrative strength and clarity that no effort of imagination is needed to realize how the first Otello of all must have electrified his audiences with those 12 bars of victorious declamation in Act 1. The firmness of voice and fervour of spirit (and Tamagno, dead two years later, was even then in troubled health) make these few seconds of recording infinitely precious; and the high A of 'dopo l'armi' must be one of the most wondrous tenor notes on record.

Not all of these early singers are served so well. Calvé's Habanera gives no clue as to what was so wonderful about her Carmen; if choice was restricted to the London session, 'Voi lo sapete' or possibly Massenet's 'Sérénade du passant' might have been preferable. I fear that Lilli Lehmann's 'Or sai chi l'onore' may also prove an incitement to ridicule, its grandeur so compromised by the frequently embarrassing inequality of registers: 'Non mi dir' would have done better. Patti too: it is hard to know what to do about her in such anthologies, for she obviously has to be represented, and yet always, even in this partially lovely 'Ah, non credea mirarti', there occurs something so regrettable that, taken on its own, one almost wishes not to have heard the thing at all. Might 'La calesera' have been risked? It is not typical, and we know that her husband is supposed to have thought it unladylike and caused it to be withdrawn: still, it remains the most animated and unflawed of all Patti's records and is the only one I feel I can play unapologetically to a chance-visitor who is curious to hear something of the legendary Queen of Song.

La Rondine

Chronologically, the last of the vocal recordings in that centenary box is of Roberto Alagna singing, with stylistic grace and in fine voice, Werther's song of Ossian, 'Pourquoi me réveiller?'. Nothing of Angela Gheorghiu is included (something from the duet record might well have been chosen, part of the *L'amico Fritz* perhaps). Anyway, the two singers are together again in *La Rondine*, and to very happy effect. Puccini's ill-starred commission from Vienna, accepted as a challenge to write something like *Der Rosenkavalier* 'but more amusing and more organic', never gained a stronghold in the general repertory and yet revealed itself as a charmer in the 1966 recording under Molinari-Pradelli on RCA. 'Charm', moreover, is a feeble word for what the opera can do at its best, which is in the ensembles of Act 2 – the most intoxicating celebration of the youthful heart in all opera. One could still see why it failed to hold the stage, principally through the weakness of its Third Act. There was also, as I remember it from that recording and from the later one under Maazel, a sense of emotional and textural thickness, a willed emotional surfeit; and one could not quite dismiss the unpleasant thought that its première was taking place in Monte Carlo within a few months of the battles of Ypres. As Edward Greenfield said in his review, the new recording effects a transformation. Act 3 comes nearer to redemption, and, more importantly the texture and with it the emotional nature of the opera are refined: the 'thickness' has been purged.

That is the achievement of Antonio Pappano, who conducts a performance never lacking in zest but more notable for delicacy. Gheorghiu is surely the ideal Magda, her tone still pure and generous in warmth and roundness, sufficiently mature to contrast with the lighter and shallower Lisette, and under fine control so that her solos have their needful poise and grace, rising to a full-bodied climax on the challengingly placed high notes. There is a lovely impulsiveness about her taking-up of the Doretta song, a recreative freedom as from the inspiration of the moment. With Gheorghiu's arrival in the opera came the thrill of recognition, so often the sign of a singer who is special in character and esteem. It was not quite so, I found, with Alagna, though he sings his praises of Paris with lyrical grace and ample resonance. In the fill-up excerpts from *Le Villi*, his 'Torna ai felice di' doesn't quite get the *tristezza* into the voice, and is surely too slow; fine singing all the same.

Almost Modern Opera

Puccini wrote tunes, and that probably explains why we are disinclined to think of his operas as being of the twentieth century. The operas which follow now, all five of them, are of their age in this respect at least: they are not without melody, but they don't go in for tunes, which are what the mythical errand-boy is supposed to whistle. Perhaps an exception could be made of Granados's *Goyescas*, premièred in the year before *La Rondine*, for it has at the opening of its Third Act the famous 'Nightingale and the Rose', best-known as a piano solo, and transmutable without undue effort into that still better-known song discouraging tears in Argentina – which presumably the mythical errand-boy might try to whistle, even if (like myself) getting little further than 'I never left you'. In fact, even this is not much of a tune (Granados's, I mean): too dependent on harmony, colour and atmosphere, and weak in melodic development. And, as with *La Rondine*, it is the Third Act that lets the opera down, the ensembles of the first and second being thoroughly enjoyable. The recording, with María Bayo and Ramón Vargas as the lovers, has plenty of life and energy, though one fancies that the tenor role may be susceptible to a little more fervour and plangency.

At least it is good to have the opportunity of hearing Granados's curiously proportioned opera at last; so too with the long-deferred first recording of his pupil Roberto Gerhard's comic opera *The Duenna* (or *La Dueña* as Chandos prefer to call it, despite its English text based on Sheridan's play with English title). Adept enough with the Spanish flavouring, Gerhard seems to have been strikingly inept in his dealings with Sheridan. The recording under Antoni Ros Marbà gives a convincing account of the orchestral score but the singing provides little pleasure – probably a matter of chicken-and-egg, for the voices might sound better if Gerhard had given them more real singing to do, and his writing for the voice might seem less unattractive if there were better voices to sing it.

Still, the mere fact of the recording earns gratitude, as does that of Zemlinsky's *Der Zwerg*, previously heard in an incomplete text with the title *Der Geburtstag des Infantas*. This also has a Spanish setting, and the opening scenes, plentiful in colour and vivacity, give hopeful promise. In the recording, James Conlon conducts, the ever-welcome Soile Isokoski plays the Princess, and a singer to look for in the future turns up in Andrew Collis, the Chamberlain. David Kuebler, in the terribly demanding role of the Dwarf, has to survive memories of Kenneth Riegel's *tour de force*, a performance of extraordinary physical and imaginative dedication. Kuebler's voice copes well, sometimes brilliantly, but he has not quite the touch that transforms story-book into reality. I'm afraid that the opera itself – the story, the composer's self-identification, the further self-torturing sweetness of the late romantic idiom – turns my stomach. There is much to admire, I dare say, but I can't get far beyond the entrance of the Dwarf.

More surprisingly perhaps, my palate also rejects *Albert Herring*. I know it is widely considered amusing and to have its deep places and subtleties too. I have seen it often enough to realize that any audible contribution on my part to the merriment arose out of sociability or an incorrigible tendency to think that everyone else must be right; but now, with a new recording to listen to in private and not the ghost of a laugh or smile coming anywhere near lips, brain or heart, I feel it has to be faced. *Albert Herring* strikes me as an obnoxious, self-congratulatory piece in which the liberalism of an audience of nice people is flattered into smugness by the invitation to laugh at a stereotyped, patronising view of village or small-town life as it is not today and probably never was. The orchestral score does its job, and no doubt with distinction, though it often seems to me a kind of superior film music. The voice-parts are said to characterize brilliantly, and perhaps they do; I only wish they were given more to sing and less to chatter. The recording, under Steuart Bedford does exactly what is expected of it. The orchestral work is fine, while the quality of singing as singing seems irrelevant, an old and wobbly voice or a young and dry one being accepted and praised in the interests of character. And truthfully I would not greatly complain about any of this if I came away from the performance with the memory of any genuine amusement or of any part of the score that seemed likely to hover in the mind for a while, eventually to take up residence as a valued possession.

No such misgivings haunt a playing of *The Rake's Progress*, and in the new recording there is much to enjoy. The Tokyo Opera Singers and the Saito Kinen Orchestra perform with infectious energy and precision under Seiji Ozawa, and among what one might call the second-line soloists (in this instance Baba the Turk, Sellem and Trulove) are first-rate performances by Jane Henschel, Ian Bostridge and Donald Adams. Sylvia McNair is a sweet Anne, just a little too sweet perhaps. But Antony Rolfe Johnson nowadays develops a raw edge to his tone when singing loudly, and though sounding young for his years still does not sound young enough for Tom Rakewell. Equally, if Nick Shadow is to be the shadow of his master, he too must sound young, and if he is sung by a bass, rather than a baritone, it must be by a slimlined, clearly defined bass such as the young Samuel Ramey: Paul Plishka suits not at all, being elderly in sound, the rotundity of voice spreading inelegantly. This is one of the disadvantages of recording on the basis of a stage production. The singers probably looked and acted well on stage, but on record all the characterization is done by voice, and the most important consideration in casting for records is timbre.

Song, and the Prospects Brighten

Opera stars do not always make good recitalists, especially when they have beautiful silky voices and the looks to match. Renée Fleming is one of those who do, working expressively by nuance and detail, allowing her own personality to colour the event but not to monopolize it. Her Schubert recital begins with a precarious exposure of intonation in *Heidenröslein*, then settles happily into *Die Forelle*, and goes on to a memorably contemplative *Im Frühling*, catching the ambiguity of mood, lingering pensively over the repetition of the last lines. As Alan Blyth pointed out in a comparison with Fischer-Dieskau, the 19-verse *Viola*, an epic in miniature, can benefit from a quicker tempo and a more sharply responsive care for words; yet this is an affectionate performance, with its address to the 'zartes Kind', and it is probable that, without comparisons, few listeners will wish away any part of the 15 minutes while listening to it.

The late romantics are well served in recitals by Anne Sofie von Otter and Angelika Kirchschlager. Von Otter's are orchestral songs, John Eliot Gardiner conducting. Zemlinsky's *Sechs Gesänge*, Op. 13 interpose their sweet sadness between Mahler's wayfarer and his Rückert settings. The orchestral textures are recorded light and clear as possible, and the vocal tone matches ideally. Just occasionally (in 'Liebst du um Schönheit', for example) the warmer fullness of some voices from the past comes to mind with gentle regret, and occasionally, too, one is aware that this fine voice, so much at the centre of musical life in our time, begins to sound worn in passages such as the climax of 'Um Mitternacht'. These are moving performances none the less. Which cannot quite be said with regard to the other recital, the one by the gifted young mezzo Kirchschlager, of whom Michael Oliver felt bound to say that she 'is not yet a Lieder singer'. It was a conclusion I came to on hearing her at the Wigmore Hall's commemorative Schubertiad earlier this year, fine as was the voice itself. On the other hand, I enjoyed her singing on this record more than did my colleague. Mahler's 'Selbstgefühl', for instance did not seem to me so utterly lacking in humour, while the songs of Alma Mahler came over very well in what for myself – as I imagine for most listeners – was a first meeting. No doubt sheer pleasure in the fresh and ample voice counted for much.

A little more freshness and beauty of tone would not have come amiss from François Le Roux, and yet his recital with Graham Johnson of songs by Saint-Saëns has also been among the season's best findings. Favourites include *Dans ton coeur*, *Marquise, vous souvenez-vous?* and the other elegant pastiches. Graham Johnson's playing and essay-writing are delightful as ever, always the working of a mind trained to be sharply specific. His observation that 'there is more sheer rage in Saint-Saëns's personality (and sometimes in the music) than in almost any other composer one could name' set me thinking about possible competitors. Beethoven? Shostakovich? Sir Edward Bairstow?

Solid Joys and Lasting Pleasures: Choral

A great joy (one shared with EG) has been the Beethoven record on Hyperion with the Corydon Singers and Orchestra under Matthew Best. In the *Cantata on the death of the Emperor Joseph I* the anticipations of *Fidelio* bring the *frisson* that so often comes when a masterwork is evoked and with it the great depth of associated feeling; but the cantata stands in its own ground, a fervour of sustained inspiration upholding it throughout. The *Cantata on the accession of the Emperor Leopold II* similarly strikes the immediate note of genius, as the introductory lamentation changes into joy. The soprano solo here is a major undertaking for any singer, and Judith Howarth commands all the needful resources of expression, tone and technique: a performance to be proud of. The late *Opferlied*, with Jean Rigby on fine form, and the inspired *Meeresstille* for chorus complete a disc which if given the chance, is likely to prove itself the quarter's best investment.

The joy in those cantatas (written at the age of 19) is Haydnesque, and later we find traces of Mozart, whose Requiem is given in what for these days is a grand, full-bodied style under Philippe Herreweghe. The solo quartet is not entirely satisfactory, with Hanno Müller-Brachmann ample in volume but uneven on the held notes of 'Tuba mirum'. The basses are also out of balance in the chorus. Notwithstanding, the performance carries conviction, strong in emotion, energy and attack. So indeed does Gardiner's recording of Haydn's *Creation*, reviewed with great pleasure by myself and subsequently heard with pleasure confirmed. It is a pity that Sylvia McNair so insists on the 'innocent' voice (as she does in *The Rake's Progress*): one wishes she would sing out with some frank earthly relish and forget about being an Archangel. The choruses are uniformly excellent.

Another Requiem, and one very rarely heard, is Delius's, completed in 1916 and dedicated to 'The memory of all young artists fallen in the War'. It had no success at its first performance in 1922, and Beecham (who did not conduct) thought it a grave error of judgement. Recorded now under Richard Hickox, it needs no apology. The musical expression runs deep and the words are no longer likely to cause offence (Delius called it his 'Pagan Requiem'). They are barely audible anyway. This is the one major criticism of the recording, a complaint which extends also to the *Mass of Life* with which it is coupled. There may be a certain appropriateness in having Delius's choruses somewhat hazily distant, but still, despite the insufferable pretentiousness of Zarathustra's utterances, the words are part of the work and cannot be left all to the soloists (why is it, I wonder, that this complaint about insufficiently forward recording of choirs has to be made so often?).

Solid joys, though? Perhaps it is too rhapsodic and moody for that; and perhaps, in one sense, the joys are not so very lasting either, for it is commonly found that though the first few minutes, or even seconds, of a choral work by Delius can transport one suddenly to Heaven's gates, they tend then to fade away and thereafter be glimpsed but fitfully. Even so, in recent years no recording has so richly provided it as this.

Terfel's Elijah

Elijah the Tishbite was 'an hairy man, and girt with a girdle of leather about his loins' (II Kings, Chapter 1 verse 8). Not so the Elijahs of my youth, who were, if memory serves, Arthur Cranmer, Harold Williams, Roy Henderson, Henry Cummings and William Parsons, all of whom played a straight bat and shaved before breakfast. Bryn Terfel's voice, on record as in the flesh, is much better at suggesting the hairy man, inspired prophet of the Lord, instigator of the Kishon Brook Massacre and the fall of Jezebel, eaten by dogs at the wall of Jezreel. He is also tender and thoughtful, and representative of a God who can, when so disposed, be 'gracious and full of compassion, and plenteous in mercy and truth'.

Most of us, I daresay, have not been too troubled by the theology of all this ('The spirit of Elijah', Dr Arnold would explain to his pupils, 'must ever precede the spirit of Christ'); but Bryn Terfel makes us think about it. He creates character as surely as Chaliapin did for Tsar Boris or Tito Gobbi for Baron Scarpia. The trouble is that there is something irreconcilable in the hairy Old Testament prophet and the familiar gentleman of Mendelssohn in E flat.

Never mind: the work, like the widow's son, liveth, and it liveth a mightily more abundant life through the singing of Terfel and the conducting of Paul Daniel. The Edinburgh Festival Chorus point their words well ('He is a jealous God'), the rhythms too (as in the fugal 'Lord, our Creator'). There is also excellent singing by soloists of the 'choruses' 'He hath given His angels charge over thee' and 'O come, everyone that thirsteth'. The Orchestra of the Age of Enlightenment produce a tone that is truly 'leaner and fitter' than usual, closer to the hither side of the composition, the age of Bach which was part of its inspiration, also intensifying the power of the brass as in the D-G sharp *fortissimo* of the awesome ninth bar.

About Terfel much more could be said, most of it (though not quite all) in his favour. Something must have prompted, after listening right through to the end, a return to those first bars of all: the marvellous opening of the whole work. Playing a succession of Elijahs (ten of them in this instance, with Fischer-Dieskau most unfortunately gone missing from my shelves), one hears none that is so strong in character as Terfel, so specific in detail, urgent in enunciation. Yet also, apart from Theo Adam, there is none who is less scrupulous about ensuring evenness of voice-production. The first notes ('As God the Lord') and the 'but according' at the end of this short utterance do not, as I hear them, sound firm: not (at least) as Thomas Allen or Harold Williams are firm. At several points later on ('Call him louder', or 'endureth for evermore' or 'the strength of the Lord') Terfel applies a pressure that loosens the note. It would be regrettable if this were increasingly to become a tendency, and, without having chapter and verse immediately to hand, I feel that some such tendency is becoming noticeable. He gives himself so completely to what he does that caution might seem a pusillanimous virtue. But think of old Battistini. With a very different type of baritone voice he also gave himself, sometimes recklessly and not always to judicious musical effect: but even in his last recordings, made well into his sixties, we hear no single spreading or beating note, or any that betrays an unevenness of vibration.

Vesselina Kasarova

Where singers are concerned, it really has been, in recent years, a matter of 'eastward, look, the land is bright'. Reviewing her new Mozart record, Alan Blyth nominated the mezzo-soprano Vesselina Kasarova 'the most exciting young singer on the international scene'. She made a strong impression in her previous recordings, but Mozart can test most revealingly and reveal most joyfully, as here. She sounds now like a singer in the prime of life, the bloom of youth still on the voice, confidence in technique allowing a boldness of style, and abundant (almost super-abundant) energy animating all. If question or caution arises, it does so because such forceful energy can sometimes go into overdrive. Dorabella's 'Smanie implacabili' is, yes, it is an outburst, and what we hear at the start of this recital fairly strikes home. Yet, slight query, would we, easily, re-attach to its context in *Così fan tutte*? Is the impact not too heroic, even tragic, in the emphasis of its defiance? The glimpse of a vulnerable woman afforded near the end enriches the characterization; but is the character really and truly that of Dorabella? And is the unsmiling, non-cajoling singer of 'Vedrai, carino' really Zerlina?

So is it because we have less distinct notions of Farnace, Cecilio, Vitellia and Sesto that the arias from *Mitridate*, *Lucio Silla* and *La clemenza di Tito* are more readily accommodated? Whatever the answer to that, let us enjoy. Here is a splendid singer, movingly expressive (hear the 'Non più di fiori'), fluent, even and precise in florid work, ample in range, lovely in quality.

1998

The American School

Into the great American pot they go, all the voices of the Western world, the national schools of singing, the *bel canto*, the *Gesangstechnik*, the *beau style*, *potencia*, *facilidad*, little Miss Mabel from the Home Counties, Sergei with the low C from Novosibirsk. Into the pot, to be warmed, stirred and tended, served with care, consumed with pleasure; a wholesome nourishment, a plenteous provision, and indeed where would we be without it? But something seems lost. A depth, an individuality, a refinement, a variety?

I'm taking up a point raised, or more truly a feeling expressed, by Hugh Canning in the Autumn issue of the *International Opera Collector*. 'A bland uniformity in the timbres of singers' is his phrase, and he applies it especially to American sopranos 'of the lighter variety', notably Kathleen Battle, Dawn Upshaw and Sylvia McNair. The quarter's listening has involved many Americans of the young-to-middle generation (though as it happens relatively little of those three), and it focuses attention on this whole question of 'blandness' and uniformity. And the singer immediately to the fore with this in mind is the splendid Thomas Hampson.

'Bland' would be too severe a word; and it would be unjust, for it is hardly possible to be bland and thoughtful (and Hampson is that) or bland and splendid (which he certainly is too). Yet the word will not quite go away. The new Lieder records (Schubert's *Winterreise* and Schumann's Heine settings) both suggest it. Alan Blyth, reviewing, obviously felt this blandness as a lurking, if unnamed, presence, especially in the *Winterreise*, which left him, as he said, 'unmoved'. He added that Wolfgang Sawallisch's accompaniments suited the singer's approach: 'bürgerlich', 'tame'. Even from the start this is true, so much so as to make one wonder whether 'Gute Nacht' is being presented as a kind of casual prologue, a walking away after a difference of opinion, the real separation then occurring between the first song and the next, 'Die Wetterfahne'. But of course, first, the songs won't bear that interpretation, and, second, one soon finds that this not-quite-casual but definitely-not-intense tone of voice and manner is to be pervasive.

Schumann suits much better, and the *Liederkreis*, Op. 24 gives the pleasure good singing in such music will always provide. *Der arme Peter*, which follows, is a different matter. This is the miniature cycle of three short songs concerning a misfit, an outsider, a poor, pale, lovelorn loner, partner in misfortune to the 'I' of *Winterreise*. The first and third of the songs observe 'poor Peter'; the second he sings himself. But Hampson doesn't differentiate. He neither 'creates' the character nor finds a voice-colour appropriate to the description of him looking 'white as chalk'. It is the kind of thing Peter Schreier does supremely well, and there lies the difference: 'bland', which might conceivably be a word to use of Schreier's vocal tone, is never one that suggests itself in reference to his art as a whole. Hampson's tone is richly beautiful, not bland at all, but the expressiveness of its use is in such instances distinctly limited.

This is all the more puzzling as the mind behind it is so active. In that same Schumann recital he gives us the original *Dichterliebe*, not heard before and fascinating in every point of detailed variation from the familiar version. In another recent recording, 'To the Soul', he presents a collection of settings of texts by Whitman: a typically enterprising programme and magnificently sung. It seems likely that these are temperamentally (as well as linguistically) closer to the singer than are the haggard romantics of Müller and Heine. And, of course, returning to that German repertoire, what has to be added to the balance is a recognition of that ever-present and critically-underestimated foundation of the European school of singing, assiduously sought-for by the best American singers, the true and difficult art of legato. In Hampson's *Winterreise* it is practised not only in 'Der Lindenbaum' and 'Einsamkeit' (where expected) but in, say, 'Die Post' and 'Erstarrung'. Perhaps this great virtue exacts its limitation (as most virtues do), and is what causes Alan Blyth in his review to refer to one of the songs as 'all too beautifully sung'.

Hail, Priory!

All morning I have sat at home, with brisk January sunlight making a pattern of Mattins on the wall, and at the same time have travelled North, South, West and East, up to Durham and down to Lincoln, climbing the hill to where the great West front of the Cathedral rises sheer and magnificent as the Beardmore glacier in *Scott of the Antarctic*, then over to Wales, treading the Dean's Steps to Llandaff, and across to where the ghost of Charles Dickens bids listen for the rich voice of John Jasper among the choristers at Rochester. And all of this is due to Priory: magic label in the service of which the Priorymen have themselves travelled (but in reality), seeking throughout the length and breadth of the land for choirs and organs, and thus from Lincoln compiling their catalogue of the recently achieved 500.

To put a tune to these wanderings of mine. At Durham I caught the fine verse-anthem by their own William Smith, of Responses fame; at Lincoln, Howells's *Collegium Regale* Evening Service, in which you might, just might, think they're a weedy lot of trebles when they start the *Magnificat*, but if so the unworthy thought perishes as they launch their 'Glory be'. At Llandaff it was Howells again, but this time the rarely-heard *Coventry Antiphon*, striving ecstatically; and at Rochester, having come for Langlais's *Missa in simplicitate*, I stayed for the *Rochester Mass* by Barry Ferguson, and was glad to have done so if only for its 'Benedictus' and *Agnus Dei*.

These cathedrals are places where young musicians are made. They are much more than that of course; but if the choral tradition were to be lost (and its sturdy survival is something of a miracle) the loss would be felt far beyond the cathedral close. Besides, the music itself is marvellous and totally underrated among ourselves, whose prize possession it ought to be. Those who don't know their Stanford in B flat from their Walmisley in D minor also don't know what they're missing. All praise to Priory for their first 500: now welcome the second.

A Great Choral Record

The record of the quarter, as far as my personal enjoyment is concerned, is also choral. This is of two unaccompanied Masses, written in the same year, 1922, by Frank Martin and Ildebrando Pizzetti. Westminster Cathedral has certainly looked after its choral traditions, and under James O'Donnell the choir give magnificent performances, as Robert Layton said in his review. But the works themselves are rich sources of interest and satisfaction. They contrast in their different backgrounds but have in common an intense commitment of spirit and skill. Pizzetti's is a Requiem, its lines lyrical and steady in their flow, evoking a mysticism that is in part medieval, part (in no derogatory sense) theatrical. Martin's is a tauter, more strenuous, exercise of the imagination, a wonderful compound of discipline and impulse. At times austere (as at the start of the *Credo*), it can at any moment speak softly from the heart ('passus et sepultus'), leave the earth ('Et resurrexit' not an apocalyptic rush or fanfare but a choral dance for Ariel), or flame with exultant rhythms ('pleni sunt caeli'). It is chastening to think of this so pre-eminently 'sounding' music lying silent for so long: Martin kept it for 40 years 'as a work between God and me' and it was not published or performed till 1963.

More Choirs

Though the leading British college and cathedral choirs sing a mainly British repertoire, they also range a good deal more widely than they used to. The Choir of King's College, Cambridge, would never in the old days have been found with a programme such as they undertake in the record called 'Credo'. This is of Russian music sung in Russian, no mean feat in itself. The sound is not 'authentic', in that the choir retains its identity rather than imitating Russian voices (though the basses establish themselves pretty promptly as masters of the low D). In his review Marc Rochester confessed to being moved to tears: stonier-hearted, I admired and enjoyed but remained dry-eyed, at least till the last item of all, where the slow, regular stepping motion leads towards a sudden floodlight of *fortissimo* splendour: Rachmaninov's *Cherubic Hymn*.

Our own groups of expert solo singers working in ensemble have played a distinctive part in our musical life for several decades, and it is interesting to hear an Italian counterpart in Alan Curtis's Il Complesso Barocco.

The respective reviewers of their two recent recordings, Fabrice Fitch and Jonathan Freeman-Attwood, like their singing more unreservedly than I do, but all must be grateful for their attention to these extraordinarily imaginative composers. Antonio Lotti is generally known only for the choral *Crucifixus* and the song *Pur dicesti*, neither of them giving adequate preparation for an encounter with the sophisticated and expressive madrigalist. Michelangelo Rossi, from a generation earlier, continues more directly in a line from Monteverdi, but in his *Straziani pur Amor* shows himself still more a high exponent of the impetuous and fantastic. Both composers are fascinating. The trouble with the singing (to my ears) lies in their assertively non-vibrating tone in combination with the 'hairpin' technique. They have one persistently unblending tenor and among the sopranos an edgy, rather sour voice that sometimes sheds these qualities but emerges troublesomely with them from time to time. They also tend to underline discords and that 'poisoned', twisted kind of vocal intertwining that is capable of speaking for itself. Even so, they are vivid and vital in their style, precise in attack and responsive in expression; and their service to these composers has been invaluable.

Both choirs in the recent recordings of Verdi's Requiem are a pleasure to hear; or perhaps one should say that the Orféon Donostiarra would be a pleasure if they could be heard properly. They sing in the version under Michel Plasson, made in Notre-Dame at Toulouse, a building in which recordings have been buried alive before now. It starts with the chorus (marked *sotto voce* we know, but perhaps not necessarily quite as *sotto* as this) in a recession from which they emerge clearly enough for their careful shading and good tone to be appreciated, and the real mischief is done to them in the *Sanctus* and in the 'Libera me' fugues, more mess than Mass. The Hungarian State Opera Chorus under Pier Giorgio Morandi seem to enjoy themselves enormously (a real smile to the *Sanctus*), and we are able to take pleasure too, hearing them in a clean acoustic which can do justice to a fine performance. The soloists here are adequate-to-good but I think not better than that. Most notable among them is perhaps the bass, Carlo Colombara, a big black Pistol (*Falstaff*) voice and a striking vocal presence but with little idea of suavity or finesse. Plasson's quartet are interesting, if heterogeneous. Julia Varady sings with characteristic tension and refinement; Keith Olsen brings musical intelligence as well as a good voice; Robert Scandiuzzi may be stylistically an improvement upon his counterpart but there is not much in it. The real interest lies with Felicity Palmer, who on this showing should have been a Verdi mezzo all along. She has probably now reached too advanced a stage in her career, but that strong-edged tone has the penetrative power of a Cossotto, and plenty of dramatic flair is ready at hand for its reinforcement.

Modern Meetings

The unique genesis of Schnittke's Requiem – a political impossibility, so brought in by the back door as incidental music for a production in Moscow of Schiller's *Don Carlos* – may well prompt a predisposition in its favour; and personally (perhaps not being adept at identifying what DJF called its 'stylistic tricks') I found that at the very least it held and rewarded attention. Certainly a sense of the dramatic is strong, almost as in Verdi: the great cavern of a cathedral (Seville, the Escorial or whatever) is almost inherently theatrical. The use of the choir is sometimes beautiful and always effective, and there is fine singing by the Moscow State Symphony Cappella. I couldn't 'make out' the *Credo*: a parody of generations of grim monks came to mind at the start.

At least with Schnittke (and really there was no 'at least' about it, for both the Requiem and the coupled Piano Concerto made a strong impression) I experienced none of the difficulty that beset the latest encounter with Arvo Pärt, which was the simple and shameful problem of keeping awake. The programme of unaccompanied sacred music performed by the excellent Estonian Philharmonic Chamber Choir has attractions of several kinds; but in all the variety or range of expression claimed for it in the accompanying booklet, conspicuously missing is anything involving the great musical enlivener, counterpoint, and very little that moves at more than a snail's pace. One does not expect works with such titles as *De profundis* and *Memento mori* to take the form of a fugal jig, but these seemed to me lugubrious and enervating. I must try again, perhaps earlier in the day.

But then comes the old dilemma – and it persists, but more obtrusively, in a first encounter with Maxwell Davies's *Job* – as to whether you are willing to throw more good time after bad in the hope that something you don't like may turn out to be likeable after all. *Job* struck me as being intolerable. With some remission during the orchestral passages, every kind of objection – musical, aesthetic, philosophical, theological, moral, psychological – arose to accumulate like yet another of Job's own plagues. Perhaps such was the intention. 'An internal drama that occurs inside Job's head', says the composer describing his concept. So God and the Devil ('the Accuser') and the comforters are not 'real'. And Job himself? The representative of poor, undeservedly afflicted Mankind? So he should be if he is to serve in this cosmic drama (however 'internal'), yet I hardly think that the drama of this century's multitudinous victims has been played out in these terms.

Don Carlo

The internal drama of all five main characters in *Don Carlo* finds exceptionally faithful expression in the new recording under Haitink, the drama which provided shelter for Schnittke's Requiem brings to mind the emotion of Thomas Mann's young Tonio Kröger on seeing the King, a character of such awe-inspiring dignity and might, alone, suffering, and emotionally naked in his private room. The solo can rarely have been more truly realized than it is as performed here. Philip is sung by Roberto Scandiuzzi, who has to enforce an almost cruel regime of self-denial. That his singing is probably improved by it is perhaps a by-product of poetic justice, but for a young Italian it must be a hard principle to accept that in the 'big' solo there is to be no sheer bigness of tone: not even in the *forte* B flat section ('Se il serto regal') is the voice to blossom, nor yet on the climactic D and E natural towards the end. It remains throughout, convincingly, the voice of a weary, ageing and unhappy man: and that is a genuine artistic achievement.

Unexpectedly allied to this is the performance of Eboli's aria at the end of the scene. Up to now it has always seemed a solo in the grand manner, the mezzo having her great moment in the house, which we hope she will fill with a proportionately great voice. Olga Borodina has indeed a fine voice, though it is not of the Gorr, Bumbry or Cossotto build, even on record. She makes an effect in the traditional manner, but more remarkably makes something of the 'internal drama'. In particular, the despairing reflections of the second verse ('Versar, versar sul passo il pianto') gain more than nominal reality, and in its louder and more turbulent way the piece stands in some sort of symmetrical relation to the King's aria as an expression of the soul's distress.

These things have their counterparts elsewhere, all presumably co-ordinated by Haitink. I rate the recording more highly than did Richard Fairman in his review. He admired much, finding 'humanity and compassion strongly affirmed, with the confrontational moments lacking in tension'. Even adding the fine contributions of the other singers and indeed of all concerned, it is true that this would not be the single recording of the opera to recommend. Yet in some respects it captures more essential dramatic truth than any of the others.

Other Operas

In the earlier Italian repertoire a good deal of interest has been aroused by the recent *L'elisir d'amore* and *La sonnambula*. The first will probably be remembered as 'the one with the different "Una furtiva lagrima"', but has other reasonable claims to a place in the annals. For one thing, the pairing of Gheorghiu and Alagna works happily, she with lustrous tone, more warm and well-rounded than the typical Italian soubrette, and conferring a more generous humanity upon a character who often seems pert and sometimes heartless. Alagna, prevented by too rigid a literalism of style from making much of 'Quanto è bella', phrases broadly in 'Chiedi al rio', draws a good, clean line in 'Adina, credimi', and disowns clownage throughout. The Romanza becomes quite a different thing in this version, the accompanying arpeggios taken not as a cue for elegiac lyricism but imparting an optimistic spring to the rhythm. Rather reluctantly, I conclude it fits better within the comedy, and also belongs more naturally to the character of Nemorino as we see and hear him elsewhere.

The *Sonnambula* is surely a prize gem in the Naxos crown. Reservations do come to mind; the resonantly named bass, Francesco Ellero d'Artagna, for instance, does not possess the suppleness and lyrical beauty of tone his role requires. Still, rejoicing prevails. Orgonasova and Giménez are delightfully cast, she with that Dal Monte-like clarity, he with such natural grace and individuality of tone. Their duets are fit to stand with Schipa's, and Zedda's conducting has the kind of 'give', the flexibility of phrase and rhythm more associated with the old days than with the present. Orgonasova may seem at first to be too bright-and-capable in her voice-character for the sleep-walker, but she develops the part tenderly and with due pathos – and with an awakening that makes even the armchair listener sit up. Time and again one is surprised to find how pictorially vivid a sound-recording can be (it's the old story of the child who prefers radio to television because 'the pictures are so much better').

The new *Oberon* regularly makes pictures on the mind, sometimes magically effective like an old illustrated edition of *Midsummer Night's Dream*. It's a pity the Rezia, Inga Nielsen, lacks the shine and firmness we were looking for, but Seiffert, Kasarova and Skovhus are attractive and, as a whole, the performance under Janowski does the somewhat underrated work grand service. It would be pleasant now to add a similar vote of thanks for the other German-English opera newly recorded, Delius's *Fennimore and Gerda*. A problem with this opera in the theatre must be how to get the voices across while preserving the naturalness of sung dialogue which the score clearly intends. On record it should be much easier to achieve, and it was done very successfully in the recently reissued previous recording under Meredith Davies. There, sung in English, the conversations were conducted with due intimacy, from person to person; here, in German, they sound too like the First Act of *Die Walküre*, sung across stage or to an audience. Besides, the 1976 recording had Elisabeth Söderström, a charming and eventually transfixing Fennimore, whereas Randi Stene, capable singer as she is, brings to this recording a dimmer personality and a more limited imagination.

Song Recitals

These months have been rich in song. Volume 2 of the Hyperion Schumann Edition brought a special pleasure and the collaboration of Simon Keenlyside and Graham Johnson is so potent that after an hour one is still ready for more. In particular, it is good to hear the Kerner cycle complete and to find that none of the distinctive flavour of this resonant voice is lost on record. So, too, with Sergei Larin. John Warrack found his 'near-falsetto' on high notes too frequent for effectiveness in his new Rachmaninov song recital, and there may be just a suggestion every now and then in his singing that he might not have been in best voice. Yet the voice is a remarkable one, and the tenor a genuine artist who can encompass a wide range of expression, from the gently meditative mood of *Lilacs* to the strong declamation of *No prophet I*.

In French song the singer's challenge is to discover comparable variety within more restricted confines. Anne Sofie von Otter responds with a finely tuned sensibility in her recital of works for singer and instrumental ensemble. She has the essential skill of combining intimacy of expression with projection of voice. And, though appreciating PO'C's beleaguered cry of 'How many recordings of Delage's *Four Hindu Poems* does a chap need?', I'm still grateful to have this one. ES's review of the Bonney-Previn recital of American songs also proved to be a good companion. I was glad he liked Domenick Argento's *Six Elizabethan Songs*, especially as I suspected that in the best circles you weren't supposed to. Good, too, to share recognition of Bonney's 'surprisingly resilient low register'. But where, I wonder, shall I find a fellow-heretic who will confess to such repeated failure as mine over the poetry of Emily Dickinson?

Vivaldi

It has been a good season for Vivaldi. *Ottone in Villa* was greeted by Lionel Salter as 'quite the best and neatest Vivaldi operatic recording yet', and Nicholas Anderson, a little less enthusiastic about The King's Consort's *Juditha Triumphans*, nevertheless expressed confidence that at least everybody new to the work would be delighted. Both opera and oratorio are refreshing fare, and despite the opening bars of *Ottone* they have little of that – what to call it? – vacuous chatter that sometimes passes for liveliness in Vivaldi. Both also put the singers through their paces. One of the most heartening developments in singing over the last 30 or 40 years has been a kind of gymnastic one, in which singers have to keep fit for virtuosic engagements of this sort. There are no 'star' names here, but simply a cast of well-exercised professionals who can sing their semiquaver runs and cover the double-octave course with ready competence and assurance. LS notes that in *Ottone* it is not always easy to tell the three sopranos (Susan Gritton, Nancy Argenta and Sophie Daneman) apart, and it is true that Monica Groop is a somewhat ladylike Caesar; still, all (including the tenor, Mark Padmore) do well, as do all four mezzos (Susan Bickley, Ann Murray, Sarah Connolly and Jean Rigby) in *Juditha*.

What then strikes one is how much more austere a form of entertainment the opera presents than does the oratorio. In *Ottone*, aria follows recitative without even so much as a duet to interrupt the succession. In *Juditha* brass and drums introduce the chorus; lengths and forms are varied, as is the orchestration. In no very serious sense can it be called dramatic, and yet the sheer range of musical colour and variety of pace make it more 'operatic' than the opera itself.

Interpreters

The quarter's best lie beyond my generally agreed landmarks, with one (Dufay) well outside, the other (John Clerk of Penicuik) just across the border. A stealthy detour is indicated.

When (then) did a performer become an 'interpreter'? When did a performance become an 'interpretation'? The dictionary (Shorter Oxford) gives 1880, which is as might have been expected. Late romanticism, with its cults of personality and aestheticism, warmed to the wild-eyed virtuoso, the impassioned maestro, the diva and divo, whose part it was to give of their own substance, transmuting the written notes into a life that was also the performer's own. In the heyday of this period the gramophone came into being, capitalizing on the celebrity-status of its artists and, with the aid of record critics, nurturing the listener's awareness of significant differences between 'versions'. These became, therefore, 'interpretations on record'. But an interpreter (in another sense) is one who translates from a foreign language, and a Mozart symphony, whoever plays it, is not a foreign language. Nor is the whole 'classic' repertoire in which for the most part the performers give us their 'interpretations'. The term is pretentious and encourages a mystique. The real interpreters of music are of a different kind and are found elsewhere.

Medieval composers do speak a foreign language. We 'understand' individual progressions and phrases, and we recognize often a great beauty. But their ways are not ours: it is often hard to tell, for instance, whether the mood is happy or unhappy, and even whether such notions as mood and expression are appropriate. This is where we need the interpreters. For a start, the scholar who translates a medieval manuscript into a score for modern reading does more by way of interpretation than any symphonic conductor. The editor or choirmaster who takes a medieval score with no indication in it of tempo or expression has more interpretative work on his hands than the subtlest of Lieder singers. And we, as listeners, need all the help we can get. With this marvellous new recording by The Binchois Consort of Dufay's *Mass for St James the Greater* and other works it is of course quite possible to 'let the music wash over you', and yet even that is more the formulation of an attitude than an actuality; for, listening, one responds to specific points and wants to know what is happening, and why. This superb group, directed by Andrew Kirkman, accomplish as much by way of genuine interpretation as lies within the power of the performing artist. We still need more, in words; and I still find that too much of what the scholars write in the booklet-notes is addressed to each other, to people who know the language already and need to be enlightened only on the finer points.

Curiously, John Clerk, though born two-and-a-half centuries after Dufay, has comparable need of an interpreter. In a splendid recital of cantatas, all first recordings, the interpreters would conventionally be said to be Catherine Bott and the Concerto Caledonia. Not so. They are the admirable performers. The interpreter is John Purser who contributes a booklet-essay which is not only fascinating but essential to the understanding of this music (which also can of course be allowed merely to 'wash over you'). Clerk (1676-1755) wrote music with arithmetical symbolism. A simple example is the exact central placing of the word meaning 'heart' in the Cantata, *Miserere mei, Deus*, 400 bars long, the change of direction occurring exactly half-way. A special vocabulary of numerical reference is elucidated, and, though the music is perfectly delightful to the ear in itself, we cannot know why it is 'thus and not otherwise' without an interpreter. Dufay is a great master, John Clerk a minor one, and both of these new records enrich the library; but the kind and degree of interpretation involved with them makes 'interpretative' differences between (say) the various singers of a song by Wolf or an aria by Verdi appear as what they essentially are – features of a performance, showing a greater or a lesser degree of understanding.

Bostridge and the Lied

An immediate challenge to this comes with the thought of Ian Bostridge and not so much the more recent Schubert recital as his

Schumann record of some months back. In this, the insights are so strong, individual and pervasive that argument about their 'interpretative status' looks like a linguistic quibble. The thing about Bostridge is that he makes these poets mean what they say. There is a difference here with even so literate a singer as Fischer-Dieskau: in fact, the difference lies partly in this, that Fischer-Dieskau, for all his intensity of intellect and emotion, remains literary where Bostridge is actual. These distinctions are too crudely made, but let's say Fischer-Dieskau gives us the condition (the feelings and events as to some extent objectified in the very act of making poetry out of them), and Bostridge gives us an 'I'. For instance, in the second song of the Op. 24 *Liederkreis*, 'Es treibt mich hin', the 'Ich' is his very self, and he hates the hours – shuffling, yawning, crawling (all the spiteful things he can think of) that stand between him and the next lovers' meeting. Then in the song 'Ich wandelte', the mood has changed to a cherished privacy of heartache: the transformation, the emotional instability, is extreme enough to be shocking. Heine through Schumann, Schumann through Bostridge, does take on here an actuality that makes something new of him (new to us, that is). Here if anywhere, you might say, the 'interpreter' in its 1880 connotation is vindicated (yet is it, when all that the singer has essentially done is to take literally and not literarily the words of his song?).

At the start of that Op. 24 I thought he was mouthing the words too much. Perhaps that too was the 'I', Heine's 'Ich'. That can't really be so in *Die Forelle* and *Der Fischer*, where, on the new Schubert record, he seems very slightly to be mouthing the story-telling as though to children. Not that this is habitual with him in narrative-songs: *Der Zwerg* is mercifully free from over-dramatization, and when a special emphasis or coloration is employed in *Erlkönig*, then it is to chilling effect. His collaboration with Julius Drake seems always to yield good results, and they work well together in the whole range of these songs, from the beautifully sustained *Nacht und Träume* to the blissful buoyancy of *Der Musensohn*.

Modern Mixtures

Schumann's Op. 24 is also the subject of *Fantasy-Pieces* by Robin Holloway (1971). After a prelude the cycle is performed (and very well, by Toby Spence and Ian Brown), then come the pieces for piano and 12 instruments based on it. Always alert (even in the movement called 'Half-asleep'), this composer commands attentive listening but lost me in the last section, an uncharacteristically repellent passage for brass and a heavy 'beat' in the piano. On the other hand, the *Serenade in C* (1979) becomes a companion (I hope) for life. It is delightfully scored and wittily allusive without being facetious: an achievement.

A rather similarly divided reaction attended the Hindemith record with *Sancta Susanna* as its supposed main attraction. In fact, any return to that disc on my part will be for the Suite from *Tuttifäntchen*, music for a children's pantomime in 1922. It was unsettling to see my colleague, Robert Layton, bowled over by the horrid *Susanna* and Three Songs, Op. 9, while considering the suite 'rather nondescript'. I found it a charming, lyrical, smiling piece and worth more than its nasty neighbours put together. To call them 'horrid' gives a poor idea of their repulsiveness, Hindemith's music doing little to redeem (as if anything could) August Schramm's *Schreidrama*, and Susan Bullock's raw-edged tone failing to justify the required expenditure of voice and other energies on the third poem, the *Aufbruch der Jugend*, which celebrates exactly the arrogant and brainless form youth's revolt should not take. Of course in all such matters – 'difficult' music experienced in what are necessarily brief encounters – one must keep an open mind. But that is a principle that works both ways. The Entartete Musik series, for example, is so insistently worthy a project that one wishes always to find in its favour. I'm afraid the further I went with Hans Krása's *Verlobung im Traum* (having more or less taken to the Overture), the harder it became to conceive that there was any profit or pleasure to be gained from it. Unlike Robin Holloway's musical allusiveness, Krása's seems snide, knowing and demeaning. The humour is heavy, the central device (the 'dream') silly, and the writing is typical of its period in that, while snatches of something like song appear from time to time in the orchestra, the singers are involved mainly in pitched chatter. There are some good singers there too – Charlotte Hellekant, Jane Henschel and Michael Kraus among them – all heroically doing what is asked of them, which is never truly to sing.

Don and Damnation

The line of British baritones – Santley its progenitor, on to Dennis Noble, Roy Henderson (now in his 100th year), Shirley-Quirk and Tom Allen – now provides both a Don Giovanni and a Leporello for the international cast-list. Bryn Terfel, the Giovanni of the 1997 set under Solti, sings his Leporello to the Don of Simon Keenlyside, giving capital performances both but affording also an interesting comparison in voice-usage. Keenlyside sings with plenty of energy but keeps his voice out of the rough; Terfel, perhaps as befits his role, is less scrupulous. Keenlyside offers what is something of a rarity, a good 'Deh,vieni alla finestra'; with an imaginative guitarist, he favours more rubato than is usual nowadays, and the effect is entirely to the good. Uwe Heilmann as Ottavio sings a sweetly lingering 'Dalla sua pace' and, to contrast, gives 'Il mio tesoro' a strong charge of energy with a forfeiture of grace. Of the women, the Elvira, Soile Isokowski, has fine moments of aristocratic distinction, Patrizia Pace phrases Zerlina's arias broadly, but Carmela Remigio is miscast: a girlish-sounding Anna who loses quality in her effort to summon the resources for 'Or sai chi l'onore'. Abbado conducts without exciting special notice, which is probably a virtue.

Terfel also sings in the new, and exciting *Damnation de Faust* under Myung-Whun Chung. His Mephistopheles appears at Faust's ear, almost as a voice in his head, almost his own voice. This is an intimate Devil, sparingly demonic, and coping well with a manic tempo for the Serenade. Anne Sofie von Otter gives a real characterization, selecting her Marguerite-voice almost as out of a vocal wardrobe, and singing 'D'amour l'ardente flamme' as still under the spell of her love. As Faust, Keith Lewis provides yet another reminder that in him we have possibly the best tenor of his kind since Gedda.

A Comparison and a Defence

Gardiner's recording of *Leonore* comes to hand with Mackerras's *Fidelio* firmly in mind. Vocally fallible, the *Fidelio* still moves deeply in a way that no other opera can do. The quality and balance of the Chamber Orchestra (the Scottish) are a great asset, the texture clarified, particularly helpful to the opening numbers, and at the start of Act 2 the brass telling with brutal force. Everyone performs with conviction. Beňačková is generous in voice and spirit and sings the quieter lyrical passages beautifully, though without quite adequate vocal resources to call upon elsewhere. Rolfe Johnson mars the legato of 'In des Lebens Frühlingstagen' and produces the now familiar rasping edge to his tone at a *forte*. Beethoven survives and triumphs. But, despite Gardiner's enthusiasm for it, the three-act version, *Leonore*, of 1805 seems essentially not more than Beethoven himself must have come to see it: an inspired draft of a yet unaccomplished masterpiece. Gardiner's strong, unportentous direction gives it every support, but the casting is patchy, Matthew Best lacking the power and firm incisiveness for Pizarro, Hillevi Martinpelto a rather light voice-character for Leonore, Kim Begley initially impressive and then seemingly forgetful of Florestan's identity as (say) a man miraculously released from Belsen. Yet it's an important recording to have, and parts of it (the wonder of 'Mir ist so wunderbar' for instance) stay long in mind.

But listening back to recapture the sounds of the quarter, I hear one voice of radiant quality shining out among all the others, and it belongs to a singer whom everybody seems to have decided to criticise. I don't know how Jessye Norman is singing these days – it was 1993, about the time when the more recent of these two new releases was made, when I heard her last. She was in superb voice then, and so she is on these records. The criticisms, in ***Gramophone*** and elsewhere, were made on other grounds: a lack of involvement, emotional, imaginative or 'interpretative'. In *Bluebeard's Castle*, not knowing Hungarian, I find that difficult to judge, and of course if one has a preconception of Judith as a mouse, Norman clearly won't do. Why, one wonders, did Bluebeard choose Judith? It can't have been for her conversation or compliance or the prospect of snuggling down to watch the sunset after supper. Stage directions describe Judith clad in a splendid robe; Norman's voice has splendour to match. The voice does in fact give an answer to our question: she has been chosen to be Queen of his realm. Almost her first words are 'Let me do it', and this imperative is her 'character-note'. Norman is not vocally shrewish, as was Elena Obraztsova in the recording immortalized by Rodney Milnes's remark that if he were Bluebeard he'd have closed the first door on her and thrown away the key. Norman's is a regal voice, instinct with will-power. This is her Judith, and if (possibly) it is uninvolved it is certainly not uninvolving; and not without depth either, for after this opulence of command it is doubly pitiful when she is reduced to hushed awe and self-deprecation at the end.

In *Das Lied von der Erde*, recorded under Levine in 1992, the richness and firmness of the voice are alone sufficient to put her performance into a special class: not even Thorborg, Ferrier, Ludwig or Baker brought quite this quality of tone to the music. Some Viennese charm would be welcome in 'Von der Schönheit' and a less heroic tone would better suit the phrase about the tired girl going homewards in 'Der Abschied'. Yet she does soften sensitively, her phrasing is broad, there is some vibrant passion of address in 'Ich sehne mich, o Freund'. But this music is so inherently expressive that it needs very little by way of so-called interpretation. Feelings are two-a-penny; everybody, or anybody, has them. The pearl of great price is the voice.

1999

Powder Her Face in the Marabar Caves

A disagreeable echo has invaded the listening room. It comes, and, thank heaven, it goes, but it has been in demonic possession lately. Readers of *A Passage to India* will remember the Marabar caves. They had an echo, which boomed most unpleasantly. To the elderly Mrs Moore they said 'Everything exists: nothing has value'.

On the occasion of its last local visit I was playing *The Mask of Orpheus*, and it was present throughout but, as it were, slyly and lurking in corners. Previously, in *Powder Her Face*, it had boomed terribly. Thomas Adès's opera about Margaret Whigham, Duchess of Argyll, has played to packed houses, winning the praise of normally judicious critics. The CD has won the approval in ***Gramophone*** of Michael Oliver who thought it 'hugely enjoyable.' For myself, I found an interest in reading about it ('everything exists') and then listened totally without benefit ('nothing has value'). Its invention may have been witty but it drew no smile and brought no pleasure. Its exposure of the scandalous (or scandalized) individual may have been meant to induce sympathy and compassion or censure or psychological and social concern, but it did not. The music should have brought some delight, and (this being an opera) so should the singing. All I found was a hollow: uncertain whether it lay in the work itself or in the listener, and with further nauseous uncertainties: whether, for instance, it was ungenerous of me to entertain a suspicion that the box-office success had attested only the power of gutter-press headlines made artistically 'smart', and whether this, as opera, has anything in common with what attracted me to the form and gave me a love of it many years ago.

I mentioned singing, but that whole aspect of opera seems to have become a borderline concern, almost expendable (as singing), almost (in terms of a responsible critic's interest) a kind of frivolity. The singing on this recording, it will be objected, is perfectly adequate, highly commendable in fact. The four singers meet the technical difficulties of their parts, three high sopranos ('Zerbinetta with knobs on' as MEO put it), the bass with his range from bottom C sharp to high F. They are firm and accurate and thoroughly in character: what more do you want?

Well, I want what most people want who go to operas. Among other things I want music in which the beauty of voices – beauty of tone and production – can be relished. There is little of that here (some phrases for the Duchess perhaps): and it is typical and telling that in press reviews of such things the actual singing of the singers is hardly mentioned. Beauty of sound in voices is about the last consideration. The critic Paul Griffiths is quoted as hailing the music of *Powder Her Face* as 'the music of the future.' The Marabar's echoes boom fearfully.

When the Future is Past

'The Vocalist of the Future' was the heading of an urbane paragraph in *Musical Times* of March 1913, referring to 'a delightful passage concluding a recent song, *Herzgewächse*, by the irresistible Arnold Schoenberg.' The final 15 bars (last six lines of the poem) were quoted, showing that the vocalist of the future was evidently 'expected to have a compass of nearly three octaves. The *pppp* F *in alt* is a touch of inspiration.' Years ago a soprano called Rita Tritter (nothing of her now on the ***Gramophone*** Database) turned the laugh backwards, singing the futurisitic phrases with accuracy, good tone and apparent ease, all to quite beautiful effect. Others have recorded the piece since, and now Christine Schäfer shows that the future is not yet past. With a voice which we do not usually think of as being of the stratospheric kind, she nevertheless advances by way of the C, D flat and E flat placed as so many stepping-stones to the F. This (set to an 'ee' of all the possible vowels) is held long and steady, even if not achieving quite the fourth degree of piano. But I would say the effect is not what Schoenberg ideally wanted. The words refer to a mystical prayer which is to rise to the crystal blue: the *pppp* shows he imagines it as a fluted tone in the *Kopfstimme*, so soft as to seem lost in the heavens. Instead, we see-hear what we should not: the face of a singer at the extremity of her range and ignoring the murderous vowel-requirement to save her life. The laugh, like the echo, booms back from one wall to the other, from the ironical MT ('the idea is obviously in its infancy') to the faithful musician-singer; but it does not stop there.

On this same disc, Schäfer also performs *Pierrot lunaire*, pitching accurately when a sung tone is required and otherwise producing a finely modulated speech-voice. The effect in this recording, with the Ensemble InterContemporain under Boulez, is exactly right: that of combining within one body a delicate beauty and a savage violation. It is strange how the mind responds while listening: I find myself attracted by the clarity and special refinement of verbal image and musical texture, and yet almost comically mindful of the woman who commissioned it and gave the first performance, enjoying the shock-effect of avant-garde stylization, while also indulging show-off effects which would have been forbidden even to the old-style 'ham' actor of the day. And that – the voice of grandiloquent 'ham' – reappears on the disc in the *Ode to Napoleon*. Declaimed here, no doubt faithfully, by David Pittman-Jennings, Schoenberg's setting of Byron's words is surely a crass distortion. Is it conceivable that he can really have believed that this is how Byron should 'go'? The poem is intelligently argued and wittily phrased. Schoenberg reduces it to high-class tub-thumping.

Music and words

Not all composers can be so sensitive as Britten in their word-setting, or so happily supplied in their choice of texts. Listening again to the *Quatre Chansons françaises* of 1928, one marvels afresh that at the age of 14 he should have known that these poems of Hugo and Verlaine existed, let alone have been sufficiently responsive to set them with such skill and feeling for idiom. In Ian Bostridge's recording they lose somewhat in cohesion and energy, as Alan Blyth pointed out, by the choice of a slowish tempo, especially in 'Sagesse'. And this, as AB also found, induces rather too relaxed a feeling in *Our Hunting Fathers*. The point is clear when Söderström's recording under Richard Armstrong is compared; similarly with 'Sagesse' as sung by Lott in her newly reissued version under Bryden Thomson. On the other hand, both comparisons confirm a preference for hearing them sung by tenor rather than soprano. More troublesome, I found, and not for the first time, are the words themselves. The note-writer for this disc gives no help towards elucidation. Perhaps none is thought necessary, but I'm afraid it is: I've tried and I don't understand them. In an essay on Britten's songs, Pears attributed the lack of demand for *Our Hunting Fathers* (he says it was performed only twice from 1936 to 1951) to a dislike of brilliance on the part of 'the English' (with whom of course we have nothing to do). Satire, he says, 'disturbs them.' But the verbal brilliance of intelligent unintelligibility is a shoddy thing, and good satire works through clear rationality, not by creating an uneasy sense of being 'got at.' The music is inseparable from the words. Britten is here the victim of his own strength as a setter of words, and that, rather than any English antipathy to brilliant satire, is why the work has never enjoyed a relatively popular success.

Anyway, the best thing on the record, I think, is something else. The orchestrated version of *O Waly, Waly* comes right at the start and is magical. The wave-motion in the accompanying motif ('The water is wide, I cannot get o'er') seems almost a physical presence. The strings are able to sustain, as the piano cannot, harmonies that grieve beneath the placid surface of the melody. It is most beautifully performed here, with Bostridge's *pianissimo* giving the ending ('and fades away like morning dew') a pictorial vividness and simple truth beyond anything we customarily hear.

The inclusion of the other early cycle of Britten's draws attention to a recital given by Ileana Cotrubas in 1978 and now issued for the first time in Orfeo's Salzburg series. *On this Island* was a bold choice and it suits her well. But the sound of that voice, particularly in her Schubert and Fauré, is not so very reassuring, considering that she was in no more than her 40th year and approaching the climax of her career. It gains real steadiness at forte and piano, so that the most enjoyable items are Duparc's *Chanson triste*, lovely in its quietness, and Debussy's song of Lia from *L'enfant prodigue*, which draws on the full operatic voice. But generally the quality is not what one might have hoped for.

In some ways a comparable voice, Yelena Prokina's also gives a slight, premature notice on the higher-and-louder notes. This is so in her recital of songs by Reinhold Glière, beautifully sung in all other respects. The songs themselves leave a pleasant, somewhat generalized memory, continuing in the line of the nineteenth-century romantics but without excessive sweetness or rhapsodic grandeur. In German song a comparably conservative, minor, but gifted composer is Othmar Schoeck, to whom Brahms and Mahler were as Tchaikovsky and Rachmaninov to Glière. Andreas Schmidt sings the 24 Lieder comprising his *Elegie*, Op. 36 with fine evenness and warmth, though the tessitura is low for him (a bass, Felix Loeffel, was the singer in the 1922 première).

In France, a contemporary was Deodat de Séverac, and he, too, finds a voice in the current lists. François Le Roux and Graham Johnson give a recital devoted entirely to this courtly, affectionate but unsentimental writer, who is certainly not well represented by *Ma poupée chérie*, the song by which he was most commonly remembered. That is charmingly sung here by Patrizia Rozario. Le Roux's voice has dried, but in feeling and expression this is good, fertile singing to match the playing – and the essay-writing – of his accompanist.

By comparison with these, Reynaldo Hahn has by now almost achieved the status of a major song-writer. Susan Graham's recital with Roger Vignoles adds lustre, the tone of her voice as lovely as any to be heard today. Lionel Salter, reviewing, found, as I did not quite, 'the verbal meaning governing the vocal colour.' In *Le printemps*, for example, radiance is present in the voice but not (I would say) in the expression: I kept thinking of how Dame Janet Baker would have caught the enthusiasm. In *Jours de vendage* the voice seems not to darken as the clouds gather verse-by-verse. A more vivid responsiveness makes itself felt in *Nocturne* and *Dans la nuit*, and the famous *Si mes vers* is sung as by an angel. But Hahn's 'subtle smile' and shared secrecy, which the lovely singer mentions in her interview with Patrick O'Connor, were the very things I could not manage to find in most of her performances.

Opera: Recitals and Rusalka

The British mezzo, Diana Montague, has been long due for a recital on record, and her programme of

French arias in English is a winner. Firm and even in production, her voice is gratefully heard though her Dalila is hardly voluptuous and her Périchole certainly not tipsy. Best, I thought, is last: Mignon's 'Connais-tu le pays?' Véronique Gens, also a welcome and somewhat overdue recitalist, sings her Mozart arias with character and apparent technical ease; also with superb accompaniment by the Orchestra of the Age of Enlightenment under Ivor Bolton. In an enterprising programme Bo Skovhus puts his fine voice to the service of dramatic expression and cares little for *legato*; he is best in *Billy Budd*. The new Argentinian tenor, Marcelo Alvarez, raises interest and hopes: he does everything well in his début recital, keeping his lyric voice light though not stinting in energy and resonance. He has a feeling for style, and there is rhythmic life in his singing. Just occasionally a query arises about intonation. That has sometimes been a cause for concern in the singing of Roberto Alagna; very rarely, however, in the programme of Verdi duets with Angela Gheorghiu. It is a most lovely record, I find, with an imaginative charge, nothing treated as routine, and in several instances (including the duet from *Otello*) bringing touches of rare loveliness. I could have done with more rubato in Alagna's verse of the *Traviata* brindisi, but generally Abbado is not restrictive, and the Berlin Philharmonic are as a gift from the gods.

Also for the shopping-list, and possibly (but according to taste) to be awarded priority, are Renée Fleming's recital of arias from American opera and the *Rusalka* in which she has the leading role. The recital gives pleasure and provides an insight. 'The American dream' is proverbial, and it usually implies wealth and status (as in *Death of a Salesman*). Opera romanticizes, and in some sense all of these excerpts have a dream and a soft centre. 'Glitter and be gay' from Bernstein's *Candide* is hard of surface but inwardly (musically) lush. Previn's *Streetcar* ('I want magic'), ending with the spoken, pathetic 'Don't turn on that light', is quintessential; 'Who wants real?' It runs deep in American culture. Stravinsky's *Rake's Progress* points it up ruthlessly, by contrast. Anne's solo is given a place in the recital ostensibly because of its part-American libretto; its music is wide-awake daylight reality. The rest of them yearn, as to her silver moon does Rusalka, and when confronted with reality (*Rusalka*, Act 2) seek refuge in dreams.

Rusalka itself exercises its spell more potently than ever in the new recording (I say this perhaps slightly rashly, not having been able, as Edward Greenfield was, to compare the Supraphon recording which memory recalls dimly but with pleasure). The score seems now a unity, and richly so, its dramatic material having depths which need no conceptual stage-production to impose lines of thought but can be explored ideally in the gramophone's 'theatre of the mind'. Mackerras's work with the Czech Philharmonic is as happy as the opera is long, and the recorded sound could hardly be better. So, too, with the cast, Ben Heppner's Prince sometimes lighting up with a glint of Björling about it, and Fleming's Rusalka going straight to the heart. What a lovely singer she is, and how very well her career is developing. Her singing in the recital is delightful throughout, her quality beautiful as was the young Kiri Te Kanawa's. Let us pray that Fleming will be as wise as Te Kanawa in her choice of roles, and that an inevitably demanding schedule does not imperil the purity of tone. Voice – sheer quality of tone – is not, it seems, a fashionable modern consideration, but for a lyric soprano, however modern, it is vital just as it was of old.

Mask and Maskarade

The Mask of Orpheus was reviewed in December 1997, but the ***Gramophone*** Awards have brought the recording back into prominence, with an urgent hopefulness. We yearn for a modern masterpiece, especially in opera, and perhaps this is it. Michael Oliver was the reviewer, reserving his personal judgement ('*The Mask of Orpheus* is, I think, a masterpiece') till the final paragraph, and opening with what indeed cries out for an immediate word from reviewer to potential listener. How do you listen? Difficult works, medieval as well as modern, have come up for comment in these pages before, but I have never known a recording which raises so many problems in the sheer act of listening to it. There are two booklets, one including some introductory essays, a brief synopsis and what appears to be a more detailed account Act by Act. The other has the libretto, but it is unlike any previous libretto: multi-layered and virtually impossible to follow while listening. So I decided I would 'just' listen, and later discovered that that was what MEO recommended. But I couldn't stay with it. Having read the introduction (and, I may say, having also seen the opera on stage), I found myself after about 20 minutes hopelessly lost. The music was not 'telling its own tale' as promised, nor was it 'working its spell', but on the contrary seemed to be music in which everything had its illustrative or referential purpose so that to make sense of it you had to identify the moment. So you try. You identify the track in one booklet, but that's not much use ('First Allegorical Flower of Reason') so you hunt it up in the 'libretto' (no track references there), and then the troubles start afresh. Myths are universal, so shouldn't be too dependent on words, and words, it is said, are here plainly and sparingly used. The words are plain to be sure (unless in the invented language), but the same cannot be said for their significance, which I found impenetrable. By this time, as a listener, you are on the road to nowhere, and so return to 'just' listening. But the circle starts up again: you want to know!

Immense wonder at the skill of the performance, and the resilience of Jon Garrison's voice: that's firm ground. *Terra firma* too, the observation that the work appears to be a masterpiece of construction (I'm trying to salvage something). One thing: it has a way of sending you back to begin again (even if another day). After three fairly long acts in which – aware that doubts or even questions risk charges of obtuseness or flippancy – you nevertheless have plenty of doubtful questions to ask. But then at the very end come some mysteriously beautiful moments that suggest an infinitely distant music, rather as a blissful slow movement from one of our earthly symphonies might dimly reach the ears of the gods in Olympus.

I shall revisit *The Mask of Orpheus* before *Powder Her Face*: ever hopeful (saying which no doubt implies the reverse). Meanwhile, because I prefer a happy ending, in Quarterly retrospects as in all things else, there is *Maskarade*. Nielsen's comedy appears, newly edited and with cuts restored, in a thoroughly enjoyable recording from Copenhagen. The humour is not, I think, very funny: following the English translation one was thankful it was being sung in Danish. But the music itself is full of fun, a Falstaffian score (Verdi's), bold and energetic, rich in melody, and saved at all points and by some kind of inner grace from commonness. In a way that is probably quite as complex as the ways of Birtwistle (and to very different effect) Nielsen establishes trust: his happiness has no painted showbiz face. The trust is confirmed when, ten minutes from the end, the Master of the Masquerade becomes Corporal Mors at whose signal the revellers throw down their masks 'and once again be dust and ashes'. The celebration is resumed with the Choric Dance 'so that earth and heaven resound'. It is Beethovenian and it silences those echoes from the caves. As in another of Forster's novels, and Beethoven's Fifth Symphony, a deadly goblin has walked quietly across the universe in the midst of its revels. Some would say the goblins, like the echoes, did not exist. But Nielsen, like Beethoven, knows they were there. 'He had said so bravely,' says Forster of Beethoven, 'and that is why you can trust him when he says other things'.

Music for Quiet Time

This is not necessarily quiet music, but it wants a quiet house (no phones ringing or people at the door), and it wants an internally quiet listener without thought for the morrow or jobs undone. To tell the truth, I think quiet music is best, or intimate music at least: the operas are for another day. Possibly even Sigismondo d'India's madrigals don't entirely qualify, or not as performed by William Christie's ensemble, with their comically dramatized 'ahi' and 'piangendo'. Still, these are things of wonder, as in the exquisite languishings of *Se tu, Silvio, crudel* or the rich enactments of *Strana armonia d'amore*. It must also be said that, though various misgivings about the performances occurred to me, the 'curiously disengaged' effect noted by Iain Fenlon was not one.

Of course it wouldn't do for us all to hear alike. Even so, it's pleasant to find companionship in listening during Quiet Time, and I was glad to read 'a charming, gentle and haunting disc' as Patrick O'Connor's description of *La naissance de Vénus* and other pieces by Fauré with the Solistes de Lyon-Bernard Tétu. The 'scène mythologique' is a heavenly work, recorded for the first time, rather over 20 minutes in length, for two soloists, choir and piano: to quote PO'C again, 'a real discovery, it suggests all the lost charm of private small-scale choral singing that belongs to the world of the late nineteenth-century Paris salons'. The whole programme, which includes the blissful *Pavane* and a happy choice of songs, combines with the performance to make the disc first choice of the quarter.

Quiet Time also brings the hour for *Winterreise*. The steady tread and downhill melody of the piano's opening measures have by now acquired the ability to summon up all that is to come, right to the final life-draining chord of 'Der Leiermann'. But too dull or portentous a pace does no service, and little pressings-forward, with a big one in verse three, make things worse; and that is how Thomas Quasthoff and Charles Spencer set out on their journey. En route, they can be vividly responsive (Spencer to the icy drip of 'Gefrorne Tränen', Quasthoff to the folk comfortably abed in 'Im Dorfe'). Much is fine, yet at the end there's too much health in the cheeks – in the voice, that is – and not enough experience fully endured.

That can never be said of the *Lamenti* in Anne Sofie von Otter's recital. She drinks her hemlock to the dregs. The cheeks now flush a hectic red and now are drained with deathly pallor. Vivaldi's *Cessate, mai cessate* is a torrent of fierce emotion, Monteverdi's lament of Arianna most moving in restraint after its outbursts. Sometimes beauty of tone is sacrificed and one fears for the voice; often the sheer quality of sound attains the utmost loveliness. Best perhaps – 'Ease after toyle, port after stormy seas' – are the two concluding pieces by Purcell; and most apt for the quiet hour is *O Solitude*, the last of all, its gracious words fitted with patient skill to the steady movement of a set ground bass.

Index to recordings

This index lists those recordings mentioned in the text where, in the original magazine, a record company and catalogue number was quoted.

Composer	Work/Album title	Artist/Conductor	Record Co.	Page
Britten	Canticles	*Langridge*	Collins Classics	**239**
	Death in Venice	*Britten*	Decca	**168**
	Folk Songs	*Pears/Britten*	Decca	**124**
		Johnson	Hyperion	**221**
	Gloriana	*ENO*	Virgin	**169**
		Mackerras	Argo	**203**
	(Les) Illuminations	*Gomez*	EMI	**166**
	(A) Midsummer Night's Dream	*Britten*	Decca	**168**
	Our Hunting Fathers	*Harding*	EMI	**265**
	(The) Rape of Lucretia	*Britten*	Decca	**168**
	(The) Rape of Lucretia/ Peter Grimes	*Goodall*	EMI	**207**
	Recital	*Ainsley*	EMI	**239**
		Hadley	Nimbus	**239**
		Langridge	Collins Classics	**239**
	(The) Rescue of Penelope	*Hunt*	Erato	**240**
	Serenade	*Rolfe Johnson*	Chandos	**166**
	Songs	*Bostridge*	Hyperion	**235**
	Spring Symphony	*Previn*	HMV	**67**
	St Nicholas Cantata	*Best*	Hyperion	**166**
	(The) Turn of the Screw	*Britten*	Decca	**118, 168**
		Davis	Philips	**118**
	Young Apollo	*Rattle*	HMV	**105**
Britten/Mahler	Nocturne/Lieder	*Tear*	Argo	**14**
Busoni	Arlecchino/Turandot	*Nagano*	Virgin	**208**
	Doktor Faust	*Leitner*	DG	**100**
Byrd	Choral Works	*King's College*	Argo	**75**
	Sacred Vocal Works	*Hill*	Hyperion	**243**
Chabrier	(Le) Roi malgré lui	*Dutoit*	Erato	**126**
Charpentier	Lamentations	*Devos*	Erato	**136**
Cherubini	Coronation Mass	*Muti*	HMV	**136**
Chopin/Liszt	Recital	*Tear*	Argo	**37**
Clérambault	Orphée/Médée	*Yaker*	Archiv	**87**
Clerk	Cantatas	*Bott*	Hyperion	**259**
Copland	Lincoln Portrait	*Thatcher*	EMI	**188**
Coprario	Funeral Tears	*Consort of Musicke*	L'Oiseau-Lyre	**90**
Crosse	Purgatory	*Lankester*	Argo	**40**
d'India	Madrigals	*Christie*	Erato	**269**
Debussy	Pelléas et Mélisande	*Karajan*	HMV	**75**
	Recital	*Fischer-Dieskau*	DG	**87**
Del Tredici	Final Alice	*Solti*	Decca	**90**
Delius	Choral Works	*Mackerras*	Decca	**234**
	Fennimore and Gerda	*Hickox*	Chandos	**257**
	Idyll	*Fenby*	Unicorn	**125**
	(A) Mass of Life/Requiem	*Hickox*	Chandos	**249**
	Requiem	*Davies*	HMV	**125**
	(The) Fenby Legend	*Lott/Allen*	Unicorn	**96**
Donizetti	(L') Elisir d'amore	*Pidò*	Decca	**256**
	Gemma di Vergy	*Caballé*	CBS	**51**
	Lucia di Lammermoor	*Callas/Gobbi*	HMV	**50**

Composer	Work/Album title	Artist/Conductor	Record Co.	Page
Hahn	Ciboulette	*Mesplé*	EMI	**169**
	Songs	*Layton*	Hyperion	**242**
Handel	Alceste	*Hogwood*	L'Oiseau-Lyre	**90**
	Alexander's Feast	*Harnoncourt*	Teldec	**135**
	(L') Allegro	*Gardiner*	Erato	**83**
	Cantatas	*Thomas*	L'Oiseau-Lyre	**90**
	Coronation Anthems	*Gardiner*	Erato	**115**
		King's College	Argo	**102**
		King's College	HMV	**115**
		Westminster Abbey	DG	**115**
		Westminster Abbey	Archiv	**102**
	Dixit Dominus	*Gardiner*	Erato	**57**
		Netherlands Radio Chorus/Voorberg	Philips	**57**
	Esther	*Hogwood*	L'Oiseau-Lyre	**135**
	Israel in Egypt	*Christchurch/Preston*	Argo	**39**
		Gardiner	Erato	**152**
		Preston	Argo	**152**
	Judas Maccabaeus	*The King's Consort*	Hyperion	**191**
	Messiah	*Cleobury*	Argo	**221**
		Gardiner	Philips	**115**
		Hogwood	Decca	**76**
	Serse	*Malgoire*	CBS	**72**
	Solomon	*Gardiner*	Philips	**135**
	Utrecht Te Deum	*Preston*	L'Oiseau-Lyre	**87**
Haydn	(The) Creation	*Gardiner*	Archiv	**248**
		Dorati	Decca	**61**
	(La) Fedeltà premiata	*Dorati*	Philips	**49, 62**
	(L') Isola disabitata	*Dorati*	Philips	**62**
	(Il) Mondo della luna	*Dorati*	Philips	**62**
	Orlando Paladino	*Dorati*	Philips	**62**
	(Il) Ritorno di Tobia	*Dorati*	Decca	**84**
	(The) Seasons	*Davis*	Philips	**61**
	(La) Vera costanza	*Dorati*	Philips	**49, 62**
Hindemith	Sancta Susanna	*Tortelier*	Chandos	**260**
	Song cycles	*Albrecht*	Wergo	**161**
Holloway/ Schumann	Fantasy-Pieces/Liederkreis	*Brabbins*	Hyperion	**260**
Howells/Stevens	Masses	*Finzi Singers*	Chandos	**193**
Humperdinck	Hänsel und Gretel	*Karajan*	HMV	**74**
		Lind/Hendricks	EMI	**179**
		Pritchard	CBS	**74**
		Solti	Decca	**74**
Janáček	From the House of the Dead	*Mackerras*	Decca	**84**
Jeffreys	A Musick Strange	*Aston*	University	**82**
Josquin	Masses	*The Tallis Scholars*	Gimell	**141**
	Songs	*Morrow*	Argo	**39**
Kern	Show Boat	*McGlinn*	EMI	**157**
Kodály	Hymn of Zrínyi	*Heltay*	Decca	**68**
Korngold	Violanta	*Janowski*	CBS	**85**
	(Das) Wunder der Heliane	*Zagrosek*	Decca	**198**

Composer	Work/Album title	Artist/Conductor	Record Co.	Page
Puccini	Gianni Schicchi	*Gobbi*	CBS	**49**
	Madama Butterfly	*Karajan*	Decca	**23**
	Manon Lescaut	*Maazel*	Sony Classical	**202**
	(La) Rondine	*Pappano*	EMI	**244**
	Tosca	*Davis*	Philips	**51, 79**
		Karajan	DG	**78**
		Mehta	RCA	**13**
		Parry	Chandos	**237**
		Rostropovich	DG	**52**
	Trittico	*Bartoletti*	Decca	**217**
		Maazel	HMV	**49**
	Turandot	*Martinelli/Turner*	EMI	**154**
		Ricciarelli	DG	**104**
Purcell	Anthems	*Christchurch/Preston*	Archiv	**102**
		King's College	HMV	**102**
	Anthems and Services, Vol. 11	*Robert King*	Hyperion	**225**
	Anthems for The Chapel Royal	*Trinity College*	Conifer	**150**
	Dido and Aeneas	*Ewing*	Chandos	**237**
	(The) Fairy Queen	*Christie*	Harmonia Mundi	**171**
		Gardiner	Archiv	**171**
	Theatre Music, Vol. 5	*Hogwood*	L'Oiseau-Lyre	**90**
Quilter	Recital	*Luxon*	Chandos	**165**
Rachmaninov	Songs	*Larin*	Chandos	**257**
		Söderström	Decca	**52**
Rachmaninov/ Glinka	Recital	*Vishnevskaya*	DG	**52**
Rameau	Hippolyte et Aricie	*Lewis*	Argo	**114**
		Malgoire	CBS	**114**
Ravel	Shéhérazade	*von Stade*	CBS	**94**
Reimann	Lear	*Fischer-Dieskau*	DG	**73**
Respighi	(La) Fiamma	*Gardelli*	Hungaroton	**130, 134**
Rimsky-Korsakov				
	Sadko	*Gergiev*	Philips	**223**
	(The) Tsar's Bride	*Nesterenko*	HMV	**47**
Rore	Mass	*The Tallis Scholars*	Gimell	**214**
Rosenmüller	Vespro della beata Vergine	*Junghänel*	Harmonia Mundi	**243**
Rossi	Madrigals	*Curtis*	Virgin	**253**
Rossini	Armida	*Fleming/Kunde*	Sony Classical	**223**
	(L') Assedio di Corinto	*Sills*	HMV	**28**
	(The) Barber of Seville	*ENO*	Chandos	**234**
	(Il) Barbiere di Siviglia	*Bartoli*	Decca	**163**
		De Lucia	Rubini	**110**
		Gelmetti	EMI	**205**
		Gui	HMV	**109**
		López-Cobos	Teldec	**205**
		Marriner	Philips	**109**
	(La) Cenerentola	*Chailly*	Decca	**205**
		Ferro	CBS	**133**

Composer	Work/Album title	Artist/Conductor	Record Co.	Page
Schubert	(Die) Schöne Müllerin	*Heilmann*	Decca	**224**
		Luxon	Chandos	**165**
		Partridge	CfP	**18**
		Protschka	Capriccio	**150**
		Schmidt	DG	**195**
		Schreier	DG	**18**
	Schubert Edition	*Johnson*	Hyperion	**225**
	Schubert on Stage	*Various*	Philips	**49**
	Schwanengesang	*Fassbaender*	DG	**187**
		Fischer-Dieskau	DG	**38**
		Luxon	Chandos	**165**
		Prey	DG	**93**
		Schreier	DG	**38**
	Song Edition	*Johnson*	Hyperion	**157, 170, 242**
	Winterreise	*Allen*	Virgin	**225**
		Bär	EMI	**165**
		Fischer-Dieskau	Sony Classical	**195**
		Hampson	EMI	**251**
		Quasthoff	RCA	**270**
		Schreier	Philips	**138**
		Schreier	Decca	**211**
Schumann	Dichterliebe	*Schreier*	Philips	**170**
	Dichterliebe/Liederkreis	*Bär*	EMI	**140**
		Bostridge	EMI	**260**
		Schreier	DG	**15**
	Frauenliebe und -leben	*Ameling*	Philips	**37**
		Ferrier	Decca	**29, 37**
		Price	Forlane	**219**
	Frauenliebe und -leben/ Dichterliebe	*Norman*	Philips	**52**
	Lieder	*Ameling*	Philips	**101**
		Baker	HMV	**37**
		Fischer-Dieskau	DG	**53**
		Mathis	DG	**101**
	Liederkreis	*Baker*	Saga	**37**
		Hampson	EMI	**251**
	(Das) Paradies und die Peri	*Sinopoli*	DG	**231**
	Recital	*Hampson*	EMI	**219**
	Requiem	*Klee*	HMV	**125**
	Schumann Edition	*Johnson*	Hyperion	**257**
	Songs	*Fischer-Dieskau*	DG	**74**
Schumann/ Brahms	Recital	*Fassbaender*	Teldec	**219**
Schütz	Motets	*Regensburg Cathedral*	Archiv	**136**
	Musicalische Exequien	*Dresden*	Philips	**135**
		Linde	HMV	**135**
	Schwanengesang	*Hennig*	HMV	**135**
	Symphoniae sacrae	*Toulouse Saqueboutiers*	Erato	**136**
Schütz/ Monteverdi	Motets	*Norrington*	Argo	**56**

Composer	Work/Album title	Artist/Conductor	Record Co.	Page
Tippett	Byzantium	*Solti*	Decca	**198**
	(A) Child of Our Time	*Davis*	Philips	**32**
		Hickox	Chandos	**194**
		Tippett	Collins	**194**
	Heart's Assurance	*Ainsley*	Chandos	**235**
	King Priam	*Terfel*	Chandos	**235**
	(The) Knot Garden	*Davis*	Philips	**16**
	(A) Man of Our Time	*Various*	Philips	**61**
	(The) Mask of Time	*Tear*	EMI	**143**
Ullmann	(Der) Kaiser von Atlantis	*Zagrosek*	Decca	**223**
Various	Agnus Dei	*Higginbottom*	Erato	**243**
	American Songs	*Bonney*	Decca	**257**
	Amorous Dialogues	*Consort of Musicke*	L'Oiseau-Lyre	**83**
	Argentinian Songs	*Giménez*	Nimbus	**155**
	Arie amorose	*Baker*	Philips	**69**
	Arie antiche	*Bartoli*	Decca	**196**
	Art of the Netherlands	*Munrow*	HMV	**42**
	Bel canto	*Alvarez*	Sony Classical	**267**
	Callas live at Amsterdam	*Callas*	EMI	**146**
	Callas Masterclass	*Callas*	EMI	**153**
	Carnaval	*Sumi Jo*	Decca	**219**
	(The) Castle of Fair Welcome	*Gothic Voices*	Hyperion	**144**
	Ce diabolic chant	*Davies*	L'Oiseau-Lyre	**106**
	Chansonnier cordiforme	*Consort of Musicke*	L'Oiseau-Lyre	**81**
	Chansons de Toile	*Lamandier*	Alienor	**140**
	Choral Evensong from Lincoln	*Lincoln Cathedral*	Priory	**252**
	Choral Festival	*St John's College*	Decca	**75**
	Credo	*King's College*	EMI	**253**
	(The) Dicky Bird and the Owl	*Previn*	EMI	**14**
	Durham Commissions	*Durham Cathedral*	Priory	**252**
	Early English Music	*Magdalen College*	Argo	**39**
	EMI Centenary	*Various*	EMI	**243**
	English Songs	*Dawson*	Hyperion	**123**
		Harwood	Conifer	**123**
		Trew	Hyperion	**124**
		Varcoe	Chandos	**165**
	Fancies	*Rutter*	Collegium	**195**
	Festival Hall 1964	*de los Angeles*	HMV	**71**
	Festival of King's	*King's College*	Decca	**75**
	(The) Fine Old Tory Times	*Martin Best Consort*	Argo	**39**
	Folk Songs	*Pears/Ellis*	Decca	**67**
		Te Kanawa	HMV	**124**
	French Songs	*von Otter*	DG	**257**
	Gala Opera Concert	*Domingo*	DG	**95**
	(The) Garden of Zephirus	*Gothic Voices*	Hyperion	**145**
	Glees from Georgian England	*The Scholars*	L'Oiseau-Lyre	**67**
	(The) Glory of King's	*King's College*	HMV	**38**
	Goethe Settings	*Fischer-Dieskau*	Archiv	**15**
	Great Cathedral Anthems	*Llandaff Cathedral*	Priory	**252**
	Great Music from Great Occasions	*Westminster*	Pickwick	**166**

Composer	Work/Album title	Artist/Conductor	Record Co.	Page
Verdi	Requeim	*Morandi*	Naxos	**254**
		Plasson	EMI	**254**
	Rigoletto	*ENO*	HMV	**119**
		Kubelík	DG	**119**
		Muti	EMI	**167**
		Rudel	HMV	**77**
		Sinopoli	Philips	**129**
		Solti	RCA	**78**
		Toscanini	RCA	**119**
	Simon Boccanegra	*Domingo*	RCA	**13**
		Gobbi	HMV	**50**
	Songs	*Price*	DG	**149**
		Takács	Hungaroton	**149**
	Stiffelio	*Gardelli*	Philips	**86**
	(La) Traviata	*Aragall*	Decca	**36**
		Bonisolli	BASF	**36**
		ENO	HMV	**93**
		Muti	HMV	**97**
		Ponselle	Pearl	**97**
		Scotto	DG	**97**
	(Il) Trovatore	*Björling*	Legato Classics	**207**
		Bonynge	Decca	**57**
		Giulini	DG	**142**
		Karajan	HMV	**57**
		Karajan	DG	**236**
	(I) Vespri siciliani	*Levine*	RCA	**19**
		Muti	EMI	**178**
		Solti	RCA	**57, 201**
Verdi/ Tchaikovsky	Recital	*Gorchakova*	Philips	**236**
		Hvorostovsky	Philips	**173**
Victoria	Masses	*St John's College*	Argo	**125**
		Westminster Cathedral	Hyperion	**125**
	Requiem	*The Tallis Scholars*	Gimell	**150**
		Westminster Cathedral	Hyperion	**150**
Vivaldi	Juditha Triumphans	*King*	Hyperion	**258**
	Ottone in Villa	*Hickox*	Chandos	**258**
Wagner	Carnegie Hall Concerts	*Toscanini*	RCA	**112**
	(Der) Fliegende Höllander	*Solti*	Decca	**50**
	Götterdämmerung	*Haitink*	EMI	**190**
	(Das) Liebesmahl des Apostels	*Boulez*	CBS	**69**
	Lohengrin	*Abbado*	DG	**223**
		Solti	Decca	**148**
	(Die) Meistersinger	*Jochum*	DG	**44**
		Sawallisch	EMI	**212**
		Varviso	Philips	**31, 44**
	Parsifal	*Goodall*	HMV	**130**
		Knappertsbusch	Decca	**130**
		Levine	DG	**215**
	Recital	*Baker*	HMV	**35**
		Flagstad	EMI	**146**